PATIENT ZERO

Helen, dressed in her white disposable containment suit, complete with gloves, mask and plastic face plate, carefully withdrew a blood sample from the poorly nun laying before her. The patient was pale, sweating and incredibly frail. Her lungs were bad, but she had not yet reached the stage of coughing blood.

As Helen glanced around the room at the others, she knew deep in her gut that some of them, at least, would not survive much longer. Like Doctor Guterra, she, too, had never seen anything quite like this. The virus was moving swiftly and it seemed the human body had no biological defense against it. They needed to confirm whether Sister Fuentez was sick with the same thing. If she was, it would mean the outbreak was swiftly turning into an epidemic. And if they didn't shut this down fast, it could potentially become a pandemic.

T0112093

ALSO AVAILABLE

PATIENT ZERO

Amanda Bridgeman

First published by Aconyte Books in 2021

ISBN 978 1 83908 021 0

Ebook ISBN 978 1 83908 022 7

Distributed in North America by Simon & Schuster Inc, New York, USA

Printed in the United States of America

9 8 7 6 5 4 3 2 1

ACONYTE BOOKS

An imprint of Asmodee Entertainment Ltd

Mercury House, Shipstones Business Centre

North Gate, Nottingham NG7 7FN, UK

aconytebooks.com // twitter.com/aconytebooks

To all the health workers around the globe; doctors, nurses, scientists, and others who help fight the good fight against viruses, epidemics and pandemics every day – thank you for what you do, trying to keep us all safe.

PROLOGUE
LIMA, PERU

Sister Valeria Dulanto waited patiently for Sister Lucila Apolo's bus to arrive. It was running late. The Gran Terminal Terrestre was bustling with people and suitcases, and she enjoyed watching them all, wondering where they were headed to or where they'd just been. Given the delay of Sister Apolo's bus, however, and the weather being so nice, she'd chosen to wait outside the adjoining Plaza Norte in the sunshine. She'd found an outdoor café beside an azure pond, circled with beautiful pink, yellow and red flowers. She sat and waited in the warmth, smiling at the children who played near the water, splashing each other and laughing with glee.

Sister Apolo had called the convent the previous day to say she wasn't feeling very well and would need help with her bags. Valeria was more than happy to lend aid to the much older Sister. More than anything, though, Valeria was simply eager to hear the Sister's tales from her annual pilgrimage to villages along the Ucayali and Amazon Rivers. Valeria had dreamed of one day making the same pilgrimage, and Sister Apolo had promised she would take her along on the next trip.

She eventually saw a large bus approaching in the distance and checked her watch. Certain this would be Sister Apolo's bus, she made her way back to the Gran Terminal Terrestre, to the relevant bay the arrivals screen told her it would be unloading its passengers in. As the bus pulled into its bay, Valeria raised her hand to shade her eyes from the sun, trying to spot the Sister through the windows. She couldn't find her, however, and thought perhaps she might be sitting on the opposite side of the bus out of sight.

People began to disembark from the bus: families, couples, workers in mining uniforms. Valeria waited patiently, smiling and nodding hello to all those who passed. The flood of people began to slow to a trickle, and then seemed to stop altogether. Yet there was no Sister Apolo. Valeria stepped back and tried to peer up through the windows again to see if anyone was still aboard.

"Hermana!" a gruff voice called, and she turned to see the bus driver approach. He was a stout man, blessed with more hair on his face than upon his head. "Venga!" He waved her forward and she followed him up the steps onto the bus. "She's ill," he said, making his way toward the back. Valeria followed him and paused when she saw Sister Apolo, laying across the back seat.

"Lucila!" Sister Dulanto gasped.

Sister Apolo was pale, sweating, coughing, weak. She looked far worse than she'd sounded on the telephone just a day ago.

Valeria bent down and felt her temperature. She was burning up.

"Come!" the bus driver waved her to hurry. "Get her off. I have another group to load."

Valeria wiped the sweat from her hand onto her dress, then grabbed Sister Apolo's bag and handed it to him. He turned and carried it off the bus, while she gently patted Apolo's cheek.

"Hermana, we must get off the bus now."

Apolo opened her eyes. They seemed to take a moment to register Valeria.

"Ah, Hermana Dulanto," she said weakly. "It is good to see you."

"And you," Valeria smiled, helping Apolo to sit up. She seemed to sway a little, but Valeria eventually got her to her feet, with the bus driver's assistance. They pulled Apolo's arms around their shoulders, made their way to the exit and down the steps of the bus. As Apolo's feet touched the ground, the fevered Sister looked up at the sun, closed her eyes and smiled.

"It's good to be home," she said.

Valeria smiled. "We have missed you, Hermana. I've been so eager for your arrival. I cannot wait to hear of your tales."

Sister Apolo took a deep breath of fresh air and immediately began to cough, ragged and wet.

Valeria's smile faded. "Come, Hermana. You're exhausted. We must get you home so you can rest."

Valeria made her way into the convent kitchen. It was a hive of activity as her Hermanas prepared for dinner. Pots boiled, knives chopped, Hermanas chatted, laughed and hummed.

Hermana Alvarez noted her arrival, wiping her hands on an already damp tea-towel.

"How is she?"

"She is weak," Valeria said. "I think nothing more than soup for her tonight."

"Shame. I've made her favorite, to welcome her home."

"I'm sure she will appreciate it tomorrow when she is feeling more rested, Hermana Alvarez. Have we had word from Hermana Fuentez?"

"Not since she parted ways with Hermana Apolo," Alvarez said.

"When she calls we should report that Hermana Apolo is unwell."

Alvarez gave a nod as she spooned soup into a bowl, then handed it to her, eyeing her with concern. "Remember to sanitize."

"Si, Hermana."

Valeria knocked on Hermana Apolo's door. There was silence and she wondered whether the Hermana was asleep given she'd been too tired to even bathe, but then she heard the awful coughing through the thick wooden door. She opened it and stepped inside, placing the bowl on the table beside Apolo's bed. She examined the Hermana and noted she looked worse still.

"Hermana, you must eat," she said softly, "to keep up your strength."

Apolo opened her eyes and gave an almost absent nod. Valeria sat beside her and began to spoon the soup into her mouth, but it was difficult for all the coughing, the soup splattering onto her hand and clothes. Valeria quickly placed the spoon down and cleaned up the mess, then used the hand sanitizer beside her bed. She studied the sick Hermana again. "I'm going to call Doctora Guterra," she said.

"No." Apolo waved her off. "Do not disturb her at this hour," she wheezed. "I just need rest… My travels were long, and they have taken their toll."

Valeria analyzed her. "If you are not better by morning, I shall call her regardless. You remember what happened with COVID, Hermana?"

Apolo waved her off lethargically. "I just need rest."

Valeria gave up on the soup. She had managed to get a little of it into the Hermana, so that would have to do. For now Valeria would grant her the rest she so desperately required.

She made her way back to the kitchen where the other Hermanas had gathered to collect their dinner plates and move to the dining tables.

"She barely touched it?" Alvarez said, taking the bowl.

"She's very unwell," Valeria replied, grabbing a tea towel and wiping her clothes and hands again.

"I'd better put that straight in the wash," Hermana Chio said, holding out her bony, aged hands.

"Thank you, Sister." Valeria handed it to her, then took a plate and began to serve herself dinner.

It was five am when Valeria went to awake Hermana Apolo to see if she was well enough for their morning prayer. She had checked on her once during the night. The Hermana was wheezing heavily, the sound of the fluid in her lungs troubling, but she was at least asleep, albeit with feverish dreams. Valeria had watched her for a while, heard her murmuring in her sleep, something about a boy, and Jesus, and eternal rest. Valeria had left her to her dreams and gone back to her own room. She'd said a prayer and made a note to call Doctora Guterra first thing in the morning.

When she knocked on Hermana Apolo's door now, however, there was only silence. Valeria pushed opened the door, noting she no longer heard the wheezing wet breaths of the sleeping Hermana. And when she laid eyes on her, Valeria knew the reason why.

Hermana Apolo lay staring up at the ceiling. Her eyes were wide open, the whites blotted with broken red capillaries, and her mouth, too, was ajar, and blood stained her neck and the white pillow beneath her.

"Lucila!" she called, racing to her bedside and grabbing her bloodstained hand.

It was ice cold.

Death had taken Hermana Apolo in the night.

Valeria gasped, raising the back of her hand to her mouth as her eyes filled with tears.

"Oh, dear Lucila…" she said softly. "May your soul rest in the arms of our Lord."

And as tears ran down her cheeks, she reached out again to hold Sister Apolo's cold, bloodstained hand.

CHAPTER ONE
EDINBURGH, SCOTLAND

Doctor Helen Taylor stood at the podium and paused briefly to take a steadying breath, glancing at her notes before she began. Despite the harsh stage lights that shone down upon her, she could just make out the faces of those in the first few rows of tables in the audience before her. She was pleased to see that she very much had their fixed attention. She smiled.

"It's an honor to be invited to speak here tonight at this fundraising gala, supporting the wonderful work that our network of researchers does." Her English accent sounded particularly crisp over the speakers in the silence of the room. "To date, so much amazing work has been done, but we need to ensure it continues into the years to come. After all our recent struggles, there is still so much to be learned.

"As Sir Terry said in his kind introduction, I am the lead epidemiologist for the Global Health Agency's European headquarters. The Global Health Agency is exactly what the name suggests. I may be based in Lyon, but my work takes me all around the world, wherever I am needed. At the GHA we strive to provide health security for everyone, everywhere, and we do this through prediction, interception and cure. When people ask me who I work for, I tell them the Global Health Agency, and they seem to understand the general nature of my work. But when they ask what I *specifically* do and I tell them I am an epidemiologist, they usually give me a blank stare. So I've learned to describe my role in the purest, most basic terms. I am a disease detective. I am a virus hunter."

Chuckles sounded from the audience and again Helen smiled.

"Disease detectives, virus hunters, they sound like something out of a Hollywood blockbuster, don't they? However, I assure you, the work that we do is far from glamorous. Then again, the most critically important jobs in our society aren't, are they? But they are *very* necessary.

"Disease detectives are very similar to police detectives, except the serial killers we chase are microscopic pathogens. But where your traditional serial killer may reach victim numbers up to the forties or so, our serial killers have the potential to kill many more. Often hundreds, sometimes thousands. Worse yet, they have the potential, if left unchecked, to kill millions, as we all saw with the last pandemic back in 2020 and 2021.

"We cannot deny the fact that our society has changed in ways that have increased the risk of outbreaks at a much faster rate than in years gone by. Wet markets and the desire to eat exotic animals aside, there are other ways in which our exposure to these threats has increased. With each passing day our cities and towns grow closer to areas of natural vegetation where complex ecosystems that have never had to come in contact with us before, suddenly do. These areas become potential hazard zones, because it's in these areas where domesticated animals may come into contact with wildlife, increasing the risk of virus mutation and transfer between the two. If a virus mutates and transfers into our domesticated animals and these animals fall sick, they may in turn transfer these mutated viruses onto humans. Just as we've seen many times before. Even before the most recent crisis that affected us all, consider the swine flu outbreak of 2009, which was a result of wild bat droppings infecting domesticated pigs. In turn, these pigs infected humans. Same again for the bird flu outbreak in 2004. Wild ducks infected domesticated chickens, and in turn these chickens infected humans. And then, of course, there's the devastating Spanish flu outbreak at the end of World War One, which one theory posits started with infected geese in a small French village. This virus passed on to soldiers, who then took it to the far corners of the Earth when they returned home from the war… The list goes on.

"When a new virus emerges like this and infects humans, we are automatically on the back foot. Our bodies haven't seen these viruses before and so with no natural immunity, our bodies succumb and it passes rapidly from person to person with often devastating effects. We then scramble to investigate the virus and work on treatments and vaccines, but that can take time. Sometimes it takes months, sometimes years. And sometimes, we struggle to find any treatment or vaccine at all. Meanwhile, people die.

"But we don't always have to be on the back foot, playing catch-up. We can stop being *reactive* and instead become *proactive*. We can invest in measures to deal with this threat now. We can identify potential hazard areas where towns and cities are pushing into areas of vegetation. We can study the local wildlife in these areas and analyze their viruses for any potential to cross over into the human race. We can study the human behavior in these areas to understand what makes them vulnerable to the risk of infection. We can then take all this data and use predictive modelling to identify the areas where the next spillover might occur. We can then focus our efforts on these areas to ensure that the at-risk human populations take the necessary care. If we study the viruses with spillover potential, we can be ready to create the necessary vaccines quickly because we'll have all the data already on hand. We'll be prepared to fight it. We'll be on the front foot, ready to save countless lives."

She paused a moment, scanned the faces in the crowd, sitting in their suits and ball gowns, eating their five-star meals and drinking expensive champagne. It was time to drive home the reason she was here giving this speech.

"But saving lives costs money," she said. "A statistical breakdown from a few years ago showed the scientific community had identified one hundred and eleven different families of viruses. Of these, twenty-five families contained viruses that were shown to affect humans or were likely to... Only twenty-five out of a hundred and eleven? That's not too shabby." She grinned. "Well, actually it is, because not all of the viruses in these families have been identified yet. An estimate of the undiscovered viruses those families contain, hovers around 1.67 million. And of that, how many would be dangerous to humans if we came in contact with them?

Estimates are somewhere between 631,000 to 827,000...
That's a *lot* of viruses!" she said, seeing a few faces in the crowd
raising their eyebrows. "And keep in mind these statistics were
from a few years ago. The number of identified viruses grows
every year... Now, keeping this in mind, it will be expensive
to find and identify all of these viruses, but when you compare
the cost of this, being on the front foot, being proactive, to the
cost of a pandemic, being on the back foot and reactive..."
She let the silence hang in the air for a moment. "How much
money am I talking? Well, to give you a ballpark, the cost of a
fairly self-contained outbreak like SARS was in the region of
thirty billion dollars."

She saw a few reactions in the front row, saw people looking
at each other, wondering if they'd heard right.

"No, you didn't mishear me. I said thirty *billion* dollars. And
that was SARS. The estimated global cost of the COVID-19
pandemic is still being counted, but believe me, the figures
would turn your hair white." It never ceased to amaze her
how it was always the cost that caught people's attention,
more so than the huge number of potential viral threats
that could cause death. Until COVID, most people had
assumed it would never happen to them, that viruses were
something that third world countries had problems with, not
them. Though some had a wake-up call during the COVID
pandemic, once the initial threat receded, many slipped back
into complacency, if not outright denial. But the thought of
it costing them money was something that always hit home
with folks like these. "That's the cost of being on the back
foot. Our society, with each passing day, becomes more and
more connected, particularly with our ever-increasing global

reach, thanks to the aviation industry adding flights to new places every day. Should another COVID-19 occur, make no mistake that it would once again spread incredibly rapidly and no corner of the earth would be left untouched. *Billions upon billions* of dollars to save ourselves, again, or we can pay *far* less than that now for preventative research to protect ourselves."

Again she let the silence sit for a moment, taking one last look at the faces she could see.

"The greater the complacency, the greater the crisis will be. Viruses know no borders, and left unchecked, they are ruthless indiscriminate killers. If unleashed, no one is safe. So, we have a choice. We can be proactive and go out there and research potential hot spots, discover where the viruses are potentially likely to develop, and figure out how to block their transmission. *Or*, we can be reactive and wait for an outbreak to occur and hope we can develop the right vaccine, fast. The former is by far the best solution. Prevention is, after all, better than cure… And it's also a hell of a lot cheaper…" She smiled warmly at her audience. "So, please, dig deep tonight and help our researchers continue the fight against these deadly viruses, before they can run rampage. Everything you give will contribute directly to saving lives – and remember, the life you save could be your own. Thank you."

Applause filled the glittery ballroom. Helen smiled, giving a wave as she left the stage, while the MC took to the podium to thank her and direct everyone to enjoy their dessert. Music and chatter filled the air as she made her way back to her table. WHO Assistant Director General, Peter Davidson, watched, applauding as she took her seat beside him. She noted the applause didn't quite reach his face, however. His blue eyes were analytical as they stared at her.

"I think that went well?" she said, wondering what was behind his analysis.

He nodded. "It was great. Well done." His American accent was calm and reserved, his years working in and around politics showing through.

"Why don't I feel convinced?" she said, studying him, as she picked up her glass of water to sip.

"You were fine. Really." He leaned back in his chair, still studying her, the ballroom's lights enhancing the silver that threaded through his dark hair.

"So what's that look for?" she asked. "You've got me worried."

He hesitated, his mind cycling over something. "It's just work stuff. After this is over, we'll talk."

"About what?" she said, placing her glass down.

He leaned forward, grabbed his glass of wine and took a sip.

"Peter?" she pushed.

"After the gala," he said. "Enjoy yourself."

"Helen!" Debbie Colson, the event organizer, called from the next table, waving her over. "Come, let me introduce you!"

Helen smiled and waved, then looked back at Davidson.

"You can't say we need to talk, then just leave me hanging," she said. "Give me a clue at least."

He considered her for a moment. "We need to talk about the team."

"What about them?" she asked, then suddenly tensed. "Oh God, you're not shutting us down, are you?"

"No," he reassured her. "No, there's just … going to be some changes."

"Helen!" Debbie called again.

"Now, go." Davidson waved her off. "Do your thing. Dazzle the audience. I'll talk to you later."

Helen stared at him a moment, then reluctantly stood. "I fly back to Lyon first thing in the morning, so whatever it is, we talk tonight."

He nodded. "We will."

Helen stared at him another moment, then straightened her dress and turned to Debbie, pasting on her best "give me all your money" smile.

CHAPTER TWO
LYON, FRANCE

Bodhi Patel sat inside a quiet little café, sipping his coffee and eyeing the architecture of the GHA building across the street. Its angular lines, white facade and mirrored windows seemed defiantly modern given the vast historical structures that spanned most of the city. The wedge of land upon which he sat, between the Rhone and Saone Rivers, was the heart of an urban renewal project; a place embracing the future. It seemed fitting, then, that this particular area, La Confluence, was going to be his new working home. At least temporarily.

He smiled subtly to himself and checked his watch. It was almost time. He had arrived early on purpose so that he could sit and curb his anticipation of the posting, rehearsing his introductions, keen to impress. He was glad to have been given this opportunity, to take some time out of the Atlanta head office and undertake some international field work. He'd been getting restless back home, the job beginning to feel stale, and he knew it was time to spread his wings and take on the next challenge in his career. His managers had identified him as "promising new talent" and had offered him a promotion but it meant staying in Atlanta. Bodhi had countered by requesting an international posting instead, stating that there was a world outside of the US and he'd like to see it. The job in Lyon had arisen urgently, so they'd offered it to appease him, knowing it was only temporary and hoping he would return to Atlanta and accept the promotion once it was over. Bodhi knew the Lyon job would give him the best of both worlds: a promotion, and an opportunity to see a bit of the world, temporary as it may be. So he gratefully accepted it and told his Atlanta bosses he would consider their offer while he was away. And he would. He would use his stay in Europe to decide what he wanted to do with the rest of his life.

He finished his coffee, left money on the table, then stepped outside into the chilly February air, pulling his coat around him. He looked out over the Saone, shaded an emerald green in this early morning light, as his breath formed clouds of mist around him. Atop the hill in the distance he caught sight of the Basilica of Notre-Dame de Fourvière. Standing white among the dwarfed winter trees that surrounded it, four large turrets bearing tall black crosses seemed to guard each corner. He recognized it from the quick Google search he'd undertaken at the airport. Given the urgency of his placement here, he hadn't had time to research the city properly, but the story behind the church had caught his eye. It was dedicated to the Virgin Mary, who had been attributed the salvation of Lyon from the bubonic plague that had swept Europe in 1643, as well as during the cholera epidemic in 1832. Naturally that had sparked his interest, given his line of work. When he had more time, he'd take a closer look, he promised himself. For now, though, it was time to see what epidemics *he* could save this city from.

He took a deep breath and exhaled long and steadily. Then he turned, grabbed his bag, and walked toward the mirrored building and his temporary future.

Bodhi stood at the door to the building but found it locked. He glanced around and spotted a security comms panel on the wall beside the door. He pressed the call button and waited.

"*Hello?*" an American woman's voice sounded.

"Hi," he said. "I'm Doctor Bodhi Patel. Reporting for duty!"

"Who?" her confused voice sounded.

"Er, Doctor Bodhi Patel. This is the Global Health Agency, right?"

"Yeah," she said, "but I don't have you on our visitor list."

"Oh..." he said, pulling out his phone and finding the email with the details. "I'm here to see Doctor Helen Taylor."

"I still don't have you on my visitor list," the woman said frankly.

"Well, I, er, I got my instructions and flew out from the Atlanta office yesterday. It's all happened a bit fast."

Silence again for a moment, before the woman said, "Hold on."

He heard a loud, deep buzzing sound and the door before him unlocked. He waited a moment, then went to push it open as it was pulled from the inside. He stumbled inward but caught his feet. Not the first impression he was hoping to give. An African American woman in her mid-fifties with short cropped hair stood there, giving him a puzzled look over the top of her red-rimmed glasses.

"Who'd you say you were again?" she asked.

"Doctor Bodhi Patel."

"And you're from the Atlanta office?"

"Yes," he nodded, smiling politely, confused over her confusion. "Er, here," he said, pulling the ID badge off his belt to show her.

She inspected it, then him again for a moment, then shrugged. "Alrighty. Come on in."

He entered a small white foyer, bare except for a simple unmanned reception desk and a sign along the back wall stating Global Health Agency, with the familiar organizational logo of Earth with an ECG line wave rolling across it, showing the peaks and valleys of a healthy heartbeat.

The woman motioned him to follow her to a double doorway set in the wall below the sign. "I'm Louise Parker," she said, "but you can call me Lou. I'm the research and data analyst here."

"It's nice to meet you, Lou," he said, following her.

Lou swiped her pass on a console beside the door. It beeped an acceptance and as she pushed one of the large doors open, a young suited man with a coffee in his hand came through from the other side.

"Jorge," Lou stopped him. "Were you expecting Doctor Bodhi Patel today?" She motioned to Bodhi who gave a smile at the young man.

"No," Jorge said, studying him as he blew on his coffee.

"Right," Lou said, waving him off. Jorge continued on, making his way to the reception desk out front.

Bodhi followed Lou as they stepped inside what looked to be the main hub of the GHA facility. It was a large oval-shaped room, filled with workstations and monitors, many already filled with its various staff members, as chatter and ringing phones filled his ears. Against the far end of the room was a wall of screens, each showing different content; some were news feeds, some were displaying data, some global heat maps and the like. There was an elevated platform, a second floor, either side of the main floor, where various other rooms seemed to feed off, and either side of where Bodhi stood now, just inside the main doors, a corridor seemed to lead around either side of the main hub, heading to other parts of the facility. It was a slightly different layout than the Atlanta office, and smaller, but Bodhi still felt right at home with the familiarity of it all.

Lou moved to a large workstation to the left, just inside the doors, and he followed, glancing at the other staff members sitting at their desks already working; some threw him curious looks, some were too absorbed in what they were doing to notice him. Lou's particular workstation seemed more kitted out than the rest, surrounded by several screens and consoles. She sat down at the desk and pulled on her comms headwear.

"I'll try to raise Helen for you," she said, tapping at a small screen embedded into the desk to make the call. "She should've been here by now."

"Lou, you seen Robert this morning?" a short, stocky guy with a receding dark hairline asked as he approached. He had Spanish features, with an accent to suit, and held an air of authority. He looked at Bodhi. "Who are you?"

Bodhi was a little taken aback by his abruptness.

"Says he's here to see Helen," Lou answered for him.

"I'm here to replace her," Bodhi explained.

"What?!" They both looked at him.

"Er, just temporarily, I'm told." Bodhi held his hand up to calm them, more confused than ever. They seemed to know even less than he did, which wasn't much. What exactly had he walked into here?

"What? Where's she going?" the guy demanded, an angry furrow in his brow.

"I... don't know," Bodhi said awkwardly. "I was just told to show up."

"He flew in from Atlanta yesterday," Lou said, tapping the screen again. "She's not answering."

"Bodhi Patel." Bodhi held his hand out to the man, trying to alleviate the awkwardness.

"Give me your pass," the man said.

Bodhi stared at him.

"I've already seen it," Lou said.

Regardless, the man waggled his fingers at Bodhi for the pass. Bodhi sighed, took it off his belt and handed it to him. The man gave it to Lou.

"Scan it."

She did so, then twisted a screen around to face the man. Bodhi's picture and profile filled the screen.

"Atlanta, huh?" the man said, reading it. He placed his hands on his hips. "And you don't know why you were sent here?"

"Well, just that I'm replacing Doctor Taylor."

The man continued to analyze him with suspicious eyes.

"Bodhi Patel," Lou said firmly, "this is Max Rojas, he's our operations and deployment manager." She looked at Max over her glasses. "Seeing how you weren't going to bother to introduce yourself." She turned to another man sitting at a nearby workstation watching them curiously. "Gabriel? You work with this guy in Atlanta?"

The man adjusted his glasses as he stood and approached. He looked like he'd just stepped out of a Giorgio Armani advert; tall, handsome and well-groomed.

"Bonjour!" he said, extending his hand. Bodhi smiled and accepted it, pleased with receiving a warm welcome finally.

"Hi. Doctor Bodhi Patel."

"Gabriel Renaud," he said. "Contingency planner."

"You're a local?"

"Oui," he replied with a smile. "Well, local enough. I'm from Montpellier."

"So, you don't know each other then," Lou said, then looked to Bodhi. "Maybe you know our quarantine expert, Ekemma Bassey? She's from Nigeria originally, but she worked in Atlanta for a bit."

Bodhi shook his head. "No, I'm sorry, I don't recognize the name. I've been there for a couple of years now. Perhaps she left before I started?"

Max grunted. "When Helen or Robert get here, tell them I want to see them," he said firmly to Lou, then walked off.

"Don't mind him," Lou said to Bodhi. "Fire is his middle name."

Gabriel smiled again. "And that's why I've been chosen to work closely with him. I am the Evian to his volcanic ash." He leaned toward Bodhi, "But it *is* only volcanic ash. Rarely do you ever see any actual lava from the man."

"But when you do…" Lou finished her sentence with raised eyebrows and wide eyes.

Bodhi smiled, amused, as the doors behind them opened and a bronzed, buff and blond guy entered in sweats and sneakers. He jogged toward a workstation, grabbed some keys off it, then came back toward them. Lou caught his arm.

"This is Bodhi Patel. Says he's here to temporarily replace Helen."

"Yeah?" The guy nodded at Bodhi, his skin shining with sweat. "Justin Thomas. I'd shake your hand but you don't want that right now," he said with an Australian accent. "Speaking of which, I better hit the shower. Talk later." He continued on his way, heading down one of the corridors.

"Ah!" Gabriel said, motioning to the doors. "The lady of the hour!"

Bodhi turned to see a woman enter, dressed in a long coat against the cold, her skin pale except for the flush of pink at her cheeks. She seemed rushed and a little disheveled as she removed her beanie and smoothed down her shoulder-length blonde hair, before striding quickly toward them.

"Call the team leads together for a meeting," she said to Lou, glancing at Bodhi quizzically.

Lou gave a nod. "This got something to do with the fact that he's here to replace you?" She hiked a thumb toward Bodhi.

The woman looked at the newcomer. "Oh! Yes. Yes, hi. I'm Helen. You must be Doctor Patel?"

Bodhi smiled. "It's nice to meet you."

"You, too. Er, great," she said, glancing around, still slightly frazzled. "Take a seat. I'll be with you shortly."

"You gonna tell us what this is about?" Max called from

the elevated platform. He was leaning on the metal railing, looking down at them.

Helen looked up at him. "Just gather the team together in the boardroom. I'll be there in a moment."

Helen moved along the corridor toward the boardroom, her mind turning over what Davidson had told her after the fundraiser in Edinburgh the previous night. Or more to the point, what he hadn't told her. She had little information to go on and wasn't sure exactly what to tell the team, especially about Robert's news. Davidson had tried to allay her fears, telling her it was business as usual, that she just had to stabilize and babysit the team, and keep the ship moving. That was all well and good, but where exactly was she steering this ship to?

"Helen?" a woman's voice called.

She turned to see Ekemma approaching, her dark eyes fixed on Helen's with concern. "What is going on? Why are you being replaced?"

"I'm about to tell everyone, Kem," she said, entering the boardroom. She moved to find a spare seat at the oval table and glanced around at those present. "Who's missing?"

"Pilar's on conference call from the US," Lou told her.

"Hi, Pilar," Helen spoke to the speaker in the middle of the table. "Thanks for calling in. I know you're finishing up leave. How are you?"

"Curious for the call," Pilar's voice said over the speaker. Pilar was always short and to the point, ever the soldier.

"Where's Robert?" Max asked Helen. "I haven't seen him today."

"Ah, he won't be making this meeting," Helen said. "Where's Aiko?"

"She's coming," Justin said, entering with wet hair, fresh from a shower.

"Aiko?" Bodhi asked Lou, as though he recognized the name.

Aiko entered, dressed in her usual lab coat, her long dark hair pulled up into a bun. Helen saw Bodhi's face fall upon seeing her, as though he'd just seen a ghost. Aiko paused when she laid eyes on him, too.

"Bodhi, this is our lead virologist, Aiko Ishikawa," Lou said. "Aiko, this is–"

"What are *you* doing here?" Aiko asked Bodhi bluntly.

Everyone at the table paused to study them both.

"You two know each other?" Helen asked.

"Er," Bodhi stuttered, "w- we… went to college together."

"Oh." Helen smiled. "Small world."

"What are you *doing* here?" Aiko asked him again.

"Aiko," Helen said. "Sit, please. I'm about to tell everyone."

Aiko moved to take a seat beside Ekemma and all eyes turned curiously to Helen.

"Right," Helen said, taking a deep breath to buy her time to figure out where to start. "Well, thanks for being here at short notice. First off, I should say that last night went very well. I think I may have got through to some people, but I guess only time will tell. I still had the usual detractors cornering me after the gala to inform me that the pharmaceutical industry is making a fortune off fearmongering and that I was only fueling the fire." She shook her head. "I wonder if they'd feel the same way after a dose of Ebola, eh?"

"Helen," Max cut off her joviality. "Spit it out. Why is he here and where are you going?"

"I'm not going anywhere, Max," she said, taking another deep breath. "In fact, as of this moment, I am the Acting Director of the Global Health Agency's Lyon office."

The silence sat a moment before Gabriel broke it. "What happened to Robert?"

"Honestly? I don't really know," Helen told them. "I've just been told that he's on indefinite leave."

"What?!" Lou said, and some of the others stirred along with her.

"I'm told everything will be fine," Helen reassured them. "Peter Davidson has asked me to step into the role to manage things until they find a replacement."

"Why *you*?" Max asked.

Helen looked at him. She'd considered that Max might have a problem with her being elevated to the role, given he was the operations and deployment manager and she was the lead epidemiologist, but how did she tell him that maybe she was better at dealing with people than he was?

"I don't know," she said, offering him a friendly smile. "It's only temporary. This doesn't mean any immediate changes. It just means that you will all be reporting to me for the time being."

"So he's here to replace you?" Aiko asked Helen, motioning to Bodhi.

Bodhi threw Aiko a glance, before returning his eyes to Helen.

"Yes," she said. "I'm sorry, I probably should've started with that. Everyone, this is Doctor Bodhi Patel from the Atlanta office. He's kindly volunteered to cover my role until we find a suitable replacement for Robert. The Atlanta office speaks very highly of you, Bodhi, so welcome."

"Welcome, mate," Justin nodded to Bodhi.

"Yes, welcome," Ekemma said.

"Thank you," Bodhi smiled. "It's great to be here. I'm looking forward to expanding my ski–"

An alarm suddenly pinged on the tablet sitting on the table before Lou. She picked it up and began to scan the data that was flowing across it.

"What is it, Lou?" Helen asked.

Lou looked up at her. "I think we need to take a look at this."

CHAPTER THREE

Bodhi followed the team out to Lou's desk. The analyst's hands darted here and there as a map of Peru appeared on one screen, weather displayed on another, a WHO alert page displayed on a third, and further data scrolled on the fourth.

Lou pointed to the map of Peru. "Report from a Doctor Guterra in Lima, Peru, about a cluster of deaths in a convent due to a mysterious virus, not yet identified. Symptoms so far appear to be along the lines of an influenza virus, perhaps even a corona-like virus. Doctor Guterra believed the virus was contained to the site, but the alert I just received was a notification of two more similar deaths at Doctor Guterra's hospital, of people completely unrelated to the nuns at the convent."

"And Doctor Guterra?" Helen asked. "Is she sick?"

"No," Lou shook her head. "She's been taking the relevant precautions. These new deaths in her hospital have caught it elsewhere."

Helen stared at the map showing the locations of the

deaths and nodded. "So we have a cluster that may potentially be turning into an outbreak."

Lou nodded. "The WHO have added it to cases in need of early investigation, and it's fallen onto our roster by default. They've asked if we can take a further look at it."

Helen looked at Bodhi. "Do you have your passport handy?"

"Er, yeah," he said. "Used it to fly here last night."

She turned to Max. "Max, we're going to need visas for Peru."

He nodded. "What team do you want to send?"

"It looks to be spreading so we may wind up with a big area to cover. I'll take Bodhi, Ekemma and Justin, and let's bring Pilar, too, in case we need her Spanish or military support. She's due to finish her leave, right?"

Max nodded, but there was a question in his expression.

"Then tell her to meet us in Lima. There's no point in her traveling back to Lyon first."

"Alright, but why are *you* going?" Max questioned. "I thought you were Director now?"

Bodhi sensed a note of dissension in his voice and wondered what it was about. Was this guy just unhappy about everything or was there some kind of power struggle between the two that Bodhi didn't know about? Helen smiled calmly at the man.

"I'd like to do a handover with Bodhi before I throw him completely in at the deep end," she said. "It could take months before they find a replacement for Robert. So, I'll manage the team in the field, and you manage the team here. How does that sound?"

He looked at her, arms folded across his chest, but didn't

answer. Instead, he looked to Gabriel, now sitting at his nearby workstation.

"Five Peru visas."

Gabriel nodded. "Coming up. I'll arrange them for the bordering countries, Bolivia, Brazil and Colombia too, just in case." Gabriel started tapping away on his console. "Alright, Bodhi and Pilar being US citizens are fine for all four countries. Pilar will travel on her personal passport and not her military one." He continued tapping away at his console and flicking through screens. "Helen's British passport is fine for all… Australia is also covered for all four, so Justin is fine…" Gabriel continued tapping away before a grimace took over his face. "Nigeria isn't covered, though, so we'll need to get Ekemma's visas sorted ASAP."

"Always Nigeria," Ekemma sighed.

"Look on the bright side… fancy a quick trip to Paris?" Gabriel grinned.

"The lengths we must go to for visas." Ekemma gave a bemused smile, then shrugged. "I'm ready when you are."

Gabriel nodded, then returned to his console, tapping away. "OK, we have two tickets on the next flight out, but we need to leave straight away." He crossed to a locked filing cabinet close by and punched in a code to open it. He searched through the hanging files, found what he was looking for and plucked a folder out. "Here are your pre-prepared documents. Grab your passport and let's go."

Ekemma nodded, and she and Gabriel left the building.

"Guess you better start packing," Max said to Helen, before he turned and walked away.

Bodhi watched as Helen stared after him.

"Wow," Bodhi said. "Barely here an hour and we're heading into the field already. That's great."

Helen looked back at him. "Not if people are dying, it isn't."

She walked away and Bodhi cringed internally at his words.

"Baptism of fire, eh?" Justin smiled, slapping his shoulder.

Lou looked to Justin. "Why don't you start Bodhi's pre-field medical, then give him a tour of our facility?" She looked back at Bodhi. "Justin's our head medic."

"Follow me," Justin said to Bodhi.

Bodhi nodded and took one last look around at the buzz of activity before him, unable to hide a smile of nervous excitement from crawling across his face. When his eyes fell on Aiko, however, staring down at him from the elevated platform, it soon faded again.

She was a complication he had not been expecting.

Bodhi followed Justin down the corridor to the right of the main doors. As they walked he heard a strange tapping sound. He looked down at the source: Justin's right foot was missing and in its place was a curved black blade. He hadn't noticed when he'd met Justin earlier as he'd been wearing sweats and sneakers, and he wondered why he'd forgone the shoe now.

"Welcome to my domain," Justin said as he swiped his pass over a console, opened the door and motioned Bodhi inside.

Bodhi stepped into a room that looked like a small hospital ward. There were four beds and various medical paraphernalia in glass cabinets against the wall. As he'd thought earlier, the GHA facility here in Lyon was a lot smaller than the one in

Atlanta, but it seemed to have everything they needed.

"Take a seat," Justin said, motioning to one of the chairs beside a small desk in the corner of the room.

"So you're a doctor?" Bodhi asked.

"Paramedic," he answered. "There's six of us based in this facility. We're here to make sure you guys are safe and healthy in the field, but mostly we support Ekemma and the quarantine folks putting their measures in place."

Bodhi nodded. "So, everyone in that boardroom – are you the heads of your divisions or something?"

"Yeah," Justin said, as he moved over to a cabinet and began fishing inside for something. As he turned around again, he caught Bodhi staring at his blade. "No, you're not seeing things," Justin said. "I've got me a metal leg. Left the other one in Afghanistan."

"Oh, I- I'm sorry," Bodhi stumbled.

"Don't be," Justin grinned. "This one's much faster."

"It is?"

Justin nodded. "I'm training for the Paralympics in my spare time. Hoping to wear the green and gold for Australia one day."

Bodhi smiled. "That's great. Well, good luck."

"Thank you."

"So…" Bodhi said, glancing around the room as Justin set about taking his blood pressure. He noticed it was neat and tidy, everything in an orderly manner, and he wondered if that was an influence of Justin's military past. "How long have you worked for the GHA?"

"Almost two years now. You came from Atlanta?"

"Yeah. I was there for a couple of years."

"What made you want to leave the mothership for an outpost like ours?"

Bodhi shrugged. "I guess I wanted to change things up. I'm looking for the next step."

"So this was a step up for you, career-wise?"

"Yes and no," Bodhi said. "They offered me something better in Atlanta, but…"

"But?" Justin said, darting his eyes between Bodhi's face and his BP reading.

Bodhi shrugged. "They've been trying to push me into management and I don't want that. I don't want to be stuck in an office. I want to get out and see the world, get on the frontlines more, you know?"

"Fair enough," Justin nodded. "Well, you'll definitely hammer the airmiles working here. I gotta say, though, we've never been sent to Peru before, so that'll be interesting."

"Mexico and the Caribbean are as far afield as I've been with the GHA, so I'm looking forward to it. Even if it is only for a few weeks."

"Yeah. So… do you know what happened to Robert?" Justin asked.

Bodhi shook his head. "No idea. He was your last boss?"

"Uh huh. He was a good guy. Big sports nut. It's weird that he would just go on indefinite leave like that. They really didn't tell you why?"

Bodhi shook his head. "No. I have no idea. I was called into the Atlanta Director's office yesterday and offered the chance to pack my bags and fly here, so I did."

"That's pretty whirlwind." Justin shook his head and narrowed his eyes in thought. "Something's definitely going

down. I hope he's not sick or something." He finished taking
Bodhi's BP and began packing the gear away. "How're your
vaccinations? We're going to need a few before we hit Peru."

"I got the usual before Mexico, so hopefully I'm good to
go."

Justin nodded, moving to his console and tapping away.
"I'll check your profile… After that, there's just a few more
things to check, then we can pack you on that plane to Lima!"

Helen entered her small office and closed the door. She
paused and wondered whether she should be using Robert's
office now. But she quickly decided it was too soon. Besides,
this was only temporary, right? Until she knew the reason
why Robert had left, she didn't want to move anywhere.

She sat down at her desk, opened her laptop, and began
to check her emails. She saw one from Debbie Colson, who
thanked her again for her talk and said she would report the
final fundraising amount soon. Helen smiled. She hoped
they'd raised a good amount. Robert had kept telling her that
the GHA's operating budget was constantly being tightened
and their research funding was being cut right back altogether.
That had to change. It was something she planned to speak to
the new Director about.

She scrolled down the other emails, saw nothing from
Robert to explain his sudden departure, so she began to check
the latest alerts from the WHO. There were no further updates
from Peru as yet. Nor anything else in the surrounding areas
that drew her attention.

An email notification popped up from Lou. It was the
details of their Lima flight booking. It was scheduled for later

that day and would route through Los Angeles in order to have them land first thing in the morning in Lima. She checked her watch. She'd need to go home and pack, but first, she had to make a phone call.

Ethan answered on the fourth ring.

"Hels?" he said. "What's up?"

"I'm flying out to Peru today."

"You are?" He paused. "How long for?"

"I don't know. You know what these trips are like."

"Yeah, I do… You disappear into thin air and reappear days, sometimes weeks later and I have no idea where you are."

"You got it in one," she smiled, trying to make light of it.

"So I suppose our weekend together is off then." The tone of his voice told her he didn't see the light side. Deep down she knew he wouldn't. She felt an uncomfortable silence settle over them.

"There's always next weekend," she offered.

"If you're back."

"Ethan–"

"I'm not sure how much longer I can do this, Hels."

She took a breath. "It's barely an hour's flight from London to Lyon, Ethan."

"You wanted space and I gave you that. But this… this long-distance marriage can't work forever. You have to come home and face the music sometime. You need to *grieve*, Hels."

Helen exhaled heavily, lowering the phone for a moment, before returning it to her ear. She did not want to get into this right now. "Look, Ethan, I have to go. I'll call you when I land in Peru."

"Of course you will. As soon as you find the time."

She paused, his sarcasm biting.

"Goodbye," she said, hanging up. Before she could process the conversation, a knock sounded on her door.

"Yes?" she said.

The door opened and Max stood there.

"Max. What is it?" she asked.

Max glanced in both directions down the corridor, then looked back at her. "What really happened to Robert?"

She shrugged. "I don't know."

"You must."

"I don't, truly. Peter just told me that he's left and he's not coming back. He wouldn't budge on telling me why."

"Are you going to take his spot permanently?"

"What?" she asked, caught off guard. "No. This is just temporary."

"But if the position comes up?"

"Max… I literally only just found out about this. I have no idea what Peter's plans are." She paused and studied him. "Why? Do *you* want the job?"

"I want to know why Robert left," he said, his eyes narrowed in suspicion.

"Well, I'm telling you all I know, and that is that I don't know."

Max stared at her a moment, skeptical, then turned and walked away.

Helen shook her head, then checked her watch. She had a lot to get her head around before she hit Peru.

Bodhi walked alongside Justin as they finished their tour. So far he'd managed to meet some of the staff, then he'd been shown the meeting rooms and the series of labs on the upper level, where Aiko kept her back to him and pretended to work. He'd made sure not to ask too many questions so they could move along on the tour. Just being in the same room with her was hard for Bodhi to take. It was uncomfortable to say the least, as though the temperature had shot up a thousand degrees and the air was hard to breathe. He hoped they would not need to work together while he was here. He wasn't sure he'd be able to do it.

Next Justin had taken him to see the staff quarters, down a corridor to the left of the main hub, which consisted of a kitchen and small recreational space with a series of tiny sleeping rooms for those working long hours. And now they had arrived at their last stop, a large storeroom filled with racks of individual equipment on one side, and large pre-packed backpacks on the other. Max was waiting there for them, tablet in hand, checking gear off. He looked up as they entered.

"He good to go?" Max asked Justin.

"Sure is," Justin smiled. "He's had the tour, knows where the fire exits are, and passed his medical with flying colors. Over to you." He slapped Bodhi on the shoulder then left.

"Alright," Max said to Bodhi. "I'm sure you're familiar with all of this from Atlanta, but I'm going over it all again anyway. Everyone is issued a standard field pack." He moved over to the large backpacks and patted one. "It's already packed with everything you need." He turned his tablet around to Bodhi to show him a list of items. "This list will be posted in your personal portal. You are responsible for everything in this kit, understand? Don't be fooled by the expensive-looking building. We fight for every cent here, so you treat it right, or you deal with me. Understood?"

"Loud and clear," Bodhi nodded, making a mental note not to get on Max's bad side. "Does Lyon work off a separate system or will I be accessing the same portal I had in Atlanta?"

"Same as Atlanta. Lou will run you through all that next. She issues the comms and IT gear. I'm all about the fieldwork equipment. I'm talking sequencers, reagents, pipettes. You get the drift. It's all in here." He tapped the backpack again. "Everyone gets a set, so we have backups in the field. It's all good gear and most of it is plug and play. You hook the gear up to your laptop, so you can upload results quickly and the team here can provide support. You go hunt down the viruses, and clean up the hot spots, and leave the analysis and cures to the folks here, like Aiko. She rarely goes into the field, does most of her work here in the lab."

Bodhi nodded again, though he felt a sting at the mention of her name.

"So try one on for size," Max said, motioning to the backpack. "Get used to the weight. I recommend a lot of back exercises to strengthen your muscles."

Bodhi grabbed the pack and pulled it on. It was heavy and a little cumbersome, but he generally felt comfortable.

"Alright, sign here." Max held the tablet out and pointed to the bottom of the screen. Bodhi raised his finger and swirled it across the screen in the shape of his signature. "Done!" Max said. "When you return, you bring the gear back to me, I check it's all there, then I sign it back in. Got it?"

"Got it," Bodhi said.

"Alright, go find Lou. She'll sort out your comms."

Bodhi gave a nod and, backpack still on, headed for the doorway.

"Oh, and Bodhi?" Max said.

He stopped and looked around.

"Welcome to the team."

Bodhi smiled. "Thanks."

Bodhi sat opposite Lou's desk on the main floor, listening intently, as she ran through the GHA software on the tablet she held. In the background the wall of screens at the far end flashed images and scrolled data, while the sounds of phones ringing and people discussing content at the surrounding workstations provided a noisy background soundtrack.

"So, this is used mainly for comms, but it's obviously small and lightweight if you need to carry it around places to work on the go." She handed the tablet to him, then slid a rugged laptop across the desk toward him. "And this is to use for more in-depth work, for things like sequencing DNA and RNA. When you have the time and space, you can set yourself up in a field lab. As you can see, with its thick casing, it's as durable as they get. So you've got flexible working options at your fingertips. The choice is yours."

"Awesome," he said, flicking through the screens on the software. It was the same systems that he had used in Atlanta, so all straightforward for him.

"Lastly," she said, passing him a cellphone, "are the phones."

"Phones? As in plural?"

"Mm-hm," Lou nodded. "This one is your GHA phone. It's pre-loaded with the team's numbers, along with home base, here in Lyon, for times where the tablet won't do." She pulled out a second, chunkier phone and passed it to him. "This one is your satellite phone, for when the standard handset doesn't work. And you've got a personal cellphone, right?"

"Yeah," he nodded.

"Then take that, too. You can never have too many handsets. We'll also give you a pre-paid local phone with SIM cards for Peru and the surrounding regions, just in case. I'm arranging that now."

"That's a lot of phones."

"You never know when you'll need to call for help."

"This is true."

"Any questions?" Lou asked, looking over the top of her red-rimmed glasses.

"No. Right now I think I'm good. I may have questions in the future, though."

"Ask away anytime. That's what I'm here for," she smiled. "You ask a question, and I find you the answer. That's my job."

"You're the oracle of the Lyon GHA," Bodhi said.

Lou laughed. "Something like that."

It was late afternoon by the time Bodhi left the GHA building. He'd spent the remainder of the day meeting more people and reading through what little information was available on the corner of Peru they were headed for, before Justin had tapped him on the shoulder and told him to call it a day, as they had to be at the airport soon enough.

He made his way for the exit, clearing the doors with ease thanks to the new access granted by his staff ID. He stepped back into the entrance foyer and paused briefly upon seeing Aiko chatting to Jorge on reception. She was wearing a long coat and scarf, and had a bag draped over her shoulder, obviously on her way home, too. She looked over at him and her smile fell away.

He walked straight past them and stepped outside into the crisp winter air. He thought for a moment about getting some food but wasn't sure where to go. He'd arrived late the previous evening and hadn't had time as yet to figure out the area, but decided he would just eat at the airport.

The door opened behind him and he felt the person exiting pause briefly before stepping onto the footpath. He turned his face and looked at Aiko. They stared at each other for a moment and she looked like she wanted to say something, but before she could find the words, another two people came out of the GHA building, and she suddenly turned and walked away.

Bodhi stared after her for a moment, then turned and walked in the opposite direction.

CHAPTER FOUR

AIR FRANCE 747, SOMEWHERE OVER THE NORTH ATLANTIC OCEAN

Helen accepted a water from the air hostess and considered watching a movie, but the truth was her mind was too distracted. She couldn't stop thinking about why Robert had left so suddenly, or why Davidson had chosen her to step into his place. If he thought she could manage the role temporarily, did this mean she had a shot at applying for the role permanently? She hadn't even thought about it until Max mentioned it. Was moving into an organizational management role a career pathway that even interested her? What would that mean for her fieldwork? Robert never left home base. And more to the point, what would that mean for her marriage? If she became the GHA Director, she would be in Lyon permanently. Ethan would be in London. That said, less fieldwork might actually help things... if they could see each other more often.

An uneasy emotion stirred within her, and she realized it was guilt. She liked staying in Lyon and she liked the fieldwork because it kept her away from London. It kept her away from the bad memories of her recent past. Away from London she could forget they existed. She could hide. But was she just hiding from the memory of Angie's death? Or was she hiding from her marriage, too? Angie had already been lost. There was nothing she could do about that. But would her relationship with Ethan follow? Did she want to save it? She felt numb to the answer, and that's what scared her.

The passenger beside her stood and moved off down the aisle. Across the aisle, Helen saw Bodhi tapping away on the GHA tablet he'd been issued with, a look of concentration on his face. He noticed her stare and looked over, then he smiled, undid his belt and crossed over to the spare seat beside her.

"I've been doing some research on the outbreak in Peru and I think–"

"Bodhi," she stopped him, "not here."

He looked at her, curious. "But we need to hit the ground running, right?"

"We do," she said, lowering her voice. "But look around. We're on a public flight. Not everyone has earphones on. We need to be discreet. This is potentially sensitive information, that could be inflammatory in the wrong hands and cause widespread panic. That's the last thing we need. We may have vaccines for COVID-19 now but the fear is still very much embedded in some people's memories."

Bodhi looked around at the passengers, then back at her. He nodded in understanding, but she could sense his disappointment.

"I know you're eager," she smiled, "and I value your opinion, I do. As soon as we land and we're in a private place you can brief me."

He nodded again; the disappointment was still present, but so, too, was understanding and acceptance.

"Our job is to investigate," she said. "That means we gather the facts first, all of them, or at least as many as possible, before we prescribe a course of action. Speculating is an important part of the process, don't get me wrong, but in this line of work we need cold hard facts more than anything. So when we land, you tell me your speculations, then we'll go talk to people, investigate the current cases, and gather the facts to see if they support your speculation. OK?"

He nodded once more as the passenger came back to reclaim his seat. Bodhi stood and moved across the aisle again. As he did, Helen's eyes fell onto a young girl, sitting on the lap of her mother, at the far end of their row, against the window. The little girl was giving a rattling, deep-chested cough before her mother wiped her running nose, and the child burrowed her face into her mother's chest. Helen couldn't help but stare at the girl as memories of Angie came flooding back. Terrible memories of oxygen masks and needles and heart monitors and tears and pain.

She noticed that Bodhi was watching the child, too. He looked back at Helen and they locked eyes for a moment. They exchanged a knowing look; *this is how easily it starts*. Helen moved her eyes to another passenger who slept soundly, a surgical mask upon their face. They weren't the only passenger wearing one either. That was one of the lingering effects of the COVID pandemic. Some people simply refused to take any risks at all now. She turned away and looked up at the air-conditioning unit that was blowing recycled air upon her. She reached up to turn it off. Bodhi did the same. She glanced around the cabin searching for Ekemma and Justin; she didn't know why but felt the need to check on their locations. She spotted the top of Ekemma's head several rows behind, and Justin's a few rows ahead.

She exhaled heavily and closed her eyes. She felt bad for shutting Bodhi down, but the truth was, she had done this for too many years now and she'd learned that on a long flight like this, nothing made her feel more useless than speculating thousands of feet in the air, far from the epicenter of the trouble. Up here she was trapped and helpless. She couldn't do anything and it drove her crazy not having the facts in front of her. So she'd learned, for her own sanity, not to think about it while she traveled.

Once on the ground, however, she would think of nothing else.

On the ground she could be useful, and she would do everything in her power to contain the threat.

LIMA, PERU

Bodhi stepped out of the terminal into the Peruvian sunshine. An electronic notice board inside the terminal had told him it was twenty-eight degrees Celsius and it felt good to be out of the airplane's recycled air, not to mention the cool of the Lyon winter. The tiredness smacked at him, though. He'd slept little on the various flights it took to get there, much the same as his flight to Lyon the day before, too eager to get to work. The lack of sleep, however, was beginning to catch up to him. Right now his body was running on anticipation alone.

"This way," Helen said briskly, tapping him on the arm.

He followed Helen to where Justin and Ekemma were greeting another woman, whom he assumed was Pilar. She looked athletic, wore mirrored sunglasses, and her brown hair was slicked back in a short ponytail.

By the time they reached them, Justin had flagged down a taxi van and had begun loading their bags in the back, while Pilar leaned in the passenger window, negotiating the fare in Spanish. Bodhi joined Justin to load his and Helen's bags, eager to get inside the van to escape the strong smell of petrol fumes surrounding the vehicle. Once the bags were loaded, he helped Justin with the large cold box they'd brought with them. They each had small versions in their field packs, but this larger container had been brought along in case they came into a situation where they needed a whole lot of sample storage. The cold boxes could be charged to hold biological samples at the optimal temperature for up to seventy-two hours, which was often required in the field.

Pilar soon reached an agreement with the driver, they piled in the back and the taxi set off. Bodhi found himself sitting beside Ekemma and held his hand out to her. As they'd sat separated on the flights and Lou had booked them such a tight schedule, there'd been little time to talk.

"We didn't formally meet yesterday," he said to her. "Bodhi Patel."

She looked at his hand, then shook it. "Ekemma Bassey." He noted her accent.

"You're from Nigeria?"

"Yes, Lagos," she said. "You?"

"The States."

Ekemma smiled. "Yes, that much I know, but whereabouts?"

"Oh, well, I grew up in DC. My parents moved out from Mumbai when I was two years old."

"I see," Ekemma nodded. In the seat across from them was Pilar. She stared back with her mirrored glasses, yet to crack a smile.

"Hi," he said, now extending his hand to her. "Pilar, right? You were the voice on the conference call yesterday."

She nodded, shook his hand.

"Sorry, Bodhi," Helen said, shaking her head as though to clear it. "This is Pilar Garcia. She's our military liaison. Bodhi Patel."

"Right," Bodhi nodded. "So we have a couple of military types in the team?"

"Hey, don't look at me," Justin said from the seat behind. "I'm just the medic. If you get in trouble, Pilar's your gal." He slapped Bodhi on the shoulder and Pilar gave a slight smile.

"What part of *liaison* says fighting to you?" she said to Justin.

He laughed. "Hey, I'm very *ex*-military. You're currently serving. You're responsible for our safety, *Sergeant* Garcia."

She pulled her sunglasses down to look at him. "I'm responsible for *liaising* with the military should you need protection." She smiled, then used her middle finger to push her mirrored sunglasses up again. "Watch your step, or I might just forget to make that call."

Justin chuckled.

"Besides," Pilar said. "My money's on Kem if we get into any real trouble."

Ekemma grunted, folding her arms. "I'll certainly give them a right tongue-lashing, that's for sure."

Pilar finally cracked a smile that showed teeth.

"No one person is responsible for the team's safety," Helen told Bodhi. "We all are. We do the job we're hired for and we watch each other's backs. If we do that successfully, we'll all go home again. It's one in, all in."

"Sounds good to me," Bodhi said.

The van stopped suddenly and Bodhi shot forward, just managing to avoid a collision with Pilar. He quickly retreated back to his seat, as the driver honked his horn and yelled abuse at the pedestrians walking in front of the vehicle. Pilar gave Bodhi a plain stare, while Ekemma fought a smile, and Justin slapped his shoulder again and grinned.

"You should probably wear a seatbelt, mate. Of all the ways you could die on this trip, a car accident is the most boring."

Bodhi laughed nervously. "Great."

Helen pulled out her tablet and opened the Global Health Agency communications software to begin making contact with the home base team.

The screen came to life and Bodhi saw Gabriel's bespectacled face, sitting in front of a desk, with Max standing beside him.

"How is the jet lag?" Gabriel asked with his subtle French accent.

"It'll hit soon," Helen said. "What time is it there? You're six hours ahead, right?"

"Oui," he said. "It's just after three pm here, so it must be just after nine am for you?"

"Yes indeed. I'm confirming that we have landed safely and everyone is accounted for. Although we almost lost Bodhi a few minutes ago," Helen smiled, shooting him a look.

"Yeah, I get it," Bodhi nodded, "make fun of the new guy."

"Are there any updates, Gabe?" Helen asked.

"As a matter of fact, there are. In the past twenty-four hours we've had six more similar deaths reported in Lima, across three hospitals."

"Damn," Helen said, her expression tightening. "It's spreading faster than we'd modeled."

"Lima's a big city," Max said, leaning in. "And it's not just the people there we have to worry about, it's the international flights, trains, roads and boats. You gotta contain this before it jumps the city border."

Helen nodded. "Agreed. We'll quickly drop our things off at the motel, then be at the hospital with Doctor Guterra in...?" She looked to Pilar, who turned around and spoke to the driver in Spanish.

"Thirty minutes," Pilar said, turning back around.

"Thirty minutes," Helen relayed to the tablet.

"OK. Your accommodation details for tonight are in your portals," Gabriel told her, "and I've provisionally booked an extension if you need to stay, as well as alternatives in surrounding cities, depending on where the investigation takes you."

Justin leaned over Helen's shoulder. "There better be no fleas this time, Gabe!"

Gabriel grinned. "But you like making friends?"

"Hey–" Justin went to retort, but Helen cut off his reply.

"I'm with Justin," she said. "No fleas!"

"You mean we don't get five-star hotels?" Bodhi asked with a smile.

Ekemma grunted.

"We're on a budget, as always," Helen said. "Oh, and we also have to share rooms. You're in with Justin, Mr Patel."

Bodhi glanced over his shoulder at Justin who grinned.

Helen spoke to the tablet once more. "Thank you, Gabriel. We'll check in again once we've spoken to Doctor Guterra."

"Good luck," Gabriel said, then the screen went black.

"Speaking of budgets," Ekemma looked to Helen, "are the millions flowing in from your little soiree in Edinburgh yet?"

"That I don't know. I'll have to follow up when we get back. I do rather hope so."

"Some of our field equipment is nearing end of life," Ekemma said.

"I hear you," Helen said. "I had asked Robert, but he told me the budgets had already been spent. He said the new portable sequencers drained us."

Ekemma grunted again, folding her arms and shaking her head as she looked out the window. "Save people, they say, but we'll give you little to no money to do it."

The van suddenly fell quiet as they passed a funeral procession on the side of the road. Dressed in black, the mourners walked along carrying a framed photo of a small child. Bodhi stared at the mourners and wondered whether the child was a victim of this recent outbreak. He glanced at Helen again, but noted she had looked away, absorbing herself in her tablet once more.

• • •

Helen packed away her tablet as the hospital approached. They'd made a quick detour to their motel near the hospital to drop off their personal belongings, then carried on to the hospital with their field kits. As the van pulled up outside the building, Pilar paid the driver and each began to don their basic personal protective equipment, being their masks and gloves. If needed, they would wear full containment suits, but until they confirmed that requirement, they would keep it simple.

Once they were kitted out with the basics, they entered the Archbishop Loayza National Hospital in the center of Lima, to look for Doctor Guterra. The hospital was a complex made up of several buildings, that surrounded a large green courtyard with walking paths in the very center. The buildings themselves, made of large gray blocks, reminded Helen of those she'd seen in Rome and Athens. Outside the main entrance, four grand pillars supported a triangular masthead bearing the hospital's name. From the information Lou had added to their case portal, Helen knew the hospital was government funded and focused on serving the disadvantaged. For the most part it was picturesque, especially with the complement of the manicured gardens, but graffiti had crept its way onto some of the external walls like ivy.

They went straight to the reception desk, where a nurse, dressed in an aqua blue uniform and also wearing a surgical mask and gloves, eyed them curiously.

"Good morning," Helen said, as Ekemma moved to stand beside her. "I'm Doctor Helen Taylor from the Global Health Agency. I'm here to see Doctor Guterra."

The nurse said something in Spanish and Pilar stepped in

to translate. Helen waited patiently while Pilar spoke with the nurse. Helen knew some Spanish from childhood family holidays in Spain, but when Pilar was around it was much easier to let her do the talking.

"We have to wait," Pilar told Helen. "They'll try to find her on the wards."

Helen nodded and they turned around to view the waiting room behind them. It was busy, certainly more patients than nurses, but that wasn't unusual for a city hospital catering to emergencies. What was unusual, however, was the number of people coughing or presenting with flu-like symptoms.

"They need to separate these people," Ekemma said, gesturing at the patients. "This man has a broken arm yet he's sitting in the same room as a coughing woman!" She walked over to them and, with Justin's help, began separating those who looked ill from flu-like symptoms from those with other illness or injuries.

The nurse behind the reception desk began calling something out in Spanish to Ekemma and Justin, but Pilar explained to the nurse what they were doing.

"The last thing they need is for this hospital to become the epicenter of an outbreak," Bodhi said.

"It probably already has," Helen said, glancing at her watch. "Unfortunately people still don't entirely take influenza-type symptoms seriously."

Bodhi yawned beneath his face mask.

"No sleep on the plane?" Helen asked, studying the tired eyes above his mask.

He shook his head.

"Been there," she said. "The first night is critical. Make sure you get an early night if you can, or it'll carry on through the next few days."

"I'll be alright."

Helen studied him. "Don't forget the altitude here, too. That can knock you about."

A woman approached them. She was short, dressed smartly with her dark hair pulled back in a tight bun, and wore gold hoop earrings. Over her surgical mask, her brown eyes looked worn with concern.

"I am Doctor Guterra," she said, her English heavily accented.

"Good to meet you, Doctor Guterra," Helen nodded. "I'm Doctor Helen Taylor, and this is my team from the GHA. The WHO sent us here to investigate your outbreak."

"Thank you for coming, Doctor Taylor." She gave a slight bow of her head.

"Thank you for raising the alarm," Helen said, then glanced at the waiting room. "You have your staff in surgical masks and gloves, that's good, but why haven't you separated the patients?"

Guterra shrugged. "We have nowhere else to put them. Our beds are full."

"Alright," Helen said. "The first thing we should do is set up a quarantine area. Perhaps we can put those without symptoms outside to wait in the fresh air and use different entrances and exits for them?"

Guterra considered this. "We did initially but it's warm outside, so people kept coming inside to sit in the shade. We don't have enough staff to police this and we need our masks for staff."

"Perhaps we could reach out to the government or

volunteer organizations to supply some umbrellas or shade structures?"

Guterra turned to the nurse and the two conversed in Spanish.

"We have some umbrellas in storage," Guterra said. "Maybe some chairs."

"That would be an excellent start, thank you." Helen turned to Pilar. "You stay with Ekemma and Justin and help them get the quarantine sorted. Bodhi and I will inspect the patients."

"Sure thing," Pilar said.

Bodhi and Helen stood on one side of the patient's bed, while Doctor Guterra stood on the other.

"They've all presented similarly," Guterra said, motioning to the elderly man lying in the bed. His eyes were closed, his breathing wet and ragged into the oxygen mask over his face. "It starts with tiredness and fever, then swollen glands, the cough sets in and it only gets worse. Our initial tests have not been able to identify the virus."

Helen nodded. "And you believe it started with a nun?"

"Yes," Guterra nodded. "Sister Apolo had returned from a pilgrimage, very unwell, to her convent. She died overnight. I was called to the convent the next day. I spoke to the other nuns and told them to report to me if anyone else fell ill, but I suspected her age played a part in her death. She was seventy-six. Two days later they reported that several of the nuns were feeling unwell also. I told them to separate the sick and ordered bed rest. Three days later I received another call to inform me that three more of the Sisters had fallen ill. I went there in person and saw that those who had fallen ill first were now gravely ill, and realized I had to quarantine the entire convent."

"Have there been any other deaths since?" Bodhi asked.

"Yes. So far, from the convent we have had four more deaths, and several in a very serious condition, and I suspect some of which won't make it. The convent is still quarantined."

The patient before them began to cough. Bodhi turned his eyes back to the man and flinched when he saw blood splatter inside the man's mask.

Guterra sighed wearily and pressed the call button. "This is how it ends," she said quietly, eyes filled with concern. "Coughing the blood. He'll be lucky to survive the night."

"We'll need samples from these patients," Helen said, "to see if we can identify the strain in our database."

"Yes," Guterra nodded. "Of course. You are welcome to do your own testing."

"We'll also need to visit the convent," Bodhi said. "It sounds like Sister Apolo is Patient Zero, but we need to be sure of that. We'll need to trace her movements and identify everyone at risk."

"Of course," Doctor Guterra said, looking back at the patient and shaking her head. "I have never seen any virus like this before. This symptoms exceed those of COVID... It concerns me greatly."

Bodhi looked back at the man's bloodstained oxygen mask and couldn't help but feel the same way.

CHAPTER FIVE

Bodhi stood beside Helen at the gates to the Convent of Santa Rosa de Lima. Plum in color with white trimmings, the Spanish Baroque-style complex bore a basilica with twin bell towers that stood connected to the large structure of the convent itself. A wide, open stone courtyard lay behind the gate, leading to the buildings, and dotted here and there were white statues of various saints, and in the near distance, a hint of lush gardens.

A nun approached the gate, her hands tucked beneath a fold in her black and white habit.

"Doctora Taylor?" she asked warily.

"Yes," Helen smiled. "You speak English?"

"Yes," she nodded. "I teach the children. I am Sister Anuncia."

"Hello," Helen said. "This is Doctor Bodhi Patel. We're from the Global Health Agency."

Bodhi and Sister Anuncia exchanged a nod, before she looked back at Helen.

"Doctora Guterra told us you were coming," Anuncia said. "Are you sure you want to enter?"

Bodhi and Helen exchanged a look of concern at the nun's warning.

"Yes," Helen said. "We're here to help. We need to trace Sister Apolo's movements."

Sister Anuncia nodded and stepped forward to unlock the gate. While she did so, Bodhi and Helen pulled on fresh surgical masks and gloves, and Bodhi wondered whether perhaps they should be using their full containment suits. As the Sister opened the gate and they stepped inside, he noticed that her eyes were red and tired.

"Are you feeling ill yourself?" he asked her, studying her carefully.

She shook her head. "No. Just sad that God has called his daughters to heaven so soon."

Bodhi saw the heartbreak all over her face. She waved them to follow her across the stone courtyard. As they did, Bodhi saw beds of colorful flowers along the wall to the left and birds dancing around a small fountain. It seemed strange to think that such a place of beauty hid such a terrible curse of death inside its walls.

They entered the convent building and continued to follow the nun as she led them along a stone corridor. They passed a smaller prayer chapel where several Sisters knelt and prayed, heads bowed to rows of candles, before they came to a closed wooden door which she knocked upon.

"Si?" a woman's voice came from inside.

Sister Anuncia opened the door and waved them through.

"Madre Superior Carmen, this is Doctora Taylor and Doctor Patel from the Global... ah..." She looked to Helen.

"Global Health Agency," Helen completed for her.

"Si." Sister Anuncia bowed. "Global Health Agency. Doctora Guterra sent them."

"Yes. Please, sit." Mother Superior Carmen motioned to two chairs on the other side of her desk. "Hermana Anuncia, you may stay also."

While Bodhi and Helen sat, their escorting Sister moved to stand beside the Mother Superior. The office was neat and clean and decorated simply. Mother Superior Carmen was a small, plump woman and aged in the face, which was marked haphazardly with moles. Her eyes looked upon them with intelligence and patience, albeit stained with a tired sadness. Neither she nor Anuncia wore masks or any other protection. Bodhi felt bad for sitting there talking to her in his mask and gloves, but it wasn't a risk he was willing to take.

"We're so sorry for your losses, Mother Superior Carmen," Helen said. "We very much want to help stop this virus before it causes any further devastation."

The Mother Superior gave a nod of thanks. "You've come to ask about Hermana Apolo?" she asked.

"Yes, that's correct," Helen said. "Can you tell us the sequence of events? Of what happened once Sister Apolo, er, Hermana Apolo, came home."

"She was quite ill," Mother Superior Carmen said. "Hermana Dulanto helped her to bed, then fetched her supper. She checked on her once during the night, then again in the morning, but unfortunately found that she had passed." Both nuns enacted the sign of the cross over themselves.

"And where is Hermana Dulanto now, if I may ask?"

"She, too, passed," again they performed the sign of the

cross, "along with Hermanas Alvarez and Chio and Cruz just this morning."

"We're sorry for your loss," Bodhi offered.

"Thank you. We pray for them. And for those who look set to follow them through the gates into heaven."

"Can you tell us how long after Sister Apolo's death did Sister Dulanto and the others fall ill?" Bodhi asked.

"Hermana Dulanto began to run a bad fever the day we buried Hermana Apolo. That was two days after her death. Hermanas Alvarez and Chio both reported feeling unwell soon after."

"And how long after reporting that fever did Hermana Dulanto pass?" Helen asked gently.

The two Sisters looked at each other, seeking the answer on the other one's face. "It was another three or four days."

"So we're looking at a week," Bodhi said, more to himself than anyone. He looked at Helen. "From infection to death. That's fast."

Helen nodded, looking back to the Mother Superior. "How many others are ill?"

"We have five in quarantine. Any who provided care to the sick, became sick. Now we are forced to leave the sick to tend to themselves and each other. Doctora Guterra has been checking on them. She has placed two on IVs and all have oxygen masks."

Helen nodded. "Where did Hermana Apolo come from? She was on a pilgrimage?"

"Si," Mother Superior said. "Every year she does this. She goes for months at a time to spread the word of God to the people."

"Do you know where she went exactly?" Bodhi asked.

"She travels along the Ucayali and Amazon Rivers mainly, sometimes even as far as the Tres Fronteras."

"Where's that?" Bodhi asked.

"The border where Peru meets Brazil and Colombia," the Mother Superior explained.

"Tres Fronteras," Bodhi repeated, feeling an unease rise within him. He and Helen exchanged another look, trying to hide their alarm. If the nun had been infected while she was there, the virus could soon be spreading through all three countries. Helen turned back to the Mother Superior.

"Did she fly in from this area, from the Tres Fronteras?"

"No. We do not have the money for that. She travels on the goodwill of God's people. Donations saw her travel by bus and ferry mainly."

"Was she traveling alone?" Bodhi asked.

"No. She joins with Hermana Fuentez in Iquitos and they travel together from there. They do this every year, together."

"Have you spoken to Sister Fuentez since Sister Apolo fell ill?"

Mother Superior Carmen's face fell. "The last that we heard, she, too, had fallen ill."

"Where was Hermana Fuentez?" Helen asked quickly. "When you heard she was ill?"

"She is based in Iquitos at another convent."

Bodhi felt his gut clench. If she had the same virus, then it was already threading through a second city in Peru. He and Helen exchanged another look, as Bodhi's heart began to race. This was a problem.

"Did Sister Apolo mention anything about how she got

sick?" Bodhi asked. "Did she say anything about coming into contact with other sick people?"

"No," Mother Superior Carmen said with sadness. "She was too ill for sensible words. Hermana Dulanto said the night before she died Hermana Apolo was having fevered dreams and talking about a boy. Or to a boy. We think she was maybe talking to baby Jesus."

"OK," Helen said, taking a deep breath. "You've done well to quarantine the sick. Please continue to keep the healthy separate for now. Assume that this illness is transmissible by both air and bodily fluids until we can confirm otherwise. We will arrange some disposable containment suits to be delivered, with instructions on how to carefully handle them. That way, you can send others in to care for your sick – but it's important you follow our instructions carefully or more will fall ill. Do you understand?"

"Si," she nodded. "I understand."

"Before we leave, we'll need to collect samples from your sick. We've brought our own containment suits. We won't need long with the patients."

Mother Superior Carmen nodded solemnly. "Hermana Anuncia will take you there."

"Thank you, truly," Helen said, standing. "We'll be in touch."

"Sister?" Bodhi said, standing. "I understand Sister Apolo's possessions will be under quarantine, but would it be possible for one of your ailing Sisters to look through her possessions and see if they can find any traces of where Sister Apolo may have been exactly? It's important we put together a timeline of her travels as it may help us identify other potential areas of infection that may not yet be apparent. I suspect some may be off the beaten track."

The Mother Superior stared at him a moment, then nodded. "Si. We can do that."

"Oh, I don't have a card." He looked at Helen as he patted his pockets. Helen fished one out of her pocket and handed it to the nun.

"That is the free-call number for our home base, back in Lyon. Call any time, it'll be staffed and they'll get in touch with us. And please don't hesitate, no matter how small you think the detail may be. It could be important."

Mother Superior Carmen nodded and watched them leave.

Helen, dressed in her white disposable containment suit, complete with gloves, mask and plastic face plate, carefully withdrew a blood sample from the poorly nun laying before her. This followed the usual nasal and oral swabs. The patient was pale, sweating and incredibly frail. Her lungs were bad, but she had not yet reached the stage of coughing blood.

As Helen glanced around the room at the others, she knew deep in her gut that some of them, at least, would not survive much longer. Like Doctor Guterra, she, too, had never seen anything quite like this. The virus was moving swiftly and it seemed the human body had no biological defense against it. They needed to confirm whether Sister Fuentez was sick with the same thing. If she was, with illnesses being reported in two cities, Lima and Iquitos, it would mean the outbreak was swiftly turning into an epidemic. And if they didn't shut this down fast, it could potentially become a pandemic.

She glanced over to Bodhi, who sat at the patient beside hers, withdrawing a blood sample.

"You alright?" Helen asked him. She felt a little sorry that he'd barely been with the Lyon team for twenty-four hours and he'd been thrown into a situation like this.

He looked up at her and nodded. "Yeah. I'm fine."

She continued to glance over, watching him, and was content that he knew what he was doing. In fact, he looked very comfortable with a needle, and his bedside manner with the patients was good, too. Peter Davidson had arranged for Bodhi to fill her shoes, so she had not reviewed his CV, but she remembered that he'd apparently attended university with Aiko, so she knew his schooling must have been excellent.

When she finished with the last patient, she took the contained swabs and vial of blood, labelled them, and placed them in the small portable cold box, set to the optimum temperature of six degrees Celsius, she'd taken from her field pack. Bodhi soon joined her and placed his samples into the unit as well.

"Let's get back to the hospital and start testing these," she said, knowing that time was of the essence. "We've got a lot of samples to get through between here and the hospital patients."

Bodhi nodded. Helen gave the patients one last look before moving swiftly for the door, ready to step outside and begin the decontamination process.

Bodhi was grateful that the Sisters had been kind enough to order a cab to take them back to the hospital, which saved them an awkward conversation in bad Spanish. With their containment suits removed and the appropriate sanitation procedures followed, they sat across the back seat with their backpacks of equipment and the small cold box between them, and rode in silence, staring out of the windows at the city of Lima as it passed by. The buildings in the city's historic center were rather picturesque, accompanied by palm trees, fountains, statues and manicured gardens. They saw horses with old-fashioned carriages and street stalls here and there, and people going about their daily business. Bodhi thought of the nuns he'd just seen and the patients at the hospital, then watched the unaware people of Lima again, wondering whether this was a stoppable threat, or whether it was the calm before a new pandemic storm.

"Have you been to South America before?" Helen asked him, breaking the silence.

Bodhi shook his head. "Not this far down. Mexico is as far south as I've been. You?"

She nodded. "Yes, we helped during the Zika outbreak in Brazil."

"That was a nasty virus."

"It certainly was," she said. "So, tell me, you coming aboard, this all happened pretty fast. I haven't even seen your CV. Summarize it for me."

"Ah, sure." Bodhi cleared his throat and straightened in his seat as though he were undergoing a job interview. "I studied medicine at Johns Hopkins. By the end of my four years undertaking the Bachelor of Medicine, I decided I wanted to move into epidemiology, so I veered off the path of becoming a standard doctor, much to my parents' disdain," he said dryly, "and did a Masters in Epidemiology. After that I got my PhD, and that led me into working for the Global Health Agency in Atlanta, and here I am."

"What was your thesis on?"

"It was a study on herd immunity and whether the rise in anti-vaxxer sentiment was affecting this, or whether it was a construct of media misinformation."

"Interesting! I'll have to read it some time." She seemed genuinely interested.

"Of course. Might I ask, what about you?"

"My pathway was similar to yours, except instead of medicine I came via the public health route. I've always felt strongly that basic healthcare is something that everyone has a right to. What's the point of having all this medicine that can cure people and save lives if people are just going to hoard it or place exorbitant prices on it and make it unattainable." Her passion for the subject was clear to Bodhi.

"I couldn't agree more," he said. "And your PhD thesis?"

"It was an epidemiological study of ageing populations affected by viruses and the associated health risk behaviors."

Bodhi nodded. "I'd like to read yours, too."

"We'll do a swap," she said with a smile. "So, you wanted to talk to me about something on the plane. Now's your chance."

Bodhi glanced at the driver. "Yeah?"

Helen nodded. "I don't think he understands English."

"Right," he said. "Well, I just wanted to share some stats, really. The presenting symptoms appear, at first, to be similar to that of influenza, right? Peru hasn't had a serious influenza outbreak for years. They were obviously affected by COVID-19 and they've had outbreaks of yellow fever, dengue fever, Zika virus and others, but nothing presenting with these symptoms that has warranted a WHO alert."

Helen nodded. "We need to keep in mind that influenza rates around the world dropped during the pandemic, so few countries have had influenza spikes since, thanks to the precautions people were taking. On the other hand, we have to keep in mind that many outbreaks go unrecorded. Especially in small regional areas. Our Patient Zero was traveling along the Amazon. God knows how small the communities were that she visited. What if she visited remote villages that rarely see people? She may have caught it from somewhere like this, where they have herd immunity already. Conversely, these villages may not have the immune experience to fight this if they're rarely exposed to the outside world. Her visit could have all but decimated these villages and the news just hasn't yet been reported." She shrugged. "Health experts are getting better each year at reporting this type of stuff, particularly after COVID, but only if they have the means, the technology and the government support, to do so. In years gone by it wasn't that great. The internet has done wonders for sharing information and enabling preparedness, although it can also spread misinformation and panic, too."

"Absolutely. I just find it strange that something like this is hitting Lima, and so hard, when it doesn't appear that an influenza virus has done this here before. Where did this virus suddenly come from? Doctor Guterra said they haven't identified it so far, which could possibly mean we're dealing with an entirely new virus, or at best a new strain of one. That in itself is a problem for us, if it continues to spread."

"Well," Helen said. "That's why we're about to sequence the DNA of the samples we've collected. I take it you've undertaken the procedure before?"

"Yes, many times in the Atlanta lab."

"Excellent. We'll split the samples and hopefully have our answer soon."

CHAPTER SIX

Helen and Bodhi returned to the Archbishop Loayza National Hospital. The nurse on reception recognized them and pointed down the corridor, so they heeded her directions. They saw two people up ahead in full disposable containment suits, complete with face masks, and from experience Helen could tell by the body shapes that it was Ekemma and Justin, wheeling a patient into one of the rooms. Helen and Bodhi, with only their surgical masks and gloves on now, followed and stood in the doorway, waiting to catch their eye.

Ekemma spotted them first and came over.

"What did you learn at the convent?" Ekemma asked, stepping out into the corridor.

"Not as much as we would have liked," Helen said, "but we did learn that Sister Apolo was traveling with another nun who left her in Iquitos. Apparently that nun also fell ill, so it's likely going to be another epicenter. I'm going to check in with home base for an update once we get the sequencing underway."

Ekemma nodded, as Justin joined them.

"Did you manage to get samples from the patients here?" Helen asked.

"Yes," Ekemma said. "This way."

She led them down the corridor to a storage room where one of their smaller cold boxes was placed. She opened the lid to show there were several samples.

"We have to work here," Ekemma said. "This is all the space they can give us." She moved a silver trolley beside Bodhi. "That's your table. Helen, you can use that small table over against the wall."

Helen checked her watch: it was just past one in the afternoon. "OK, we'll start processing all the samples now. I'll take care of the convent," she said to Bodhi, "and you handle the hospital."

Bodhi nodded and he moved to Ekemma's cold box

Justin stepped to and began spraying the surfaces with a hospital grade cleaning agent and wiping them down. Once the surfaces were clean, Helen and Bodhi grabbed their backpacks and began to unload their field kits. Helen placed down her portable DNA and RNA sequencer, her laptop loaded with the GHA software, cables and battery pack, a mini thermocycler and battery operated benchtop microcentrifuge, pipettes and sample rack, along with the necessary reagents and of course the portable heavily insulated cold box with the samples from the convent.

She glanced over at Bodhi and saw that he had set up the trolley in a similar vein, giving her confidence that he knew what he was doing. They began to process their samples in silence, starting with the swabs, soaking in the reagents of their containment tubes, collecting the required material for extracting the identity of the virus.

Helen heard Bodhi's stomach rumbling from across the small room. She checked her watch. It was mid-afternoon. They'd been so eager to start working on the samples that they'd been subsisting on coffee and tea alone. Maybe it was time for food. They had begun processing the swabs of their first patients with their two sequencers, and had now separated the serum from the blood samples in the centrifuges, ready to initiate DNA sequencing on Ekemma and Justin's sequencers as well, which could take some time to finish processing. Once processed, they would upload the results to the GHA portal, where Aiko and her team could start their analysis.

"After you load the first sample, Bodhi, why don't you take a break and ask one of the nurses where you can grab a bite to eat?" she told him. "It could take a while for the results to come in."

"You heard my stomach from over there, did you?" he smiled through his surgical mask.

She smiled back through hers. "I'm sure if it wasn't for our stomachs groaning we would forget to eat sometimes. I'll keep an eye on things, you go eat and I'll check in with home base."

She watched as Bodhi nodded and turned back to his trolley, taking Ekemma's portable sequencer and carefully loading the first blood sample. Once it was locked and loaded in the small handheld device, he double checked it was cabled into Ekemma's laptop correctly and the software was turning over and doing its thing. Sequencing the swabs, should they return a match, would help identify what virus they were dealing with, and then hopefully how to also stop it. The analysis of the patient's blood, at this stage, was merely supplementary data to provide Aiko's team with as much information as possible.

"Can I bring you back something?" Bodhi asked her when he was done.

"I'll go when you come back, stretch my legs."

Helen watched him leave, then brought up the comms channel on her laptop to connect with the team in Lyon.

Max soon appeared alone on screen, and Helen felt a little apprehensive, wondering if he was going to push for more answers she couldn't provide.

"Hi Max," Helen said. "Gabe's finished his shift?"

"Yeah. You got me until Lou joins us at ten pm, which is four your time."

Helen nodded. "We're processing samples from both the convent and the hospital now. Is Aiko still there?"

"Yeah." He picked up a handset and spoke into it. "Aiko? Main floor data comms. Site team online." He hung up again and looked back at her. "So what are we dealing with?"

"We've just loaded our first sample, so hopefully we'll know soon," Helen said, "but it's definitely highly infectious. Our suspected Patient Zero, Sister Apolo, was traveling with another nun and they parted in Iquitos. Can you check the data in that area?"

"For sure," he said, turning his face to look at another monitor, as Aiko joined them.

"Aiko, excellent," Helen said. "We're processing the samples now. Hopefully we'll have an answer in an hour or two." She checked her watch. "Can you log into the software at your end and be ready to start taking a look at things?"

"Yes," Aiko nodded. "Do we have a case definition yet? Incubation period, decline rate and symptoms?"

"From what limited observations we've been able to make so far, the symptoms appear most similar to that of influenza, but we can't rule out a coronavirus either. It's highly infectious, starts with tiredness, temperature, swollen glands. It appears to move into the chest rapidly, resulting in pulmonary edema. Patients appear to be coughing blood toward the end also. Incubation is looking like two days at best. We're still working on the official decline rate, but initial findings based on some of the deaths at the convent suggest that the timeline from infection to death looks to be seven days."

"Seven days?" Aiko asked, looking confused. "Are you sure? Deaths from the bird flu outbreak of 2004 took almost two weeks from infection to death."

"That's what I'm being told."

Aiko nodded, scribbling down notes. "OK. I will keep watch for the results at this end."

"Helen," Max said, reading one of the screens, "there are reports of eight deaths bearing similar symptoms in Iquitos and six in other surrounding towns between there and Lima. That I can see. This our virus?"

"By my count that's … twenty-seven deaths to date," Helen said, feeling a sense of pressure in her chest. It was plain to see that the virus was no longer just in Lima or Iquitos but spreading through towns like a fire in a dry forest. "It's moved from cluster to outbreak to epidemic fast. Max, according to the information Doctor Guterra gave us, Sister Apolo arrived in Lima by bus at the Gran Terminal Terrestre from Pucallpa. I'm sending you the details. We need a passenger list so we can trace and quarantine everyone aboard and their families."

"On it."

"We're waiting to hear how she traveled from Iquitos to Pucallpa. We're hoping to find evidence in her belongings, but she apparently kept her route to boat and bus. In the meantime can you get the team to start looking into the possible scenarios of how she might've traveled there?"

"No problem," he said.

"Thanks, Max."

"No wonder it spread so quickly," Ekemma said, entering the room with Justin in tow. "If she took public transport all the way?"

Helen nodded. "Yes, that's what worries me."

"We're nearly done establishing the quarantine zones here," Ekemma said. "We'll hand over to the hospital and they can take it from there. I've asked them to put out a call to the other hospitals to see if they need our help."

"We've had similar deaths across several towns," Max said, looking off to the side at another screen, as Aiko watched over his shoulder. "If it continues this way, Peru's going to need more than the GHA to help them."

Helen nodded. "Max, it's time to raise a health alert for the affected cities, and a warning to the entire country's health system that we may have linked epidemics. Copy in Atlanta and WHO," she said.

"On it," he replied. "How's the Lima accommodation?"

"We were only there long enough to drop off our bags."

Justin leaned over Helen's shoulder. "Like I said to Gabe, Max, there better not be any fleas."

"Hey, it sounds like fleas are the least of your worries right now."

"Ain't that the truth?" Justin said before he ducked back out of sight.

"Aiko, let's touch base again once we have an answer on the virus's identity," Helen suggested.

"Yes," Aiko said, and walked off screen.

"Talk soon. Good luck," Max said, and the screen went black.

"I need a coffee," Ekemma said, as she and Justin left the room again. Helen watched them leave, then turned to load her first blood sample into the sequencer.

Bodhi sat in the small room at the Archbishop Loayza National Hospital, staring at his laptop. He checked the time in the corner of the screen. It had been over three hours and still there had not been a match in the system. He knew the extracted swab sample would also include bacterial and human RNA, and the viral RNA would be hidden within that soup, so the software would take time to discard any human or bacterial signal. Still, with each passing minute, he became more certain that it would eventually return no match, which meant they were dealing with a new virus. The waiting was agony. At least once they knew what they were dealing with, be it a recorded virus or a new one, they could start taking action. But until then, all they could do was wait.

"Ever heard the saying, a watched pot never boils?" Justin said, standing in the doorway with his hands on his hips.

Bodhi gave a tired smile. "Yeah." He looked back to the screen. "It's just bugging me it hasn't found a match yet. It's looking more and more like we're dealing with something we haven't seen before. And if we are, and it's spreading this fast, then–"

"We might be in trouble," Justin finished his sentence, face falling as he entered the room.

"Yeah." Bodhi's mind turned over and he looked back at Justin. "What if we're dealing with the new COVID?"

"That was a coronavirus," Justin said. "Our virus appears to have a shorter incubation period and a shorter serial interval, which makes me lean toward an influenza virus."

"I don't mean literally, I mean figuratively. This could have the potential to be the next great pandemic."

Justin sighed and placed his hands on his hips. "Then we stop it. We stop it before it becomes that."

"Yeah," Bodhi nodded. "Easier said than done."

"Well, staring at the thing isn't going to make it cough up a result, if that's not a horrible image to use at this point. I don't know about you, but I'm hungry. Let's find the others and get some dinner, eh?"

Bodhi looked back at the laptop, hesitant. "I only ate a few hours ago. Take Helen, maybe? She never ended up having any lunch. I'll stay and keep watch on the results."

"Sure?" Justin asked.

Bodhi nodded. "Yeah. Besides, Max strikes me as someone who would be real pissed if our equipment got stolen."

Justin laughed. "Would he ever? We'll bring you something back, then. Any allergies I should know about?"

Bodhi shook his head.

"Alright. Back soon." Justin pointed at him. "Stop staring at it."

Bodhi smiled and turned back to the screen. Right now he couldn't think of anything else but these results. He'd taken a walk earlier when he'd grabbed some lunch, and it helped to clear his mind and shift some of the tiredness. The summer air was warm, but not too hot, and it was nice to get some sunshine and fresh air. If he could call it that. The pollution haze hanging over the city was of concern. The last thing sufferers of this virus needed, with their lungs already struggling for air, was to have to weed out the oxygen from the pollutants too.

He sighed, feeling useless, and decided to review the patients' files again, that Doctor Guterra had granted them access to. He had to keep combing over the detail until he found something, anything, that could help them. If this virus had the potential to become the next pandemic, he did not want to be the one responsible for letting it slip through his grasp and spiraling out of control.

Helen walked along the Avenida Alfonso Ugarte with Justin, Ekemma and Pilar, heading toward a nearby restaurant one of the nurses had recommended for takeout. Dusk was settling over the city and between the pink-orange sky, twinkling building lights, and sporadic palm trees, it felt rather tropical and somewhat soothing, despite the traffic that whizzed past them.

"The new guy seems alright," Justin said, walking along with his hands stuffed into his pockets.

"Yes, I think so," Helen said. From what she'd seen and heard,

Bodhi seemed more than capable, and most importantly, attentive. He was listening and learning, and picking up on things like an epidemiologist should. "So far, so good."

"What is his background?" Ekemma asked.

"He started in medicine," Helen said. "Almost became a regular doctor but wanted to branch into epidemiology instead."

"Was it just me," Pilar said, "or did Aiko sound a little... surprised, maybe unhappy, at his arrival? At least, that's how it sounded over the conference call. Did I miss something?"

"No," Ekemma shook her head. "I picked up on that, too."

Helen shrugged. "They went to school together, but at what point or for how long I don't know. Virology is a different path to epidemiology. But he was confident gathering the samples, seems to be asking the right questions and he's eager, that's for sure. All good qualities."

Ekemma nodded. "I think he'll fit in fine. The real question is, what the hell happened to Robert?"

"That, I still don't know," Helen said. "It's a mystery and Peter is remaining tight-lipped about it."

"Maybe he's sick or something," Pilar said. "Maybe he wants to keep things private."

"I wondered that, too," Justin said.

Helen shrugged again. "Maybe." She ran her eyes across the team, wondering what things would be like in the future, once there was a new Robert. Or perhaps, even, if *she* became the new Robert. Would things change? Would she no longer have moments like this to walk and eat field dinners with the team?

They continued on as the sun set and the temperature

cooled. They came across the restaurant they were looking for and let Pilar do the talking as they each ordered their meals, ready to top up their fuel tanks for another couple of hours, before they crashed and shed what they could of the jet lag and altitude that burdened each of them.

Bodhi, still waiting for the results, decided to check his personal email. He saw one from his mother and opened it. He smiled when he saw the word "banar". It was Hindi for monkey and that was what she called him; her term of endearment. He read her update on things back home in DC with his father, and their two Pomeranians, Raja and Mani, before she moved her thoughts onto his life and his future. Bodhi's smile soon turned into a cringe as she began talking about her friend's single daughter, and he realized the attachment on the email was a photograph of said single daughter. Bodhi groaned. His mother was always trying very hard to find him a wife, wanting to get him married off like his older brother, but the truth was their tastes couldn't be farther apart. Besides, his focus right now was on his career. He'd done the serious relationship thing and it had done nothing but leave him with a broken heart. It had taken him a long time to heal from that, so the last thing he wanted was to go through that again.

Aiko's face appeared in his mind, and he felt his chest tighten a little at the thought of her. This temporary assignment was not going to be great for keeping old wounds sealed, seeing her face every day. Despite him wanting to be here, doing this, thoughts of returning to Atlanta were suddenly solidifying in his mind.

He went to close down the email but hesitated and decided to open the attachment. What could it hurt? He was glad he'd opened it. The woman inside, dressed in a traditional sari at someone's wedding, was pretty and had a nice warm smile about her. Before he could stare at it too long, however, an alert sounded on his laptop.

He closed down his emails and pulled up the GHA software.

Bodhi stared at the words blinking on his screen, confirming what his gut already knew: NO MATCH. The virus spreading here in Peru did not match any of the viruses catalogued in the GHA software. And every known active virus afflicting humans had been catalogued on their system.

"Shit…" he breathed. He looked over at Helen's sequencer, still running her first sample. He checked his watch. Based on how long it took his sample to return the finding of NO MATCH, he figured it could be anywhere up to another hour before the same was reported on hers too. If the cases were related, that is. But given what he'd seen so far, he had no reason to suspect otherwise. He thought about the team phone he'd been issued with but decided against calling Helen just yet. By the time the second one came through, they'd be back from dinner anyway, and she'd made it clear to him that she wanted cold hard facts, not speculation.

He removed the sample from his device, then took the necessary stringent measures required to wash the cells of the portable sequencer, so that it could be reused for a fresh sample. It was a little time consuming given the urgency, but obviously very necessary. Once the device had been thoroughly cleaned, he prepped the next sample, loaded it and started the process all over again. With that underway, he turned back to the software on his laptop and the sample reading NO MATCH. He set about renaming the sample: *Lima-Hospital-ALN-1* and saving it in the database. This now gave all the future samples a chance to be matched to this sample, which would hopefully mean a faster turnaround in results.

Sure enough, eighteen minutes later the second sample on Helen's laptop, *Lima-Convent-SRL-1*, returned no match for the database at large, but a match to the *Lima-Hospital-ALN-1* sample, which confirmed the convent cluster and the hospital patients had the same virus.

An incoming call sounded on Helen's laptop. He scooted over and maximized the comms portal screen and answered it. Aiko's face appeared, and they both froze upon seeing each other.

"Is Helen there?" she asked.

"Er, no… But, hi, Aiko. I'm well, thanks for asking," he said, unable to hide the sarcasm in his voice.

She stared at him, surprised and a little awkward. He exhaled measuredly.

"They're all out grabbing a bite to eat," he said more professionally. "They'll be back soon."

"Oh," she said. The silence sat for a moment and he realized that this was the first time they'd had time to talk without other people around.

"Look, are we going to pretend we don't really know each other?" Bodhi asked. "Is that how you want to play this?"

"You already told everyone we went to school together so we can't do that."

"Right," he said, feeling as though she'd just plunged a dagger in his chest. "So what *do* you want to do then?"

"Well, you're only here temporarily, aren't you?"

Bodhi gave a laugh and shook his head. "Forget I asked." He looked away, too tired to get into this now. What more was there to say? They'd dated for two years, then she suddenly ended their relationship, returned to Japan, and he hadn't heard from her since. Clearly what they had had was a lot more disposable to her than it had been to him.

"I'm sorry..." she said awkwardly. Her apology made him turn his eyes back to hers. "I just wasn't expecting you to turn up in my team like this," she said.

"Yeah, well, I wasn't expecting to see you either, but here we are... And it's fine, 'cause I know how you work. You made a clean break like what we had was nothing, so why would you treat me any differently now? It was only two years of our lives." He stopped suddenly. "Um... no one else is listening to this, are they?"

"Do you think I'd let you keep talking if they were?" Her mask of calmness was betrayed by an underlying flicker of emotion, before it quickly ebbed again.

He smiled and shook his head. She wasn't the cold, closed book she was making herself out to be. He knew better. But for the sake of keeping the peace he'd keep her secret to himself.

"Look," she tried again, "it wasn't going to work. I had to return to Japan. You got the posting in Atlanta, you were staying in the States."

"That wasn't the reason and you know it, Aiko."

"This has nothing to do with my family."

"No, it doesn't. This is all about *you* not standing up to your family and telling them what you really want. You sacrificed me for them. I hope it was worth it."

She looked away and he saw her cheeks flush pink with anger again. She took a second and looked back at him again. "Never speak to me about this over the team comms again. Now," she steadied herself, "the virus hasn't matched to any on file."

"Yes, I know. I was the one actually doing the sequencing here, Aiko. I know what I'm doing. I was top of my class, too."

"Hey, Aiko," Helen said just then, entering with Ekemma, Justin and Pilar. "Are the results in?"

Bodhi looked around at them, wondering if they'd heard anything. "Er, y-yeah," he stuttered, angling the two screens toward them and reducing the size of the comms screen so they could see the data. "The first two samples have been processed and there's no match in the database, but they have matched to each other."

"So we have got a new strain?" Ekemma asked. "Or a new virus altogether?"

Bodhi shrugged and looked back at the comms screen. "I guess that's what Aiko needs to figure out."

Aiko nodded. "I'm reviewing the results as we speak, but I'll also need live samples to study here in the lab."

"We'll get them out by courier to you tonight," Helen said.

"Good. Talk soon," Aiko said, then abruptly ended her comms.

Bodhi looked back at Helen as she moved to take in the results.

"Let's run a few more before we call it a night," she said. "I want to be sure."

Bodhi nodded and they set to work.

It was ten o'clock by the time they finished up. Having been on the go since yesterday, Lyon-time, and with little sleep on the plane, the team were looking weary and sleep was calling them. Bodhi himself was beginning to struggle greatly and could not stop yawning.

Several more results had come through, much faster now, each returning a match to the *Lima-Hospital-ALN-1* and *Lima-Convent-SRL-1* samples, which confirmed that they were very much dealing with an outbreak of the same virus here in Lima, but given there appeared to be a similar outbreak in Iquitos and other towns, it was most likely already an epidemic. Sequencing samples from Iquitos patients would confirm this, but if proven, that meant an epidemic was already raging across Peru.

Bodhi walked up the stairs to their accommodation, a motel close to a busy freeway. His arms were laden with his backpack full of field equipment and the strong scent of disinfectant permeated from his skin as well as that of his colleagues. Helen, Ekemma and Pilar bade them good night, then disappeared into their room, while he followed Justin to theirs.

The room was small but clean and comfortable enough, with white walls, and brightly colored bedspreads and curtains. He placed his backpack on the floor beside the nearest bed, and slumped face down on it.

"That tired, huh?" Justin asked.

"Mm-hm," he murmured. As Justin disappeared into the bathroom, his mind began to wander over the past two days: of joining the Lyon team, and of his first day on the ground in Peru. It had been a whirlwind and there was a lot to process, but right now, more than anything, his brain begged him for sleep.

Helen stood on the balcony overlooking the freeway close by the motel, as cars traveled past to and fro. Pilar was in the bathroom and Ekemma was already fast asleep in her bed. Helen closed the glass sliding door behind her for privacy and held the phone to her ear, waiting for the call to connect.

"So you're alive then," Ethan answered roughly as though he'd just awoken.

"It's nice to hear your voice too," she said.

He sighed heavily down the phone. "Of course I love you, Hels," he said. "I just wish you'd phone your husband more when you're out on site. I always worry, you know that. You said you'd call as soon as you landed."

"I know. I'm sorry. We had to hit the ground running." Making this call had been nagging at her all day. She'd felt bad, which was odd, because normally she was so absorbed in her work that, frankly, all thoughts of Ethan came second. But that was what was niggling at her. Their last conversation hadn't ended so well, and she felt like a terrible wife. He deserved more, but at the same time, she wasn't sure she had it in her to give.

He sighed again. "I'm sorry for what I said before… the way I said it…"

Helen was silent. The truth was, she had nothing to say back to him. That part of her life, losing Angie, was numb. That part of her life was something she didn't have the strength to begin looking at. She just couldn't. It was still too raw. She wasn't ready to grieve. She wasn't ready to let her go.

"So, how bad is it?" he asked, changing the subject.

"It's not looking good. The virus already seems to have spread across the city and possibly farther afield. Our potential Patient Zero was a fan of cross-country public transport, so…"

"Bugger. That's not helpful."

"No. But it's all she could afford. And now she's infected countless people."

"What kind of outbreak is it?"

"We can't find a match as yet, but it feels like an influenza-type virus to me. The way it's looking it has the potential to surpass swine flu and bird flu put together. Maybe even COVID levels."

"Shiiit," he breathed. "So what's the plan?"

"Well, right now, I'm going to sleep on it and try to kick some of this jet lag out the way. I'll decide in the morning."

"That sounds wise."

"I am a wise woman."

"You are. But you're also relentless, Hels. Take care of yourself, you hear?" He grew quiet. "I don't want to lose you, too."

Helen stared out at the freeway lights in the darkness and felt her eyes suddenly sting with tears. "You won't."

Silence hung thickly between them. A truth neither wanted to speak.

"Alright… Well, it's near on four-thirty in the morning here," he said. "I might like to go back to sleep now."

She laughed. "Sorry."

"Don't be. It is good to hear your voice."

"And yours… Goodnight."

"Goodnight."

Helen ended the call and sighed. She stared up at the Peruvian moon and wondered just what news tomorrow would bring.

CHAPTER SEVEN

Bodhi awoke to singing. He opened his eyes and heard water running. The shower. Justin was singing in the shower. He wasn't much of a singer, either. Bodhi took his pillow and threw it over his head.

"Rise and shine!" Justin said loudly. Bodhi opened his eyes and moved the pillow as Justin threw back the curtains, flooding the room with early morning light. Bodhi looked through sleep-crusted eyes as Justin smiled down at him. He was dried and fully dressed. Bodhi must have fallen back asleep for a bit.

"Sleep well?" Justin asked. "You were out like a light by the time I got out of the bathroom last night."

Bodhi grunted.

"Not a morning person, huh?" Justin grinned.

"No, but you obviously are," Bodhi said, not seeing anything to smile about. Justin laughed.

"Mate, I've been up for ages. I've been for a run and everything. You can take the man out of the military, but you can't take the military out of the man!"

Bodhi groaned and Justin chuckled.

"I can see we'll get along well this trip." He moved for the door. "Don't sleep in too long, or you'll miss breakfast."

By the time Bodhi made it down to the café adjoined to the motel, Justin and Pilar were already on their way back to the rooms.

"Boss wants to see you," Pilar said, hiking her thumb back to the café. Bodhi could see Helen and Ekemma sitting by the window at a table bearing dirty breakfast plates, both looking at something on her tablet. Bodhi nodded to Pilar and picked up his pace. He was obviously the last one out of bed and hoped he had time for something to eat before they got moving.

He entered the moderately busy café and the scents of coffee and pastries made his stomach cry out for some.

"Good morning. How did you sleep?" Helen greeted him, as he arrived at their table in the corner of the cafe.

"Fine, until Justin started singing this morning."

Ekemma broke into a toothy smile. "Poor thing thinks he can sing."

"He can't," Bodhi said.

"You go order something and we'll update you," Helen said. Bodhi nodded and walked up to the counter to place his order. He wasn't sure what half of the things on the menu were, but he saw some delicious looking pancake-style dish on another diner's plate and ordered that along with a coffee.

"Aiko's sent her initial findings," Helen said, as he slid into the chair beside hers.

"Yeah?" Bodhi said.

Though the immediate tables around them were empty,

Helen still kept her voice low. "It's a Type A influenza virus, as we suspected. It has similar characteristics to an avian flu but there's also strong characteristics that appear to belong to bats."

"Bats?" he asked. "There's no record of bat-borne influenza transfer to humans before."

"No," Helen said, showing him the sequencing software.

He studied Aiko's notes and nodded to himself in thought. "The Spanish flu was an ancestor of human and swine viruses, but it also had avian-like qualities, so I guess it's possible to now have a human-avian flu with bat virus qualities."

Ekemma nodded. "This is the danger with mutations."

Bodhi nodded in agreement. "I read in the background notes on the portal that Peru has had an increase in rabies cases in recent years due to bites from vampire bats. Mostly children, but I guess you never know. It does suggest more contact between humans and bats. We could be dealing with our very first direct transfer of a bat-borne influenza virus here."

"We certainly can't rule it out," Helen said. "Either way, this has the potential to be big. We may have discovered a new mutated strain of an avian virus, or we may have discovered an entirely new virus altogether that's somehow emerged from the ecosystem."

"Which would normally be an exciting discovery except for the fact that we have no protocols in place to fight it," he said. "No vaccines, no treatments, nothing."

Helen nodded. "That's why within a matter of days it's moved from cluster to outbreak to epidemic. It's spreading incredibly quickly because we have no immunity to it."

"Which means, we could soon have a pandemic on our hands," Ekemma finished.

"All being well, Aiko will have the live samples by this afternoon," Helen said. "Hopefully she can tell us more about it once she has the chance to study things further. Until then, I think we need to get to Iquitos, follow Sister Fuentez's movements, and see if we can find out where and how Sister Apolo caught it."

Ekemma nodded. "There's not much else we can do here in Lima. Doctor Guterra said she would send her nurses to the other hospitals to ensure they were following our quarantine procedures."

Helen stood. "I'll tell Max to alert the WHO to the fact that the outbreak is potentially a new strain of influenza, and all safety measures need to be put in place urgently across the country. We're past a warning now. If we're not careful this will become a full-blown emergency."

The café owner placed Bodhi's plate down on the table, as Ekemma stood also.

"You better eat fast, Bodhi," Helen said. "We're heading to the airport just as soon as Gabe gets us on a flight."

Bodhi nodded and hurriedly began to scoop the food into his mouth as the two women left the café.

Helen was pleased with how quickly Gabriel had issued their tickets to Iquitos, cancelled their Lima accommodation and advised of their new arrangements. The flight time from Lima was two hours and took them into the north-west pocket of the country and into the heart of the Peruvian Amazonas. Based on the notes Lou had added to their case portal, Iquitos was the largest city in the world not accessible by road. Thanks to the Amazon River, the only way to get there was by plane or boat.

Through the airplane's windows, Helen saw a carpet of lush green trees as far as the eye could see, broken only by the mighty Amazon River snaking through it. From up high, the river looked blue as it reflected the sky overhead, but the closer they came to the ground, she could see its true color was a muddy brown. The sunshine looked warm, however the horizon was dark gray and laden with rainclouds. According to the portal information, it rained an average of seventeen days in February, so it wasn't a surprise to see the incoming rain, despite it being summer in this part of the world.

Helen looked back to the carpet of trees below and wondered what bird or bat could be lurking within that carried this potentially deadly virus that was now wreaking havoc on the local human population. And more to the point, just how did this virus pass from them into the human race? Had it been contaminated food or water? Had it been some kind of bite or scratch? Or had it transpired another way, like through eating contaminated meat?

When they stepped outside the terminal, Helen noted that Iquitos, well inland, was much warmer than Lima, which had the benefit of an ocean breeze to cool it.

They split across two small taxi cars and headed into the city's center. Iquitos, she noted, was a buzzing metropolis, that despite not being accessible by road, was not short of vehicles. Home to over 430,000 people, most traveled by motorcycles or motocarros – a motorcycle-style vehicle with an added back seat, similar to a pedicab. Referred to as the 'Capital of the Peruvian Amazon' she saw many tourists walking about Iquitos. Again, this was to be expected from the information Lou had logged in the case file portal. Many used Iquitos as a port from which to undertake one of the many tours offered into the Amazon rainforest. For Helen, this was a major point of concern. If any of these tourists were to pick up whatever killed Sister Apolo, they could easily take the virus back home to their native countries, infecting hundreds of others along the way, and resulting in a full-blown and possibly unstoppable pandemic.

Although she was eager to track down Sister Fuentez, who Sister Apolo had traveled with, their first priority was to visit the local hospitals to see how they were faring and check on their quarantine processes. Gabe had alerted them to three more deaths in the area, including one in the town of Tarapoto, south-west of Iquitos, that had previously reported no cases. By Helen's count, the death toll was now at thirty people, but she knew that probably wasn't an accurate figure, given they had only just identified the virus in their systems. She knew there were bound to be other influenza deaths that the relevant health professionals just hadn't realized belonged to this epidemic as yet – if they even yet realized there was an epidemic to contend with. And that worried her. The faster they informed the Peruvian health networks, the better.

Helen's team traveled together to the Hospital Regional de Iquitos, the largest in the area, to gauge the temperature of the outbreak in these parts and figure out their next steps. Painted in a duology of yellow shades, the hospital was large, standing at four stories high, and a good city block lengthways. Palm trees were dotted here and there as though a reminder that they were in an exotic clime. Not that the reminder was needed with the humidity in the air. Helen had a sheen of sweat on her forehead by the time she reached the doors.

Donned in their surgical masks and gloves, they entered the hospital and Helen knew they were facing a real problem when she saw over forty people in the waiting room, all presenting with signs of influenza; coughing or blowing their nose or looking as though they were running a fever. The numbers looked just as bad as Lima, maybe worse. Helen began to reconsider whether Sister Apolo was indeed their Patient Zero. What if Sister Fuentez was? That could explain the numbers here. Or was it just a matter that she arrived home first and spread it about in the one area sooner, whereas Sister Apolo had infected small amounts of people as she traveled through towns and cities before arriving at the convent and creating the cluster there?

"This is spreading faster than we thought," Ekemma said beneath her face mask. "If there are this many here, the other hospitals will be burdened, too."

"Should we split up?" Justin asked beneath his.

Ekemma nodded. "Yes. Gabe said there were three main hospitals catering to emergencies. You take the next hospital on the list, EsSalud. I'll deal with this one."

"Agreed," Helen said. "Bodhi, why don't you go with Justin, and I'll head to the third one, Clinica Ana Stahl." She turned to Bodhi. "Do you speak any Spanish at all?"

"The basics. Enough to get by, I think. You?"

"Summers in Spain with my family," she said. "Yes, enough to get by, too."

"Is it a good idea to split up?" Pilar said, eyes staring at Helen over her face mask.

"I think it spread here in Iquitos first," Helen said. "They're looking worse than Lima right now. We can't afford to bunch together. We need to assess the quarantine measures at each hospital and ensure they're heeding the GHA's health emergency alert."

"Iquitos has international flights, too," Justin said. "This zone could be catastrophic if left unchecked."

"It might already be too late," Helen said.

Pilar sighed. "Alright, who has the worst Spanish?"

They looked at each other, then Ekemma shrugged. "Me."

"I'll stay with Kem, then," Pilar said. "But I want you all to check in with me hourly. Got it?"

"Yes, boss," Helen smiled beneath her mask, before turning serious again. "From this point forward we all wear our containment suits. Got it? Don't take any risks."

The team nodded, then went their separate ways.

Bodhi was trying to maintain his calm and patience. It was hot, he was sweating, and the language barrier was taking its toll, despite finding someone who did speak English, although a very broken form of it.

The hospital itself was busy, verging on chaotic. The waiting room was full and the staff were beginning to feel overwhelmed. It was clear to him this epidemic was reminding them of COVID and the worry showed in their eyes.

He assisted Justin as he helped ensure the health workers were using best practices for handling such a virus. For the most part they were already adhering to them, but it was clear that being overwhelmed and understaffed, anything could fall through the cracks. And if that happened, with an unstoppable virus and one misstep, the tables could turn in an instant. Taking care of the patients was incredibly important, but the priority was to keep the healthcare workers safe. If they fell ill, it would have devastating effects on the community at large.

After conferring with the nursing staff and one or two doctors, he left Justin attending to the quarantine zones and set about taking a random selection of samples from the admitted patients, who were for all intents and purposes displaying symptoms of the newly identified virus. As expected with influenza outbreaks, the three groups most vulnerable to this type of illness were presenting: the elderly, young children, and those with underlying pre-existing medical conditions. But they weren't alone. There were many patients outside of these groups. Many were in their prime, and for the most part, appeared otherwise in good health. This only seemed to cement the fact that they were indeed dealing with a virus that the human body had not encountered before. And worse, the virus was killing many of its victims before their bodies had a chance to build resistance and fight back.

He took samples until the small cold box that came with his backpack was full, then he set about undertaking another round of the wards, eager to observe the progress of the current patients, study the new patients, and most importantly, ask each of them questions on their movements and interactions – tracing their contact and trying to find a link. And he did find a link with some, although not all. Some of the patients attended a local church and had all been to the same mass almost a week ago, or knew someone who had. Bodhi was sure if he looked further, he would probably find that Sister Fuentez had attended the same mass.

•••

Helen was as satisfied as she could be with the hospital she'd been assigned to. Several hours had passed and she'd been lucky that there was an English-speaking doctor on staff, so she was able to easily communicate how to improve their quarantine. She helped them set up the standard three zones to assist with triage: a low probability ward, high probability ward, and a full quarantine ward. She also assessed their decontamination processes and questioned many of the patients about their symptoms, the timeline of when they first fell ill and whether they knew where they had caught it, and everyone they had been in contact with for the past few days.

As she walked down the corridor to leave the hospital, a body in a cadaver bag was being wheeled along beside her. From what the doctor had told her, this was their eleventh fatality in the past few days. She exited the hospital, free of her containment suit and smelling of disinfectant, as she pulled her phone from her bag. She'd done what she could to reassure herself that the hospital was doing everything it could to contain the spread, but now she had to get back to the investigation at hand and find further information on Sister Fuentez. That is where she could provide the most benefit in stopping this virus, by tracing it to its source, which would hopefully help them to find a cure.

"Bodhi?" she said when the call connected.

"Hi," he answered. "Are you ready to head to the convent?"

"Yes. Are you done there?"

"Yeah. Justin's almost done with the quarantine zones and they've been receptive to his suggestions for improvement, so it's as good as it can be here."

"How many dead there?"

"Seven."

"I had eleven at this one."

"From what I can tell, a lot of them attended the same church. I bet Sister Fuentez attended it, too," he said.

"Yeah, I got the same here. I'll come and get you."

Helen hailed a motocarro, as her own personal concern elevated from an alert to an emergency, thinking about what danger the Peruvian people were in, and quite possibly the rest of the world. She would need to start considering all manner of options. Did she recommend the WHO announce an emergency? Did she keep the alert targeted at Peru or did she make it a global alert? Should she recommend they step up airport surveillance or shut down the airports in the infected towns entirely? She knew from experience that many of the top-level recommendations could take time and a lot of political red tape to action and enforce. If she waited too long, it could be too late. They couldn't make the same mistakes they did during COVID.

En route to the convent, Helen collected both Bodhi and then Pilar, in case she needed the latter's translation skills at the convent. Before joining them, Pilar had managed to find an English-speaking nurse and assigned her to take over as Ekemma's translator.

They drove the busy streets in two motocarros, weaving in and out of traffic, passing all kinds of stores and street sellers along the way. Though the hospitals were taking the relevant precautions, word had not reached civilians as yet. They were still mingling, and none wore masks or gloves. Helen swallowed as she thought once more about elevating the emergency so people were aware of the grave risks.

They passed an open green park space opposite a large cathedral. The gardens were well manicured around a central fountain and a large white war memorial, with all sorts of palms and other trees offering shade. Some of the surrounding buildings looked very worn and ready to tear down, but among them were newer buildings; banks, hotels and the like.

"Plaza de Armas," Bodhi said, reading an app on his GHA phone, as they passed the park.

"It means Weapons Square or Parade Square," Pilar told them from her motorcarro, which had pulled up alongside theirs at a set of traffic lights.

"What's the name of the church?" Helen asked Bodhi.

"According to this, it's St John the Baptist Cathedral."

Helen nodded, studying the neo-gothic architecture of it. The cathedral, like many buildings here, was painted a pale yellow, with white trimmings and maroon roofing. She wasn't religious herself, but hoped those who were in Peru, started praying.

They traveled onward for another fifteen minutes until they arrived at the Convent de Augoustus de Iquitos, where Sister Fuentez resided. As they pulled up out front, an incoming call sounded on Helen's tablet. She answered it while Pilar and Bodhi paid the motorcarros drivers, which then went on their way.

Helen watched as the faces of Max and Lou appeared on screen, which meant they were in the process of a shift change back in Lyon. According to their portal, Gabriel had the six am to six pm shift, Max had the four pm to midnight shift and Lou had the ten pm to eight am shift, which allowed a two-hour period of crossover between each shift, while Aiko worked whatever hours were required of her.

"What do you have for us?" Helen asked them.

"Mother Superior Carmen made contact," Max said. "She passed on details of the few travel tickets that were still in Sister Apolo's possession."

"I'm going through them now," Lou said, "but among them I've already found one for Brazil, and I got bad news for you."

"What is it?" Helen asked, as her body stilled.

"Since we released the health alert for Peru, we've had a spike in influenza-related death reports coming in from Brazil. We're looking into them now, but I thought you'd want to know that it's–"

"Already jumped the border," Helen said, feeling her chest compress with the news. Bodhi and Pilar joined her, studying her face, sensing something was awfully wrong. "Alright, see if you can get access to samples and get Aiko onto the sequencing of the Brazil cases straightaway, so we can confirm it's our virus. Did she go home?"

"No, she slept in the staff quarters here, just in case," Max said. "I'll go wake her now."

"Thanks. We're about to head into the Iquitos convent. Hopefully we'll get some more answers, but I think in the meantime you should call Davidson. I think we need to elevate the status and make it global. We need the airports on alert and close all borders in the region."

"Alright. Shit," Max said, his face showing what Helen felt inside, the alarming knowledge of all the work that would need to be done to stop this, that this wasn't any ordinary influenza. Like everyone else on this planet, they each had their own COVID stories burned into their memories, ones they did not wish to revisit.

"We'll check in again in a few hours, if not before," Helen said.

"Max is heading home soon, but I'll be here," Lou said. "Call me if you need me."

"Thank you, Lou," Helen said. She shut down the comms and put her tablet into her bag.

"Did I hear you say it's jumped the border?" Pilar asked.

Helen nodded. "We have confirmed reports of a spike of influenza deaths in Brazil."

"Outbreaks in two countries," Bodhi said, eyes filled with concern. "Our epidemic is now officially a pandemic."

"Well, potentially, yeah," Helen said gravely. "But first we need to confirm this is the case by testing samples, and even if they are found to be the same, you know the WHO doesn't pull out the P-word that easy. They'll call them linked epidemics."

"Yeah," Bodhi nodded. "Because one P word sparks the other P word. Panic."

Helen nodded, and Pilar added, "And we do need to bear in mind that some politicians hereabouts have been known to question whether viruses and pandemics even exist. What if they do the same with this one as they initially did with COVID?"

They exchanged concerned looks, before Helen said, "Let's get our containment suits on, and see what we can find out about Sister Fuentez."

CHAPTER EIGHT

Bodhi studied the convent as they approached in their disposable containment suits, surgical masks and gloves. The convent was much older and a lot less grand than the one they'd visited in Lima, and he noted there seemed to be fewer people about in the area. Whether that was typical for this convent or whether it was an effect of the virus, he wasn't sure. As they approached the double entrance doors and saw the sign posted on it, however, it became evident. He didn't understand the entirety of what the sign said, but he did pick out two words he knew: "enfermedad" and "muerte", which meant "illness" and "death".

When they knocked on the door, a voice eventually answered from behind it in Spanish. Pilar listened then looked at Helen and Bodhi. "They say there's illness here and to go away." She looked back at the door and spoke in the woman's native tongue. Bodhi heard Pilar requesting someone that spoke English. After a few moments and more

Spanish voices in conversation behind the door it opened. A middle-aged nun stood there, unable to hide her initial surprise, and perhaps fright, at the sight of them in their containment suits.

Once the surprise slipped away, the nun soon appeared old and tired. She stood back and waved them through. They entered a corridor and followed her to a sitting room. She motioned for them to sit, then disappeared. They remained standing. Eventually the nun came back with a young girl, obviously a novice in training to become a nun. She looked to be in her late teens, with olive skin and brown eyes.

"My name is Sister Maria," she said, her English strong. "How can we help?"

"We're from the Global Health Agency," Helen said, and Bodhi sensed relief in her voice at not having to struggle with communication. "We're here to help with the influenza outbreak. We want to speak with someone about Sister Fuentez."

The young nun performed a sign of the cross over herself. "Sister Fuentez has passed." Bodhi wasn't surprised to hear this, nor were Helen or Pilar based on their reactions.

"I'm very sorry to hear that," Helen said. "May I ask, how long ago?"

"Eleven days."

Bodhi's mind turned quickly. "That would make it about a day after Sister Apolo," he said.

"Would you happen to know where she went with Sister Apolo on their travels?" Helen asked the girl.

"They traveled mainly along the Amazon to the borders."

"Do you know all the places they stopped?" Helen asked.

"They stop wherever they can."

"Did Sister Fuentez tell you of their travels? Who they met with?"

"Not me, no."

"But someone else?"

The girl thought for a moment. "She roomed with Sister Chavez. They were close."

"May we speak with her?"

Sister Maria shook her head and performed another sign of the cross.

"I'm so sorry," Helen said, and Bodhi saw her shoulders slump. He'd have felt his own fall, too, if they were not so tense. "Is there anyone else here who may have spoken with Sister Fuentez after her travels? We do really need details."

Again the girl thought. In the background, the elderly nun who had answered the door said something in Spanish to the girl. The girl looked around at her and for a moment they conversed between the two of them, as though the girl were catching the elder Sister up. The elder Sister mentioned a name and the girl looked back to Helen and repeated it.

"Sister Manuel may know," she said. "She helped care for Sister Fuentez, but she is very sick."

Bodhi felt a sense of hope fill him, but it was immediately followed by despair when he heard the Sister was ill. He saw Helen's eyes fill with the same duo of emotion. All their leads, all those who may hold any useful information were dying or dead. "May we speak with her?" Helen asked.

The girl nodded and motioned them to follow.

Bodhi, Helen and Pilar followed Sister Maria down several corridors and a set of stairs to the basement. When they came upon the room, the girl knocked softly and opened the door. As she went to enter, Helen caught her arm.

"Have you been inside this room before?"

The young woman shook her head.

"Then you must stay out here," she warned. "Never go in there. Not while they're sick. Understand?"

Sister Maria looked at Helen, the worry evident in her eyes. "Is it like the corona?"

"It's a different kind of virus," Helen told her, "but you should treat it as though it was. Stay away, sanitize thoroughly, and wear masks if you can."

Sister Maria nodded and stayed by the door with Pilar, as Bodhi and Helen entered.

Sister Manuel lay propped up on several pillows in the dark room, lit only with candles. The cough was ragged and seemed to rattle her frail ribcage. Bodhi knew she was in a bad way before he even had the chance to study her.

"Sister Manuel?" Helen said softly.

The woman murmured something in Spanish.

"Pilar?" Helen called. Pilar stepped into the room but held back a little, despite her surgical mask, gloves and containment suit. "Tell her we're here to help. Tell her we need to know about Sister Fuentez's travels."

Pilar nodded and began to speak gently. The woman opened her eyes. Even in the dim light, the whites looked all pink. They seemed to roll around the room, but eventually they fell on Pilar. The GHA military liaison continued to speak in Spanish, carefully stepping closer to the woman.

Finally the woman responded, but she only managed a few words before the fluid in her lungs somehow cut the air off from her throat. They waited patiently while her weakened body struggled to clear itself. Once able to breathe again, Sister Manuel closed her eyes and continued murmuring. Bodhi and Helen waited patiently while Pilar and the woman conversed slowly.

"She's not making much sense," Pilar eventually said. "I'm not sure if she's dreaming or talking to me."

Bodhi felt a sense of urgency spike within him. "Ask her if Fuentez mentioned them meeting anyone sick."

Pilar spoke. The woman was silent. Pilar stepped forward again and repeated what she said. The woman opened her eyes and said something, before her wet lungs tried to choke her again. This time the attack was much more violent than the last, and blood sprayed across her lips and down her chin. They all reacted silently.

"What did she say?" Helen asked, stepping closer and wiping the woman's mouth with her gloved hands.

"I don't know," Pilar said, her brows knotted in puzzlement. "She said something about a boy. A young boy."

"A boy?" Bodhi asked, feeling his spine straighten, his mind turning over. "Mother Superior Carmen said that Sister Apolo spoke of a boy in her fevered state, the night before her death. They thought she was talking about baby Jesus. Was the boy ill?" he asked Pilar.

Pilar turned and asked the woman, while Helen moved to support the Sister's head and helped her to sip some water.

The woman croaked something out. This time, Bodhi made out the word, *Benjamin.*

"Benjamin," Pilar confirmed. "The boy's name was Benjamin."

"He was sick?" Bodhi asked. Pilar nodded. "Where? Where did they come across him? How old was he?"

Sister Manuel's body seemed to fall limp in Helen's hands, and she lay the woman's head back on the pillow, her eyes closed in rest. Pilar asked more questions but all they received in return was slurred, quiet murmurs. She looked so incredibly weak. Bodhi predicted she wasn't far from death, that perhaps she might not make it through the night. He looked to Helen and saw the same resignation in her eyes.

"She needs to rest," Helen said softly. "We can't keep pushing her."

Reluctantly, Bodhi nodded in agreement.

They moved out into the corridor and followed the young girl, at a distance, back up the stairs. As they stepped outside, Bodhi discarded his mask, looked up into the sunlight and breathed the fresh air, glad to be alive.

Helen's mind fired rapidly, trying to beat back the hopelessness that tried to claw its way inside her. The confirmation that neither Sister was their Patient Zero only meant they were back to square one, while the spreading virus only grew stronger. They carefully removed their masks, gloves and disposable suits, placing their waste into sealed biohazard bags from their field packs, then carefully cleaned their hands and sprayed their entire bodies with a sanitizer.

"We need to find this boy," Bodhi said. "They both mentioned him. They were trying to tell us something. He must be our Patient Zero."

"We need a last name," Pilar said. "There's bound to be a lot of Benjamins in this country."

Helen nodded, rubbing her neck. "Let me check in with Lyon," she said, pulling out her tablet. "Pilar, ask Ekemma and Justin what they've found, would you?"

Pilar nodded. She walked away a few steps as she pulled out her phone, while Helen contacted the home base team.

Lou's face appeared. "How did it go?"

"Not good, Lou, and it's getting worse by the hour. Aiko filled you in on what we're looking at?"

"Yeah. An unknown strain. Some kind of avian-bat influenza virus."

"Yeah," Helen said. "Our human bodies have some familiarity with avian influenza viruses, but less so with bat-borne influenza viruses. Which means we could be in for a world of pain. Literally."

"How can I help?"

"We thought Sister Apolo or perhaps Sister Fuentez were our Patient Zero, but they're not. We think they came in contact with a sick boy named Benjamin. But we don't have a surname. We need to try to find him and see if he's our Patient Zero. We need to trace the infection and see where and how he caught it."

"You want me to search for Benjamins in Peru?" The look on her face was part questioning, part surprised, part "you must be joking?"

Helen smiled grimly. "I know it's crazy, but we have to start somewhere. Just try to search for this immediate area around Iquitos to start with. Perhaps we can narrow it down a little, at least. Has any other information come through?"

Lou checked the screens at her desk, tapping here and there. "I've applied the travel ticket details sent through from

Mother Superior Carmen onto a map of the area, along with the reported deaths and patient numbers."

"Anything of interest?"

She looked back into the camera. "Well, nothing that we didn't already guess. There are definitely correlations between Sister Apolo's journey with the reported outbreaks and it's all spiraling outward from there. With each new report that comes in, as you can imagine, our chain of infection tree is growing branches like there's no tomorrow. Three towns in Brazil have now reported cases, and I'm about to check on Colombia and Bolivia now."

"And each reported death is being updated into our timeline for the predictive modelling to assess, right?"

"Yes," she said, looking at the other screen. "I've been keeping it updated. You can access it through the GHA software as normal. Though, I'll add, Brazil is currently only listing these as standard influenza only. They haven't issued any health alerts to their country as yet."

Helen sighed. "OK, keep in touch." She ended the conversation and looked around at the streets. Bodhi joined her.

In this area the buildings looked very aged and worn. Helen stared, almost trance-like, at a group of young children, playing some kind of hopscotch game down the street. She heard their laughter and squeals, saw how much fun they were having.

Angie flashed into her mind again. Angie in the end days. Angie pale, skinny, and so, so, weak.

"Helen?" Bodhi verbally nudged her. She looked at him. "What are you thinking?"

She continued staring at the children.

"I'm not thinking anything right now," she said. "I'm just feeling fear. The kind of fear only the threat of a pandemic can bring. If I'm thinking anything, it's of the countless innocent lives at risk. Innocent lives who, right now, have no idea of the invisible killer that's knocking at their door." She looked back at him. "Peru is a developing country, not a third world country, but that doesn't make me feel any less troubled. They'll have some structures in place from the COVID pandemic, which is good, but if this virus spirals past COVID, will they have the necessary infrastructure in place to handle a pandemic of that magnitude?"

"Probably not," Bodhi said quietly.

She nodded and exhaled heavily as she continued to look around the streets. "Where are you, Benjamin?" she said quietly.

"Justin reported another death," Pilar said, approaching. "Both he and Ekemma say there's not much more they can do where they are. The quarantine zones are in place, so it's just a day by day fight now for the health workers to contain it. Ekemma thinks we should probably get WHO volunteers on standby ready to deploy."

Helen nodded. "Let's get Kem and Justin and head to our accommodation. We'll go over our interviews and see what else we can piece together. Hopefully Aiko will report in soon with further information on the virus."

Aiko Ishikawa sat on a stool in her lab and checked her watch. It was one am but her brain was still firing on all cylinders; she did her best work in the quiet early morning hours. She'd been searching the database for known links to bat-borne viruses, eager to leave no stone unturned.

She knew bats were known carriers of over sixty-five human pathogens. They were a primary cause of rabies, after all. Bats were believed to have been the cause of the severe acute respiratory syndrome (SARS) outbreak, although recent evidence now suggested that SARS may have possibly originated from civet cats. Bats were also suspected to have originated the virus that caused the Middle East respiratory syndrome (MERS) outbreak, both of these involving a type of coronavirus. On top of this, bats had been linked to several other virus outbreaks in humans, such as the Nipah virus, Lassa virus, Ebola virus and Marburg virus, among others. Her focus, however, was tracking down information on bat flu viruses, which were only first discovered by scientists in 2009. In 2012 it was discovered that the way bat flu viruses infected their host's cells were very different from other A type influenza viruses.

She found herself reading a 2013 CDC study on the A/bat/Peru/10 flu virus. It was identified as an influenza A type virus and named H18N11, however the researchers had not been able to grow it in the lab, which indicated that it may not be able to infect humans. But Aiko knew that mutations could easily occur that could enable this virus to jump species and eventually find a way to enter humans. As always there was much more study to be undertaken in this area, particularly with regards to a bat's immune system and why these creatures were especially adapted to tolerate viruses and not fall sick themselves.

She flicked screens on her laptop to check the latest casualty statistics and how these affected their predictive modelling. The numbers had grown further since she'd checked just a few hours ago. Seventy deaths had now been officially reported in Peru, and forty in Brazil. The number of deaths had now exceeded one hundred. And they were rising every day – and so, too, was their modelling, exponentially so.

Aiko switched to the map showing the location of each outbreak, indicated by red circles of various sizes. The larger the circle, the higher the casualty rate of the hot spot. There were so many red circles now. They would only grow as more hospitals in the regions became aware of the problem and posted their statistics. And that was just two countries. Lou was about to update the figures from all surrounding countries that shared borders with Peru: Bolivia, Ecuador, Colombia and Chile.

Her eyes drifted back to one of the larger circles, resting over Iquitos. She thought of the GHA team being right in the middle of it. Of course, they'd been in hot spots before and she knew they would take the necessary precautions, but she wasn't sure that they'd been in the midst of a pandemic that had moved this fast before, or killed so swiftly. And that concerned her.

She thought of Bodhi then. Given all that had happened, she hadn't had time to process him suddenly being back in her life. She closed her eyes briefly, admonishing herself for talking to him the way she did. Their break-up hadn't been his fault. She'd been the one to end it, and she'd regretted it every day since. She'd had a great career, but it had been a lonely one. After a while she had tried to date again, but it had only made her realize just what she'd given up.

And now Bodhi had suddenly re-appeared in her life, just like that. Was this her opportunity to make amends for past mistakes? Was this a second chance? Or was this her self-inflicted loneliness tormenting her? Bodhi had come back into her life, but now he was in a hot spot that was rapidly turning into an inferno. What if she lost him for good?

"Hey," Lou said, entering the lab, startling her. "The live samples have arrived from Lima."

"Finally!" Aiko said, all focus returned. She jumped off her stool and took the refrigerated box from her.

"Let me know if you need anything," Lou said.

"I will," she replied, but she was already halfway out the door.

Helen and the team were gathered in Bodhi and Justin's room, spread out across the two beds, each with their laptops or tablets out; all except Ekemma who paced the room, thinking aloud. They'd grabbed a quick bite to eat for dinner and were now going over everything they had learned to figure out a way forward. It had been a long day.

"So, Sister Apolo was the first reported death in Lima," Ekemma said, "and Sister Fuentez was the first reported death in Iquitos. And together they were the first two reported deaths according to our current timeline."

"Yes," Helen said, "because they were traveling together and came across this boy, Benjamin."

"Well," Justin said, "if Aiko thinks this new virus could potentially be a bat-borne virus, where, along the Amazon, where Apolo and Fuentez traveled, might they or this boy have come in contact with bats?"

"Let me check," Bodhi said, tapping away at his laptop. "Good news!" he said sarcastically, reading the notes posted by Lou. "They're found all over Peru and there are one hundred and fifty-two known species of them, of which approximately sixty per cent are found in the northern Amazon Basin in Peru." He looked up at the team. "We're apparently dealing with one of the most diverse ecosystems of small mammals in the world." He sighed, moving his laptop aside. "My biggest concern here is that the Sisters traveled as far as the Tres Fronteras, which is the area where Peru, Colombia and Brazil meet. If they were sick when they were there, then it won't just be Brazil reporting deaths, but Colombia will be, too. We need their data."

"Let's see if Lou has had a report from Colombia yet," Helen said, as she accessed the GHA link to the latest WHO data. They sat silently while she searched for the answer.

"We need to close the airports," Ekemma said.

"The bigger problem we face," Pilar said, studying her own laptop screen, "is that a lot of the borders around here are open. From what I've read, you can walk straight through from Colombia to Brazil and back again. They ask you to visit the office and get a stamp, but there's no real form of border control. And Peru is joined to five countries. There's almost five thousand miles of boundary to control. There's no way, with its typical staffing, that you can have any form of quarantine policing. It's already jumped the border and if we want to stop it spreading any further, the Peruvian government might just need military assistance to insist on a country-wide lockdown."

Ekemma nodded. "Without tight border control, they can't

stop people passing between and infecting countless others. It's a prime area for a pandemic to spread."

"This is the one good thing about living in an island nation," Justin said. "Australia has just over sixteen thousand miles of coastline. Aside from the occasional small boat of refugees, people arrive there by airplanes or large ships that pull into ports, so we have a better chance of stopping contagions before they hit land. And they learned a hard lesson about cruise ships during the COVID-19 pandemic, that's for sure."

An alert sounded on Helen's comms software and she answered it.

"Lou?" she said. "What do you have for us?"

"I wanted to let you know that the live samples have arrived and Aiko is working on them as we speak," she said.

"Excellent," Helen said, feeling a little of the pressure in her chest ease. Knowing that Aiko was working on things and would do so with their extended GHA network if necessary, gave her some hope.

"I've also been taking a further look at all Sister Apolo's movements. So, you know I've looked through the details of the few travel tickets that Sister Apolo had and I've marked these places on the map." Lou shared the relevant screen with them, so theirs split in two, showing Lou on one side and the map on the other. "Most of the stubs, according to the dates and times printed on them, show a path from Iquitos back to Lima. Although from what I can gather on the travel possibilities, there are other towns she would've needed to pass through to return home, so there must be some stubs missing. But more interesting than that," Lou said, as the map's data cleared, "based on the influenza deaths reported in the past few days now the warning is out, we can clearly trace Sister Apolo's path back to Lima, by the number of deaths. Though perhaps not one hundred per cent accurate, we could presume the areas of greater numbers as having been affected the longest, and the lower number of deaths having been affected the least amount of time." A series of red circles appeared on the map, dotting between Iquitos and Lima. Each dot tracing from Iquitos to Lima grew smaller in size. "But *most* interesting of all," Lou said, "since we sent out the elevated health alert, we've been watching the influenza deaths recently reported in Brazil and now in Colombia." She tapped another button and more red circles appeared. Much larger than those in Peru. "And going by the numbers and dates of death, they're much older than many of those in Peru."

"Which means it started there," Bodhi said, straightening. "Not in Peru."

Helen nodded, feeling her heart begin to race as the path of infection became clearer. "Sister Apolo went to the Tres Fronteras, caught the illness, then took it all the way home to Lima, infecting countless people along the way. This didn't start in Peru, it just ended up there."

"Yes," Lou said. "And it's now threading its way through three countries. I have no doubt it will appear elsewhere across the globe very soon, as information on the South American alert spreads."

"We need Davidson to get the WHO to push the alert worldwide," Ekemma said. "We need to declare an international health emergency and offer other countries the opportunity of turning away people with symptoms at their borders if they can. We cannot have another COVID-19 so soon."

"Absolutely," Justin agreed.

Bodhi nodded. "Meanwhile, we need to get to the Tres Fronteras to find the source."

Helen agreed. "We need to find this boy, Benjamin."

"I don't suppose you know his age?" Lou asked. "The number of Benjamins in Peru is staggering and that's just the ones with birth certificates. We may have a general location of the Tres Fronteras now, but it's still three countries I need to search."

"If he was the source of infection it's unlikely he would still be alive," Justin said. "That narrows things down a bit. We're looking for dead Benjamins."

"And he would be one of the earliest, if not *the* earliest death recorded," Bodhi said. "If the timeline from infection to death is approximately seven days, then we're looking at up to a week before Sister Apolo died."

"We should try the convent here again," Helen decided, already pulling out her phone. "See if we can get more information from Sister Manuel." She paced the room nervously waiting for the call to connect, hoping they could still get some sense out of the dying Sister before it was too late.

"While I'm waiting for more information on this boy," Lou said, tapping away at her console, "I'll see what I can do about getting you to the Tres Fronteras, in Gabe's absence. Knowing our contingency planner, I'm sure he's thought ahead and booked something for you."

Helen heard her call connect and asked to speak to Sister Maria, the young nun who spoke English.

"What I'm confused about," Pilar said in the background, "is how we were directed to Peru first? If the infection started in Colombia or Brazil, shouldn't we have been notified to the outbreak there first?"

Ekemma shrugged. "It can depend on a number of things, politics and red tape being one. Some countries don't want to admit they have a problem and accept outside help until it's too late. You remember what happened. Plus each country has different reporting processes and escalation procedures. Another factor is having a doctor who keeps abreast of the WHO and follows their advice and reports things accordingly. We were lucky that Doctor Guterra was very aware and responsive."

"Hello?" Sister Maria came to the phone and Helen turned away from the team.

"Hi, Sister Maria. It's Doctor Helen Taylor. I'm wondering if you can ask Sister Manuela whether Sister Fuentez mentioned the age of the sick boy, Benjamin."

"I am sorry," Sister Maria said softly. Helen heard her sniff and realized she was crying. "She passed not long ago."

Helen exhaled, lowering her head and closing her eyes. Should they have persisted earlier despite her fragility? She looked up and saw Bodhi staring with fixed eyes, trying to read hers. "OK. Thank you," she said to Sister Maria. "I'm very sorry."

"Damn it," Bodhi said, slumping back against the wall as she hung up the call. "She passed?"

Helen nodded, and Justin stood.

"Then we've got no choice but to head to the Tres Fronteras

and see what we can find out," he said. "There's nothing more we can do here, so let's start packing."

"Wait!" Lou said, her eyes fixed on something. "Hold the damn phone…"

"What is it?" Helen asked, returning her eyes to her laptop screen.

"What did the nun say about Benjamin, exactly?"

"Sister Apolo apparently talked about a boy in her final stages," Helen said, "and the nun we spoke to today, here in Iquitos, said she overheard Sister Fuentez talking with another about an ill boy they came across. Sister Manuel said the name Benjamin."

"And you're sure his name was Benjamin?" Lou looked over her red-framed glasses into the camera. "You sure it wasn't *in* Benjamin?"

"What?" Helen's brow furrowed.

The map on one of their screens zoomed in to show the tri-country borders.

"This is the Tres Fronteras," Lou said. "Look there, at the bottom of the screen. In Brazil, and right on the border with Peru."

Helen's mouth fell open and her heart rate shot up again.

"Benjamin Constant…" Bodhi said, staring at it.

"It's a town?" Justin asked.

Ekemma smiled. "We're looking for a sick boy in Benjamin Constant. We're closing in on the source!"

"Yes!" Justin said, pulling Ekemma into a hug. She laughed and so, too, did Bodhi and Pilar.

"Lou," Helen said earnestly, "I love you and you're worth every penny!"

Lou smiled. "Yeah, just make sure Robert hears th– Oh wait. *You're* the boss now. Yeah, I am worth it, ain't I, boss?"

Helen grinned. "We'll discuss that later. Right now, I need you to get us to Benjamin Constant!"

CHAPTER NINE

Bodhi stood behind Helen in the queue to board the fast boat to Tabatinga, Brazil, calling at Benjamin Constant. Even more remote than Iquitos, Benjamin Constant was really only accessible by boat. In some ways, Bodhi was relieved there were no airports or roads, but he still knew how many people the boy or the nuns could have infected on the journey to or from, or simply while they passed through the town.

It was six am and already warm, with the humidity very present. He felt something tickle his neck and slapped it, then looked at his fingers to see the remains of a mosquito. The process to board had been time consuming. There were maybe a hundred passengers, and so far, their passports, tickets and Peru visa had been checked no less than three times. This was obviously not one of the lax border control areas. They seemed to be stirring some interest for wearing their masks, too.

Given time was of the essence, they had been hoping to travel by air to Tabatinga, as the flight was just an hour, but it only departed on Mondays and Fridays. Given it was a Wednesday, an eight-hour fast boat was now their best option. They could've taken several other flights and detours to get there, but the time they spent doing that would be just as long, when including the time spent waiting around at airports. Besides, it was along the river that Sister Apolo traveled, and if they were to investigate this properly, it made sense to follow a similar route.

They filed aboard via the gangway at the bow, then entered the cabin and followed the aisle down the middle of the long, narrow enclosed boat, filled with rows of seats. Bodhi took a seat on the right-hand side of the aisle, as the team and a swarm of tourists filled the area around him. The seats themselves were comfortable enough, with more leg room than an airplane and Bodhi's row had a power outlet for recharging their electronic devices, which was good given they'd be stuck on this boat for eight hours.

Helen sat in the aisle seat beside Bodhi, while Ekemma and Pilar sat in front of them, and before them, sat Justin against the window. With shouts back and forth from the Peruvian crew, the boat finally got underway. Bodhi was glad they'd opted to sit toward the front of the boat as the engine at the rear was loud.

He felt a little restless as he stared out the window at the passing brown Amazon waters. Knowing the virus was raging through three countries now and that they were trapped on this boat for eight hours with little more to do than speculate, frustrated him. He watched the team around him to gauge how they were dealing with the forced stagnation. Pilar had slumped down in her seat, looking as though she was going to snooze behind her mirrored sunglasses. Justin had put earphones in and was nodding his head to music as he watched the passing scenery. Helen had pulled her tablet out and looked to be scrolling through Lou's notes on Benjamin Constant, while Ekemma just stared out the window, thinking.

Bodhi regarded Ekemma for a moment, then leaned forward. "Have you been to South America before?"

She glanced over her shoulder at him, then back out the window again. "Brazil, yes, but not to the places we are going."

"Did you work the Zika outbreak with Helen?"

Ekemma's eyes smiled over her mask. "Yes. That was our first field case together."

Bodhi nodded. "I just got bitten by a mosquito, so I hope I'm not about to become another case."

"As long as you're not pregnant I'm sure you will be fine," she said dryly.

Bodhi smiled. "I sure hope I'm not. Zika would be the last of my problems if I were."

Ekemma chuckled. "Do you have kids?"

"Oh, no. I'm far too young for that."

Ekemma turned to view him again. "What are you? Late twenties?" She scoffed a laugh and looked back out the window again.

He smiled. "What about you?"

She gave a single nod. "I have a son. Tayo. He is at university in Oxford."

Bodhi flinched in confusion. "You ... don't look old enough to have a son at university. What are you? Like, late twenties, too?"

Ekemma grunted. "You flatter me. I am thirty-four, but yes, I had my son when I was very young." She fell silent and her face stilled as her eyes became lost in a memory. There was something about the tone of her voice that made him not want to push that line of conversation any further. He decided to change the subject slightly.

"What is he studying? Tayo?"

"Political science," she answered. "He wants to follow his grandfather into politics."

"Your father is a politician?"

Ekemma gave a nod. "One who believes he is making a difference in Nigeria. But I think he could do much more." Bodhi sensed disapproval in her voice. He made a mental note to perhaps avoid talking about her family from this point forward.

Distraction came and he was relieved. Breakfast was being served; some kind of fried pork and sweet potato dish. While Bodhi ate, he watched other boats pass them, and the towns on the banks float past. Most looked to be fishing villages with small children out front, splashing in the water, while parents and grandparents watched over them. Curiously he pulled out his phone and opened up the pre-loaded geographic app that would hopefully tell him what each village was called, trying to educate himself on a part of the world he knew little about.

Soon enough the rainforest canopy was all around them. He was amazed that even from the middle of the Amazon River, despite the loud motor and conversations around him, he could hear a symphony of insect, bird and monkey sounds emanating from the dense coverage of trees beyond the banks. He eyed the rainforest, intrigued, wondering whether somewhere within the tiers of trees perched the bird or bat that had been the source of this new virus beginning to sweep through the South American population.

The boat stopped at a couple of the villages along the way. The stops were brief, however, only long enough to let those departing off, and to let street vendors on to sell food and drink, before they were on their way again. Occasionally the team got up to stretch their legs, or turned in their seats to chat, but mostly they spoke of the scenery or of their past travels. Bodhi noted that none of the team spoke of their work or why they were here or where they were going, and he recalled his conversation with Helen on their plane journey to Lima, about talking of such things in the public arena.

Still, Bodhi felt a little strange, sitting there cruising the Amazon on this boat, feeling the sun reflecting off the water onto his face, seeing all manner of colorful birds squawking and flying across the skies, feeling somewhat relaxed like he were on holiday, but knowing underneath why he was really here. To think about the people who were dying, and the countless more who would die soon. He couldn't really take in the scenery like he wanted to or allow himself to enjoy it. It just didn't feel right.

They'd been traveling for about six hours before the boat's driver began to talk over the speakers in Spanish. Pilar listened, then translated for the team.

"Delfin," she said. "Dolphin. He says to look out for pink dolphins in this area."

Bodhi studied the water but couldn't see anything. After about twenty minutes a young German tourist started talking excitedly and pointing at the water in the distance. Bodhi stood in his seat to look through the far windows to see the arcing of the dolphin's light body as it disappeared beneath the waves.

"Did you see it?" Helen asked.

He nodded, before sitting again. "Briefly."

Helen glanced at him. "One of the few perks of this job. I mean, other than saving lives, of course. We see a lot of horrible things… but we also get to capture moments of beauty and wonder. They help make the bad more tolerable."

"I'm struggling to enjoy it," he confessed.

"Let yourself," she said. "Don't deny absorbing any of the good. It counteracts the bad." She turned her face away and stared off into the water. "You should never feel guilty for being alive… Embracing life is exactly what helps us fight for other people's lives." She looked back at him. "They need us to hold on to hope. They need us to fight for it on their behalf." She turned back to stare at the river and fell silent. Bodhi watched her, curious for what memory her mind was recalling, but he decided not to ask.

A short time later, Bodhi felt the boat begin to slow and looked up to see another vessel approaching. As it neared and turned slightly, he saw 'Policia Federal' emblazoned along the side of the vessel. He straightened in his seat and watched as they pulled alongside, then boarded. An announcement was made over the speaker and Pilar translated for the team.

"Brazil National Police," she said. "It's a passport check. Have them ready with your tickets."

The team produced their passports and waited patiently. Two men eventually entered the passenger cabin dressed in green fatigues, black bullet-proof vests and helmets. Bodhi noted they were both heavily armed. They began to make their way down the aisle, each taking a side. The younger officer took their side and being seated near the front it didn't take long for him to reach the team.

Justin was first to be checked and he pulled his mask down to show the officer his face. The officer eyed him and his mask carefully, then handed his passport back. He moved onto Ekemma next, scrutinized her for slightly longer, then held his hand out for Pilar's passport. He studied it carefully, then moved onto Bodhi. After studying Bodhi's passport a moment, the man motioned to Pilar and said something in his native tongue. Bodhi looked to Pilar as she narrowed her eyes in concentration trying to decipher his words.

"Brazilians speak Portuguese," she told Bodhi, noting his curious look, "not Spanish." She looked to the guard and spoke in Spanish. He repeated his statement, this time in Spanish.

"Si," Pilar answered, and motioned to their group. "Estamos junto. We are together."

The officer said something else, and Bodhi picked up the word "ocupación?" He heard Pilar respond: "Global Health Agency". The older guard glanced over in interest as he continued to check passports on his side. The younger officer continued with his questions. This time Bodhi picked up the word "vacación?"

Pilar shook her head and spoke some more, before the younger officer turned to ask the more senior officer a question.

"What's wrong?" Helen asked, leaning forward, as Justin

and Ekemma watched on carefully. Pilar held her hand up to quiet Helen as the older officer looked back at them and asked a question of his colleague. The younger officer nodded and motioned for Pilar's passport again. She handed it over.

"Pilar Garcia," the younger man called to the elder, reading her passport, then Bodhi's. "Bodhi Patel." The older guard asked another question, before the younger one read their tickets and said, "Tabatinga."

The older guard said something, and the younger officer handed their passports back and moved along to the next people.

Bodhi gave Pilar a questioning look and she shrugged in return.

The officers continued on down the aisle, studied each passport carefully, flipping the pages to find their entry visas, and studying their faces and tickets, before handing them back again. After thirty minutes or so, they eventually finished and, satisfied, they left the boat and boarded theirs again. Bodhi watched them pull away and move off down the river.

"That was… weird," Justin said, and Helen nodded before looking back at her tablet again.

Bodhi suddenly wondered whether he should have asked those officers if they'd seen Sisters Apolo and Fuentez. Had the Sisters enough money to catch this boat down the river? Or would they have taken a cheaper, slower boat?

Again he thought of the tragedy it was, that the two nuns had picked up this virus, unlikely to have ever been seen by man before, and then inadvertently taken it all the way back to their homes, leaving a trail of destruction in their wake. Their pilgrimage to help people, had turned out to be a pilgrimage of hurting people.

He looked out upon the thick green canopies spanning into the distance beyond the banks, wondering again whether something within had caused this virus to be unleashed. He suddenly recalled a quote he'd once read by the American author, Belva Plain. She'd said: "danger hides in beauty and beauty in danger". And right now he couldn't help but think how right she'd been.

Another hour or so had passed when Bodhi, looking back at his app, could see that they were now traveling along the invisible border between Peru and Colombia. If he looked out the window to his right, he was looking at the banks of Peru. If he looked out the windows to the left, he was now looking at the banks of Colombia. From where he sat, though, they were identical. Merely two banks of the same river, each filled with dense forest either side.

Before too long they were passing the large island of Santa Rosa, laying in the middle of the river, which, according to Lou's notes, belonged to Peru. If they continued straight down the river, they would soon be in Brazil; if they turned around the island, they would pass the border into Colombia. Though their destination was the former, their portal notes advised that they needed to stop in the village of Santa Rosa to clear Peruvian immigration.

Soon enough he felt the boat begin to veer left around the island and the village of Santa Rosa came into sight. He saw a cluster of wooden houses with thatched roofs, elevated on stilts above the water line. A large blue and white sign was emblazoned with "Bienvenidos al Peru" and "Welcome to

Peru". Beside the sign stood a red and white striped beacon tower, and beyond that were more palm trees and the rest of the village.

While some tourists departed at this point, the rest stood in line to get their passports checked and receive their Peruvian exit stamps, before loading back onto the boat, to travel the short distance across to the other shore. They all received their stamps without any bother, though officials did scrutinize Ekemma's a little longer than the rest of theirs. Bodhi started to wonder whether it was because she traveled on a Nigerian passport and didn't have the travel freedom the rest of the team had. But soon enough they were on their way again.

Halfway across the river to Brazil, Bodhi smiled.

"Right about now," he said aloud to the team, while looking at his app, "we're crossing over the point where the three borders meet. Behind us is Peru, to the left is Colombia and to the right, our destination, Brazil."

"We're in a tri-country state of being," Pilar glanced over her shoulder at him, her mirrored sunglasses reflecting both the brown waters below and the gray skies above.

"Indeed," Helen said quietly. "And so is our virus."

Bodhi's smile faltered at her words. He stared at the land mass before him comprising of both Colombia and Brazil, and thought of the country behind him, Peru. Joined by land or the river flowing between them, this was the Tres Fronteras and it was a prime area for a virus to spiral out of control.

Helen was glad to have finally reached Tabatinga. Although the journey along the Amazon River had been scenic and interesting, after over eight hours on the boat, she was ready to hit dry land permanently. And more to the point, she was itching to find the boy and trace the source of infection.

The boat pulled up to a two-story wooden building. It was painted a pale blue and seemed to sit atop the water, about twenty meters from the nearest bank. As they drew closer she saw it was connected to the bank by a long walkway of wooden planks cobbled together. The sky was gray, though they'd seen no rain so far, and it didn't seem to deter the people on the bank or in the surrounding smaller boats. She wondered whether the number of people milling about was normal, or whether perhaps the numbers were down thanks to the virus. She did spot a couple of people wearing bandanas across their noses and mouths.

While waiting to disembark, she studied the bank and saw a presence of law enforcement. Two vehicles emblazoned with the words "Policia Federal" were parked up by the nearest road and four officers, heavily armed with bullet-proof vests, were waiting on the wooden platform as the boat pulled alongside. From what she'd seen so far, the border patrol hadn't been lax in these parts at all. Then again, there was a lot of border to patrol and she suspected most of it was concentrated in the more populated areas with tourists, while the rest went unmanned or with little staff. She eyed the large guns the officers displayed and wondered how often they had to use them.

The four officers waiting on the platform boarded the boat and filed into the passenger cabin. They spread out, two at the front and two halfway down the aisle and began checking everyone's passports again. It wasn't long before the officer seeing to their quadrant of seating, a man named Braga according to his uniform shirt, made it to Pilar.

"Pilar Garcia," Officer Braga said, reading her passport aloud, then studying her, before his eyes found Bodhi. "Bodhi Patel?"

Bodhi nodded with surprise that he knew his name. The guard held his hand out for his passport, and Bodhi passed it over.

"Juntos?" Officer Braga said, studying the two passports again. "Together? Yes?"

Pilar nodded, exchanging a look with Bodhi. The officer nodded, then waved their group off the boat, departing with their two passports as he did.

"Hey, our passports!" Bodhi said anxiously, standing. Braga turned around and said something, waving them to follow.

"What's going on?" Helen asked Pilar, concerned.

"I don't know," Pilar said, "but he wants us off the boat."

The team filed off the boat onto the dock platform, where they waited for the boat crew to hand them their backpacks of field equipment and bags of personal belongings; all the while the remaining officers continued checking those on the boat. Pilar negotiated with Braga to hand back their two passports, and once they had their bags, Braga waved them to follow him again.

"Maybe someone announced our arrival?" Bodhi said, tucking his passport away again. "Maybe they're expecting the GHA?"

It was a possibility, Helen thought, and they followed

the man curiously. Braga led them to the wooden walkway
sitting precariously over the brown Amazonian waters, and
they followed him, balancing carefully with their large packs
until they hit land. Waving them forward again, he had them
follow him to a van parked near the road and pulled the door
back, motioning them to get in.

"Wait, where are we going?" Ekemma asked firmly, refusing
to get in.

"No one get in," Helen ordered, making her way to the
front of the group. "I want some answers first. Pilar?"

Pilar spoke to the man, and he replied with a spark of
impatience and motioned again for them to get in.

Pilar looked back at Helen. "He's taking us to the
immigration office."

"Why?" Helen asked.

"I don't know," Pilar said. "He won't say. But I think he's
legit. Let's get in and find out."

"Very well," Helen conceded. "Just stick together and stay
alert," she said, then climbed into the back of the van. She
found a seat and pulled out her tablet, while the rest followed
suit.

"It was the earlier passport check," Justin said quietly. "They
radioed ahead and told 'em we were coming."

"But why?" Ekemma asked.

"Pilar told him we were with the GHA," Bodhi said. "It
must be to do with that."

"I can't see any notes from Max," Helen said, tucking her
tablet away again. "I don't think our arrival was announced
by him." The team exchanged nervous looks as silence filled
the van.

It was only a short drive to their destination, located on the Avenida da Amizade. Officer Braga pulled over on the side of the road and beckoned them to exit the vehicle. He then led them inside the building and made them stand in the waiting room while he knocked on an office door and spoke to another man in uniform, who looked to be senior. The senior officer, mustached with a head of thick dark hair, nodded to Braga, who then moved back toward them.

"Passports," he said, motioning them into the senior's office. "Come."

Helen and Pilar led the team into the office. The man behind the desk studied them as they entered, resting back in his chair. He seemed big in stature with a round belly that pressed against his desk.

"What seems to be the problem?" Helen asked the senior officer, reading the name on his uniform as Rocha. He didn't answer her, as the team filed in and lined up before his desk and two other officers filled the room behind them with Braga, closing the door.

"Passports!" Braga said again, motioning for them to hand them over to him. He collected the passports one by one and placed them down on Rocha's desk. The first passport Rocha picked up was Justin's.

"Australia?" he said, looking up at Justin.

"Si," Justin nodded.

"Sim," Pilar corrected him. "It's 'sim' in Portuguese."

"Sim," he corrected himself. Rocha motioned for him to lower his mask. Justin did so briefly.

The officer dropped the passport on the desk and picked up the next one. It was Helen's.

"English?" he asked, looking up at her.

"Sim," Helen nodded, exposing her face briefly, too. "Is there a problem? Why have we been brought here?"

Rocha ignored her and collected the next passport.

"Nigeria," he said, looking up at Ekemma.

"Sim," she said. He stared at her a moment, then tossed her passport aside for the next one.

"United States," he said, looking up at Bodhi.

"Duas pessoas," Braga said, pointing to Pilar's passport. Rocha took that one as well, looking between the two passports and then up at both Pilar and Bodhi.

"United States?" he said again, looking between the two. They both nodded at him.

"Please, why did you bring us here?" Helen said again, more firmly.

Rocha said something to Braga that Helen didn't catch and she watched as the officer moved to the door and called for another officer to join them. This one was female, and she entered and moved to stand beside Rocha's desk. He spoke to her in Portuguese and she turned to the GHA team.

"You travel together. Why?" she asked, obviously their translator.

"We work for the Global Health Agency," Helen said. "We're a relatively new organization, but we report into the World Health Assembly."

The woman turned and translated this to the man. He asked another question.

"Why are you here?" she asked.

Helen looked back at Rocha. "We're investigating an outbreak of influenza in Peru. We believe the earliest patient of the virus, what we call Patient Zero, was in Benjamin Constant. We're trying to trace how they contracted the virus so we can help stop it."

Again the woman translated and the man asked another question.

"The virus you seek," the female officer said, "it is the same as the one here?"

"We believe so," Helen nodded, "although we're awaiting official confirmation of this. You have many sick here?"

The woman gave a single nod. "What is this virus?"

"We're not entirely sure just yet. It's either a mutation of an existing strain of influenza, or an entirely new virus altogether. That's what we're trying to figure out, but we need to trace Patient Zero, the first person to have contracted the virus. We think this person, a boy, was in Benjamin Constant across the river. The only way we can get there is from here in Tabatinga."

Again the woman translated. Rocha spoke once more to Braga, who collected their passports and left the room.

"Hey!" Ekemma said. "Where are you taking our passports?"

"What is going on here?" Helen asked Rocha firmly. She knew they were visitors in this country, so she had to keep calm, but at the same time, she wouldn't just stand by and let them walk over her either.

Pilar held her hand up to halt Helen and spoke in broken Portuguese to Rocha. The female officer replied to her.

"We are checking your credentials. You must wait."

"How bad is the outbreak of influenza here?" Helen asked the woman. "Have many died?"

The woman hesitated. "Some."

"Well, *some* will soon become *many*," Helen said. "The virus is spreading swiftly and it's knocking down everyone in its path. We are experts, but we need to act fast. You need to let us go so we can get to Benjamin Constant and investigate this."

The woman turned and spoke to Rocha again. He eyed each of them carefully as he smoothed down his moustache, deep in thought, but said nothing. They waited several minutes before the officer came back with their passports. He placed Pilar's down open in front of Rocha and Helen heard the words "militares" and "United States".

Helen stiffened, wondering what the problem was with Pilar being military. Helen looked to Pilar who stood rigid and tense. Justin did, too, his eyes sharply on Rocha.

Rocha spoke rapidly to the woman.

"You are US military?" she asked Pilar.

"Yes," she said. "But I work with the Global Health Agency. I am employed by them in this instance."

The woman relayed the message and the man rapidly fired back.

"Why do they need US military personnel?" she translated.

"To enable a fast response when required," Pilar told her. "If a crisis hits, I call on military support to help quarantine areas and also lend aid to the sick."

"But you are United States military," the woman said. "Not Brazil military, not Peru military."

"No," Pilar said evenly, "but my guys generally know how to get your guys on the phone real quick." Pilar looked back to Rocha. "We're here to help," she emphasized. "If the Brazilian government needs US or other outside assistance, we can arrange that. Swiftly."

The woman relayed the information. Rocha stared at her, then eyed the team again. He picked up Pilar's passport, handed it to Braga and gave him some instruction. The officer left the room with Pilar's passport again, while the other passports remained on the table.

"I really don't understand what the issue is," Helen said to the woman. "We're here to help you. We're here to stop this virus."

"No one has notified us of your help," the woman said.

"Things have moved fast," Helen said. "We thought the outbreak was centered in Peru, but new evidence leads us to believe that it started in this area. I'm sure the GHA through the WHO are making contact with your relevant people as we speak."

Rocha gave the female officer an instruction and she began handing the other passports back.

"Garcia…" Justin said to Pilar, as he looked over his shoulder through the office window, "they're making a copy of your passport."

Pilar looked through the window, then locked eyes with Justin, before turning to look at Helen.

"Why are they targeting you?" Helen asked.

Pilar turned back to face Rocha. "This isn't a US military operation. This is a global health initiative. We're here to stop the virus," she said. "We're here to help. That's all."

Rocha waved them off, dismissing them. The woman opened the door and ushered them back into the waiting room. Pilar was handed her passport back and each was stamped with their Brazilian entry, before they were released from the building.

They stepped silently back into the street, all a little confused and concerned about what just happened. They didn't have time to dwell on it right now, though, Helen thought, as she checked her watch. It had just passed three-thirty. They were running out of daylight.

"Let's just get back to the dock and catch that boat to Benjamin Constant," Helen said, motioning the team to start walking back to the river.

"I don't understand," Bodhi said, brow furrowed as he walked alongside her. "What the hell was that about?"

"They were probably checking to see if I'm with the CIA or something," Pilar said, pulling her mask down to rest around her neck and giving a smirk. "They'll be so disappointed when they confirm that I'm actually with the Global Health Agency."

"I'm worried about them copying your passport," Helen said, not seeing humor in the situation.

Pilar shrugged. "What can I do about it? I'll make a call and let my superiors know that I'm on the Brazilian government's radar. They'll give me a heads up if there's anything I should be aware of. They're probably just flexing their muscles. No one likes the thought of the US interfering in their country's affairs."

"I'm going to put a call into home base," Helen said, pulling out her tablet, "make sure Max and Gabriel are prepared to pull us out if needed."

"I'm sure it won't get to that," Pilar said, stuffing her hands into her trouser pockets.

"The border with Colombia is maybe eight blocks from here," Bodhi said, looking at his app. "It's crazy to think that people can just walk down this road and through the open border to Colombia. No wonder people are edgy."

"Let's hope the boy did not come through here," Ekemma said.

"Lou said the only way to Benjamin Constant was by boat," Justin said. "There's a real good chance he passed through here."

"I think he definitely came through here." Bodhi nodded, staring off into the distance ahead, mind turning over. "And I think this is our worst-case scenario."

"Boa tarde!" Max appeared on Helen's tablet. "So you arrived in Tabatinga OK?"

"Yes and no," Helen said. "We're here, but we seem to have drawn the interest of the Brazilian police."

"You've been upsetting the locals?"

"No, just me, Max," Pilar leaned into the camera. "They somehow found out I'm US military and they're suspicious."

"But you were traveling on your personal passport," Max said. "How would they know that you're US military?"

Pilar shrugged. "I guess they have their ways."

"Well, that's not a great start," Max said. "You don't need any roadblocks slowing you down. I'll see what I can find out from this end. Keep an eye on things and let me know if you want me to push this up the chain and alert Davidson." He checked the time on his screen. "You're about to board for Benjamin Constant, yes?"

"At last," Helen said. "Can you give us an update on the influenza reports in the area?"

Max's face took on a serious look. "Not good," he said. "There's been a spike in reports but that could be in relation to us releasing the global WHO alert. It could just be the local health authorities joining the dots and finally reporting all influenza patients just in case."

"How many deaths?" Bodhi asked from beside Helen.

"Well, Brazil numbers are now higher than Peru's," Max said, reading the data. "We've got eighty-one influenza deaths there now and most look to be concentrated in Benjamin Constant and Tabatinga and spreading outwards from there. We've had four deaths reported in the city of Manaus, which means it's already traveled halfway through Brazil. The numbers in Colombia are also rising and I suspect that'll climb higher as the numbers are only just starting to flow in. We've got forty-five reported so far. Again, mostly reported from Leticia which shares the open border with Tabatinga. Peru deaths are now sitting at seventy-five."

"Shit," Bodhi said. "That's over two hundred people."

"And climbing," Max added.

"Two hundred people in, what, twelve days?" Justin said.

Helen nodded, feeling the intensity of the situation pulling at her shoulders. "And I guarantee you not all the relevant deaths have been reported yet. But there's definitely a higher number of deaths in this area now. It sounds more and more like it definitely started here."

"The emergency warning has been pushed out to all South American countries now," Max said, "and the global alert has been issued as you know. We've warned everybody, now all we can do is hope they all quarantine their patients sufficiently and contain their outbreaks as best they can so it doesn't spread any further. Let's hope they learned a thing or two from COVID, huh?"

"And hope in the meantime we find a way to stop it," Helen said, exhaling heavily as though trying to release some of the pressure she felt within. "Thanks, Max. We'll be in contact after we check out Benjamin Constant."

Max nodded. "If you catch that boat, you'll be there in thirty minutes. Stay safe."

CHAPTER TEN

Helen and the team bought their tickets to Benjamin Constant, then had to wait another thirty minutes until there were enough passengers to fill the small boat. It appeared that the operators never left until they had enough fares for the trip. Understandable from a business perspective, but frustrating for the GHA team. When they finally had enough passengers, though, they loaded everyone on board, laden with their full backpacks and bags, and headed east along the river.

The boat cruised at speed, the wind rushing past and through the open sides, blowing them about. Pilar pulled on a cap and held it down to stop her hair whipping about, while Helen pulled out a hairband and tried to contain hers. Soon enough, however, the boat began to slow, and up ahead Helen saw small green hills that sloped down to the river, where rustic wooden buildings appeared to float at the edge.

The boat pulled up to one of the larger wooden buildings that seemed to be the Benjamin Constant dock. They climbed out and Helen checked the information on her tablet.

"There are two hospitals here," she said. "One is close by,

one is perhaps a bike ride away. Let's split up." She turned to Bodhi. "You and Ekemma check out the farther one with Pilar. Justin, you come with me."

They all agreed, and the two groups went their separate ways.

Helen and Justin made their journey down the main street, searching for the local hospital. There were cars, motorcycles and bicycles, and people walking along the street, and Helen noted that many people here were wearing scarves, bandanas and other materials over their noses and mouths. The people here knew that death was lurking and not to take the risk of exposing themselves to it. It saddened Helen, though, because she knew those bandanas weren't guaranteed against the minute particles of virus if transferred through the air, but they were sure better than nothing.

As she walked along, she pulled out a fresh mask and put it on, followed by gloves, and Justin followed suit. They almost walked right past the hospital before they found it. It was a very small and unassuming building with worn paintwork and a waist high metal grille fence out front.

"This is the government hospital?" Justin asked, eyeing it with concern.

Helen nodded, checking her own tablet. "Apparently so. The hospital the others went to is the general hospital. I think it's larger than this one. According to Lou's notes, there's just over twenty-six thousand people in the area."

"Two hospitals for twenty-six thousand people," Justin said, exchanging an apprehensive look with her.

Helen dropped her bag to the ground and began to don a disposable containment suit, and when they were both dressed, they finally entered the hospital. As they expected the small waiting room was filled with people coughing and fevered. This time they exchanged a look of dread as they approached the small, worn, reception desk. It took them trying with five different staff members before they found one with very broken English who at least understood theirs.

"A boy," Helen spoke as clearly as she could through her mask, reading off a translation app on her phone. "Menino. Boy... Doente. Sick... A semana passada? Last week? Er... duas semanas? Two weeks?"

After several minutes of both Helen and Justin trying to converse with the nurse, they were taken through crowded corridors to an equally crowded ward where a young boy, maybe nine months old, lay sleeping with an adult oxygen mask over his face.

Helen paused on seeing the child, so small, so poorly. She felt heartbreak slice through her chest, to see a child so young stricken with this virus; to see that the hospital was not equipped to handle this outbreak. The baby's mother sat close by, her eyes filled with concern as they looked at Helen. Helen immediately felt pity for her. If this mother knew what Helen knew, her eyes would not be filled with concern right now, but instead with terror. This woman was most probably going to lose her child soon.

Memories of Angie came rushing back; of heart monitors and oxygen masks and pain and crying; her skinny bones too fragile to hold herself upright any longer. Memories of Angie begging Helen to stop the pain.

"No..." she said quietly to the nurse, before finding her voice again. "This isn't him." She turned to the nurse. "He would be dead by now. Morto. Menino Morto. Semana Passada, duas semanas."

The nurse shook her head and walked away.

"What if it was a teenage boy?" Justin asked Helen. "The word 'boy' covers a hell of a lot of an age range."

"But the Sister said 'young boy'," Helen said.

"Yeah, but he would've been young to her? That still doesn't help us narrow it down."

The nurse came back and thrust a book at Helen. She took it, confused, but opened it.

"Morte," the nurse said, pointing at it. "Lista."

Helen saw that the book was a register of patients and a column on the far end was marked "morte". She read it as best she could, given it was in Portuguese, but at least the ages were written numerically, so she could understand that easily enough. She ran her gloved finger down the list as Justin read over her shoulder.

"I see babies… kids under five," Justin said, "and I see an older teenager, but nothing in between. How can we find out the boy's age?" He hissed, his voice weighted with frustration. He was clearly feeling the suffering of those around him, too.

"What if he didn't even make it to hospital to die?" Helen asked Justin. "Some people may have chosen to die at home. What if there are no records of his death?"

"Don't say that," Justin said, his blue eyes staring at hers over his surgical mask. "There has to be a way for us to trace him. There has to be a way for us to figure out what started this."

Helen looked around the crowded ward again, feeling as though she was standing in a waiting room for death. She nodded at Justin, needing to get outside into the fresh air to give herself time to think.

"Let's see if Bodhi had any luck," she said, taking a photo of the register for upload, so the home base team could help them review it.

Bodhi stood before the hospital's cool room door, beside Ekemma and Pilar, dressed in their containment suits, gloves and masks. He swallowed as the door opened and they stepped inside. He saw five bodies covered in sheets. The nurse moved to one and pulled the sheet back. The boy's face was pale, a white crust had settled around his mouth and nose, along with dried blood. Bodhi picked him to be about eight or nine years old. Aside from the crusted fluids on his face, the boy almost looked like he was sleeping. It was hard for Bodhi to wrap his brain around the fact that he was staring at a dead child.

"When did he die?" Bodhi asked Pilar. She translated as best she could in her rough Portuguese. The nurse answered and Pilar exhaled, disappointed.

"Two days ago. This isn't him."

Bodhi nodded and Pilar instructed the nurse to put the sheet back in place.

They left the cool room and made their way back into the hospital corridor again.

"Let's check their records," Ekemma said. "They've had a lot more deaths here than those five bodies in the cool room. The rest must already be buried or cremated. We might still find trace of him yet."

Pilar nodded and the two women moved to talk to the

nurses. Bodhi didn't follow, however; instead, he stepped outside needing some fresh air.

Unfortunately the boy's face traveled with him.

He'd seen dead bodies before but not outside of the study arena, and certainly not a child's body before. He stared out at the river before him, saw children playing by the water. He watched them laughing and singing, not knowing what danger they were in.

An older woman was approaching the children, moving slowly, her body slightly bent over as though she were sick. She coughed, and Bodhi tensed, his eyes darting to the children by the water. He wondered if the woman knew the children, whether she was about to infect them or whether she already had. Thankfully, she shuffled on past them and he breathed a sigh of relief.

"You alright?" Pilar's voice sounded as she stopped beside him. He hadn't heard her approach.

"That woman just coughed." He pointed. "We should quarantine her."

Pilar spotted the woman, then nodded. "I'll get Kem and the nurses on it. Kem's checking on their quarantine procedures now." She studied Bodhi carefully for a moment. "You sure you're alright?"

He nodded. "Yeah." Then he paused, looking out at the river again. "I just… hadn't seen a dead child before."

Pilar stood silently, nodding to herself as she looked down at the dirt.

He looked back at her. "Have you?"

Pilar nodded, shoving her hands into her pockets. "Yeah. More than I'd like to have."

Bodhi studied her curiously, wondering whether she'd previously been stationed in a war zone or something to have seen that. "Were you stationed overseas before this?" he asked gently, trying not to pry.

"No." She shook her head, turning her eyes to the kids playing by the water. "I was working down along the US-Mexico border."

"Right…" Bodhi said, his mind turning over, wondering whether that had been where she had seen the dead children. "What made you decide to join the GHA?"

She looked back at him. "What makes you think this was *my* decision?"

He stared at her, waiting for her to elaborate. The wind stirred her brown hair as she looked out to the river again. "I didn't decide. I was sent here." She looked back at him. "Apparently my views down on the border were unwelcome." She turned and began heading back toward the hospital. "I'll let Kem know about the woman."

Bodhi watched her walk away, suddenly wanting to know more about her, but his thoughts were interrupted by his phone ringing. It was Helen.

"Helen?" he answered.

"Hi," she said. "Any luck?"

"Not so far. The only dead boy they have here died two days ago so it can't be our Patient Zero. You?"

"No luck here either. It's like searching for a needle in a haystack, without his name or age."

"I know. What do you want to do?"

There was silence before Helen sighed heavily.

"I don't know what else to try right now and it's getting late."

Bodhi checked the time. It was approaching five-thirty. "Why don't we head back to Tabatinga, drop our things at our accommodation, regroup, and try to figure out where to go next?"

"Yeah…" Helen's voice sounded distant.

"Are you alright?" he asked.

"Yes, I'm just… I feel like we're close but there's just so much cloud cover I can't make out the sun, you know?"

Bodhi looked to the skies at the gray clouds overhead. "There is a lot of cloud cover," he said, "but it hasn't yet rained. We've still got time to stop this."

"Your optimism is timely."

"We're tired." He smiled softly to himself. "We just need to rest and clear our thoughts, that's all. We'll find this kid."

"Yeah," Helen sighed. "We'll meet you at the dock in an hour."

Bodhi, Pilar and Ekemma made their way back to the dock, after they had done all they could to help improve the quarantine measures in the hospital. His optimism was fading, though. He felt a sinking feeling as they'd left, like throwing a single life ring to a boat of drowning people and wishing them luck. But there really wasn't anything else they could do. What these people needed now was WHO reinforcements to bolster the containment methods. What the GHA needed to do was find the boy and trace his movements.

It was already twilight when they arrived at the dock. Helen and Justin were waiting for them. While Justin sat on a bench seat alone, Helen stood staring out at the darkening river before them, that had departed from the Amazon to become the Javara River.

Bodhi moved to stand beside her. "We'll find him," he said. "We have to."

"If he's not here, where did he go?" Helen asked, looking at him.

"Well, he went somewhere. With the amount of deaths in the region he spread it far and wide."

"I don't think he was a local," Helen said. "He must've been visiting. The hospital staff would know who we were talking about, I'm sure. He would've been the first death. They would remember that."

"So he traveled through here, crossing paths with Sisters Apolo and Fuentez, but what we need to know is where he came from and where he went next."

Helen nodded. "That makes sense. Let's ask around here at the dock. Someone might remember him."

Bodhi agreed and they went up to the ticket counter, waving Pilar to assist them. Ekemma and Justin followed, but stood back a little as though in support.

"Can you ask if they saw a sick boy come through here, about two weeks or so ago?" Bodhi asked Pilar.

She nodded and translated. The plump woman behind the counter listened thoughtfully, her brows catching every now and then as though stumbling over Pilar's phrasing. But thankfully she understood enough. Bodhi saw her shake her head and point to the boats. A brief discussion ensued, before Pilar nodded at the woman.

"Obrigada," she said, thanking her, then turned to Bodhi.

"She doesn't work every day, so she doesn't recall, but she said the boat operators are our best bet. They're generally here every day."

Bodhi looked around at the boat operators present. Most were packing up for the day, but some were still taking passengers aboard. Whether they would remember the boy from almost two weeks ago, or even the nuns, he wasn't sure, but they certainly had to try.

Pilar began asking them one by one. Bodhi saw a lot of shaking heads and what sounded like "no", until one, after shaking his head, elaborated to Pilar, pointing across the water.

Pilar's face seemed concentrated at first, but it soon lightened with what looked like a spark of hope. She turned to Bodhi and Helen who waited eagerly to hear what the man had said.

"This guy remembers another boat operator talking of a very sick boy on his boat, a week or so back."

"Where's the boat operator now?" Bodhi asked, straightening, though fearing the worst.

"He's on a run across to the other bank. We'll need to wait until he returns."

Bodhi's adrenaline-filled eyes caught with Helen's before they fixed their sights across the water, waiting anxiously for the man to return.

After several minutes, Bodhi saw the other man preparing to leave in his boat. He quickly jogged toward him.

"Wait! You can't leave. Who is this man? You need to point him out?"

Pilar was quickly at his side and the conversation was thick and fast. Bodhi only caught one word: "Paulo".

"Paulo?" Bodhi said. "He's the one we want?"

"Sim!" the man said, climbing aboard his tourist-filled boat and starting the engine. He pushed the boat back from the dock, then began to motor away, only to suddenly slow down, turn around in a semi-circle to swing back past the dock. "Paulo!" he pointed toward another boat heading in. "Paulo!"

"Sim! Obrigado!" Pilar called back with a wave.

They stood on the dock and waited anxiously for Paulo and his boat to arrive. As soon as the passengers disembarked, Bodhi, Helen and Pilar quickly boarded the boat to Paulo's surprise. He yelled something at them, motioning for them to get off his boat, but Pilar cut over his protests. The man listened, his angry face soon smoothing out as he nodded occasionally. Bodhi saw him look off to the left, as though recalling something, before he looked back at her and nodded again, talking animatedly and pointing to the seats in his boat.

"Sim… Sim," Pilar said again. "Obrigado!" She turned to the team, her eyes alight over her mask. "The boy was on his boat! He was gravely ill but Paulo says two nuns were taking care of him!"

"Apolo and Fuentez!" Bodhi said, his eyes almost popping from his skull.

"Yes!" Justin fist-pumped as Ekemma gasped with glee.

"So what happened?" Helen asked urgently. "Where'd they go?"

"His boat stops at the Leticia dock," Pilar said. "The nuns said they were taking the boy to the Leticia hospital!"

"Then that's where we go!" Helen said, her eyes lightening with hope again.

Bodhi nodded, as he slapped one hand against the other. "Colombia, here we come!"

Helen paced anxiously. They had to wait another anxious twenty-five minutes before the next boat was ready to cross to the other side. This one was headed to Tabatinga, but with the open border between it and Leticia, getting dropped off at Tabatinga was just fine – anything to get them to the other bank.

It was an unusual feeling to be crossing the Amazon in the darkness with only one light aboard the vessel and just a sprinkling of lights visible on the other bank. The team sat in silence. Helen shook her leg, trying to contain the excitement and tension within her. She felt it in the whole team. To have finally narrowed down on the person they thought was Patient Zero, was something else. It gave her hope that they could trace the boy's illness to its cause.

Once they knew exactly how the boy caught it, they could collect the relevant samples and it would help Aiko and her global network break down the virus and find a way to stop its invasion of the human body, and hopefully avoid further future infections. Information was power, every data point was important, and they were getting closer to their source of truth.

As Helen walked along the wooden planks from the dock to the Tabatinga bank once more, and stepped onto dry soil, she saw the Brazilian police officer, Braga, waiting for them.

"Shit…" Pilar muttered under her breath, lowering her mask, before forcing a smile and moving toward him. The team stood back patiently and let them converse. When they were done the man moved off and Pilar came back to the team.

"What's the problem now?" Helen asked her.

"There's no problem," Pilar said. "He just wants to know what we're doing back here so soon. I've reassured him we're heading into Leticia. He says we need to report in whatever we find out."

"We really don't answer to him," Helen said.

"While we're standing in their country they say we do. Come on, let's get to the border."

They hailed three tuk-tuks and piled in with all their gear, then headed up to the Avenue di Amazade, where they turned left, then headed straight for about two kilometers until they came across the open border. It was marked with a simple wooden sign affixed to two metal poles that Helen probably would've missed completely, especially now it was evening, if it hadn't been for the tourists taking photos in front of it.

She was amazed that there appeared to be no law enforcement presence at all. Whether that was because of the time of day, or perhaps the virus, she wasn't sure.

"The hospital is about one and a half kilometers from here," Ekemma said, checking the app on her phone, before she groaned. "Dammit. The Wi-Fi is patchy!"

They arrived at the Hospital San Miguel de Leticia around seven-thirty. Painted white, it was a relatively large complex covering about a block, albeit only a single-story development, that was surrounded sporadically with palm trees and the like. An array of motorcycles were parked out front and several people seemed to be milling about, some smoking in the night air.

When they entered, dressed in their full containment suits, they were surprised at just how many sick filled the waiting room there. There were even patients on beds lined up in the corridor and from what they could see, quarantine zones were non-existent – most likely due to the sheer numbers.

Helen paused and looked at Bodhi. "This could be our epicenter."

"Yeah," he said through his mask. "I'm starting to think we should be wearing our containment suits permanently from now on, like even sleeping in them."

Helen shot him a look that didn't disagree. As with every hospital they'd attended so far, their first priority was to find someone who spoke English. Pilar moved straight to the modest wooden reception desk and began conversing with the masked nurse. As Colombians spoke Spanish, it was somewhat easier than in Brazil.

They finally met their English speaker in the form of Doctor Ramirez, although they waited a good forty minutes until he came to see them. Ekemma and Justin had grown impatient waiting and had started assisting the nurses as they separated the incoming patients into the three risk categories, having already established as best they could the relevant quarantine zones to match.

Doctor Ramirez was tall, maybe early forties with a receding hairline that he opted to shave altogether. The hospital light shone off the brown skin on his skull, though Helen guessed it may have also been sweat from the workload he was handling.

"Yes?" he asked curiously, his dark eyes piercing over the top of his mask.

"Doctor Ramirez, I'm Doctor Helen Taylor and this is Doctor Bodhi Patel. We work with the Global Health Agency, reporting to the WHO and the World Health Assembly. We're investigating the outbreak of influenza, which we believe to be responsible for the patients you have here. I'm sure you've heard that it has spread not only through Colombia but also Brazil and Peru."

"What do you want from me?" he asked.

"We're still trying to find out whether this virus is either a stronger, mutated strain of an existing virus or a new virus altogether. Either way, that's why the casualty numbers are so high, because our bodies haven't experienced this before. We've been trying to trace Patient Zero and we believe we might know who that is, but we're hoping someone here can help us place the pieces of the puzzle together."

"Why here?"

"There was a boy, gravely ill with the virus. He came into contact with two nuns from Peru who helped care for him. They boarded a boat in Benjamin Constant and traveled here to Leticia with the boy. They parted ways and the two nuns then carried the virus into Peru, where it has spread. The two nuns were the first patients reported in Peru. We think this boy they met is our Patient Zero and responsible for the spread in all three countries. We're trying to find out if he came to this hospital. It would've been almost two weeks ago. Can you confirm this?"

"I don't know," the doctor said. "There are over a hundred thousand people in the Leticia and Tabatinga region. I would need to check the admittance records."

"If he's our Patient Zero, he would stand out," Bodhi said

calmly. "Assuming he died from the virus, he would've been the first death recorded before the outbreak started. You would remember him."

The man's brows furrowed as he stared at Bodhi. "I'll check the records," he said, walking away abruptly.

Helen stared after him. There was something about his manner that made her think he knew exactly which boy they were talking about.

CHAPTER ELEVEN

Helen figured it was almost another hour before the doctor came back to them with a folder in his gloved hands.

"A boy was admitted around the time you mentioned. He was in a critical condition, suffering from pulmonary edema. He died soon after."

"And you have no other recorded deaths prior to that?" Bodhi asked, trying to take a closer look at the folder.

The doctor shook his head, holding the folder against his chest, brows furrowed again as he stared at Bodhi. "No. He was the first in our hospital."

Helen sighed with relief, nodding and smiling beneath her mask. "Thank you. We finally found him…" She looked at Bodhi and his eyes smiled back at hers before he turned to the doctor again.

"Do you know who he was?" Bodhi asked. "Was he from these parts or visiting?"

The man glanced at Bodhi, then turned his eyes away. "He was local. His family collected the body. We recommended a fast burial."

"Do you have their details?" Bodhi asked.

"Why?"

"Because right now he's our Patient Zero," Bodhi said. "We need to try to find out how he became infected. We need to trace his movements. That will help us map possible outbreak areas and predict the future chain of infection. We'll need to set up quarantine areas in suspected future hot spots to stop the spread and if we find out how he first became infected it might help us find a way to stop this virus."

"I'm sure you understand all that, Doctor Ramirez," Helen said, feeling Bodhi was stating the obvious.

Ramirez looked at her. "I'm not at liberty to give out that information." He turned and began to walk away. For a moment Helen was surprised, but she quickly shook it off and moved after him, catching his arm.

"Wait a moment. What?" she said, confused.

Ramirez turned around and shot her a hard look and she released her grip.

"You're 'not at liberty'?" she asked, perplexed. "You're not at liberty to help save lives?"

"I don't know who they were. Try the nurses."

"But you would have been the one to process the death certificate," Helen said.

"Try the nurses!" he said again more firmly, then turned and walked away.

Helen stared after him, bewildered.

"Come on," Bodhi said calmly to Helen. "He's probably been working double shifts thanks to the outbreak. Let's try the nurses instead."

They tried the nurses but got the same response. No one

seemed to want to talk about the boy; who he was, nor who his family were. Helen had tried to argue reason, but she kept coming up against walls. She couldn't understand it. They were so close to finding out what started this, but no one wanted to help them. Sensing the hostility, Bodhi encouraged her to step outside the hospital, and the team followed.

They moved outside into the humid night air and stared at each other dumbfounded and questioning, as the sound of insects in nearby bushes sang songs to each other.

"Patient Zero is *right* there," Ekemma hissed frustratedly, "but we cannot get to him!"

"You think they just don't want us foreigners interfering?" Justin asked.

"They can't want this to go on," Pilar said. "No one wants another COVID."

"No, but I've been in places where pride takes precedence over common sense," Justin said. "Some people would rather suffer and handle things themselves than let a foreigner step in and help."

"This isn't a war zone, Justin," Ekemma said.

"Isn't it?" he said.

"Let's try home base," Helen said. "See if they can find any electronic records of his death."

"But they won't give us a name to search," Ekemma said.

"No," Bodhi said, "but we do now have an approximate date and location of his death."

"Try dock," a woman's voice said with uneasy English. They turned to see a nurse standing by the door, smoking a cigarette. "The dock," she said again. "Ask there."

"Do you know who the boy was?" Helen stepped toward

her, but the nurse threw her cigarette butt away, pulled up her mask and quickly walked back inside.

Helen stared after her, then shook her head in frustration. "I don't understand why they won't just bloody tell us!"

Justin narrowed his eyes. "Let's go to the dock and find out."

"I'm not sure that's a good idea," Pilar said, checking her watch. "Do we want to be walking around and asking questions this late at night?"

Helen checked her watch, too. It was almost eleven. As much as she wanted answers now, it probably wasn't wise to do so in a foreign country this late at night. Besides, they had been up since four-thirty that morning in order to catch the boat from Iquitos and needed to rest. She had a feeling they were going to need it tomorrow.

"We'll do it first thing tomorrow," she decided. "Let's go check into the Leticia accommodation Gabe booked for us and make camp for the night. I'll call home base from there."

They headed to the accommodation Gabriel had arranged for them. It wasn't too far from the hospital, which made it convenient. The hotel itself was very modest, but it would do, and they had two rooms side by side, with doors that led directly onto a small parking lot out front.

While Helen contacted home base on her tablet, Bodhi and Justin quickly dropped their backpacks and bags in their room, then returned to hers. It took Helen a while to connect to home base, as the wireless internet device she had kept dropping out, but eventually she got a signal and connected. Lou appeared on the screen and Gabe quickly joined her. They were obviously in the process of a shift transition.

"How're things?" Lou asked, as Gabriel watched on intently.

"Humid," Helen said, "and frustrating, frankly, because no one will talk to us about this boy and tell us who he is."

"Where are you now?" Gabriel asked.

"We're in Colombia. We found where the nuns crossed paths with the boy. They took him to a hospital here in Leticia. We're struggling to find out more than that right now, because no one seems to want to talk to us. But it's late here, so there's nothing more we can do tonight."

"How can we help?" Lou asked, adjusting her glasses.

"We've narrowed down the hospital where the boy died, but they won't release his name. I'm hoping you can trace death records for him and find out his name, so we can use that to ask around to ascertain his movements prior to infection."

"Sure thing," Lou nodded. "I'll see what I can do. I'll need the date of death and an age."

"We can't give you an age because they won't tell us, but we can tell you it was approximately twelve to fourteen days ago. He would've been the first influenza death around that time. Cause of death was pulmonary edema."

"The hospital," Lou said, tapping away at her console, "is it the San Miguel de Leticia?"

"Yes, that's it."

"Leave it with me and I'll see if I can arrange access to the records."

"Thanks, Lou," Helen said, ending the connection.

"So, now we wait," Justin said.

"No, now we sleep," Helen said, rubbing her neck.

"I need to eat," Ekemma said. "I'm starving."

"Me, too," Pilar said. "I could eat a horse."

"I think you have to go to Chile to get that," Bodhi said.

The team paused and looked at him. "So I've read," he added.

Justin chuckled. "Max is Chilean. I wonder if he's eaten horse before?"

Pilar grinned. "Dare you to ask him."

"I've been to war, Garcia, but I am not brave enough to ask him that."

The group broke into laughter that seemed to last much longer than the joke deserved. Helen knew it was a purging they all needed; a release of frustration, of fear, of helplessness. It had been an incredibly long day, but they had made some headway and they had earned some joy.

"There are protein bars in your packs," Helen said. "Eat that for now and I promise I'll buy you a proper breakfast. Right now I'm exhausted and I need to sleep."

There were no arguments from the team, as Justin and Bodhi vacated to their room and Helen fell back onto her bed and let the exhaustion sweep over her.

Bodhi and the team sat around a wooden table outside their hotel rooms, eating a simple breakfast of fruit, arepas rellenas and strong coffee. As it was early, it wasn't too warm or humid yet, and above them now, the skies were relatively blue. Justin was talking about his morning run down along the river and seeing people walking around with bandanas over their noses and mouths, and others coughing. Bodhi only half-listened, as his coffee hadn't taken effect as yet. Mostly he watched a couple of colorful birds perched close by in a tree. They had a loud cry as they nibbled at the bark and defecated on the ground below. He wondered just what other wildlife came into daily contact with humans like these ones did.

An incoming call sounded on Helen's tablet, which lay on the table beside her food. She quickly wiped her hands and answered it. Gabriel appeared, still on shift in Lyon.

"Bonjour!" he smiled.

"Tell me that smile is because you have good news for us?" Helen said, as Bodhi suddenly felt awake.

"His name was Sebastian Dias," Gabriel announced. "Thirteen years old. He's the first influenza-type death registered at the hospital around the predicted time."

"Sebastian Dias," Helen nodded. "Any luck with a family address?"

"No. It's just listed as the hospital address."

"How can that be?" Ekemma asked, brows knotted. "The doctor said the family came to collect his body. They must have needed those details to release him?"

Gabriel shrugged. "He might've come from a small rural village for all we know."

"The doctor said he was local, though," Bodhi said.

"The name should be enough to ask around," Justin said. "A sick boy named Sebastian Dias, who died nearly two weeks ago?" He shrugged. "Can't be too many fitting that description."

Helen nodded. "Thank you, Gabe, truly. We'll start asking around." Helen ended the comms and grinned at the team. "We have a name!"

"We have a name!" Justin repeated, holding up his coffee

and tapping it against Helen's. Bodhi smiled and they each raised their takeout coffee and tapped cups in celebration.

After breakfast, they began making their way toward the Leticia dock on the banks of the Amazon. The heat and humidity were now beginning to rise and it was promising to be another warm day.

They arrived at the dock some fifteen minutes later and studied all the different boats pulled up to it; most were in the form of long wooden canoe-type boats complete with oars, however one or two were motorized with a shaded covering overhead. The dock itself was similar to that at Tabatinga, with a wide wooden platform with overhead roofing that sat on the water about ten meters from shore, linked to the land by a series of long wooden planks. The visible wood was painted a dark green, the tin roof rusted, and the sides open to provide relief from the humidity. Close by on the banks of the river itself, more boats were pulled up onto the sand. The banks themselves, Bodhi noted, were lined with litter, mostly variations of plastic. It made his heart sink to see it.

He noticed curious stares from the locals that were milling around. Tourists obviously weren't rare in the region, but Bodhi knew the GHA team didn't look like tourists to these people. They didn't appear relaxed like the tourists, nor were they wearing shorts, t-shirts and sandals like them either. They had their surgical masks hanging around their necks and gloves in their pockets, ready for quick deployment if needed. Had they not been in the fresh air, they would've been wearing both already. But here in the open air and standing well back while speaking with people, they could risk not wearing their masks. He knew how alarming it could look to some people. That said, he noted that some of the locals did have scarves and bandanas around their own necks anyway. Clearly these people were wary of another coronavirus scenario.

As they approached the dock, Bodhi noted that any of the locals he made eye contact with, would quickly look elsewhere, and any they approached began to move away to avoid talking with them. The few who didn't automatically move away, he noted, began to listen when Helen or Justin or Ekemma spoke, but as soon as either he or Pilar spoke, they quickly walked away. Bodhi was starting to realise that their American accents weren't exactly welcome in these parts.

"These people don't appear to want to talk to us any more than the hospital staff did," Bodhi commented.

"Yeah," Justin said, eyes narrowed in suspicion. "And I got a feeling it's not the virus they're scared of, it's us."

"They love tourists here, but they're not so keen on the United States," Pilar said, scanning over the people at the dock. "Let's stick in groups as we ask around, alright?"

"Indeed," Helen said.

"Justin, you go with Helen," Pilar said. "I'll go with Bodhi and Kem."

Bodhi, Ekemma and Pilar had been asking around after the boy for almost an hour but were having no luck. With each boat that departed, so, too, did a little of their hope. Though each time they saw a new boat approaching, their hope would buoy again, but it would soon sink once more. They found a lot of people claiming not to understand English and when Pilar offered to speak in Spanish, they got a lot of waving hands and people walking away. Some even physically tensed or looked guarded or aggressive when Sebastian's name was mentioned, which Bodhi found strange. The more people they spoke to, the more he got the feeling that it wasn't talking to outsiders that these people were opposed to, it was simply talking about this boy, Sebastian.

They eventually gave up on the dock and the banks and began moving toward the road, Calle 3, that would lead them back into the town proper. Before they hit the town, however, they veered left onto a path that connected with a dirt road that ran parallel to the river. Along this road were many houses that, although a good hundred meters back from the river, may just have seen Sebastian Dias before and known of his movements.

They approached some people who were milling about in front of the houses; a woman watching her kids play in their yard, a man smoking a cigarette on his front steps, two men fixing a car. They began asking questions, but the response was the same. The people suddenly moved indoors or walked away from them. No one wanted to talk to them. Only the woman mentioned "enfermedad", sickness, staring at their surgical masks before waving them away and gathering her children and taking them inside. While Pilar was calling after the latest group of people who were avoiding her, Bodhi noticed someone standing by the corner of one of the wooden, stilted buildings, watching them carefully as he spoke into a cellphone. He was a young man, early twenties, lean but toned with a thin face and high cheekbones that gave him an intense look.

"We're just trying to help your people," Pilar called out in

English after the group that was walking away from her, "stop them from getting sick and making you sick!"

Bodhi walked up and tapped her on the shoulder and motioned to the man watching them. The man ended his call, then he turned and disappeared around the corner of the building out of their view. Bodhi and Pilar caught Ekemma's attention, from where she'd been looking down at her tablet, and they began to walk hurriedly after him, but once they turned the corner of the wooden building, he was nowhere to be seen. Somehow he'd just disappeared. They walked along for a few minutes more, looking down each walkway between the wooden buildings, but saw no trace of him. They weren't game to enter any of those pathways between the houses either. Several aggressively barking dogs dissuaded them of that idea.

"He must've taken shelter in one of these buildings," Bodhi suggested, studying them.

"But which one?" Ekemma asked.

Pilar called out something in Spanish again, talking to the buildings and empty walkways. Upon hearing silence in return, she placed her hands on her hips, sighed and looked back at Bodhi and Ekemma.

"They're not going to talk to us," she said.

Ekemma nodded. "We're strangers. They don't know us. We need to find a local to help."

"Who, though?" Pilar said. "The hospital staff weren't interested."

Ekemma's phone rang and she answered it.

"Justin? No, we've had no luck. You?" she asked. The silence sat as she listened to them. "It's hopeless here. I know the nurse told us to ask around the dock, but we're getting nowhere. It's time we tried the local police," she said, glancing at her tablet. She listened again, then nodded. "Alright. We'll meet you there."

She hung up the phone.

"The police?" Pilar said.

"We could try the nurse again?" Bodhi suggested.

Ekemma shook her head. "The nurse wouldn't tell us anything accept to ask around down here, but no one here will talk to us. We need to find the boy's family. The police are our only option now."

CHAPTER TWELVE

Helen and Justin met up with the rest of the team en route to the police station. There was one close by, an inspector's office, further down the palm tree lined Calle 3, heading back into the town proper. They had no luck there, however, and instead were directed to try the Estacion de Policia Leticia, which was a tuk-tuk ride away down Carrera 11.

When they arrived they saw a handful of officers behind the reception counter, with several people in the waiting area, some with their faces covered in bandanas and scarves. Helen and Pilar waited patiently for their turn to speak with a member of the National Police of Colombia, while the rest of the team waited outside, checking the latest outbreak data and discussing their conversations with the locals.

It felt like an age had passed, while those behind the reception counter sat together in discussions, typed two-fingered into their computers, answered ringing phones, or walked around with cups of coffee in hand. Eventually, a bored or perhaps tired looking officer came over to speak with them. He appeared to be late thirties in age and seemed relatively fit beneath his dark green uniform. According to the patch on his chest, his name was Major Andres Perez.

After he declined to speak English, Helen waited patiently for Pilar to explain their situation and ask for information on Sebastian Dias. The man listened patiently, sipping his coffee every now and then, but he seemed to be attentive. A discussion ensued in Spanish, back and forth, Perez seeming to ask more questions of Pilar, than she of him. After a moment, he shrugged, said something, then walked off to a desk and sat down behind a computer and began to type something into his console.

"Is he helping us?" Helen asked Pilar

Pilar nodded, watching Perez. "Said he'd see what he could find out."

"Well, that's more helpful than anyone else so far."

Another fifteen minutes passed before Perez stood and walked over to a printer. He picked up whatever it had spat out, studied it, then brought it over to them. Another conversation ensued in Spanish, while Helen tried to read, upside down, the data on the print-out before the man. Perez showed them a list of names, but he would not let them take it. The list was several pages long, but from what Helen could gather from the body language of each party in the conversation, Sebastian Dias was not on the list.

"What's this list?" Helen asked.

"It's a list of Dias' in the immediate region," Pilar explained, as Perez moved back to his desk with the list in hand.

"According to that, a thirteen year-old Sebastian Dias doesn't exist."

"How can he not exist on police records, but did on the hospital records?"

Pilar shrugged. "Maybe he was born in a village or something and not recorded. The hospital only had a record of him because he died. Maybe prior to that, he wasn't recorded anywhere."

Helen's mind turned over. "Doctor Ramirez said he was a local. How did he know how to contact the family to collect his body?"

"It's strange, isn't it?" Pilar said. "I'm starting to think we're not going to find him no matter how hard we try. The kid's a ghost and no one wants to talk about him. We're chasing shadows."

Helen nodded, the frustration rising again. "And in the meantime, this virus is doing Lord knows what."

Bodhi, Ekemma and Justin waited outside the local police office, while Helen and Pilar spoke to the officers inside. Bodhi watched them through the windows, saw their expressive hand movements, but he could tell they weren't getting anywhere. The faces on the local police officers were flat and unemotional in return. The frustration was starting to build again. For every piece of information they uncovered, for every small win they had, the setbacks and walls they hit seemed innumerable in comparison. The death toll was quickly approaching two hundred and twenty-five people across the three countries, with many more ill, and these people seemed to be going out of their way *not* to help them.

Justin nudged Bodhi's shoulder and he looked at the medic.

"Two guys on the motorcycle," Justin said quietly. "Three o'clock. I think they're watching us."

Bodhi glanced over Justin's shoulder to see two men sitting on the cycle, blatantly staring at them.

"I don't think they like us talking to the cops," Justin said.

"We had no choice," Ekemma said. "How can we trace the boy's movements if no one will talk to us? We need to know where he caught this virus. It's an important data point. Every day we don't have this information, is another day this virus spreads. It's moving fast and we're moving too slow." It was clear Ekemma shared Bodhi's frustration.

"I hear ya, Kem," Justin said calmly, "but for some reason, we seem to be ruffling feathers and I don't like strange guys staring at us."

Helen and Pilar exited the building.

"Let me guess," Bodhi said. "No luck?"

Helen shook her head, as Justin motioned Pilar away to talk.

"They said he could be anyone," Helen sighed. "They said a lot of villagers come into town and they don't know everybody out there."

Bodhi nodded and sighed as well, wiping the sweat off the back of his neck. He looked over at Justin and Pilar talking low and quiet and Pilar subtly eyeing the motorcycle guys. She moved back over to Helen.

"I think we should get off the streets for a while."

"We have to keep asking around," Helen said. "It's our only option."

"No, I really do think that we need to get off the street for a while and stop asking questions," Pilar said insistently. "Let's head back to the hotel and lay low for a few hours and work from there."

Helen looked at her. "What's going on?"

"It's my job to keep you safe, Helen, and right now I recommend we go back to the hotel."

"Agreed," Justin said. "Let's go check in with Aiko and see where she's at with the virus samples from Lima."

Bodhi looked at the two men on the motorcycle again, then nodded. Having seen the young man on the phone earlier watching them, and now these two men on the motorcycle, he was starting to feel uneasy.

"Come on," he said to Helen. "A break will be good to clear our heads."

Aiko, watched by Max who stood close by, split her screen so that both she and her data could be seen.

"Can you see both?" she asked the hot spot team.

"Yes," Helen replied. Aiko darted her eyes to their screen, where Bodhi sat beside Helen. Aiko felt Bodhi's stare more than Helen's; judging her, appraising her. Was he curious to see just what she'd left him for? Was he curious to see if pursuing her career had been worth the sacrifice of their relationship?

"I'm still working on things, of course," she said, "but the virus appears to be a distant relative of another virus recently studied, called the Peru Bat virus. Studies, at the time, showed that transference to humans wasn't able to occur, but it was concluded that it could be a future possibility. So either the time has come and this virus has finally mutated and evolved to infect humans or we've discovered a brand new virus that just happens to be distantly related to the Peru Bat virus. If it's a new strain of the existing virus, then what we're seeing is an antigenic shift. Somehow the virus has suddenly found a way to invade our human cells, undergo some kind of reassortment, and replicate at an extremely fast pace. Now, a recent study by University of Zurich scientists identified a gateway receptor that let bat flu viruses enter host cells and cause infection, isolating a protein called MHC-II as the reason. This is a troubling discovery because these protein receptors are found across a number of species, including mice, pigs and chickens, which means these animals could possibly become a 'bridge' of infection into humans. We obviously still don't know how our Patient Zero contracted this virus, but a bridge species is a possibility. We need to focus on birds, particularly chickens, and bats."

"So…" Helen said as though to herself, "we're dealing with a bat-borne virus that has avian qualities. A bat-borne influenza type A virus that has likely undergone an antigenic shift event in order to have infected humans."

"Yes. And that bothers me. New World bats harbor more influenza virus genetic diversity than all other mammalian and avian species combined. We have so much to learn in this area and the problem we have is one that is going to require years of study."

"I guess we're about to undergo a steep learning curve then," Bodhi said.

Aiko's eyes shifted to his. "Perhaps, if we're lucky. But my concern is that it could take us months, even years to understand this virus and find a way to successfully block the transmission. Look how long it took to get the COVID vaccine. This virus is showing potential to be even more contagious. We don't have that time."

"No," Helen said, "we really don't."

Aiko saw the concern on Helen's face and took a breath. "I'm trying to find out how the virus invades our human cells, but this is bigger than just me. I've called on other labs in our network to assist. We have a team working on this, around the world. Now the global health alerts are out, we should see the infection rate begin to stabilize as quarantine measures come into play and hospitals prepare themselves to treat the patients, but the numbers will continue to rise until those measures take effect."

Helen nodded. "The health alert is raised to its highest level and it's properly global now. The WHO knows we can't afford to tread lightly with this. Not after last time. This virus is going to clear just about everyone in its path, unless we can find a way to stop it."

"As you can imagine, it's starting to hit the media," Max said, leaning into view. "The news here had a full story on it last night. We need to make sure we don't incite panic. That can cause just as much damage as the virus will if we face another economic collapse."

"I know, Max," Helen said, "but better people be panicked and careful, than lax and dead. I know that sounds bloody harsh, and I hope we can get the message out calmly, but that's the truth of it."

"You will need to be extra careful," Aiko told them. "Don't take any chances. Use containment suits wherever possible."

"We are."

"It would be helpful if I could get a biological sample from

Sebastian Dias," Aiko said. "Especially if he's our Patient Zero. Is that possible?"

Helen exchanged a look with Bodhi. "We'll try, but right now we can't find out anything about him. The kid's a ghost."

"People simply aren't talking," Bodhi said.

"Then you need to find a way to make them talk," Aiko said. "Those samples would give us the starting point of the virus, which will enable comparisons to the latest victims. We need to know if this virus is still mutating, and we need to know if there are asymptomatic people out there that are spreading this without knowing."

"Helen," Max said, "there's something you should know. I got a call from Davidson. He's on his way here to Lyon."

"Why?"

Max shrugged. "I don't know. I got the feeling that something's gone down and he's coming in to clear up the mess."

"Mess? To do with Robert?" Helen asked. "Or to do with our operation here?"

"I don't know any of the details, but I got a feeling maybe you've been upsetting the locals down there."

"Upsetting the locals?" she said. "Trying to save people's lives is upsetting them?"

"Hey, hey." Max held his arms out. "I'm just warning you that Davidson's on his way here. You're not the one that has to deal with him, I do. So whatever you're doing to piss people off, stop it, alright? 'Cause I'm the one that has to get your ass out of there if you do."

"Alright, Max," she said in appeasement. "You deal with home base, and I'll deal with the hot spot, alright? That was the arrangement. Aiko? Contact me soon-as if you find out anything else."

Helen ended the comms and she and Bodhi disappeared from view. Aiko looked to Max who exhaled heavily and rubbed the back of his neck.

"We're all under pressure, Max," she said. "But we're all doing everything we can. Especially them," she motioned to her laptop where Helen and Bodhi had just been. "And they're the ones in the hot spot. They're the ones at risk."

"Yeah, I know," Max said, looking up at her. "And I don't want anything to happen to them on my watch. Do you?"

Aiko didn't answer. Max turned and left the lab, and she returned her eyes to the blank laptop screen.

Bodhi watched as Helen tossed the tablet aside onto the hotel bed and exhaled her frustration.

"They're still out there," Justin said, peering through the curtains.

Pilar moved to peer out also. "Alright, enough of this bullshit," she announced. "I'm going out there."

"I'll come," Justin said.

"No, this one's mine."

"Pilar, this is Colombia," he said. "You're not on US soil, your uniform means shit here."

"That's why I'm not wearing one," she agreed, "but I think this Cuban-American girl stands a better chance talking to these guys than an Australian gringo."

Justin stared at her, unhappy, but conceded her point.

"I'm just gonna talk to them," she said calmly. "Besides, you're not responsible for our safety, right? I am. You're the medic."

"Yeah, well, you can take the boy out of the military but you can't take the military out of the boy, I guess." He tapped his temple. "It's up here for life."

"I'll call you if I need you, soldier," she said, slipping out the door.

Helen looked at Justin. "I appreciate you want to help, but I think she's right. If these guys are somehow a threat, then we don't want to seem a threat to them."

"We need to go back to the hospitals and help them," Ekemma said. "We can't just sit around here hiding and doing nothing."

"We need to trace Sebastian Dias," Bodhi said. "That's where we can add value."

Helen nodded. "Bodhi's right. But we do also need to know what these guys outside want from us."

Justin peered out the window again, watching Pilar carefully, clenching his jaw and shaking his bladed leg. Ekemma moved to stand beside him and placed her hand gently on his shoulder. Justin looked at her, and the two seemed to have a silent conversation that instilled calm within him.

Bodhi watched them for a moment and it only seemed to remind him that he was the new guy here. This team had worked together for a while. From what he could gather Pilar was the newest among them, but even she had been with the team for nine months or so. There were relationships here that had long histories that he didn't know about. The tension between Helen and Max, the friendship between Ekemma and Justin. He knew it was par for the course with any working relationship, especially when you worked as many hours together in the field as they did; some relationships grew deeper, some grew strained. If you spent enough time with people, it was bound to happen. And he hadn't spent enough time with these people yet, to know who they really were. Or how they would handle the pressure.

He paused for a moment, suddenly realizing that maybe he wasn't that different from the rest of them, after all. He had a history with Aiko. A history that lasted two years, and most of those two years were the best times of his life. That was, until she ripped his heart out. Still, that was a long time ago now. He had no idea who she was today.

Bodhi stood and joined Justin and Ekemma at the windows, wanting to shake the thoughts from his mind. They watched in silence, as Pilar spoke with the two men. It seemed friendly at first, but Bodhi saw her face flatten out a little and her shoulders tense. She nodded and started heading back toward the room but stopped and looked back around when one of the men said something to her, which the other man laughed at. Pilar just stared at them for a moment, then smiled and said something with her arms spread wide. Then she turned back and headed for the room again.

"What happened?" Justin asked as soon as she reentered the hotel room.

"I got nothing but a recommendation on where to eat," she said.

"Did they threaten you?" Justin asked.

Pilar's face fell a little. "It's fine."

"What did they say?" Helen said with concern, standing up.

"Nothing. They laughed at my Spanish. Apparently the accent is all wrong. It's not Colombian."

"You talked for longer than that, Pilar," Helen said.

Pilar sighed, relenting, as she placed her hands on her hips. "They asked what a US soldier was doing here asking questions. I told them I'm here with the Global Health Agency, but they don't seem to buy it."

"How do they know you're a soldier?" Ekemma asked, straightening. "Only the Brazilian police know that."

Pilar shrugged. "Open border. I assume the transfer of information is like the transfer of people here."

"This is a problem," Justin said.

"Did you speak to your superiors about this?" Helen asked Pilar.

"Yeah."

"And what did they say?"

"They're looking into it. Relax. Forget about that now, we need to focus on finding this boy."

"It doesn't seem we're going to be able to do that with so much heat on you," Bodhi said carefully.

"It just means they're going to watch me." Pilar said. "They'll see soon enough that we're just trying to help."

"But *who* are they exactly?" Ekemma asked.

Pilar shrugged again.

"This is probably why people won't talk to us, because of these men," Bodhi said. "Maybe if we go out there alone without you, Pilar, they might stop following and then people will talk to us."

"No." Pilar shook her head.

"We're epidemiologists," Bodhi said, motioning to himself

and Helen. "We work in public health, we're no threat. Ekemma is a quarantine specialist. She's no threat. They clearly don't trust the military and they know who you are. It's probably only a matter of time before they find out Justin is ex-military, and we're blocked even further. I think maybe we need to try things with you two staying out of it." Bodhi knew it could be a risk, but without any other options, they had to try. "No offense," he added with a shrug.

"This is Colombia, Bodhi," Justin said. "You could get yourselves killed."

"We could get ourselves killed just as easily back home, too," he debated.

"I rather agree with Bodhi," Helen said. "We're not a threat, but you could be, Pilar. Even you, Justin."

"They've seen you with us," Justin said. "You can't pretend to suddenly not be with us."

"Look," Ekemma said firmly, "we're not getting anywhere arguing amongst ourselves like this. We need to put our egos aside for the good of our investigation. We're here to help save lives. In order to do that, we need information. Let us go, on our own, and try. We will stay together, the three of us, but let us talk science and quarantine to them, and see if they will talk to us. We must try this."

"The voice of reason," Helen said, grabbing her tablet and putting it in her bag and hiking that bag over her shoulder. "You're quite right, and as the new leader of this team, my recommendation as to the course of action stands. Kem? Bodhi? Let's go and try it on our own. You two stay here. That's an order."

Bodhi stood and followed Helen to the door, while Pilar

and Justin shot each other a look that lay somewhere between frustration and concern.

Max watched as Peter Davidson entered the GHA facility. He rose from Lou's desk and turned ready to greet him.

"Peter," he said.

"Max," Davidson shook his hand. "What's the latest?"

"Well, they're still trying to find out about this boy, but they've got a strong feeling he's their Patient Zero, so that's good news."

"It is, but the numbers are spiraling, yes?" Davidson said, casting his eye over the screens at Lou's desk.

"They are."

"It's hit international media so as you can imagine I've got a lot of people asking questions, and I need to give them answers. There's a lot of PTSD from last time and everyone's worried panic will take over again."

"That why you're here?" Max asked, unable to contain his curiosity, though it may have sounded more like an accusation.

Davidson looked at him. "Why the hell did Helen go into the field? She's the Acting GHA Director, she should be here dealing with this."

"I asked her the same thing. She said she'd handle things in the field, and I was to handle things here."

"No offence, Max, I know you're capable, but I left her in charge. She should not have left her post."

Max tried not to bristle at his words. "I guess that's something you need to take up with her, then. I'm not her keeper."

Davidson studied him but ignored his response. "I'll be in Robert's office."

Max watched him leave, trying to contain his annoyance. The last thing he needed was Davidson looking over his shoulder, pissed at what Helen had done.

Helen, Bodhi and Ekemma walked along the humid streets somewhat despondent. They'd tried asking around for another couple of hours, but even without Pilar and Justin they still had no luck. Talking science and quarantine hadn't worked either – especially with their limited Spanish. Even those they came across who looked sick wouldn't listen when they tried to urge them to go to hospital and stay away from their loved ones. They seemed scared of the hospital. Maybe they knew if they went there, they may not come home alive.

Tired and hungry, they now walked to collect some dinner for the team before heading back to their hotel. They found a small grocery store but its shelves were bare. Panic buying was well underway. Their only option for food was a little restaurant not far from the hotel, so they placed their orders. The restaurant was even more hot and sticky than the climate outside, so they opted to wait on the street. They'd noticed the two men on the motorcycle hadn't followed them that afternoon and a phone call to Pilar confirmed that they'd stayed at the hotel to keep an eye on her instead. That was something, Helen thought. However, it seemed they'd picked up some new followers of their own. They noticed two teenagers had been trailing them instead. They looked to be about fifteen or sixteen. One was skinny with a long fringe that hung in his eyes, the other was meatier with acne. Helen wasn't sure whether they were linked to the men on the motorcycle or not. And now as they waited outside the restaurant, the two teens stood on the other side of the road, trying to look inconspicuous, although not successfully.

"What do you think – are they linked with the motorcycle guys?" Helen asked Bodhi and Ekemma quietly.

"Should I go talk to them?" Bodhi suggested.

"It didn't do Pilar much good," Helen said.

"No, but these are kids," Bodhi studied them. "I'm going to give it a try."

"Bodhi–"

Helen watched as he started crossing the street toward them, but the teens quickly got on their bicycles and took off. Bodhi exhaled heavily, then turned and came back.

They got their food and started walking back to the hotel. Though the sun had set, the temperature had not. Helen's clothes were damp and stuck to her body. She longed to remove her gloves and mask and have a long shower but she was so hungry, the spices emanating from the takeout bag called more strongly to her. She couldn't wait to tuck in.

"Hey," a voice called from behind. The three of them turned to see a boy, about ten, standing there. He wore a baseball cap and had a yellow gold chain around his neck. He motioned with his head for them to follow and made his way down a darkened walkway between two old wooden buildings. Helen, Bodhi and Ekemma exchanged a quick look, then watched as he stopped. He looked back at them, then motioned with his head again for them to follow.

Helen studied the darkened walkway but couldn't quite

see down to the end. There were parked cars and piles of rubbish against the walls of the buildings. Plenty of objects she couldn't see behind. She shook her head firmly. "No."

The boy stared at them, then moved forward a few steps. Two figures suddenly appeared beside him, stepping out from behind structures either side of the walkway. It was the two teenagers who had been following them. Helen tensed.

"Come," the skinny teen said in heavily accented English.

"No," Helen said even more firmly, her heart beginning to race, thinking they were about to be mugged.

"You want know about Sebastian Dias?" the teen asked.

Helen felt her heart stop for a moment before starting up again. She quickly exchanged a look of shock with Bodhi and Ekemma, then turned back to the boys. "Yes, we do."

"Come." The teen waved them forward.

Helen looked ahead at the darkened walkway again, wedged between two rundown weathered buildings. Was it a trap? Were they luring them into the alleyway with a promise of information on Sebastian, only to rob them? Or were they telling the truth?

"Helen," Ekemma said. "I don't like this."

"Neither do I," Helen said, swallowing, "but if someone finally wants to talk about Sebastian, then I really should hear what they've got to say. Just stick together," she added. "We'll be fine."

They followed the boys down the walkway to an area behind a row of houses, where an older woman waited sitting on an upturned crate. The woman was small, her face creased with sun and sadness, and framed with pepper-gray hair. The boys ushered them closer toward her.

"Sebastian grandmother," the skinny teen said.

Helen's eyes lit up, and her heart swelled with hope. She stepped forward eagerly but stopped when the other teen flicked a knife out at her.

"No closer!" the first said.

Helen's heart nearly leapt into her throat. She quickly held her hand up in calm. "OK. OK. Si."

The woman spoke in Spanish to the boy, who turned and spoke to Helen.

"Why you ask about Sebastian?"

"We're doctors. We're trying to find out what caused his sickness."

The boy relayed her words. The woman spoke again, then the boy translated.

"He's dead. So is sister and mother. They don't know cause."

"Please tell her: we're very sorry for her loss. Please tell her we want to stop other people from dying, but in order to do that we need to trace Sebastian's movements. This will help us find out what made him sick in the first place and how the spread of infection might evolve."

The boy studied her for a moment, then turned to the older woman. He spoke, pausing now and then as though trying to find the right word, but eventually finished his spiel. The woman eyed them in contemplation, before she spoke again to the boy.

"He traveled all over," the teen told them, "between Colombia and Brazil. Very far."

"Why?" Helen asked.

The teen studied her. "He work. Deliver for boss."

"Did he mention that he was bitten, by a bat or anything

else? Or that he felt sick after eating some food?" Helen asked, then waited for the translation.

"No." The boy shook his head. "He was too ill to speak when he return to Leticia. He went straight to hospital. Then he die. Very quick."

"Can you tell us where he traveled exactly? Where to find this boss? It's important we know the boy's movements."

The teen stared at her.

"If we know where he went," she explained, "we can help the people in those areas, as they will likely be the hardest hit. If not, the sickness, it will," she used her arms to demonstrate, "move out from these areas. And the threat, whatever caused this, might infect new people and the cycle will start again. Soon there will be too many people infected for us to stop it."

The boy translated as best he could. The woman closed her eyes and shook her head. She said something, then waved her arm as though sending them away.

"No one knows where he traveled," the boy said. "You must stop asking questions. It is dangerous."

"Why?"

The woman said something angrily, and Helen heard the words "gringa" and "muerte", then she stood and began to walk away.

"Wait! Please!" Helen said. "I'm sorry to ask this, but can we take a sample from Sebastian's body? We need to study the virus he had."

"Go!" The teen waved Helen off. "Leave! No more questions." He followed the woman, along with the other teen and the boy.

Helen moved after them, but Bodhi's hand on her arm stopped her.

"Helen," he cautioned quietly. "Don't. I think we're done here."

"Let's get back to the street, somewhere safer," Ekemma said, pulling her other arm.

They began quickly down the darkened walkway back toward the streetlights.

"Did anyone else pick up what that boy was putting down?" Ekemma asked.

Helen looked at her, confused.

"He *delivered* things for his boss," Ekemma said. "No one wants to tell us anything about him because they're scared to. What is Colombia well known for, aside from coffee and rainforests?"

Bodhi looked at Helen as a realization seemed to sweep over him. "Drugs…"

The realization swept over Helen, too. She nodded absently as her heart and mind began to race. "The boy was a drug mule."

CHAPTER THIRTEEN

Helen peered out the hotel room window. The two men and the motorcycle were still there. They were parked by the road, their bodies shadows beneath a Chontaduro Peach-Palm tree, which offered some shade from the lone streetlight close by. Helen spotted them easily, however, as one man's face lit up briefly in the orange glow of his cigarette lighter.

As soon as her team had returned to the hotel, they had gathered with Pilar and Justin and told them what they'd learned from the discussion with Sebastian Diaz's grandmother.

"It makes sense," Pilar said. "Explains why no one wants to give us any information about the boy."

"It does," Helen said, "but that's not going to help us trace the infection or find out what started this."

"Do you think the doctor knew?" Bodhi asked, eyes narrowed in thought. "Ramirez. He was just as hesitant to tell us anything."

"But he's a doctor," Ekemma said. "Surely he knows the risks if this continues to spread. This outbreak is already working its way through three countries."

"That we know of," Helen added.

"I guess it depends whether his life is at risk if he talks," Justin said. "What help can he provide these people if he's... silenced?"

"There's only one way we find out," Helen said. "First thing tomorrow, we go back and talk to him."

Bodhi sipped his coffee in the early morning light. He'd snuck out of the room he shared with Justin, grabbed a coffee from a café just down the street, then took a seat at the wooden table out front of their hotel, gathering his thoughts before the team awakened. He hadn't slept well. Too many thoughts had circled through his mind as he lay in bed the previous night. Thoughts of the virus spiraling out of control. Thoughts of their Patient Zero, such a young boy being a drug mule. Thoughts of the roadblocks facing them to find out the information they needed. The language barrier. Scared civilians. A drug baron they'd inadvertently pissed off. This was no ordinary virus they were facing, nor was it an ordinary Patient Zero.

He glanced over to where the men on the motorcycle had been. The motorcycle was gone, and in its place a car where one man slept, open-mouthed, while his companion stared straight at Bodhi.

"Can't sleep?" Ekemma's voice sounded behind him, making him jump. She smiled. "I'm sorry. I didn't mean to sneak up on you."

He smiled and shook his head. "No, couldn't sleep."

"Me either," she said, taking a seat beside him. As she did, she eyed the men in the car carefully.

They sat in silence for a moment, just looking around, soaking up the peace and quiet.

"I like sleep very much," Ekemma finally said, "but I also like the solitude the early morning brings."

Bodhi nodded. "I'm more of a night owl, but it is nice on occasion."

A moment of silence passed as they each soaked in the morning.

"I don't like our chances of finding information now we know this boy was a drug mule," she said flatly.

"It's definitely a hurdle," he said, then shrugged. "But who knows, maybe his boss will see the devastation this virus is causing and help us?"

Ekemma grunted and crossed her arms.

"You don't think so?"

She looked at him, then back to the road to see a motorcycle pass, laden with boxes. "I don't know what Colombia is like, but I know what the gangs in Nigeria are capable of. They care little for anything outside of what they want."

Bodhi studied her. "When did you leave?"

"Nigeria?"

He nodded.

"As soon as I could," she said, staring off at the trees across the road. "But I still have family there and they are very entrenched in the country, so I go back from time to time... Part of me wants to stay away, but part of me cannot look away from what happens there." She glanced back at Bodhi. "If we all stand back and let the gangs and militia of the world do what they want, what will happen to our society?"

"It's not an easy thing to stand up to them."

"No, it's not. But they rely on fear and intimidation to hold their power. The first step any country must take is to stamp out corruption in the government and in the police. When there is no one to buy off, these criminals will fall. But to rid the governments and police of their cancer is in itself a monstrous task."

Bodhi nodded, wondering what Ekemma's life must've been like when she was young. He didn't know much about Nigeria except for what he had seen on the news. Ekemma spoke as though she had intimate knowledge of hard times. She glanced at him again, then smiled. "Look at us, talking so deep at this hour." She stood and stretched again. "Right now we have a monster of our own to defeat. And I must do this on a full stomach. Shall we eat breakfast?"

Bodhi smiled and stood. "I think that sounds like a very fine idea."

Justin emerged from their room in his running sweats and paused upon seeing them. "What's this? You beat me up?"

Bodhi shrugged. "Anything to avoid listening to you singing in the shower."

"What do you mean?" Justin shrugged back, walking toward them. "I sing like an angel."

"One that's being strangled perhaps," Bodhi's reply came.

"Justin, you cannot go for a run," Ekemma said.

"Why not?" he said, stretching.

"We're being watched," she said, motioning to the car.

"Exactly," Justin said. "They're just watching. So they can watch me jog."

"You can't miss one day?"

Justin shook his head. "Jogging is my daily medicine, Kem. It's not just for the body, it's also for the mind." He tapped his temple. "It's a proven stress reliever. Trust me, if I miss a day, I get grumpy, and no one wants that."

"Don't go far, *please*," she pleaded gently.

"I won't," he said reassuringly, then jogged away.

Helen entered the hospital's waiting room with the team in tow, dressed in their disposable containment suits, gloves and masks. The number of patients seemed to have swelled overnight. They had run out of chairs in the waiting room and people now sat or lay on the floor and some were even queuing outside. Justin and Ekemma immediately set about helping the nurses where they could, while Helen, Bodhi and Pilar sought out Doctor Ramirez.

Helen walked straight past the nurses who started yelling at her in Spanish. Pilar said something appeasing back to them, and all three continued down the corridors in search of the doctor. They couldn't afford to have him ignoring them, or worse, disappearing on them.

They found him in a small room crammed with eight beds of influenza-stricken patients. Helen moved up behind him and tapped him on the shoulder. He looked around in annoyance and upon recognizing who it was, his look soon turned to one of frustrated anger.

"We need to talk," Helen said firmly, frustrated herself that if he'd just been honest with them when they first came here, they wouldn't have wasted all that precious time.

His brows creased further in anger. "How dare you barge in here like this? Can't you see I'm busy?" He motioned to the patients around him.

"Yes, we can see that. And you're only going to get busier if you don't talk to us."

"I've told you all I know!" He turned his back on her and continued his work.

"Have you?" Helen asked. "You're telling me you didn't know about Sebastian Dias?"

The doctor paused then looked back at her.

"You know who he is and what he does for a living, don't you?" Helen said.

The doctor grabbed her upper arm tightly and began to lead her toward the door.

"Hey, hey!" Pilar blocked his pathway, squaring her shoulders. "Take your hands off her."

Ramirez let Helen go, then pointed angrily to the door. "Out!" he said, then barged past them into the corridor. He snapped off his gloves as they followed him to a break room, where he ushered them inside, then checked the corridor both ways and closed the door behind him.

"What are you doing?" he hissed beneath his mask.

"Trying to stop this outbreak turning into a pandemic!" Helen said.

"You're going to get yourselves killed asking all these questions!"

"We need to stop this virus!"

"And I understand that, but you cannot ask about this boy.

You must find another avenue."

"There is no other avenue. He's our Patient Zero. He's the first death on record from this virus. We need to know how he caught the infection."

Ramirez exhaled in frustration.

"Look, we know he was a drug mule, and we don't care," Pilar said.

The doctor looked at her. "You may not care, but the people he worked for will."

"You know a lot more than you're letting on, don't you?" Bodhi asked, studying him.

"What I know," he said stepping closer to Bodhi, "is that you cannot come here and ask these questions, Mr American. I'm sorry if he's your Patient Zero, but you cannot pursue this line of investigation."

"We're outsiders, I get it," Bodhi said calmly. "No one wants to give us answers, but what if you helped us, discreetly? What if you asked the questions on our behalf?"

Ramirez looked away, pacing a few steps.

"You know this boy," Bodhi said, "and you know his boss, don't you?"

Ramirez looked back at him.

"What he does for a living is none of our business," she said gently. "We just need to know where the boy went, that's all."

"Where the boy went?" Ramirez's eyes turned angry again. "Where he went would uncover his Patron's drug routes. Do you think they'll give up that information?"

"We don't need specifics," Pilar said. "What if you just give us general areas? Just narrow our search area down."

The doctor laughed sardonically.

"What about exhuming the boy's body and taking samples?" Helen said.

"What?" Ramirez said. "You need to leave this boy alone!"

"I know you're in a precarious position right now," Bodhi said calmly. "And we're sorry to put you there, but what you're seeing now in the hospital is just the tip of the iceberg. It's spreading fast and the fatality rate is through the roof. It's hit us hard and fast because it's a new strain of virus that we have no immunity or treatments for. And because it's hitting hard and fast, people aren't getting to hospitals in time to receive treatment. The numbers are astounding and that's just the ones that have been recorded. We're talking potentially thousands upon thousands of deaths yet to come if left unchecked. Maybe more. At worse, we're talking a pandemic that equals if not exceeds COVID." Bodhi stepped toward him. "Here in Leticia you have hospitals, but what about all the smaller villages out there? And not just in Colombia, but in Peru and Brazil, too. Even the rest of South America or the world at large. These people may not have the health systems in place to treat them, or they could become completely overwhelmed and collapse. This virus could potentially wipe out whole villages. Everyone is at risk."

"Doctor, you know as well as we do, that information is power," Helen said. "With information we can contain the projected spread. We can help the sick, we can work on a treatment, a vaccination. But we need information in order to do these things."

The doctor exhaled heavily, lowered his head. He looked tired, he looked worn, he looked tense with the stress of it all.

"We believe the virus started here," Bodhi said, "with this boy, in this region. Do you want Leticia, Colombia, to be known forever more as the origin of the pandemic that wiped out millions of lives across the world? Do you want the world to know that you stood by and watched it happen?"

Ramirez suddenly looked up, Bodhi's potential allegation hitting home. Ramirez looked angry briefly, but it quickly washed away with guilt and remorse. He looked away to the door, turning his back on them.

"Surely this *Patron* would want to help his people, too," Bodhi said.

Ramirez exhaled heavily again and turned back to face them.

"I don't know the boy's route. Not all of it," he said then seemed to hesitate.

"But?" Pilar asked, narrowing her eyes.

The doctor looked at them. "I treat some of the Patron's workers."

Pilar straightened. "The ones who work the drug labs?"

The doctor turned his eyes to her but did not answer.

"We're not here to judge, truly," Helen reassured him.

"I treat *people*," the doctor said. "That's my job. I don't ask questions, I just treat people."

"And you're doing what you should," Bodhi said reassuringly. "You're fulfilling the oath you took when you became a doctor."

Ramirez turned to stare at Bodhi again as though trying to gauge whether he was being genuine or patronizing.

"I studied medicine," Bodhi explained.

"I treat the people," Ramirez repeated. "That's it."

"Have any of the Patron's people had symptoms of this virus?" Bodhi asked.

"Some, yes. Not all."

"When you say, not all," Bodhi asked, "what do you mean?"

"Some have reported illness, some have not. The ones deep in the forest have not."

Helen felt her body still briefly. "Wait, they've reported no illness or they haven't reported in at all?"

The doctor looked at her. "They haven't reported in."

"Did Sebastian go there?" Helen asked. "Into the forest?"

Ramirez nodded. "I believe so."

"So, they could all be dead by now…" Helen said, terrorized by thoughts of entire villages razed by the virus.

"No." Ramirez shook his head adamantly. "I would have been notified."

"But if they're ill they wouldn't–"

"If they were ill, production would slow. *I would be notified,*" he said the last part slowly, accentuating each word as though explaining something to an imbecile.

"But if you're sure they're fine–" Helen began.

"The boy couldn't have gone there," Bodhi said, finishing her thought.

Ramirez shook his head. "I don't know the specifics, I told you. But the boy travels to this village, this lab, regularly. He doesn't skip it."

"And this lab, this village," Bodhi said, "do you know if the boy visited them while he was sick?"

"That I cannot say."

"How remote is this village?" Helen asked.

The doctor looked at her but didn't respond.

"Would the boy need to stay overnight?" Helen added. "Spend some time there?"

The doctor nodded.

"If he was infected," Bodhi said, straightening, "and he stayed overnight, the virus would be sweeping through them right now. And if you're sure they're not–"

"They're not," he said adamantly. "I would be called immediately."

Helen felt her body tighten with adrenaline, which she could see mirrored within Bodhi's. "If they're not infected, if they're fine and he was there for several hours while infected, that could mean they have some kind of rare natural immunity to the virus."

The doctor looked at her, as though it were something he hadn't considered. Given the whirlwind of the crisis over the past few days, it would've been easy to overlook, especially given his workload.

"We need to get to this village and study them," Helen said urgently. "Everyone else who came in contact with the boy is dead or very ill, because their bodies have never experienced this virus before. If these people have been exposed and are fine, they could help us treat this virus."

"No." The doctor stepped away from her. "No, you cannot. You cannot do this."

"You don't understand," Bodhi said, equally urgent. "This may be our only hope to stop the virus. Why has everyone else who's come into contact with this boy fallen sick, but not them? This could be a breakthrough."

"Patron won't allow you!" Ramirez said. "Leave it to your scientists to find a cure."

Bodhi stepped closer to him. "You know as well as we do that it could take months, even years, to develop antiviral meds and vaccinations for this virus, and we may never find a cure at all. How many will die in the meantime?"

Helen tried to keep the pleading from her voice. "Doctor Ramirez, if the villagers have a natural immunity, we can study their blood and replicate their antibodies. We could develop a treatment that much faster. Even if it's only short term, thousands of lives could be saved."

"Maybe the boy wasn't sick when he visited there," Ramirez said, unsure, searching for answers, a way out of this mess. "Maybe I was wrong."

"But what if he was?" Helen said. "What if you're right?"

"Cases like this have occurred in the past," Bodhi said, nodding to himself. "Next door in Peru, there was a remote village, the people of which were discovered to have a natural immunity to rabies... And take a look at the HIV virus. One per cent of the northern European Caucasian population appear to have a natural immunity to the virus, thought to have traveled down through their ancestry from the plagues of the Middle Ages. This remote village in Peru, immune to rabies, obviously had a similar immunity passed down through the generations. There is *every* chance this remote community here in Colombia has the rare immunity for this new virus. Except maybe it's not a new virus, but a long forgotten one that has reemerged from the forest?"

"I do understand what you're saying," Ramirez said, "but you cannot put me in this position. I cannot tell you where it is, because not even I know. People are either brought to me from the lab or I meet them elsewhere. I have never been there exactly."

"Then tell us who the Patron is," Pilar said, "and we will ask him ourselves, to let us go there."

The doctor laughed with disbelief and shook his head like she was crazy. "I cannot tell you that either. This is not some drug pusher standing on a street corner. This is *El Patron* and you interfering in his affairs."

"We are very sorry that you're in a tight spot here," Pilar said, "but you put yourself in this position when you agreed to work for a drug dealer."

"I had no choice!"

"Well, now you do," Bodhi said calmly, cutting off any reply from Pilar. "You're a doctor. You're the one who has to deal with all these patients. This will help you, too. Do you want to clear that waiting room out there? Do you want to clear the beds in the wards?"

"I cannot tell you what you want," Ramirez said, his forehead beginning to break out in sweat as the stress levels boiled within him.

"We don't care about the drugs," Helen said. "We just care about containing this virus. This virus that has, in a matter of weeks, turned from a cluster to an outbreak, to a series of linked epidemics, and threatens to become a global pandemic. Let us do our job. Let us help you save lives."

The silence sat a moment as Ramirez's mind turned over rapidly.

"With all due respect, sir," Pilar said, "you're not in a position to be unhelpful."

The doctor turned his back to them again, wiped his

forehead with his sleeve. "The only person who can grant you access to that village is the man himself, and not even I have met him."

Pilar nodded. "So put us in touch with whoever you deal with, and we'll take it from there."

The man hesitated again.

"Sir," Pilar said, "you must've misheard me. You don't have a choice in this. Give us a name and tell us where to find them."

CHAPTER FOURTEEN

Helen waited patiently with the team in her hotel room. Pilar thought it best now they knew the reason behind everyone's resistance, and why the men on the motorcycle, the Patron's men, were suspicious about Pilar's presence and watching her closely. They must have thought she was working undercover for the Central Intelligence Agency or the Drug Enforcement Agency. The streets had suddenly become that much more dangerous to them.

In the end, Doctor Ramirez had agreed to make contact with the person he dealt with but promised no more. So now they waited to see if they would be granted an audience with the Patron. With each passing hour, they were starting to lose hope, however. It was now late afternoon.

"We can't stay holed up in this hotel much longer," Justin said. "If this Patron guy won't help us, we're going to have to figure out another way."

"Aiko's great at what she does," Helen said, "but even the greatest scientists have been unable to find cures to some diseases. And even the ones who have, for some it has taken them years. I really hope Aiko and her network can crack this virus, but it's foolish of us to wait and hope on only one course of action. If there's a chance that village has a rare immunity, we have to try to get to them."

A knock sounded on the door and Pilar stood instantly to answer it, while Justin moved to wait close by.

Pilar opened it a crack, then opened it wider.

"Doctor Ramirez," she said, as Helen stood from the bed and moved closer.

"I've arranged a meeting," he said.

"When?" Pilar asked.

"Now. Just one of you."

"No." Pilar shook her head. "We travel in twos."

"Fine, but not you."

"Excuse me?"

"The two doctors," he said, motioning to Helen and Bodhi.

Helen exchanged a glance of trepidation with Bodhi. Though this was what she'd hoped for, it didn't make the course of action any less daunting. The thought of meeting with a drug dealer scared the hell out of her, but right now this was their best shot. She had to do it.

"Very well," she nodded, swallowing as she moved to gather her things. She felt a nervousness shoot through her body, her hands suddenly feeling sweating and shaky. Her mind raced to find another option, but it came up blank.

"Helen–" Pilar began, stepping toward her.

"We're just going to talk, yes?" Helen said to Ramirez. He nodded and she looked back at Pilar. "We'll be fine." She turned to Bodhi. "Are you OK to come with me?"

"Er, yeah," Bodhi said, as though shaking off a brain freeze.

"We're meeting in a public place, right?" he asked Ramirez, wiping his palms on the side of his trousers.

The doctor nodded. "I will be there with you."

"I'm not comfortable with this," Justin said, looking to Helen.

"We'll be OK," Bodhi said, nodding, although it sounded like he was reassuring himself as much as anyone. He turned to Pilar. "Maybe just let home base and your… *friends* know."

"Goddamn it," Pilar hissed and turned for her tablet as Helen and Bodhi walked out the door.

Max, sitting at Lou's desk with Deputy Director Peter Davidson standing beside him, stared into the comms screen at Pilar and Ekemma.

"They what?" Max said, eyebrows jumping to the top of his forehead. He darted a glance at Davidson, worried how this might transpire. "Why didn't you go with them?"

"I tried to, but it got shot down," Pilar said. "It seems my presence is hindering things here, not helping."

"So you let our two epidemiologists just walk off to meet with a drug dealer?"

"When did they leave?" Davidson cut off Pilar's reply.

"Just now."

Davidson exhaled. "Alert the local police. Have them on standby."

"Sir," Pilar held up her hand, "I don't think that's such a good idea. We don't want to spook these guys. They're meeting in a public place and they're just talking."

Davidson clenched his jaw. "As soon as Helen returns, I want her to call me. Understand?"

"Yes, sir," Pilar said.

"I'll see what I can find out from this end about El Patron," Davidson said, "but maybe ask your guys, too, and have them on standby."

"Sir," Pilar said, "if they sniff military or foreign interference, they're not going to cooperate."

Max leaned forward. "For all we know, we've just let them walk into a hostage situation, Garcia!" he said. "I wonder how much ransom a British and US scientist are worth?"

"Or maybe they're genuinely just going to talk," Ekemma, sitting beside Pilar, said firmly but calmly. "Doctor Ramirez went with them. They were not alone."

"You keep me posted," Davidson said firmly. His tone was even but Max was sure he could see steam pouring out his ears. "And you get Helen to contact me the second she returns!"

"Yes, sir."

Max ended the comms. "This is a dangerous, stupid idea."

"It is," Davidson said, placing his hands on his hips, his mind turning over, "but at the same time, if this village does have a rare natural immunity…"

"I know," Max nodded, conceding the point and finishing Davidson's thought, "we could replicate their antibodies and fast-track treatments that could save a lot of lives." He sighed and looked at Davidson. "But it could also cost two of our own."

"Max–" Davidson began.

"I grew up in Chile," Max said. "No offense, but I know South America a little better than you. And I know what these men can do. There is some peace in Colombia now, but there are leftovers of the paramilitary and guerrillas that still have major strongholds in the Amazon regions. Our guys are at major risk of kidnapping if they go in there."

"I understand," Davidson said, "but right now, that's not helping."

"I am *trying* to help."

"Then stop focusing on the worst outcome and start focusing on solutions to steer us to the right one. If you want to help, then give me a map of every known village in Colombia, and every outpost of Colombian police and military, along with every hospital and every known route that we can get them out of there if needed. Understood?"

Max nodded. "One step ahead of you. Gabe's already been working on it."

"Good," Davidson nodded, then walked away. Max watched him for a moment before he turned back to his screen.

He pulled up the latest outbreak data and felt his chest sink upon seeing the results. "Shit…" he breathed. The number of towns reporting illness had grown, and both Ecuador and Panama had just reported their first cases. That meant the virus was not only spreading its way across five countries, but it had now entered Central America. A global pandemic was looking inevitable, and Helen and Bodhi were having to meet with drug dealers to try to combat it. He wasn't sure which threat terrified him more.

Max exhaled heavily and rubbed his face, trying to wipe away the sense of helplessness. He stared at the map before him, at the red circle showing over Panama, then his eyes drifted upward to the United States of America, where his eyes rested on Los Angeles; the city where his ex-wife and son were now living.

He took out his personal phone and made a call. He wanted to hear Nicholas's voice, to know he was OK.

"Dad?"

"Hey, Nicko," he said, trying not to sound glum. He always made a point of trying to sound strong and positive around him after what he'd been through. He never wanted his kid to lose hope again.

"What's wrong?" Nicko asked.

"Nothing," Max lied. "I was just calling to check in."

"OK…" Nicko said, though his voice didn't sound like he believed him. "Well, I'm fine."

"Your mom's there?"

"Yeah, she's here. Barely leaves my side. When are you coming to visit?"

"Not for a while," Max said. "We're in the middle of something right now."

"That the something I saw on the news? The virus hitting South America?"

Max hesitated. "Yeah."

"They're saying it's going to turn into another pandemic. Is that true?"

"It's a possibility," Max sighed.

"So, that's why you're calling," his son asked. "You're worried, aren't you?"

"I always worry about you," Max said. "You know that."

"I know," Nicko said, as the silence sat a moment. "But you know your worrying can be suffocating sometimes."

Nicko had always been average at school. He was never going to be a maths kid, but he'd always loved music. He was a hell of a drummer and that's why he moved with his band to Los Angeles, to try and score a record deal. He was on the path to success, but unfortunately, it was also where he'd discovered drugs. And everything had gone downhill from there.

Max rubbed his tired eyes again. Nicko had been seeing a counsellor and it had mostly been doing the kid good, but Max was still getting used to this whole "let your feelings out and tell it like it is" deal he now had going on. Max was trying hard to embrace it for the sake of his kid, though he had no idea what he was doing. He'd never had this kind of relationship with his own father.

"I know you care, but I'm past the worst, Dad," Nicko said. "You gotta let me breathe."

"I know," Max said, quietly. "I know… I just want you to know that I'm here, alright?"

"I know you are… But I'm twenty-three now. You need to back off a little. Alright?"

Max didn't respond. He couldn't expect Nicko to know what it was like to be a parent who had almost lost his kid. To be a parent who had watched his son from afar, slowly destroying his life and feeling helpless to stop it. To have seen his kid waste away. To get a phone call in the middle of the night saying his son had overdosed… Max had packed his bags then and moved to Los Angeles to sort him out. It was Max's toughness, his constant shadow, his refusal to let the drugs win and take his kid that had seen his son survive. Even if it had left a few scars on them both in the process.

"Just stay vigilant," Max said at last. "And wash your hands. Often. Maybe wear a mask, too. I'll send you some."

Nicko laughed. "Alright."

"I love you, kid," Max said.

"Yeah, I know," he said. "I gotta go. Talk soon."

The call ended and Max sat there staring at the screen. He studied the various red circles indicating the areas of infection across the five countries. The growing circles of doom.

"Alright," he said to himself. "Let's focus on Colombia."

He'd saved Nicko from drugs, now he had to find ways to save Helen and Bodhi from this drug dealer.

Bodhi and Helen, under Doctor Ramirez's escort, headed to an area of Leticia, popular with tourists. It was late afternoon and somehow the town seemed less welcoming or friendly. Every now and then Helen and Bodhi exchanged a look, as though checking the other was still there. After all, it wasn't every day they went to meet a drug dealer.

Eventually they came to an open public space called Parque Santander. There were some other people around, which made Bodhi feel a little better. If he was going to meet a drug dealer, he wanted plenty of witnesses. Though he sensed the mood of those present was perhaps not as buoyant as it ought to be. Whether their minds were perhaps on sick loved ones, he didn't know. Many wore masks or bandanas.

The parque was roughly square, although at its center was a large oval pond, where giant green lily pads floated atop. As they walked to its center, they passed dark statues dotted here and there, depicting villagers carrying baskets of fruit and hunting gear. He also saw rustic, worn statues of pink dolphins standing atop blue pillars, and they'd passed a faded mural showing the Amazon rainforest. At the far end of the parque, bright umbrella stands were placed here and there selling food and drink and souvenirs, and across the road stood a white church with a tall bell tower. From the front, the church almost looked like a rocket ship, triangular in shape with curved yellow edging. Bodhi hadn't seen anything like it before.

They came to a halt beside the oval pond beneath a shade structure that looked reminiscent of a fish spine which curved around the water feature. While Doctor Ramirez glanced around for his contact, Bodhi's eyes fell onto a nearby garden bed where a wooden sculpture depicted a Jaguar eating some kind of deer-like creature. He wondered just how many jaguars prowled through the nearby rainforest.

Despite the hour the humidity was thick in the air, and he wiped the sweat from his brow. The sun was beginning to set, turning the sky a bright neon pink that promised a beautiful palette as the sunset wore on.

"Here he comes," Ramirez said. "Let me do the talking."

Bodhi and Helen tensed and stood back from Ramirez, close together.

A man dressed in sweatpants, t-shirt and gold chains approached. He eyed Helen and Bodhi with an intimidating stare, made even more so by the three companions he had trailing him. If this was how the doctor's contact made Bodhi feel, he wondered just how fearsome El Patron would be. It wasn't something Bodhi wanted to find out.

The man stopped in front of the doctor and the two began to speak in Spanish. Bodhi started wishing for Pilar to be there to hear what they could not. The conversation sounded heated, despite the hushed tones, but he wasn't sure whether that was just because he didn't understand the language.

Having grown up in DC with Anglo-Indian parents, English and Hindi were the only two languages he knew.

He watched as the man stepped right up to the doctor, nose-to-nose, and whispered something fiercely to him, poking him in the chest. Panic shot through Bodhi, that this might turn violent.

"We're just trying to help," Bodhi blurted, stepping toward them with his hands out, asking for calm. The last thing he wanted was for Doctor Ramirez to get hurt. The man turned his fierce gaze to Bodhi. "We're just trying to help," he repeated, holding his hands up peacefully and speaking calmly. "We want to help your people."

The man dropped his hands to his sides and stepped toward Bodhi, subtly flicking out a knife. Bodhi automatically stepped backward, his gut clenching, but Ramirez caught the man's knife-wielding arm, stopping him. Another heated conversation started in Spanish. Bodhi felt Helen's hand on his arm, tugging him back.

The man put his knife away, shot them one last fierce scowl, then left with his followers. Ramirez exhaled heavily, took a moment, then moved back toward them, running his hand down over his mouth.

"What did he say?" Helen asked.

"They're not happy that I brought you here to meet them."

"But you told him what we're trying to do?" Helen said. "You told him we don't care about the drugs."

"Don't say that aloud!" Ramirez warned.

"I'm sorry. What else did you say?" Helen asked.

"I told him people were dying and that El Patron could help."

"And will he?" Helen asked.

"We have to wait and see."

"So, what happens now?" Bodhi asked.

"We wait," Ramirez said. "We wait and hope he cares to provide us with a sympathetic ear."

"And if not?" Bodhi asked.

"Then we pray he will not punish us for asking questions he does not wish to answer."

Before Bodhi could imagine what that punishment might look like, the sound of screeching birds suddenly filled their ears. They looked up to see swarms of them filling the sky, wings flapping, beaks chirping. Bodhi and Helen stared amazed at the scores of them, turning around to see them almost fill the sky.

Ramirez noticed their wonder.

"Every day they do this," he said. "Every day they fly across the skies on their way home to roost for the night. You can set your watch by it."

"There's so many," Helen said in awe. "And they're so loud!"

Ramirez shrugged. "This is the Amazonas. There is much wildlife in the rainforest. Most of it stays hidden but some venture out."

Bodhi turned back to him. "What about bats? Do you see many of them around here?"

Ramirez stared back at him. "Of course. This is the Amazonas," he repeated. "Now come. I will take you back to your hotel to wait."

Helen sat alone in her hotel room and stared into the screen of her tablet, at Peter Davidson's scowling face. She understood why he was upset with their actions, but he was safe back in Lyon, he wasn't here in the hot spot watching people die.

"We had no choice," she said firmly.

"Helen," Davidson said, "you're there to stop this outbreak, yes, but dealing with drug dealers is beyond your scope of work. It's too goddamn dangerous!"

"We've just asked for a meeting to talk, that's all."

"We don't have as much pull there in Colombia as you think, Helen," he said. "What you're doing is extraordinarily risky."

"What I'm doing is saving lives. That's our job, right? We face danger and death every day."

"Yes, but viruses and diseases we can understand and mostly predict. Men with guns we can't."

"Come on, you've seen the latest figures, right? The virus is now present and taking lives in five countries across both South and Central America. At this rate it's only a matter of time before it hits the US and jumps the Atlantic to Europe. The only way we can fight it is with information. Education and quarantine, yes, absolutely, but at the very core of stopping this virus is information that will help us establish protocols and find a treatment or vaccine. This village may potentially have a rare natural immunity. We need to get there and examine their blood, we need to confirm if they do. It will save us a lot of time and lives if we can create a treatment based on their natural immunity."

"Or you could wind up getting killed by drug dealers for asking too many questions."

"How is Aiko progressing with studying the virus?" she

asked. It sounded like she was changing the subject, but she wasn't.

Davidson paused. "She's working on it, everyone is, all the GHA teams and their affiliates worldwide."

"But they can't figure it out yet, can they? How the virus invades our human cells? How to block its entry?"

Davidson hesitated but relented with a nod.

"And it could take them months to figure it out, Peter. Maybe years. Maybe never. You know what that means."

"I do, Helen, I really do, but the safety and management of the Global Health Agency is of my concern. We have to report into the World Health Assembly. What am I going to tell Greta Meier about this? I'm already getting calls from the Peruvian and Brazilian governments about what we're doing to stop the spread."

"You tell Greta we're doing everything we can. And that includes talking to drug dealers."

Davidson exhaled in frustration.

"You left me in charge of the team, Peter. Let me do that. I'm not going to put anyone's life in danger. These people are like family to me. But it's my job to do everything we can to stop people from dying. Let me do that. Let me do my job."

He stared at her as his mind turned over the situation. "Have you had any luck with exhuming the boy's body for samples?"

"No. I'll try again, but right now getting access to that village is my primary goal."

He nodded.

"I'll handle the hot spot," Helen said, working to keep her voice steady. "You handle Greta Meier and the World Health Assembly."

Davidson studied her a moment, then nodded again. "Alright, but I want you to report in every hour. Without fail. Don't make me regret this decision."

"You won't. I promise."

"And we're going to talk about this when you get back," he said. "You should never have gone into the field and left the GHA unattended."

Helen eyed him carefully, wondering whether her Acting Team Director role would be passed to Max after this, but she didn't have time to dwell on it right now.

First, she had to make it back to Lyon.

CHAPTER FIFTEEN

Bodhi sat crammed with the hot spot team in the small motel room Helen shared with Ekemma and Pilar. Takeout containers were around them and the room smelled like empanadas. He felt exhaustion creeping in, but like a firefighter battling a raging inferno, he couldn't lay down the hose just yet.

"Sebastian had been dying on the boat back from Benjamin Constant," Ekemma said. "The question is, how long was he in Brazil? Did he catch it there, or did he travel there sick then return? And if he traveled there sick, then where did he catch it?"

"It would have to be here in Colombia," Justin said.

"The problem we face," Helen said, "is that we are in a Tres Fronteras region. From what we've learned so far, it sounds like he didn't enter Peru. We don't know that for sure, of course, but it is fair to assume that the spread there was caused by Sisters Apolo and Fuentez. However, being a tri-border region, he could've come across anyone with symptoms. What if he wasn't our Patient Zero? That's what scares me."

"He was the earliest death reported for the Tres Fronteras countries," Bodhi said, "where we know for sure that it started. That has to mean something. We need to exhume his body and take samples."

"He was the earliest death reported," Helen nodded, "but who knows what happened out in those villages off the beaten path? Maybe it actually started there?"

"The biggest threat here in the Amazonas must be the wildlife," Bodhi said. "You saw those birds today at Parque Santander. Somehow avian flu has mixed with bat flu and created this new strain. But with so many birds and bats around, in all three countries, it could take us forever to figure out which specific animal is responsible and how he actually caught it. And worse still, how to stop this from happening again."

"Which will be nigh on impossible give the vastness of the Amazonas," Pilar said. "These people, especially those living out in the jungle, can't avoid the wildlife. Which means this virus is now a permanent threat. Even if we beat it back now, it could raise its head again."

"That's why finding a treatment has to be our top priority," Justin said. "Until Aiko and her network can come up with a vaccine, finding a treatment is all we have."

"If we can just find out his route," Helen said with a tinge of frustration that the group shared, "it would narrow the possibilities down for us. We could follow it and see just where he might've come in contact with it. We can get our animal specialists down here testing all the creatures until we find which one was responsible. Biological samples from the original source of the virus will be incredibly useful to us."

Bodhi nodded. "Maybe. But we need to face the fact that this El Patron may not let us see the route. And if he doesn't let us near those villagers of his? If our hands are tied, then all we can do is hope that the live human samples are enough for Aiko and her network to unlock a vaccine to the Constant Strain."

"The Constant Strain?" Ekemma asked him.

Bodhi shrugged. "Well, Benjamin Constant Strain is a bit of a mouthful."

Helen smiled and Justin chuckled.

"Think about it," Bodhi said. "Our first connection with this case is the dying boy leaving Benjamin Constant and infecting the Sisters. As far as I'm concerned, right now, it's the Constant Strain."

Ekemma nodded. "The Constant Strain."

"But hopefully," Helen said, resting back against the wall beside her bed, "it will have a Colombian cure."

They sat in silence for a moment, thinking their thoughts. Bodhi saw many pathways ahead that could help them: getting access to the villagers to test for their natural immunity, getting samples from Sebastian Dias' body, and finding the source animal to study the original virus and map the mutations it made to invade the human body. The key was in the mutations. They had to find a way to block the virus entering human cells.

Pilar stood and moved to the window, glancing out again.

"The Constant Strain..." Justin said, exhaling heavily. "Doesn't that just about sum up our job perfectly? The constant strain of fighting against these viruses, the constant strain for funding, the constant strain against the politics, the constant strain of fighting for people to see sense…"

Bodhi nodded in agreement at his words. Helen studied him, tilting her head to the side in examination. He looked back at her curiously.

"So is your first trip with the GHA all that you imagined it to be?" she asked him.

Bodhi gave a laugh. "Er, yeah, boss. An incredibly deadly virus, the rough terrain of the Amazonas, the language barrier, and our Patient Zero being a drug mule for a potentially even deadlier drug dealer." He placed finger to chin. "Let me think…"

Pilar smiled. "Did you really think it would all be lab work?"

"No," Bodhi said, settling into seriousness. "And that's not what I wanted. Otherwise I'd be a virologist like Aiko."

"You went to school with Aiko, yes?" Ekemma asked curiously.

Bodhi looked at her. "Yeah. She was studying biology and I was studying medicine but we had classes that overlapped."

"So what made you switch to epidemiology in the end?" Helen asked.

Bodhi considered her question. "Honestly, I just found the human body fascinating and I wanted to learn more about it. My parents wanted me to become a regular doctor, but that didn't satisfy me for some reason. I wanted to be out there doing something. Exploring, solving puzzles. Maybe I read too many mystery novels as a kid, but I found myself enjoying the challenge of tracking down the reasons why." He stared up at the ceiling. "I wanted to know why people got sick and how they could avoid it, how we could cure it. And I studied myself, you know. I traced back the reason why I chose to do this, to a family trip I took with my parents back to India. I was about thirteen at the time. We went there for a family wedding. It took place right after a bad flood. Many people were sick and they nearly called off the wedding. I mean, most of my relatives were fine, but the poor on the streets... sickness was spreading fast through them. It just stayed with me, you know?" He shrugged. "I had a natural affinity for science and medicine and loved solving a good mystery, so the investigation element just came naturally and lead me to epidemiology." He studied Helen. "What about you, Helen?"

She smiled. "I've always likened it to my competitive streak. If I see a challenge I've always wanted to overcome it. I see these tiny viruses and bacteria and I refuse to believe that something so small can beat us. It's my objective to win."

"And do you have a good record on that score?" he asked.

She looked at him as her smile fell away. "Mostly."

Bodhi noticed the other three exchange a knowing glance among themselves, as though understanding what Helen was referring to. He looked back at Helen, saw her blue eyes staring off at nothing.

"Mostly?" he asked gently.

Helen seemed to come out of the memory and glanced at him. "I lost my daughter to leukemia last year." Bodhi felt his heart fall into his stomach. "I've helped save so many lives," Helen said softly, staring off at nothing again, "but I couldn't save hers."

"Oh..." Bodhi said, stumbling for the right words. "I'm so sorry."

"She is not lost, Helen," Ekemma said, tapping her chest. "She lives on in here. Whatever we lose, we have a choice. We can hold onto it in here," she tapped her chest again before moving her hand to her temple, "and in here. Or, if holding that loss does us no good, then we can choose to set it free."

Justin nodded in agreement. "Life is sometimes about loss and learning how to pick up the pieces afterward," he said, staring down at his bladed leg, then looked over at Helen. "You lost Angie. I lost my leg." He turned to Pilar. "What have you lost, Garcia?"

Pilar, looking out the window, glanced to Justin, then shrugged. "My last posting?"

Bodhi remembered her saying that she didn't choose to work with the GHA, that she had been sent here. He wondered what exactly had happened down on the US-Mexico border that had seen her sent away.

Justin nodded at Pilar and looked to Ekemma. "What about you, Kem?"

She stared back at him. "What have I lost?" She looked away to the curtained windows. "More than I care to mention."

Justin's face filled with sympathy before turning to Bodhi. "And you?"

Bodhi's mind turned over, wondering whether he had lost anything in his life like these people had. He couldn't complain. He'd had a good life. He hadn't lost any family members or limbs or jobs he cared about. Strangely enough, though, searching for loss in his life, Aiko came into his mind. He realized then that he'd experienced loss, too. Perhaps not on the same level as the others, but she'd been the love of his life, he'd lost her, and it had scarred him. He'd perhaps felt it in the same way Justin may have felt the loss of his leg, or Helen had felt losing Angie. He had lost a part of himself. But he couldn't tell them that. He couldn't compare a broken heart to their pain.

"Nothing, yet," he lied. "And hopefully that will extend to this trip. Touch wood."

"There's plenty of wood in the forest, if you care to venture," Ekemma said, before smiling. "But there's also birds and bats with a deadly virus there."

Justin chuckled and raised his leg. "Perhaps we can touch blade instead."

Ekemma grinned, then leaned forward and tapped his blade. Helen, chuckling, followed suit, as did Pilar trying to contain her smile.

Justin smiled over at Bodhi. "Works every time. Chicks dig the blade."

Ekemma laughed louder and hit his blade harder this time, and the rest followed suit, throwing pillows and anything else they could get their hands on while Justin ducked and weaved.

Eventually their laughing ceased, and the silence hung in the room like the humidity outside.

Bodhi was the first to break it. "I can't stand all this waiting around. Drug dealers or not, we can't sit in this hotel room while people out there are dying."

"Maybe we should talk to Doctor Ramirez again," Ekemma suggested. "See if he can help us talk to Sebastian's family about exhuming his body. If these drug dealers won't help us, we need to help ourselves to fight this."

Helen nodded. "We've already asked a lot of him, but right

now, he's our only hope." She checked her watch. "It's late now. Nothing will happen at this hour. We'll speak to him in the morning."

Bodhi nodded in agreement, casting his eyes once more to the latest casualty figures on his tablet. Five countries, two hundred and sixty-four dead.

Helen, Ekemma and Justin entered the hospital at eight the next morning, seeking out Doctor Ramirez. Pilar and Bodhi had remained behind at the hotel, where Pilar would check in with her superiors and Bodhi would undertake more research on the region, in particular on the local birds and bats.

When Helen found Doctor Ramirez he looked even more exhausted and frustrated than when they'd last seen him. There were more people lined up in the corridors and Helen saw the nurses turning some people away. This was now very much a worst-case scenario: the hospitals were full and their resources were stretched to their very limits. The sick would now start dying in their homes, where Helen knew the quarantine measures would be lax, and the virus would only accelerate in its spread.

When Ramirez saw Helen, Ekemma and Justin, his shoulders slumped. "I've not heard anything yet," he told them.

"We're not here about that," Helen said. "We have another favor to ask."

Ramirez exhaled heavily. "I'm doing everything I can for you already."

"We know you've got your hands full," she said, gently. "And we know that you've already done so much for us, but if El Patron won't help us, we need to find another route for answers. We really do need to exhume Sebastian's body and take samples to confirm our theories, and hopefully trace the virus back to its very origin."

"The boy is buried. As is his mother and sister either side of him. His family is grieving."

"We know," Ekemma said softly, stepping forward. "But if they let us do this, his death will not have been in vain. Sebastian Dias can help save many other lives."

Ramirez sighed again, placing his hands on his hips.

"They'll listen to you," Helen said.

"We can come and support you when you visit the family," Ekemma said.

"And I'll help you take the samples we need," Justin said.

Ramirez rubbed the back of his neck and sighed. There was no denying how destructive this disease was nor how fraught Ramirez's hospital was. Helen saw it in his eyes. The doctor's walls had come down and his fight had receded. This was a man who realized he couldn't fight this alone. This was a man who realized he needed help. Just like they did.

"Let me go alone," he said. "I'll have better luck on my own."

"Thank you," Helen said. "Really, thank you."

They watched Doctor Ramirez walk off down the corridor, then left the hospital.

Back at the motel, Helen sat on her bed, studying the latest notes from Aiko. The GHA network of scientists had been studying the live virus particles sent to them from several of the hot spots, including Lima and Iquitos in Peru, Benjamin Constant and Manaus in Brazil, and Leticia in Colombia.

The virus was presenting in a similar manner across the board, confirming that this was indeed the same strain traversing these three countries, and that so far, no further mutation had occurred. That was a good thing. If the virus was mutating and changing, it would be near on impossible to keep up with the changes to counteract it and stop further deaths. If the virus continued as it was, they stood a chance of defeating it. That is, if they could find a cure. Right now, Aiko was focused on isolating how the virus invaded the cells of the human body. Once she isolated and confirmed the suspect processes, she could then commence working on how to block the transmission. It was a step-by-step process.

Helen's local cellphone rang. It was the hospital.

"Hello?" she answered, as Pilar stepped closer.

"It's Doctor Ramirez," he said. "They're sending someone to take you to a meeting."

Helen paused a moment, surprised. She'd been starting to think it wasn't going to happen. Her heart kicked up a notch. "With El Pat–?"

"Don't!" Ramirez cut her off. "Don't say it."

"I'm sorry." She lowered her head into her hands. "Sorry. I'm not used to this sort of thing."

"Neither am I," he confessed.

"So we have a meeting?" Helen said, locking eyes with Pilar.

"Yes. You must not take anything with you. No phones, nothing, or they will not see you."

"OK," she said. "Will it be public again?"

"No. This one will not be, and I won't be going with you."

Helen felt a spike of fear shoot down her spine. "And we

can't take anything with us?"

"If you want to talk, this is how it must be done. So long as you do not offend him in any way, you do not have anything to worry about."

Helen nodded, placing her laptop aside and standing, her heartbeat slamming against her chest now. "Thank you, Doctor Ramirez. Thank you."

"Be careful. This meeting is just to talk. Do not push too hard."

"I won't," she said, then took a moment to catch her breath. "Did you have any luck with the Dias family?"

"I arranged to meet with them this afternoon. I'm on my way now."

"OK. Thank you."

"We'll talk again soon," he said, ending the call. Helen lowered the phone.

"You've got a meeting with El Patron?" Pilar asked.

"They're sending someone now to collect us."

"Where is it?" Pilar asked.

"I don't know."

A banging on their hotel room door sounded. Pilar quickly moved to it, while Ekemma stood ready to take any action necessary.

Pilar spoke through the door in Spanish. The response came in the form of a husky male voice.

Pilar peered through the window to check the speaker.

"What's going on?" they heard Justin's firm voice sound from the doorway of the next room.

"Shit," Pilar said and quickly opened the door.

Helen saw one of the motorbike men, staring at Justin.

He turned back to Pilar, glancing briefly at Helen, then said something in Spanish to Pilar, before moving back to his motorbike.

"Is this it?" Helen asked, joining Pilar by the door.

"He said they want the blonde gringa woman to go with them."

Helen stared at the man in the parking lot; his angry scowl, his accusing eyes that stared right at her. She nodded. "Doctor Ramirez said they would come."

"You're not going alone, Helen," Ekemma said.

Helen looked at her. "I'd prefer not to."

Pilar opened the door and approached the guy on the motorbike, where they continued to speak in Spanish. Justin and Bodhi appeared in the doorway to Helen's hotel room.

"What's happening?" Justin asked.

"We have a meeting," Helen said. "They're taking me to him."

"What, now?" Justin asked. "You can't go alone."

"I'll go with you," Bodhi said hurriedly. Helen looked at him.

"Are you sure?" she asked.

Bodhi nodded, though he looked nervous, his eyes wide with adrenaline. "We went to the parque together. Justin's right, you can't go alone."

"No, I'll go with you," Justin said firmly.

Helen shook her head. "No. Doctor Ramirez was on his way to speak to the Dias family. If he gets the OK to take samples, I need you there with him."

"Then take Pilar," Justin said.

"No offense taken," Bodhi said to Justin.

"I'm sorry, mate," Justin said, "but Pilar's been trained to kill a man. You haven't."

"I studied medicine," Bodhi said weakly. "I know a few ways to kill a man, too."

"Justin," Helen said, "we can't be seen as a threat. They know Pilar is military and they'll know from one look at you that you're ex-military. The deal will be off the moment you step out of this room." She looked at Bodhi. "Are you sure you want to do this?"

"Not really," Bodhi swallowed, "but we started this, so let's finish it."

Helen nodded and Bodhi hurried back to his room.

Pilar came back into the room.

"What did they say?" Ekemma asked her.

"They'll take you and Bodhi to him, but they'll only do it if you go blindfolded."

"Blindfolded?" Justin protested, as Ekemma shot Helen a worried look.

Pilar nodded. "If anyone follows you or tries to track you in any way…"

Helen nodded, pulling on shoes and socks. "Understood."

"You're OK with that?" Justin asked, gobsmacked. "You cannot agree to this, Helen. You can't go off blindfolded to meet a bloody drug dealer with nothing but the clothes on your back."

"Do you think I *want* to do this, Justin?" Helen snapped. "I'm doing this, because right now this is the best course of action we have. If that village has immunity we can fast-track a resolution to this virus. If we don't do this, then it's only a matter of time before we all die!" She stared at Justin as both their chests heaved with emotion. "We're just going to talk," she said more calmly. "No one is going to follow us, so there is no risk to our lives, right?"

"These are career drug dealers, Helen," Pilar said, placing her hands on her hips and broadening her shoulders. "You realize lives are expendable to them."

"Well, they're not to me, and that's why I'm doing this."

Bodhi reappeared in the doorway. "Should we take our packs?"

"No," Helen said. "No gear. This is just a meeting to talk. They don't want us taking anything."

"Nothing?" Bodhi asked, his face flushing a little paler.

"We have to go with them," Justin said to Pilar. "They can't go alone."

"We don't have a choice," Helen said.

"So let me go instead of Bodhi," Justin said. "Kem can work with Doctor Ramirez while I'm gone. I get that we can't send Pilar, but right now they don't know I'm ex-military. I'm just a medic to them. I'm no threat."

"And what are you going to do, Justin?" Ekemma asked, crossing her arms. "Protect Helen against a horde of men with guns?"

Pilar tightened her jaw and paced. "I don't like this," she said, shaking her head. "It's my job to keep you safe, Helen."

"We've been through this, round and round. We need to act," Helen said firmly. "I'm Acting Team Director and I'm pulling rank. This is our best course of action right now. It's just a meeting, and yes, we'll be blindfolded, but I actually prefer that because if I don't see their faces or where their lair is, then I'm not a threat to them."

"And what happens if he says yes?" Pilar said. "Then what? You'll head out into the jungle with these criminals?"

"If necessary, yes," she said. "These men aren't stupid, Pilar. If they know you're in the US military, they will have looked into the GHA and seen our affiliations with the WHO and a whole variety of international governments."

"Aid workers go missing all the time, Helen, if not killed," Justin said. "Just let me come."

"I appreciate your loyalty, Justin, but you're to stay here with the others. Bodhi and I will go. We're just going to talk. That's all."

"We're not going to do anything stupid," Bodhi said to Justin, wiping his palms on the side of his trousers. "Trust me. We want to come back."

Helen looked at Pilar. "We'll be back soon," she said, squeezing Pilar's arm, then moved out the door toward the motorbike. Bodhi followed, and Pilar, Justin and Ekemma's eyes trailed after them.

CHAPTER SIXTEEN

Max and Lou stared into the comms screen, listening to the update from the hot spot team in Leticia. Max felt his body tighten with stress, while Lou sat glued to the screen, her face pasted with worry.

"I hope they know what they're doing," Lou said.

"Me, too," Ekemma said on the screen.

Max sighed heavily. "I'll update Davidson now and hope he doesn't shoot the goddamn messenger."

"Maybe…" Ekemma said, "maybe just hold off until they return."

"And if they don't return?" Max asked. "Nuh-uh. I'm not withholding this from him."

"He can't interfere," Pilar leaned into shot beside Ekemma. "They sniff police or military, that puts their lives in danger."

"And if they need police or military to get them back out alive?" Max asked.

"We cross that bridge when we come to it," Pilar said.

Justin exhaled and leaned in on the other side of Ekemma. "I'm on your side, Max, but as much as I hate to say it, Pilar's right. Hopefully they'll return from this meeting with the information we need and we can all move on."

"We'll have to tell Davidson regardless," Lou said. "We can't keep this from him, but we'll caution him with your comments."

There was a pause. "Alright," Ekemma said at last.

"Keep us updated," Lou said, then ended the call. She looked up at Max, concern all over her face.

Max, a ball of tension, cursed under his breath. He leant on Lou's desk. "Show me the contingency map."

Lou's hands darted about her console as she pulled up the map of Colombia that Gabriel and Max had set up for the hot spot team. The map was made up of several layers, each featuring one element that could either be viewed separately or overlaid with the others. One layer showed all the transport routes, major roads, airports and airfields, etc. Another layer showed hospitals, police stations, scientific labs and research stations that the GHA had access to. Another showed the locations of Colombian military posts, along with foreign national assistance they could pull from. Another indicated the various hot spots with death tolls and patient numbers. And so forth. It had everything they could possibly need in terms of evacuation or sending in assistance if things came to the worst. Max sure hoped it didn't come to that.

"Did you check this?" Max asked.

"Yes," Lou nodded confidently. "You and Gabe have got all the bases covered. Everything's there."

Max reached out and clicked through the various layers, checking one last time, as though to reassure himself. But it wasn't just himself he needed to convince, it was Peter Davidson and possibly Greta Meier and the World Health Assembly.

"It's all there, Max," Lou said again confidently and calmly.

Max looked at her and nodded. "OK. I'll go update Davidson and hope this gives him a level of comfort."

He stood upright and made his way for the stairs to the upper level of the facility. He tried to instill within himself some of Lou's confidence and calmness, despite the dread that swirled in his belly and the acidic bile that threatened his throat. If there was one thing that both angered and terrified him more than killer viruses, it was killer drug dealers. He had to make sure he kept his past dealings out of this and kept his head clear. If he didn't, the people he cared about might not be so lucky this time.

Helen and Bodhi rode silently in the back of a tuk-tuk, following the motorcycle ahead. She had been told they would be wearing blindfolds but had not been given any so far. They drove down several streets, zigging here and zagging there. She wondered whether they were purposely driving around aimlessly in case they were being followed. She even entertained the thought that perhaps they were playing with them, having a laugh at their expense. Either way, her stomach clenched, her heart raced, and her body sweated, and glancing at Bodhi, his body seemed to be having the same response; the textbook reaction to stress.

Eventually they came to a wooden house painted a pale

blue. It was probably bright once but looked as though it had faded with the sun and humidity. Though she was happy to leave their transport, her stomach seemed to tighten at the thought of what would happen next.

They were pulled from the tuk-tuk and motioned to enter the house. They did so. Once inside two men waited there with the blindfolds in their hands. They were dressed casually but bore gold watches on their wrists and expensive chains around their necks. The men threw the blindfolds to the motorcycle men, now standing behind them. Spanish words were spoken and the motorcycle men placed the blindfold over their eyes, tightening it at the backs of their heads. Helen's heartbeat raced faster.

She was grabbed by the arm and ushered through a different door. She listened for sounds to confirm that Bodhi was following, as they were then forced into what Helen could only assume was the back of a car. Their heads were pushed down between their knees as though keeping them out of sight from passersby. Helen now felt her heart echoing in her throat as the vehicle started and began to move. There was silence at first – the only sounds were her and Bodhi's heavy breathing – before more Spanish words were spoken, someone patted her on the head and it was followed by laughter. They were mocking their fear.

It's a means to an end, she told herself. It's a means to an end.

Or was it sheer stupidity?

Guilt suddenly struck through her as she realized it had been days since she'd called Ethan. What if she disappeared?

She felt the urge to vomit, but breathed through it, ignoring the men's laughter. The vehicle drove around for what felt like twenty minutes or so, until it finally stopped at what Helen hoped would be their destination.

They were pulled from the car and led, still blindfolded, up some stairs to another building. They moved down a corridor or two before they were stopped. Strong hands clasped their shoulders and pushed downward until they were on their knees.

Then the blindfolds came off.

They were in a bare room surrounded by several men, all heavily armed except one who held a cellphone as though he were ready to call in an air strike. In front of them, in the center, was a man, wearing a white cotton button-up shirt, light summer trousers and a pair of sandals on his feet. His face was handsome enough, though it bore a scar down his cheek, and his dark eyes looked as though they had seen much violence.

He spoke to them in Spanish, and Helen and Bodhi exchanged a glance to see if the other understood what was said. They did not.

"H-habla usted Inglés?" Bodhi stuttered in his best minor Spanish.

The man stared at Helen's colleague, stroking the three-day growth that lined his jaw.

"Lucky for you, I do," he eventually said in English.

"Thank you for seeing us," Helen said. "We appreciate it."

The man turned his eyes to her now. She paused, curious as to why they no longer wore the blindfolds. Was it only to hide the location of their destination? Why did this man allow them to see their faces?

"What do you want?" he asked. "Why are you asking questions on matters that don't concern you?"

"We work for the Global Health Agency," she said. "We report to the World Health Assembly. We're investigating an outbreak of a terrible new strain of influenza. You've seen the spike in deaths in the area, yes?"

The man nodded. "So?"

"This virus is new and so far it has spread into five countries. It's fast and it's deadly. We're trying to find a way to stop this pandemic."

"So why do you need to talk to me?"

"You're El Patron, yes?" she asked.

Silence sat heavily as the men in the room stared fiercely at her, as though it were an insult or act of heresy to speak the name 'El Patron'.

"No," he eventually said. "But you may speak to me on El Patron's behalf. Why do you ask questions of this boy, Dias?"

"We believe him to be our Patient Zero," she said, fighting for breath against her rattling heart, "the first victim of the virus. We need to trace his movements to discover what infected him. If we find the source, it could provide us with vital information that may help us with a cure."

"A-and if we know where he went," Bodhi said, "it will help us predict the spread of infection, which areas will overflow with patients. Once we know this, we can focus our quarantine efforts there, and in any predicted future hot spots, to stop it spreading to other areas."

"To save lives," Helen added.

The man studied them both, mind ticking over. "I cannot tell you this."

"We don't care about your…" Helen stopped herself, corrected her course, "your operations. We just care about the people this boy interacted with along the way."

The man stared at her venomously.

"Did you know the boy personally?" Bodhi asked him calmly.

The man turned his face to Bodhi but gave no answer.

"Did you see him sick?" Bodhi asked. "Did he tell you or anyone about any wildlife he came across? Bats? Birds? Was he bitten by something? Did he eat contaminated food?"

"No," the man said simply. "He said nothing."

"How often does he go to Benjamin Constant?" Helen asked.

The man shifted his eyes back to her, but again did not answer.

"Does he go far into Brazil?" Bodhi asked. "Or does he just cross to Benjamin Constant?"

"These are our private affairs," the man said firmly, shutting him down. "And you have no business sticking your noses into our affairs."

"We've been trying to work out a timeline of the boy's movements," Helen said, quickly but calmly, scared the man would close the conversation, "trying to work out when he became infected, and when he was showing symptoms or contagious. We think he may have infected a lot of people on his route, including your workers. Have your workers fallen sick?"

The man stared at her, then spoke in Spanish to another of the men, who replied. And so it went back and forth for a few moments. The well-dressed man eventually looked back at them.

"Some have fallen ill, yes. Not all."

She nodded. "You need to quarantine them immediately or they will kill the rest of your workers."

The man stepped forward. "Do you threaten my people?"

"No," she said, her throat constricting in fear. "No, *we* don't, but this virus does. If your workers are sick and they don't seek help immediately, they may die and they will certainly infect others. This is a fact. But it's a fact you can help change. You remember COVID-19. All the precautions you took for that will need to be taken again."

Bodhi nodded. "Doctor Ramirez mentioned that he tends to the people who work your…" it was Bodhi's turn to recalibrate his words before speaking them, "*operations*. He said they haven't reported illness, but that the boy visits there."

The man turned to another and spat violent words in Spanish.

"No!" Bodhi said. "Please don't get angry at Doctor Ramirez. He told us no more than that. It's just that if we knew a timeline, if the boy was sick when he visited there, contagious, and yet the workers are not sick, this could mean they may hold a rare natural immunity to this virus. If they do, we can study their immunity and replicate it, and use it to fast-track short term treatment for the greater population, while we develop a vaccine." Bodhi pleaded with the man. "If it's true, your workers could save thousands of lives."

"You think we're stupid? You think we're going to fall for this story, so the American government can find out about our… *operations*?" He said the last word as he held his hands up in quotations.

"We don't work for the American government," Bodhi said. "We're not the CIA or DEA."

One of the men standing behind Bodhi grabbed a handful of hair and yanked his head back. Helen heard the sound of a knife flicking out and saw the shine of it as it pressed against his neck.

"We're just health workers!" Helen said desperately, feeling the perspiration roll down her back. "I promise you! We're just health workers!"

The well-dressed man stepped toward Bodhi and leaned right down into his face.

"*He* is American," the man said.

"I'm just an epidemiologist," Bodhi gasped as the fist tugged his head back further. "I-I swear!"

"It's true," Helen said, licking her lips and catching her breath. "We fly around the world and help stop outbreaks before they spread and become pandemics. We're disease detectives. Virus hunters. That's all."

"Virus hunters?" the man said, amused. He turned to the others, spoke in Spanish and they all broke out into laughter.

"We hunt viruses," Helen said weakly, knowing how it must sound to them. "We trace them to their origin in order to find ways to stop them."

The man's smile fell away and he turned back to stare a threat into Bodhi's eyes, before looking back to Helen again.

"Then why haven't you stopped this one yet?" he asked.

"We're trying to," Helen said calmly. "Please… do we look like we're military trained to you?"

The man looked at her. "Spies are not so obvious."

"Look, I'm telling you," she held her hands out and clasped

them together as though in prayer, "we don't care about your operations. We just want to study the blood of the villagers working for you. That's all. They could be the key to stopping this pandemic from killing millions."

"You will find other drugs to work," the man said, straightening to stand again.

"You don't understand," Helen said. "This is a new virus, a new strain not seen anywhere before. We're possibly experiencing what's called an antigenic shift, an abrupt, major change in an influenza type A virus. This happened with the bird flu and swine flu outbreaks. Even COVID. These viruses emerged with a new combination of genes that quickly spread, causing a pandemic. When an antigenic shift like this happens, the reason it's so destructive is because most people have little or no immune experience against the new virus."

"Except your workers," Bodhi said, breathing heavily and sweating profusely now, his head still pulled back by the man standing behind him, the knife still at his throat. "If the boy was infected, and they did not become ill, that means they were immune. Their immunity could be incredibly rare."

"The village is remote, yes?" Helen asked. "I assume it's cut off from the outside world? If so, this could mean they've been exposed to the virus for years, where no one else has. They've possibly built up an immunity over time, that the rest of the population doesn't have."

"They're our only hope," Bodhi said. "We need to study their blood and replicate the antibodies."

Again, the scarred man stared at them in silence as his mind turned over.

"You find cures all the time," he eventually said, his voice emotionless. "You will find this one without them."

"Vaccinations and treatments take time, years even," Helen said, a feeling of hopelessness weighing her shoulders down that he wouldn't listen to them. "Sometimes we fail to ever find one. The Nipah virus, West Nile, Marburg, Hantavirus, Lassa Fever…" Helen shook her head. "There are so many that we've not been able to cure as yet… and this could be one of them. Hundreds are already dead. Soon it will be thousands. And your people will die. And if they die, who will work your operations then?"

The man stared at her as silence filled the room.

"If we don't do something," she shook her head in despair, eyes pleading, "the virus will only accelerate and we'll see an upward epidemiological curve as the new virus infects more and more susceptible people. It will grow and spread like the branches of a tree in that rainforest of yours. Tier after tier until there is no sunshine left on the ground. It's already doing this. And we're already too late to save some people. But your villagers could help us slow the spread. They can help the sick fight the battle against this invader, this serial killer, and stop them from wiping out your friends, your family, your whole community."

The man stared at them unmoving, his face still emotionless. He casually shoved his hands in his pockets, then ordered the men behind them to do something. A blindfold suddenly slapped across Helen's eyes.

"No! No, please…" Devastation drowned her. This man would not listen to them. "Please…" she fought hard not to cry, but tears wet her eyes.

"Please!" Bodhi joined her chorus of pleas.

Her blindfold was tied tight, and she was yanked back up to her feet. "Please..." she said again weakly.

"We tried, Helen," Bodhi said, his voice heavy with sorrow, as they were led to the exit. "We tried."

They suddenly heard another voice, then. It sounded as though it came from a cellphone speaker. The voice was deep and measured, confident, and for some reason it sent a ripple of gooseflesh up Helen's arms. It was in Spanish, of course, so she couldn't understand what was being said, but the scarred leader before them seemed to have a passionate discussion with the voice for a moment, before the man on the speaker raised his voice in what Helen could tell was an order. Their guides stopped them from walking and began to pull them back into the room at the scarred leader's commands.

And they stood there, blindfolded and waiting, for what they didn't know.

Would they be killed now?

Suddenly the scarred leader was in front of Helen, his voice startling her.

"You have your wish. El Patron will let you study the villagers," he said tightly.

"He will?" she gasped, realizing the voice on the phone's speaker had been El Patron. He had listened to everything they had said. She heard Bodhi's breathing increase rapidly beside hers.

"We will take you there now," the scarred man said.

"Thank you..." Her mind raced. "But wait! We need supplies," she said, panting. "Medical supplies to take blood samples, to check for immunity, and supplies to bring blood donations back."

"You ask a lot," the man said.

She nodded then gave a saddened, blindfolded smile. "It takes a lot to save lives," she said. "That's what I'm always telling the benefactors."

The man spoke to El Patron for a moment longer, then turned back to Helen.

"You have one hour to get what you need, then we leave."

Helen burst through the hotel room door, heart thumping against her chest.

"What happened?" Pilar asked, jumping up from her bed.

"They're taking us!" she said. "We've got one hour to get what we need."

"Taking you where?" Pilar asked. "To the village?"

"They're letting you go to their lab?" Justin asked, dumfounded. "Seriously?"

Helen nodded. "I need you and Ekemma to go to the hospital and speak to Doctor Ramirez. We need supplies to take blood samples and donations. We're going to need a lot more than what we have in our field packs."

"Let's go!" Ekemma said, pulling Justin out the door.

"But, Helen—" Justin began.

"Justin!" Ekemma raised her voice. "Let's go! Now!"

He turned, not happy about it, but followed her out the door.

Pilar watched as Helen moved around grabbing her things. "We're going with you, right?" she asked carefully, staring at Helen as though she already knew the answer.

"No," Helen said, darting a nervous glance at her. "It's just me and Bodhi."

"Helen…"

"Pilar," Helen said, shoving things into her bag, then moving into the bathroom. "They're not going to let you come. I don't think they mean us any harm. If they did they would've killed us already. I think we got through to them. They're just as much at risk of dying as everyone else here."

"Did you meet this El Patron?"

"No. We dealt with one of his lieutenants. I think they had El Patron on speaker though. His voice on the phone gave the order to take us to the village."

"Helen, if you go to their lab, you'll have seen too much. They can't let you just walk away."

"They blindfolded us. And they'll do the same on our way to the village. We won't be able to tell anyone where it is."

"Did you see any of their faces?" Pilar asked.

Helen didn't answer the question. She avoided looking at Pilar but didn't need to. She could feel Pilar's steely stare piercing through her.

"They have reason to kill you," Pilar said. Her voice was low, but not soft.

"If they kill us, they die, too," Helen said. "If not from the virus, then from whatever international fallout occurs because of our disappearances."

"How far is the village?"

"I'm not sure exactly, but I was told we'd be back in three days." Helen nodded, making her way back into the main room. She pulled out her sequencer and connected it to her laptop, double-checking the software was working correctly.

"Davidson is going to utterly lose his shit at this," Pilar said, shaking her head. "I can't let you go off into the jungle to an unknown destination with a group of armed drug dealers."

"It's basic human survival instinct, Pilar, that's all. El Patron doesn't want to die. He doesn't want his men to die. If they die, who will work his labs? Right now, he needs us to find this cure, so he can stay in business."

"Yeah, well, my basic human survival instinct says that what you are about to do is incredibly dangerous. I can't let you go. Send Doctor Ramirez to do it."

"And who will tend the hospital?" Helen said, staring at her. "Bodhi and I are better equipped to run these tests. This is what we do for a living. Doctor Ramirez is better equipped to tend to the sick at the hospital. That's what he does for a living."

"If I let you go and you get killed–"

"Then it's on me," Helen said, standing. "We all knew the risks when we joined this organization."

"The risks of working with diseases, yes."

"No, with everything. We often go to places where people and situations are desperate. I've been to natural disaster areas before. There is risk in everything we do!" Helen sighed. "Pilar, I don't want to go into the jungle with these men. If there were another way, I'd do it. But right now, this is our best option and the fastest solution. The virus is moving too swiftly, and we need to as well."

Pilar exhaled heavily and began to pace, rubbing the back of her neck. Helen saw the sweat staining her shirt.

"I'm just going to take blood samples," Helen said. "If we find traces of the virus present, then we'll know they have immunity. If they do, we'll take as much blood as we can, bring it back to the hospitals and send Aiko and her network what they need, so they can work on replicating the antibodies and commencing a roll-out."

"So, three days?" Pilar said. "Three days that we leave you in the hands of some drug lord in the Colombian jungle."

"If that's what it takes."

Pilar stared bewildered at Helen, and Helen stared resolutely back.

"Our job is to make a difference, Pilar. Prediction, interception, cure. That's the GHA motto right? We didn't predict this, and we're too late to intercept this. But we *can* cure this."

Pilar sighed. Helen could tell that Pilar knew she wasn't going to change her mind. Instead, Pilar moved to her bag. She pulled out a pocket-knife and held it out to Helen.

"It's not much, but it'll buy you time," Pilar said.

Helen looked at the knife, then shook her head. "They'll check everything. I can't risk the operation. They need to trust me. They need to believe I'm not a threat, that I'm just a health worker. They need to believe that they're in charge and they hold the upper hand." She moved to Pilar and closed the military liaison's hand over the knife. "I won't do anything stupid, Pilar. I won't risk my life or Bodhi's. I promise you that."

"I don't suppose they'll give you a phone or some way we can contact you?"

Helen shook her head. "They can't risk someone tracking us. We'll go out there, run the tests and upload everything once we're back in civilization."

"So you'll be completely off the grid for a few days," Pilar said. Helen could still see the concern and resistance in her eyes.

Helen nodded, then shrugged. "We've done this before, Pilar. It's part of the job. Sometimes we're out in the middle of nowhere and we're not contactable. But we always make it back."

Bodhi knocked and quickly entered. "The hospital supplies?"

"Kem and Justin are on it," Helen told him. "Let's double-check our equipment."

Bodhi nodded, then he and Helen began to go through all the necessary field supplies in their backpacks that they would require, while Pilar watched on.

Helen and Bodhi waited outside with all their gear, as El Patron's men searched their bags carefully for any items they did not want them to take. They'd already had an in-depth discussion about taking their laptops, with Pilar needing to explain that they required them for the software needed to produce the results of the sequencing. In the end they allowed the laptops but tossed out their wireless internet thumb drives. Helen stared at the devices laying on the ground, as the immensity of what she was about to do filled her with fear. But she would not show it. There had been times in the field in the past where she'd had to deal with armed groups. She had survived those cases and she would survive this, too. She just needed to keep a level head.

Before too long, Justin and Ekemma arrived back in Doctor Ramirez's vehicle with all the supplies.

"Are you sure about this?" Ramirez asked Helen quietly.

She nodded. "How did it go with the Dias family?"

"They need some time to think about it."

Helen nodded. "We may have access to the village now, but we still need to exhume his body. Keep trying. Do your best."

Ramirez nodded.

"Helen," Justin said, taking her to the side a little, "meeting them in a public park is one thing, heading out into the Colombian jungle and going incommunicado with them is another."

"I'm not arguing with you, Justin."

"When you met with the last lot, were they carrying weapons?"

She looked at him but didn't answer.

"I'll take that as a yes," he said, his eyes more intense then she'd ever seen them; the happy-go-lucky Aussie was nowhere to be seen. "Were they automatic weapons? Semi-automatic? Do you know what they can do to a person? Have you seen it? 'Cause I have and it's not pretty!"

"Justin," Pilar said. "I've already tried. She's not budging."

"This is incredibly dangerous!" Justin hissed quietly to Helen, then looked to Bodhi. "What happens if it turns to crap out there? No one will know where you are. We won't be able to help you."

"Nothing is going to happen," Helen said firmly, making herself believe it so the others would, too. "We're just scientists trying to keep them alive. They know this. Now, I've made my decision and I'm *seriously* not arguing with you anymore."

"They know you have international connections," Doctor

Ramirez said to Justin, placating the situation. "I don't think El Patron is foolish enough to make you disappear with such attention on him."

Justin exhaled, tense, turned away and began to pace. Helen heard his blade tapping on the cement. A splash of sympathy hit her. She wasn't entirely sure what Justin had been through during his time in the forces, but whatever it was, it was clearly still very present in his psyche.

Ekemma moved to Helen and pulled her into a tight hug. "Stay safe. Call us as soon as you can and we'll come get you."

Helen nodded and gave her a grateful smile, thankful that Ekemma wouldn't give her a hard time about this. She looked back to Justin pacing and to Pilar who stood arms folded, biting her nails. She needed to put them to work, to keep their minds occupied and stop them from worrying or doing something stupid.

"What you can do while we're gone," Helen said to them firmly, "is to keep trying to get Sebastian's grandmother to allow us to exhume his body, talk to people and see if you can find out where he might have come into contact with this bat or bird. We'll do the same."

Ekemma nodded.

Helen looked to Bodhi. "You ready?"

Bodhi took a deep breath and exhaled long and slow. He nodded but said, "Not really."

Helen gave an empathetic smile. "Come on. Let's go."

"Should we check in with home base before we leave?" Bodhi asked.

Helen's face fell and she shook her head. "No. Pilar will do that for us."

"Gee, thanks," she said sarcastically, probably imagining what Max and Davidson's responses would be, as Helen and Bodhi walked away.

CHAPTER SEVENTEEN

Max watched the video link intently as Pilar updated Lou on the situation in Colombia. He stood rigid, his jaw clenched so tight he thought he was going to break his teeth. Davidson stood beside him, his hand to his chin, his face a ball of concentration as he processed the update.

"Are you *kidding me*?" Max barked. "Why didn't you talk some sense into her?"

Pilar gave a shrug of resignation. "She's doing her job, Max."

"So they've gone into the jungle with these drug dealers," Davidson asked carefully, "we have no way to make contact with them, and they won't be back for a few days?"

Pilar nodded. Davidson exhaled heavily, closed his eyes and bowed his head into his hand.

"Helen's not a fool," Pilar said. "She'll be careful."

"I wouldn't call heading into the jungle with armed drug dealers careful!" Max said. "Why didn't you try to get them to bring the villagers to you?"

"And slow production?" Pilar said.

"Justin, why didn't you go with them?" Max asked.

Justin leaned into shot. "I tried. She wouldn't let me."

"First of all," Pilar said, holding up her hand to stop them, "security is *my* remit, Max, not his. Secondly, I talked it over with her and she wasn't budging."

"Are you telling me a currently serving soldier and an ex-soldier couldn't restrain her?" Max asked.

"Trust me, it crossed my mind," Justin said.

"Perhaps you should both trust that the woman knows what she's doing," Pilar said firmly. "Helen's in charge for a reason. And she's got Bodhi with her. They'll look out for each other."

"Yeah, that's great, Pilar," Max said, "let's get the new guy killed on his first trip with GHA."

"Max," Davidson warned. Max looked back at him but decided to close his mouth.

"What's happening?" Aiko's voice sounded from behind. Lou looked around at her, peering over her red-rimmed glasses.

"Helen and Bodhi have gone into the jungle with the drug dealers," Lou explained.

A look of concern washed over Aiko's face, sending it a shade paler. "What?"

"Look, Pilar's right," Lou said calmly to them all. "We've all seen Helen diffuse seriously tense situations before. She won't take any unnecessary risks. And Bodhi seems pretty switched on. He's not the type to do anything stupid, right?" She looked to Aiko, who shook her head. "So we just gotta wait and let them do their jobs, which we all know they are good at, otherwise they wouldn't have those jobs. We've worked with them long enough now. We need to have faith, because that's our strength, right? We work together and we each do our bit. We stick together, we trust each other, and we do what we do best. Helen and Bodhi are best placed to go into that jungle. They'll find us an answer, I know they will," she said, then her face became even more serious. "Besides, we're out of other options. I just checked the latest figures. The virus has jumped to Mexico. It's now spreading in six countries, and if it continues at this rate, we'll lose the fight for the Americas within a matter of months."

Davidson stared thoughtfully at Lou.

"What?" Lou asked.

He broke into a small smile. "You should work in international relations."

She laughed. "And leave these guys? No way! This is my family, right here." She squeezed Max's arm. "We just need to stay calm and provide the support we are paid to give."

On screen, Pilar's face lightened a little. "We'll let you know when to expect the blood sample data, Aiko."

"Of course." Aiko gave a nod, and the comms screen went black. Max looked to Aiko and watched as the virologist's mind seemed to turn over something. He didn't like the concern showing on her face. If their virologist was concerned, that didn't instill him with a whole lot of hope. She locked eyes with him briefly, before turning and heading straight back to her lab.

"I'm going to need to update Greta on this," Davidson said to Max. "I think you should join me. I'll let you know when the video link is happening."

Max gave a nod, surprised, then watched as he walked away.

•••

Aiko examined the results before her, showing across four screens. Upon three she displayed the virus particles from three of the live samples sent to her; the Lima strain, the Constant strain and the new sample she'd received from Panama. On the fourth screen was a DNA comparison between the three. All three samples were virtually identical in DNA coding, confirming what they already knew, that the new sample virus was indeed spreading through all the six countries. She focused her attention on the DNA strands, because she was sure the answer to its origin lay there. And if they knew its origin, if they studied the parts it was made up of, that might just help them find a way to break it down.

One possible theory to explain the antigenic shift, that she was starting to lean toward, was that their Patient Zero, if it was Sebastian Dias, was already carrying an avian based Influenza Type A virus, when he contracted the bat-borne Influenza Type A virus. These two viruses then swapped genetic material, hybridizing to form a brand-new virus. One that now had the ability to run rampant within the human population.

If this theory was correct, then that meant Aiko and her team of scientists here and around the world were, in fact, facing two problems to resolve. First, understanding how the original bat-borne virus had managed to invade human cells in order to swap genetic material with the avian virus, when no others had done so before, and secondly, how to block the transmission of this brand new avian-bat virus. She believed, given sufficient time, that she and her network could solve these questions. But time was against them. It was incredibly unlikely that they could resolve this before thousands, maybe many more died.

But first she had to confirm her theory. There was only one way to do that and prove once and for all that Sebastian Dias was their Patient Zero and how the antigenic shift occurred. They had to exhume his body and take the samples they required. She needed Doctor Ramirez to make this happen for them.

She felt a helplessness wash over her that was foreign. She always saw viruses as a puzzle to unlock and relished the challenge. She'd always been confident in her abilities, but this virus was nothing like any influenza virus she'd seen before, and it was unfolding in ways that were all too familiar from the COVID pandemic – something they could not allow to happen again. Perhaps it was because the virus now had a human face. That of Bodhi and Helen, deep in the jungle, risking their lives to find a cure, because Aiko could not.

Max sat nervously in the boardroom beside Davidson, as he logged into a video link with WHO Director General, Greta Meier. It had just gone midnight. Davidson had asked Max along to assist with any questions Greta may ask, filling in the empty shoes that Helen had left behind when she went into the field.

When Greta appeared she looked a little tired around the eyes but otherwise her hair and modest make-up were neat, the blouse and jacket she wore stylish.

"Peter," she nodded, her German accent noticeable, yet her English refined. "And this is?"

"Max Rojas," Davidson answered. "He's the operations and deployment manager here at the GHA in Lyon."

"Max," she smiled.

"Ms Meier," he nodded back.

"Please, call me Greta," she said.

"Thank you," he said.

"I take you have an important update, Peter, given the hour?" she asked.

"Yes," Davidson said. "I know it's late, but I wanted to inform you that the team in Colombia have made contact with the drug dealer, and he's agreed to take them to study the villagers."

"When do they leave?"

Davidson exchanged a glance with Max. "They, ah, they've already left."

"Where is the village?"

"We don't know."

"But your team will make contact when they arrive?"

"No," Davidson said. "They weren't allowed to take any comms gear with them."

Greta stared at him a moment, her brown eyes searching for the truth. "Are they being held hostage?"

Again Davidson exchanged an apprehensive look with Max. "We don't believe so. It was simply part of the deal to let them go there. El Patron is obviously concerned about, er, jeopardizing his business."

"And how long do you expect them gone?" she asked.

Davidson looked to Max.

"We've been led to believe it'll take about a day to get there," Max answered, "then it'll take a day to run the tests and take the blood if the tests are positive, then it'll be another day until they return. Or so we've been told."

"So, you expect them gone for days with no contact from the outside world."

"Yes," Davidson said.

Greta stared at them, considering the situation.

"Have their families been informed?" she asked.

"Not that we're aware of," Max answered, nervously. "Things happened pretty quickly. This El Patron obviously didn't want to give them too much time to alert any authorities or put other options in play. They basically had enough time to grab what gear they needed, then they left."

Again Greta considered the situation. "The families should be told," she said. "If anything happens… the GHA will be held responsible. You know this."

Davidson and Max exchanged another uneasy look.

"Greta, I think we should wait," Davidson said. "Let's wait three days. If they don't return we inform the families then. Right now, they're simply following a line of investigation that will see them incommunicado for a few days. This isn't out of the ordinary for their line of work. If they don't return in three days, we call the families then."

Greta mulled over his suggestion, eyes examining them carefully, then nodded.

"I'll have our legal team look into this. Regardless of that, we'll need to ensure every support is provided to the families should they not return."

"Of course," Davidson said.

Max looked down at the table, not sure he agreed. Although he didn't want to alarm their families, he knew how he'd feel if this was him. Especially if someone knocked on his door telling him that his loved one had gone missing in the jungle with drug dealers, and that their company had known about this for days. He knew what it was like to get hard calls in the night. Would this be any different?

"Max?" Greta said, studying him. "You have thoughts on this?"

He looked up at her. "No, ma'am."

"Surely you must?"

Max thought things over. "It's true, our guys often go offline and we often have to work in hazardous situations."

"And how do you feel your team members will cope in this situation?"

Max inhaled deeply, buying time to find the right words. He didn't like being in the hot seat with the biggest wig of the WHO. "Helen's had plenty of experience," he admitted. "She's been doing field work for years. The new guy, Bodhi, I don't know, but Helen... She's passionate but level-headed. She's good at what she does..." He felt a resignation wash over him. "The team listens to her. They believe in her, trust her... and we have to, too."

Greta nodded and looked to Davidson. "This is a hazardous situation, Peter," she said. "For all involved."

"Yes, it is," he agreed. "But they are very capable epidemiologists and we're certain they'll get to the bottom of this and return safely."

"If they return with immune-rich blood, if they help slow this pandemic, they will be hailed heroes," she said. "If they do not return, they are still heroes to our organization."

Davidson nodded.

"But," she added, "putting their lives in danger like this, is not something I wish to become a requirement of their work, Peter."

"I couldn't agree more," he said.

"Seconded," Max said.

"We shall discuss this further at a later date," Greta said. "For now, continue to keep me updated with their progress."

"Most certainly," Davidson said.

The video link ended and Max turned to him.

"That went better than I thought it was going to."

"You haven't met Greta personally before?" Davidson asked him.

"No."

"She's a good leader," he said. "She has the right balance of business smarts and people skills. She's cool, calm and collected under pressure. She thinks things through. She has a lot of compassion, but she's not soft. She'll stand up and fight for what she believes in. She makes things happen. And she'll make things happen if we need her to."

"You admire her," Max commented.

Davidson nodded. "Yeah, I do. I've learned a lot from her over the past couple of years. She's a good ally to have on our side."

"Allies are hard to come by in this business sometimes."

"They are. That's the fun of politics, Max. So we need to keep the communication lines open with her."

"Understood," Max nodded.

Bodhi's blindfold loosened and he shook his face free of it. It fell around his neck as one of El Patron's men pulled him from the vehicle. His body ached from being crammed up for hours on end, and he was sweating hard, his shirt saturated. He wasn't sure whether that was because the humidity in the jungle was that much heavier than in Leticia, or whether it was pure anxiety. Either way, he could use a shower or at least a can of deodorant.

He searched for Helen and saw her on the other side of the vehicle. They smiled briefly at each other from across the roof of the car, glad each was OK, before the man next to Helen motioned her into the trees.

"Bano. Bano!" he said.

Bodhi looked at her confused.

"I think this is a bathroom stop," she explained to Bodhi.

"Right," he breathed with relief.

Helen looked at the line of trees close by and started moving toward them. Bodhi turned and started moving toward the ones on his side. He looked around carefully, saw the men were staying back by the car. He wasn't sure he was happy about that. He thought of the jaguar sculpture he saw in Parque Santander. He didn't know what animals this jungle hid and thought an automatic weapon might be nice to have close by. He was certainly wishing he had his snake gaiters handy, to protect his legs. He could just see a big python biting him or choking him death. Or worse still, some bat or bird nipping him and infecting him with the Constant Strain.

He stopped by the first tree he came across and did his business, grateful he didn't need to get too close to the ground like Helen did. He looked overhead and realized he could barely see the sky it was so covered with branches and leaves from the various tiers of trees.

He heard another vehicle and looked around to see a van approaching from the other way. He zipped and turned around, pulling a small bottle of hand sanitizer from his pocket and using it. As he did, he saw one of the gunmen waving him back. He moved toward them and saw the back doors of the van opening. He was motioned toward it.

"What about that car?" He pointed to the one they'd just traveled for hours in. Another man grabbed his arm and pulled him to the van and pushed him inside. With no other choice, he climbed in, then looked around for Helen.

"Helen?" he called.

"Bodhi?" she called back.

For a moment he panicked, thinking they were being separated, but another gunman was soon pushing her into the same van. He grabbed her arm and helped her aboard.

"You alright?" he asked.

She nodded. "Yeah. You?"

He nodded back and the men started transferring all their equipment into the back of the van they were in; their large field backpacks, their smaller bags of personal possessions, their large cold box to hold the blood donations if it came to it.

"Why are we transferring vehicles?" Bodhi asked.

Helen looked out the doors into the shaded sky. "In case someone's following us, maybe? They won't see through these trees, but they'll be looking for that vehicle, not this one."

They were handed bottles of water and quickly took a drink to quench their thirst, as the back door closed and locked on them. Suddenly they were in virtual darkness, the only light coming from a small window into the driver's seat.

"At least we don't have to wear the blindfolds anymore," Bodhi tried to look on the bright side of things.

"This isn't much different," Helen said in the dim light.

"No, I guess not."

The silence sat a moment as their vehicle started up, and the convoy continued onward.

"How long do you think it'll take to reach the village?" Bodhi asked.

"I don't know." Helen gave him a confident, calming smile through the gloom. "We just need to be patient."

"I have to say, this isn't how I pictured seeing the Amazon rainforest," Bodhi said.

Helen laughed and Bodhi smiled, enjoying the tension relief, however brief.

"That's the GHA for you," she said. "Never a dull moment."

Silence settled over them again, as they both sat staring at the small window into the driver's seat and awaiting their fate.

Justin's phone rang. He checked his watch: it was a little after ten pm. The number showing on his cellphone screen was that of the Leticia hospital.

"Doctor Ramirez?" Justin answered, glancing to Ekemma and Pilar who straightened at the sound of his name. "Is everything alright?" he asked, feeling his heartbeat kick up a notch.

"Yes," he answered. "The family have agreed to let us exhume Sebastian's body. We will do so first thing tomorrow."

"That's great news," Justin said, feeling a sense of relief. "We'll be there to help you. We'll need everyone in full containment suits obviously, and we'll want to keep as few people involved as possible."

"Understood. I will collect you in the morning. Seven o'clock."

"No problem. Have you, er, heard any news on Helen and Bodhi?" His body stilled waiting for the answer.

"No. I don't expect we will until they return."

"Right."

"You don't need to worry," Ramirez said. "Not now. If they don't show in three days, you worry then. But now, you must focus on Sebastian Dias and what the boy's body can tell us."

Justin nodded to himself, knowing Ramirez to be right.

"OK," he said. "I'll see you tomorrow. Thank you."

Justin hung up the phone and looked to his eager colleagues.

"What is it?" Ekemma stood and moved to him.

"Helen and Bodhi?" Pilar asked, her face a sheet of concern.

"No," Justin reassured them, holding his hands up to calm them. "The Dias family have been in contact. We're exhuming Sebastian's body tomorrow morning."

Ekemma and Pilar both exhaled with relief.

"That's good news," Ekemma said. "This will help Aiko a lot."

Justin nodded. "Yeah." He slumped back down on one of the beds and forced Helen and Bodhi out of his mind. Instead, he turned it to thoughts of exhuming their Patient Zero.

Helen sat in the back of the van opposite Bodhi, swaying gently with the movement of the vehicle. It was very dark now, only the slightest light coming through the small window of the driver's cabin; the headlights showing the way.

She checked her watch. It had been four hours since they'd switched vehicles. Every now and then they stopped for toilet breaks, or to have packaged food or water shoved at them. The stops were very short but they appreciated the chance to stretch their legs all the same.

Despite the men being heavily armed and her general nervousness, Helen sensed no immediate threat. They had not been mistreated or manhandled in any way. It would seem, so far, that El Patron was accepting their help with honor. But Helen wasn't fool enough to think their lives weren't in danger at all. One wrong step, one misguided word, could mean the tide turning against them. They had to be smart and measured in everything they said and did from this point on to ensure they made it home.

Ethan sprang into her mind again, and she silently admonished herself. They'd been in such a rush to gather all they'd needed, she hadn't called him… She hadn't thought to call her husband and say goodbye.

"What's the toughest case you've worked on?" Bodhi asked, breaking the silence. Helen could just make out the side of his face from the small amount of light that shone through from the headlights. He was studying her curiously. Perhaps he'd sensed the dip in her mood and was trying to take her mind off things. "This one?"

"Maybe," she smiled gently. "Ask me again when this is all over."

He nodded.

"Every case has its moments," she offered. "There have been times in Africa and Asia where I've been tested. It's never easy to watch people die, to not be able to help the sick. Or worse, know there is a treatment or vaccine but that funding or politics stop it from passing through to where it's needed. We just have to do everything we can. Even the smallest thing can have a huge impact and make a difference. Even if we only save one life, that's still a life saved. That's all we can hope for."

He nodded again.

"What about you?" she asked. "You haven't done a lot of international field work before, have you?"

"Outside of the States, Mexico and the Caribbean, no. I've certainly never worked from a jungle lab before."

Helen chuckled tiredly. "I worked from a mountain cabin once, in the snow. It had the most beautiful views… That was something else." Her mind drifted to memories of her standing in the snow with her tablet and turning around in a circle to show the beautiful landscape of mountains in the background, to Angie back home in London. She heard her daughter's giggles and her smile faded again.

Helen felt the vehicle begin to slow. They both tried to peer through the driver's window to see what was happening but saw only shadows passing across the headlights. The vehicle came to a stop and the driver spoke to someone outside, before they started moving again. A short time later, they stopped once more and footsteps approached the rear of the vehicle before the back doors of the van opened.

Three men with very large guns stood there, waving them out. Helen suddenly felt wide awake as a stab of panic shot through her. She and Bodhi exchanged an apprehensive look but obeyed. As they stepped down onto the dirt floor of the jungle and looked around the opened van doors, they saw a village ahead. *The* village. It was a small cluster of maybe fifteen or twenty huts, each on stilts, surrounded by dense rainforest. Obviously large enough for what El Patron needed, but small enough to stay hidden from the authorities. The volume of sound the insects and creatures within the trees made, was something else. Although in the distance, Helen made out the sound of a generator.

The men waved them forward and they moved toward the huts. In the center of the village was a fire, and several faces staring at them. Faces that held curious and suspicious eyes that appeared not to have seen many outsiders before. They all looked in good health, she noted. She stared at them, eager to start taking swabs and testing their blood, but the armed men pushed them toward a hut on the outskirts of the group. They opened a door and ushered them inside, throwing their personal bags onto the floor and shutting the door behind them.

Helen quickly opened it again and the men raised their weapons to her. She held her hands up peacefully. "The cold box," she said, pointing to the van. "We need power to charge it. We need to freeze it overnight, so we can use it for the samples tomorrow."

The men looked at each other, neither apparently speaking English. They called for someone and the scarred lieutenant appeared. She explained the situation to him, and eventually they brought the cold box to them. She confirmed it was the item they needed, then they disappeared with it again, hopefully to connect it to power like she'd asked.

Once again, the door to the hut was closed on them. Helen and Bodhi exchanged a hesitant glance in the darkness, the only light being the moon itself, pouring in through open hatched windows either side of the hut.

"Well, I guess this is where we're staying for the night," Helen said, looking around.

"Looks like it," Bodhi agreed.

There were no beds, but two hammocks strung up over the bare floor, either side of the hut.

"I've slept in worse places," Helen said. She sat down on one of the hammocks, then rummaged in her bag and began to spray herself with mosquito repellant. Bodhi followed suit in the other hammock, and plumped his bag to use as a pillow.

They lay down and closed their eyes, listening to the night sounds of the forest around them, and trying not to think of the armed men at their door.

CHAPTER EIGHTEEN

Bodhi awoke abruptly in the early morning to a loud banging and an armed man pulling open the door to their hut. For a moment he panicked, thinking something was wrong, but the man simply stepped outside again. Despite being only half-awake, it didn't take a multi-linguist to understand the man was telling them to get up.

He glanced over at Helen, his heart still thumping against his ribcage. He saw the alarm on her face slide away, too. She looked slightly more rested than he felt, but tiredness was still pasted across her face.

"Morning," she said, rubbing her eyes. "Sleep alright?"

"Not really," he said roughly, rubbing his face, too. "Colombia has the loudest insects on the face of the Earth."

Helen chuckled. "Welcome to the Amazonas."

Bodhi saw something move in the corner of his eye and turned to see a skinny spider, the size of his hand, on the window ledge beside him. He let out an unintentional squeal and threw himself out of the hammock, onto the floor.

"What is it?" Helen sprang up from her hammock. She saw Bodhi staring at the window ledge and caught sight of the spider heading outside. She bent over, hands to knees and laughed. "Like I said, welcome to the Amazonas."

"Jesus Christ…" Bodhi breathed as though trying to restart his heart.

The man banged on the door again, making them both jump. Apparently they were taking too long to get up.

They quickly made their way outside to see that mist had filled the landscape and visibility beyond a few meters was nil. It looked eerie.

A figure emerged through the mist. It was El Patron's scarred lieutenant.

"You sleep, yes?" he said as he approached them.

"Yes," Helen lied. "Thank you."

"You will eat, then do what you must," he said. "Then you will leave. You must work fast."

Bodhi exchanged a look with Helen. They were both happy with the idea of leaving as soon as possible and didn't want to stay here any longer than they had to. The guards pulled them toward the open fire area in the center of the village and handed them bowls of food. Bodhi saw it was some kind of rice dish. Helen began to eat, so he followed suit.

They ate in silence, pausing only to accept the coffee offered to them. Bodhi mostly kept his eyes down, not wanting to risk looking at one of the men with guns the wrong way, though every now and then he would glance up at the passing villagers. Most were male and between the ages of fifteen and fifty, but there were female workers and children about, too. Despite their basic living quarters, they mostly wore nice clothes, wore expensive watches and jewelry. And he realized then, that although this village and these people had probably lived here for generations, El Patron had bought them. He owned the village now. Whether it was by providing them with food, protection, or simply nice things, or whether they were prisoners, he wasn't sure. Bodhi started to wonder whether this village could even be found on any official Colombian maps. That thought made him uncomfortable. Firstly, if there was any trouble, no one would know where to find them. Secondly, he was seeing things the DEA and Colombian officials would probably kill to find out about. Bodhi thought of his parents, then, and wiped the thought from his mind. He didn't want to see any more than he had to. He just wanted to run their tests and make it back to Leticia as soon as possible.

When their bowls were empty, they were snatched away and once again they were pulled to stand and led toward the other side of the village. There, a larger wooden hut stood, on stilts like the rest, with open sides, essentially forming a raised platform with a roof and nothing more. It appeared to be a communal space where many of the villagers now sat or stood, staring at them, waiting.

Helen looked to the lieutenant who walked with them. "Our equipment? In the van. We'll need it to run the tests."

The lieutenant nodded and ordered his men to fetch it.

"Be careful!" Helen called after them, glancing to the lieutenant. "It's fragile. Expensive."

He nodded and called after the men, then pushed Helen and Bodhi up the steps to the communal hut. One young man eyed Bodhi venomously and spat onto the ground as he passed. Another muttered something in Spanish, and all he caught was the word "gringo". Bodhi exchanged an uneasy glance with Helen. Bodhi may have brown skin, but he was just as much an outsider here as Helen was.

"What do you need to do?" the lieutenant asked them.

"We need to speak to those who had direct contact with the boy," Bodhi said.

The man turned to the workers and voiced their request. Six people stepped forward.

"These people had direct contact with the boy?" Bodhi asked.

"Si."

"In what capacity did they deal with the boy?" Bodhi asked.

The lieutenant pointed to an older woman with graying hair. "She cooked for him. Cleaned up after him." He pointed to two other men. "They shared a hut with the boy." He moved onto the next two. "They exchanged packages with the boy." He gave Bodhi and Helen a hard look, then turned to the last young man and asked him a question, which the boy answered. "And this one," the lieutenant said, "played football with him."

"And they've had no flu symptoms in the past two weeks?" Bodhi asked.

The lieutenant spoke again to the six, who responded in Spanish, along with a couple of the others in the group. He looked back to Helen and Bodhi.

"Some sniffles, that's it."

Helen nodded, excited by the thought. "OK. We'll start with them. We need to take swabs and a blood sample. Not much. Just to run an initial test to see if there are traces of the antibodies in them. If there are, then we'll want to take blood donations."

Bodhi suddenly paused, looking at the gathered people, then back to the lieutenant. "They don't, er, partake in your product, do they?"

The lieutenant stared at him. "If they did, they would not be here to tell you about it," he said darkly.

"Good to know," Bodhi swallowed.

"Why are you asking this?" the man asked.

"Because if they are found to carry a rare natural immunity, we can use their blood for direct transfusions with the most critical of patients, to enable transfer of the antibody response to fight the virus. We'd prefer it if the blood wasn't laced with a narcotic."

"We could help at least one patient per person here," Helen added. "It won't save many in the short term, but it can save some, and in the long term, once we replicate their antibodies, it can save thousands, maybe more."

He nodded, then motioned them forward. "Commence."

Justin, dressed in his full containment suit, observed Doctor Ramirez and his colleagues as they set about performing the necessary procedures to obtain samples from the exhumed body of Sebastian Dias.

It had been a tough morning, seeing the remnants of Sebastian's family mourning as these strangers, dressed in full containment suits, dug up his body. It was almost as though they were killing their boy all over again. He understood their grief. Having lost him so tragically, having to bury the boy, having said goodbye and put him to rest, only to have his grave disturbed like this, it was adding insult to injury. Salt to their wounds. But at the same time, it was so very necessary.

They'd escorted the body to the hospital, where they immediately set about undertaking the autopsy. Justin, at Helen's request, had volunteered to be the one to assist Doctor Ramirez and control the chain of custody, while Ekemma and Pilar waited outside, helping the hospital staff with their overflowing number of patients. The number of deaths in Leticia alone had now hit a hundred and sixteen, and based on the latest data from Lou, a new case had been detected overnight in Miami, which led them to believe that an infected person had caught a flight there. This not only meant that an entire plane full of people had been exposed to the virus and were potentially spreading it throughout the United States and possibly beyond, but that it was now confirmed as circulating in seven countries.

Things were spiraling out of control and the team felt helpless. Ekemma, desperate to help Doctor Ramirez and the local hospital staff after the death of two nurses, had arranged for an emergency shipment of disposable containment suits, so that now all the nurses at the hospitals in the region were wearing them permanently. In response to the growing crisis, the WHO had confirmed they were sending in volunteers to the heavily affected cities, so that was something at least.

Justin stared briefly at the face of Sebastian Dias, as Doctor Ramirez and his colleagues worked, wondering how such a young boy had become a drug mule. Necessity, he figured. Lack of money, and desperation. This boy's life was a world away from Justin's childhood, growing up in a small country town in Australia. He'd loved the town as a child but had grown restless in his teenage years, wanting something more. More excitement, more adventures. He'd wanted to see the world and thought joining the army would satisfy all these needs. And for a while it did. Until he was sent to the frontlines in Afghanistan.

Justin glanced down to his bladed leg. Memories of the explosion made him flinch. Memories of excruciating pain. Of fire. Of screams. He'd lost two of his team in that explosion. He had been one of the lucky ones.

Justin focused back on Sebastian Dias' face. In a strange way he felt like he was giving the kid moral support. *Just hang in there,* he said in his mind. *We'll put you back to rest soon, mate. We just need to find out what started this. You might hold the key to ending this.*

Though he tried to keep his eyes on the boy's face, he couldn't help but look at Ramirez and the others from time to time, seeing what they were up to. There were times, however, when Justin had to look away. Even as carefully as they treated the boy, seeing them take the necessary samples from his lungs and other organs, from his nose and throat, from the dried blood in his veins, was not pleasant. Despite the faceplate or the filtered air regulator he wore, he still felt the urge to throw up.

"I think we have all our samples now," Doctor Ramirez said to the other man assisting him, who nodded and began to finish up.

Justin focused back on them and took a step closer to examine the boy.

"Can you see any marks on his skin?" Justin asked. "We need to know if he was bitten by something or whether he contracted it another way like through contaminated food or water."

The three men leaned over the boy and began examining his legs, his feet, his arms, his hands. They saw what looked like bruises and other markings as a result of decomposition, but even with a magnifying glass, they struggled to find any trace of a bite wound.

"Wait," Justin said, leaning closer and pointing to what looked like two very small dots barely an inch apart, on the side of the boy's hand. "Could that be a bite?" It was hard to tell given the discoloration in the area. Whether that was due to bruising from the bite or simply from lividity or the marbling that came with decomposition, he didn't know.

"It's hard to say," Ramirez said, narrowing his eyes in study. "Possibly?" He motioned for one of his colleagues, the man who led the autopsy, to take a closer look. He stepped forward, studying the boy's hand through his surgical loupe, a small magnifying device attached to his glasses. He spoke to Ramirez in Spanish, relaying his findings.

Ramirez looked at Justin. "He says it could be, but we'll take samples from the area and know for sure once the results come back."

"Well, that's something," Justin said. "If we can narrow this virus down to a bat bite, that gives us a starting point."

"It does," Ramirez said. "But you still need to find the offending bat, if that's the case. The Amazon is filled with them."

"And that's not going to be easy," Justin said, nodding. "We need Helen and Bodhi to confirm that immunity."

Ramirez nodded and looked back to the boy.

"Let's finish up and return him to his family," Justin said, "and pray we both get the closure we need."

Helen smiled at the elderly woman as best she could with the surgical mask she wore. She made sure the smile reached her eyes, protected as they were beneath clear plastic glasses. Carefully, she showed the woman the small syringe that she would soon poke her with. The woman stared back without reaction. Helen continued, using slow, careful movements to take the woman's arm, swab the skin with the cleaning agent, then insert the needle. The woman didn't flinch, just stared back emotionless with her lined, sunbaked face.

Helen took the sample and handed it to Bodhi who waited beside her, ready with an empty vial. The blood was transferred, then Helen bandaged the woman's puncture wound, while Bodhi labelled the sample and placed it in the cold box the lieutenant's men had brought back to them.

"Gracias," Helen said to the woman, who stood and went about her day.

Next in line was the venomous young man that had spat at them earlier. She waved him forward to the chair. He sat down, staring at them both with hate. Helen wondered where his hate came from, wondering if he was simply raised to hate outsiders, or whether outsiders had done horrible things to make him feel this way.

They heard a giggle and turned to see a group of children close by watching them. Two boys and a girl, no older than five or six years old. Bodhi smiled beneath his mask and gave a small wave. In return, one of the boys lifted a toy gun in his direction and pretended to fire. Helen saw the smile leave

Bodhi's eyes, as the other villagers laughed and cheered the boy on.

"Bodhi?" she said. "Keep your focus here."

He nodded and prepped the next vial, and Helen continued on.

Aiko moved hurriedly down the stairs toward the comms desk where Gabriel waited. Max was there, too, so he must've just arrived for his evening shift. She saw they were linking with Colombia; it was just after ten am there.

"What's happening?" she asked.

Gabriel waved to the screen, where Justin was front and center.

"We have the samples from Sebastian Dias," Justin said. "Gabe's arranged us flights and I'm heading to Bogota now with Doctor Ramirez, where they have the facilities to analyze them and send the results to you."

"That's great news!" Aiko said. "Did anything unusual stand out on the boy?"

"We found what we think was a bite mark, but due to the decomposition it was hard to be absolutely sure until we get the test results."

"What kind of bite? A bat bite?"

Justin shrugged. "We're hoping so, but we won't know until those test results come back."

Aiko nodded. "Alright. Good to know. I won't rule out that he ingested it somehow until the bite is confirmed."

"No." Justin checked his watch. "We've got to go. I'll be in touch."

"Good luck," Gabriel said, ending the comms.

Gabriel turned to Max and Aiko and smiled. "We have samples from our Patient Zero. This is good news."

"It is," Max agreed. "Now we just need to hear from Helen and Bodhi."

"Are there any updates from Miami?" Aiko asked.

Gabriel nodded. "They have tracked down most of the passengers on the plane with the sick man and have put them and anyone they've come into contact with into quarantine, but some are still out there."

"The Atlanta team is all over it," Max said.

Aiko nodded, but it still didn't make her feel good. She knew in her heart of hearts that once a virus like this hit international flights, it would be all over the globe within a matter of days. She swallowed her fear, then turned back to her lab.

Bodhi took the vial from Helen and began to label it.

"That's the last one," she said, standing and stretching.

It had taken a couple of hours, but they'd obtained samples from thirty-nine people. The scarred lieutenant told them that the village held seventy-eight people, but that the rest were currently unavailable for testing. What that meant, Bodhi didn't know, though if he were to hazard a guess, he'd suggest the rest were working in or around the lab and couldn't be spared. Still, sampling these thirty-nine would tell them what they wanted to know. And if they had immunity, then thirty-nine blood donations were better than none.

Bodhi placed the final sample in the cold box with the others, then he, too, stretched, looking up at the sky. The mist had cleared, but from what he could see of the sky, it had now grayed with clouds. Rain was on the way. He could feel it in the air.

With the samples in hand, they headed back to their hut, and requested two small tables be brought in. They rolled up their hammocks and put them aside, then placed one table against each side of the hut. They propped open each of the woven window coverings with the stick provided, letting the dappled sunlight filter through and began to set up their field lab with everything they needed from each of their large backpacks.

Bodhi pulled each item out and placed it down in position on the sanitized table. First was the portable DNA/RNA sequencer, then the laptop with cables and battery pack, then the battery operated mini-thermocycler and benchtop centrifuge, then he laid out the pipettes and sample rack, then the necessary reagents for preparing the samples. Together, he and Helen placed the heavily insulated cold box inside by the door. They knew it would keep their samples at the optimal temperature until they could attend to them. At best, the cold box would hold their specimens for up to seventy-two hours.

"I think we're ready," Helen said, looking around at their field lab.

Bodhi nodded, and they began to step into their white containment suits, a fresh pair of gloves, surgical masks and large clear plastic face shields. They then each took one of the vials and began the process to sequence the DNA using their thermocyclers and benchtop centrifuges, which would separate the serum from each blood sample.

They worked in a ball of concentrated silence, the only sounds coming from outside; the rainforest's loud insects, birds and monkeys in the near distance, along with the occasional sound of laughter or yelling in Spanish. The guards took it in turns to stand by the hut's door and watch them; some curiously, some menacingly, some completely bored.

After a while, they took turns to step outside the hut and eat lunch. Bodhi went first, escorted by one of the guards to the communal area where he was given some kind of egg and bread dish. He sat alone and ate quickly, watching as some of the children played soccer in an open area in front of the housing huts, impressed by their footwork. He couldn't help but wonder what would become of these children. And what might've become of them if they weren't being raised in El Patron's village drug lab. Then again, would this village be poor and starving if El Patron had not come to them with money in hand? Had El Patron become their savior? Or jailer?

A brightly colored bird flew overhead squawking loudly. He watched it soar and come to land in a nearby tree. It appeared to be some kind of parakeet, bright green in color with yellow highlights. It walked up and down the branch until it found the place it wanted to perch, then it sat and seemed to watch him back. He saw the bird defecate onto the ground and Bodhi's eyes stared at where it landed, tempted to grab a sample and test it for the Constant Strain.

A gust of wind tossed Bodhi's hair about and he saw the nearby trees move with it. The sky overhead was turning a deep gray now and Bodhi was sure that rain was imminent.

He hoped it wouldn't last too long. He hadn't seen the state of the roads that had brought them here, but it worried him to think their return might be delayed or cut off due to a torrential downpour.

He stood and returned his plate to the women who were serving the food, graciously accepted a cup of coffee, then turned and made his way back to the hut to continue his work, eager to leave before the rain set in.

Ekemma checked the bag of IV fluids, then looked at the patient laying in the bed before her. The woman was elderly and her lungs sounded awful. Ekemma knew that she would not be saved.

As more patients arrived with each passing hour, and more patients were turned away, it was hard not to feel helpless or grieve for these people. Lou had told her that WHO volunteers would arrive shortly, and Ekemma knew the nursing staff here would welcome the relief, but still she felt like they were treading water in the middle of a stormy sea. There was little they could do but ease the suffering of those dying.

Still, Ekemma pressed on. She knew from her training and from years of working in hot spots that no effort was wasted. If their quarantine measures saved just one life, then it was a life well-saved. If her aid helped to make someone's last hours more comfortable, then it was time well-spent. Helping the weak, helping those who could not help themselves had always been the force that had driven her. And now, more than ever, she was needed.

After working for several hours without a break, though,

her body and her mind especially were telling her to take one. She found Pilar and told her she was going to take a break in the fresh air. The military liaison nodded and joined her. The weary duo moved into the corridor and down to the series of rooms that had become their biohazard disposal and cleansing areas. They carefully stepped out of their disposable suits and took all the necessary precautions before exiting with just a surgical mask and gloves.

Once outside the hospital, Ekemma lowered her mask to inhale a deep breath of fresh air. It was late afternoon, but the humidity felt warmer than before and as she looked into the sky she saw that gray clouds had taken over the blue.

"More rain on the way," Pilar said, looking up at the skies as well.

"Feel like a walk?" Ekemma asked her.

Pilar nodded. "Where to?"

"Let's go down to the river. I need it to wash over me. Metaphorically speaking."

Pilar nodded and they began to make their way toward the Amazon. As they walked, a message sounded on Pilar's phone. She checked it.

"Justin's arrived in Bogota and the analysis has commenced."

"That's good," Ekemma said.

Pilar nodded. "I wonder how Helen and Bodhi are doing?"

"It won't do any good to dwell on their absence," Ekemma said.

"It's kinda hard not to think about it, Kem," Pilar said.

"I know." Ekemma gave a sad smile. "But I have learned it never helps to focus on the things that are outside of our control. We cannot control what Helen and Bodhi do, nor what El Patron will do. Nor even what results Sebastian Dias' body will return. All we can focus on is here and now, what difference we can make in that hospital. How we can help Doctor Ramirez after all he has done for us."

Pilar nodded, shoving her hands into her pockets as they walked. "I guess that's always been my problem, wanting to control things I can't."

Ekemma looked at her curiously. "Why did you join the military? That does not seem like a good career choice for someone who likes to be in control, when you are paid to take orders."

Pilar chuckled. "In a way it is control. Controlling safety, controlling the right to freedom... but yeah... sometimes it can feel like you're in a cage and all you want to do is bust out." She glanced at Ekemma. "So what about you? How'd you get to be so pragmatic?"

Ekemma exhaled heavily. "I was forced to grow up young, saw a lot of terrible times where my control was taken away from me." She stared out at the river as it came into view. "But I fought my way through it and I learned to survive. And part of that was learning to focus only on what I could control. Everything else was out of my hands and it would do me no good to tear myself up over it. So, I let it go." Ekemma looked back at Pilar. They'd worked together, on and off, for about nine months now, but she still knew very little about her. "You are passionate, Pilar, I see that." She smiled. "Never lose that passion. But learn how to channel it before it drives you crazy."

Pilar threw her a glance and a smirk, and they continued on

in silence for a moment, until they came to the banks of the river. They saw children playing by the water's edge, splashing each other. Close by, locals hung around boats, unpacking from the day, cleaning fish and the like.

The loud squawking began and they each looked behind them to the town and saw the skies filled with birds. They watched silently for a moment, at the daily display, amazed by the sheer numbers of them. After a moment, Ekemma looked back around to the water and her eyes fell on a man selling fruit from his boat. In his hands he held several yellow green fruits, the size of oranges, joking with some men standing around him, he started juggling them. It made Ekemma smile. She felt a craving for some sugary fruit and began looking in her bag to find change. As she looked back to the man, however, she paused at something she saw. In the back of his small canoe, amongst the piles of bananas and other fruits, she saw something move. Something black.

Ekemma grabbed Pilar's arm. Pilar turned back from the birds and looked at her.

"There!" Ekemma whispered, eyes wide as she pointed.

Pilar turned to the juggling man by the shore, who was now jogging to the back of his canoe and waving something away. A creature took flight, and as they looked carefully, they saw a bat soaring up into the air.

Ekemma looked back to the man and saw him inspecting the fruit the bat had been eating. He muttered something in Spanish, then threw the piece of the nibbled light green fruit to another man who caught it and cheered. The man turned the bitten side of the fruit away and raised the other side to his mouth.

"NO!" Ekemma sprinted for the man. "No!" She snatched the fruit before he could place it in his mouth. "No! Bad! No eat!"

The man began to yell, as did the fruit seller, but Pilar was soon there calming them. She held her hands out in apology, explaining in Spanish that the fruit might just be tainted with the Constant Strain.

CHAPTER NINETEEN

Aiko tapped away at her keyboard, logging into the software, as Lou stood by her side.

"It must be late there?" Ekemma said on her comms screen.

"It's just on midnight here," Lou said. "I'm alright, this is my shift, but Aiko here might need some coffee."

Aiko smiled. "I'm fine. I've been working a later shift to suit the hot spot. So what do you need?"

"I need you to instruct me on how to upload a sample of fruit DNA," Ekemma said, holding up a gloved hand containing the yellow green piece of fruit that had been nibbled at. "I'm hoping you're going to find bat DNA on there, too, and maybe even the Constant Strain."

"Bat DNA?" Aiko asked. "The Constant Strain?"

"That's what Bodhi named our virus, given our Patient Zero crossed paths with the nuns there."

"So why do you think this fruit is linked?" Aiko asked.

"Down at the Leticia dock, there was a man selling fruit,"

Ekemma explained. "There was a bat on his boat nibbling at the fruit. Pilar asked him if it happens often, and he said it never used to, but it has been happening a bit lately. He said he normally had a covering over the fruit but takes them off at the end of the day when he's packing up. He said if the bats get to his fruit, he can't sell it, so he gives it away. I'm going to try to get a photograph of Sebastian Dias to see if the man ever gave fruit to him. It's a long shot, I know, but if Sebastian ate some…"

"We may have just found our cause." Aiko finished her thought, nodding to herself. "This is how the Nipah virus in Bangladesh is believed to have started. The bats got to the raw deep palm sap at night, left saliva and urine on it, the villagers ate the sap and fell sick."

"But there's no known cure for Nipah yet, is there?" Lou asked.

Aiko shook her head. "No."

"So we might have found the cause, but that does not ensure us a cure," Ekemma said.

"No," Aiko said, "but it's a start. Although Justin did report finding what he thinks was a bite mark on the boy, so we can't rule that out either. Did Helen and Bodhi take all the DNA sequencers or did they leave you the spare?"

"We have the ones from our packs," Ekemma said. "I've seen it used before plenty of times, but I normally leave the testing to Helen or Justin."

"That's fine. I can walk you through it. You'll need to take a swab of the fruit where the bat has eaten from it. You'll need to mix it with an ionic solution to prepare it for sequencing. Do you have the solution and a pipette?"

"Yep," Pilar said, holding up the pipette in a gloved hand. "And a couple of vials."

"Good," Aiko said. "Do you have a surface to work on?"

"Crappy motel desk, cleaned and readied," Ekemma said.

"Good," Aiko said. "Who will be doing the honors?"

Pilar pointed to Ekemma. "This is Kem's ballpark, not mine."

"OK," Aiko nodded. "Essentially we're going to take a swab of the fruit, add it and the ionic solution to one of the vials, then we'll use the pipette to carefully extract a sample of the fluid and place it into the relevant sequencer cell. Then, we let the sequencer process it to see if it can find traces of the Constant Strain, which is now recorded in our database. If it's present on the fruit, it will return a match in our system."

"Sounds simple enough," Ekemma said.

"It is, but every step must be carefully undertaken. Let's begin."

Lou patted Aiko on the shoulder. "I'll get you some coffee."

Bodhi checked his watch. It was late afternoon, the first series of blood samples had had its serum separated, and they had now commenced the DNA sequencing with their portable devices, which would confirm whether they had been infected with the virus and if so, confirm that they had the antibodies present to fight it.

It would be a slow process, however. One by one the thirty-nine prepared samples would need to be uploaded. The sequencing could take minutes or hours, they didn't know, but they needed to proceed with care and clean the devices thoroughly between each use. And that would take time in itself. It was going to be a long night. Regardless, he felt a sense of nervous excitement, or perhaps anxiety, as they waited for the first results to come in. While they waited for the current samples to return results they stepped outside the hut for some fresh air, sitting on the steps with another mug of Colombian coffee, while their guards stood close by.

Bodhi watched a small lizard scuttle across the ground nearby, then felt another breeze and looked up at the skies. "Rain soon," he said.

Helen nodded, closing her eyes and taking in a deep breath. She held it for a moment then exhaled and opened her eyes. She glanced at Bodhi.

"Just getting a hit of oxygen," she said. "They say the Amazon rainforest is the lungs of the earth. It apparently supplies around thirty per cent of the Earth's oxygen. Did you know that?"

"No," Bodhi shook his head. "I didn't." He, too, inhaled deeply, closing his eyes and holding it in his lungs a moment before exhaling again and opening his eyes.

A few huts over, two young women giggled and whispered, looking over at them. Helen glanced at them then smiled.

"I think you might have some admirers."

Bodhi looked at her, then the women. He shook his head. "I doubt it. They don't seem to be a fan of outsiders here."

Helen shrugged. "I don't know. Think about it. Just like the Amazon around us, this is a closed ecosystem. They wouldn't get fresh faces around here too often. That's potentially why they all have the immunity. It's been passed down and around their small community for generations. But that aside, it's a natural evolutionary urge, a survival mechanism, to want to widen the gene pool."

"Yeah, I'm good all the same," Bodhi said. "I'm skipping town as soon as I can."

Helen chuckled. "Do you have a significant other? Back home?"

"Me?" he asked, surprised by the question. "No. I'm very much married to my job at present. You?"

Helen nodded. "My husband, Ethan. He's in London. He's an architect. We met on a community project, rebuilding houses destroyed in a landslide in south-east Asia. Many years ago now."

Bodhi looked at Helen's left hand and saw no ring. She noticed.

"It's not wise to wear expensive jewelry to places like these," she said. "I learned that a long time ago, so I just don't wear it anymore."

Bodhi nodded, curious to her flippant attitude, wondering whether it was an emotional survival mechanism. "How do you make that work when he's in London and you're in Lyon?"

Helen looked at him and shrugged. "A lot of weekend visits." She stood suddenly. "Come on, let's get back to it."

Bodhi watched her head back inside, noting Helen's avoidance of the topic. He thought of her daughter's passing and decided not to push any further. He sat there staring at the trees as he thought of Aiko again, wondering just how they would've made their relationship work with her being in Japan and him in Atlanta. Perhaps it wouldn't have worked. Perhaps ending it had been the right thing to do.

But still, deep in his heart, he struggled to reconcile with that.

He sighed, finished his coffee, then stood and followed Helen inside.

Helen handed her dinner plate back to one of the women and gave a slight bow.

"Gracias," she said. "It was delicious." She wasn't sure what it was exactly, but from what she could tell it was some kind of deep-fried plantain dish stuffed with cheese.

"It is," the lieutenant's voice sounded behind her.

She turned to see him returning his plate as well.

"What's the dish called?" Helen asked, making conversation.

"Aborrajado," he said.

"Aborrajado," she repeated, nodding. "Is it local to the region?"

He shook his head. "You will find this all over Colombia."

"Do you need to ship ingredients here or do you grow most of this locally?"

He stared at her but didn't answer.

"I'm sorry," she said. "I was just curious. This is my first time in Colombia. Forgive my questions."

"Coffee," he said, holding his mug out to one of the women, who filled it and handed it back to him. He took it without a thank you.

"If I can ask ... how many families live here?" Helen asked him.

"There are about five lines, but they have mixed over the years."

She nodded. "They don't have much contact with outsiders, do they?"

He looked at her curiously, a furrow in his brow as though he were annoyed with her incessant questions.

"Forgive me," she repeated. "I've just been thinking about their immunity. That's part of what I do. I ask questions to investigate the reasons why a virus has traveled the way it has, or why a village such as this potentially has the immunity it does. I trace virus contact and I trace virus causes and cures. The only way to get answers is to ask questions."

He continued to stare at her curiously, sipping his coffee.

"These five family lines," she continued, "they've mixed with each other, but no outsiders, yes? For many years?"

He gave a nod.

"The villagers," she said, "if they've been so isolated for years, what brought them to let El Patron in?" She hesitated, thought her next words through carefully, wondered whether she should speak them. "Did they have a choice? Or are they his prisoners?"

The lieutenant's face hardened.

"I'm sorry," she began.

"He saved them!" he said, stepping toward her. "There are armies in these jungles. Armies that abide by *no* laws. They were the ones looking to imprison them. Use them for slaves, steal their children, rape their women. El Patron offered them protection. He has kept them safe from these armies."

Helen nodded, swallowing her fear of the lieutenant. "And in return they… make his product."

The lieutenant sipped his coffee, staring at her but refusing once again to answer her questions. Helen sensed it was time to stop asking them.

"I, er, I should get back to the hut and see how Bodhi's

going." She looked back at the man hesitantly. "Would... that be OK?"

He waited a moment, staring her down, before nodding, clearly wanting to reiterate the power structure between them. She moved to leave, but then paused and turned back to him.

"I don't know your name," she said. "What should I call you?"

He gave her a dark look. "Sir."

Helen nodded, then turned her eyes away and made her way back to the hut.

Aiko studied the results displayed before her on the GHA software. The DNA from the fruit swab had been analyzed and the sequencing arranged before her. Three types of DNA had been identified on the swab. The first was of the fruit itself, which had been identified as a Champagne Orange, typically found in Brazil. The fruit had been in the back of a boat, so perhaps the owner had brought this to Leticia from Brazil. The second source of DNA was from the bat, which had been identified as belonging to the Phyllostomidae family, normally found further south in Brazil. The third source, although not matching anything in the GHA system, was a virus of some kind that did share similarities to the Constant Strain, but not enough to have it return a match. It left Aiko uncertain about its link to their pandemic. It could potentially be a distant relative, or it could perhaps be the original source of the virus before it underwent several mutations into the Constant Strain. Either way, she was curious to find out more. She wasn't in a position to leave any stone unturned.

Aiko checked the time. It was two am in Lyon, which

would make it eight pm in Leticia. She looked at Lou, who stood beside her.

"I need to call Ekemma."

Lou nodded. "Do what you got to."

Aiko set about contacting Ekemma. When the video link connected, Aiko saw Ekemma and Pilar gathered in front of her screen.

"Aiko, Lou," Ekemma greeted them. "What did you find?"

"I need you to catch the bat," she said.

"I'm sorry, what?" Ekemma asked. "Did you say catch the bat?"

Aiko nodded. "I've analyzed the sample you sent. There were three sets of DNA present like you hoped, the fruit and the bat, along with an unidentified virus. There were definitely characteristics of the DNA sample that align with our virus, but not enough to provide me with assurance. It may or may not be linked, but in order to eliminate it as a suspect I need a blood sample. I need a live virus to study."

"Wait," Pilar said, "you want us to capture a wild bat and take a blood sample?"

"Yes," Aiko said frankly. "And take a series of swabs for me. I need to extract a live virus from the source so I can compare it to our virus and study its behavior. If I can distinguish it as a distant relative or perhaps the origin prior to mutation, then I'll need to study what changes it has undergone to be able to invade our human cells. Once we know what changes have occurred, we can concentrate on those changes and hopefully find a way to block them. That is, if it is even related to ours. It may well not be. Regardless, Helen and Bodhi may find that those villagers don't carry a natural immunity to the virus, so we need to investigate all avenues." She shrugged. "And if we end up with both the source and the immunity, that'll only help us to stop this pandemic even faster."

"Huh," Pilar said. "Normally it's bats taking blood from us."

Ekemma chuckled. "I think maybe Aiko is talking in her sleep. She can't want us to catch a damn bat."

"Yes," Aiko said in all seriousness. "I do."

"What I don't understand is," Pilar said, "why now? Why has this strain broken out now? Surely bats have eaten the villagers' fruit before?"

"Not necessarily these particular bats, carrying this particular virus," Lou said, angling Aiko's laptop screen around. "You remember those fires that raged deep in the Amazon last year? Well, no doubt they displaced a lot of animals, pushing them into new areas. This would have a domino effect, an impact on the ecosystem at large and may have forced these bats out from deep within the heart of the rainforest to areas of human crossover."

"One catastrophic event leads to another," Ekemma nodded to herself.

"Exactly," Lou nodded.

"Catch the bat," Aiko said. "Extract a blood sample and get it to me as soon as possible."

"We'll do our best," Ekemma said, "but Lou? I don't suppose you can put us in touch with a local animal specialist, can you?"

Lou smiled as she adjusted her glasses. "Gabe's already sourced several in the area as a contingency measure. I'll contact one and see if I can get them to Leticia first thing tomorrow for you."

"Thanks, Lou."

"Now go eat and rest up," Aiko said. "You've got some bat catching to do tomorrow."

Bodhi stared at his screen. Their first sample had been sequenced and uploaded to their software, but the program was still analyzing the sequencing against the virus data on file, searching for an alignment.

"I wish they would let us upload this information to Aiko," Helen said to Bodhi. "I always like her reviewing the data."

Bodhi nodded. "She has a talent for analyzing this stuff."

Helen glanced at him, then back to her laptop. "We just need this software to tell us if traces of the virus are present in their blood, which will confirm their immunity."

Bodhi nodded in agreement, then stretched his body out. He stood and headed for the door. "I'm going to make a bathroom stop."

He stepped outside, moving quickly, eager to get back to the hut to see the results. He found a spot close to the hut, glancing over his shoulder at the guard who stood close by watching him. Lightning flashed in the distance and thunder rumbled soon after. Bodhi looked back around at the darkened rainforest, darting his eyes here and there, seeking out any creatures that he should be wary of.

A rustling overhead caught his attention and he looked up into the trees in the direction of the sound. Hanging on the branch of one of the trees was a bat, holding some kind of small fruit in its claws.

He quickly zipped and stepped away, eyeing it carefully, swearing the bat was staring back at him. The guard behind him called out something in Spanish and Bodhi looked around to see him motioning him toward the hut. Another "hurry up," Bodhi guessed. He heard a fluttering of wings and spun back to the bat, but it had disappeared. He scanned the trees again to make sure it had gone, then he turned and quickly made his way inside again.

Justin held the phone to his ear as he paced the corridor of the Bogota lab where they'd processed the samples from Sebastian Dias.

"Justin?" Gabriel's voice sounded.

"Hi Gabe. Is Aiko about?"

"She's resting. Do you need me to wake her?"

"Yeah, sorry. The samples from Sebastian Dias have been rushed through. Doctor Ramirez got some strings pulled for us. I've uploaded them to our portal. Aiko might want to take a look."

"I'll alert her now."

"Have there been any updates?" Justin asked.

"On Helen and Bodhi? No. But Ekemma and Pilar discovered a bat eating a seller's fruit at the Leticia dock. Aiko wants them to catch it and get a live sample."

"Catch the bat?"

"Oui. Don't worry. We've arranged an animal handler to assist you. I'll have him there first thing tomorrow. I take it you need flights back to Leticia?"

"Sure do. Don't want to miss the bat-catching action!"

"Just one moment…" Gabriel said, tapping away at his keyboard. "Alright. I can get you on the first flight out in the morning. Is that good?"

"That's great, Gabe. You're a star, you know that?"

"Well," Gabe's voice smiled down the phone. "That's what my husband tells me!"

Justin laughed. "Alright. Talk soon."

Helen was tired and considering resting when she finally heard an alert sound from her laptop. Both she and Bodhi moved quickly to view the screen, to see the results they'd desperately waited to see.

When Helen saw the results, emotion swelled within her.

"It matches!" Bodhi said, looking as she felt; his chest buoyed with delight and electricity buzzing through his body with excitement. "At least in part. It's isolated the bat-borne characteristics of the Constant Strain!"

Helen nodded hurriedly, unable to stop the smile spreading across her face as she studied the results before them. "Traces of the bat-borne virus are most likely present in this person's blood. But they're not sick!"

"Nor is anyone else," Bodhi said, "and we know how contagious this thing is. This indicates the presence of antibodies against the pathogen. These people carry immunity to the bat-borne type A influenza that's at the heart of all this!"

She looked at Bodhi. "They dodged a bullet of death from Sebastian Dias."

Bodhi nodded. "If they didn't have this immunity, the whole community could've been wiped out."

"Assuming they all have the antibodies, thirty-nine blood donations will help, but it's not enough," Helen said. "Yet, if these people have immunity, there's a strong chance the rest of the workers have it, too. And there could be others out there in surrounding villages that do as well. We need to start testing everyone in the area."

Bodhi nodded. "I suspect we're going to need the WHO's help. We don't have the capacity to do that."

"No. Prediction, interception, cure, that's what we focus on. The management and treatment of outbreaks falls to the WHO and their network of other medical organizations."

Bodhi nodded.

Helen exhaled tiredly. "I have a feeling El Patron isn't going to like further probing though."

"No," Bodhi said, then exhaled, too. "But maybe we can convince him. These people have the ability to save many, many lives."

"But will they if it risks their operations?"

Bodhi shrugged. "He let us come here."

Lightning cracked across the sky, startling them, and it was followed by an almighty deep booming roll of thunder that seemed to rattle the hut around them. Almost immediately the rain began to slam down heavily upon their hut. They both watched through the doorway to see it pelting down.

"We'll start the blood donations in the morning," she said, rubbing her neck, "and aim to be back to Leticia by nightfall."

Bodhi nodded, looking at the water outside, then down at the shirt he'd been wearing for two days now. He grabbed it and held it to his nose, then turned his face away.

"Speaking of showers, I could really use one."

Helen smiled. "Well, there's one right outside the door."

Bodhi looked at the rain, then smiled, too. *What the hell?* he thought and headed for the door. As he stepped outside into the warm air, he felt the power of the rain, thundering against the dirt floor. It was loud, drowning out the insects and birds now. He held his hands out and stepped beneath the torrent, instantly saturated.

"Hey!" Helen called. He turned around, squinting through the rain, and she threw him some soap. He caught it, just, then looked back at her as she stepped down into it, too, while their guards looked at them strangely.

He began to lather the soap in his hands, washing himself and his clothes at the same time. Then he handed the soap to her as she did the same.

And they both laughed at the madness of it all: standing in a drug dealer's den in the middle of the jungle and showering in an Amazonian thunderstorm.

CHAPTER TWENTY

Helen stepped outside their hut into the muddy morning. Despite the thunder and lightning, she felt like she'd had the best sleep in a long while. Knowing they had discovered a natural immunity to the pandemic currently sweeping through the Americas, gave her hope they could defeat this virus and had allowed her to relax enough to sleep. Of course, they still had a very long way to go before this pandemic was stopped, but at least now they actually stood a chance at fast-tracking a treatment to slow the devastation.

She turned to one of the guards outside.

"Lieutenant?" she said. "I need to speak to the lieutenant. Sir?"

The two guards looked at each other, then one yelled to another in the distance. The other man nodded and walked away. When the lieutenant finally came, Helen led him inside the hut and tapped their heavily insulated cold box.

"We'll need to plug this in to freeze it again," she told the lieutenant. "That will ensure the blood donations we collect today will be OK until we return to Leticia."

He nodded and ordered his men to remove the box.

"Where are you taking it?" she asked.

"To the generator."

"And where is that? We'll need access."

He stared back at her but didn't answer. She didn't like not knowing where their cold box was being stored. They had to ensure it was being handled correctly, especially now she knew it had to hold all these blood donations.

"We'll need to place the blood inside as soon as possible, so we'll need access to it for the thirty-nine blood donations."

"My men will take the blood there for you," he replied.

She exchanged an uneasy look with Bodhi but nodded at the lieutenant. What choice did they have? They were close to treating this virus, but they needed El Patron's cooperation in order to do it.

"Very well," she said.

"How long for the donations?" the lieutenant asked.

"We have thirty-nine people to do. Unless we can access your remaining villagers?"

"No," he said bluntly.

"OK, well, thirty-nine donations will take a while as it is, but if all goes well, we should be done by mid-afternoon. So we should be good to leave after that. Is that timing alright with you?"

"Eat breakfast, then get started," he said, turning and walking away.

They watched him leave, before Bodhi stepped closer to her.

"Did you notice that he completely ignored the part about us leaving?" he said quietly.

Helen looked at him. "I'm sure there's nothing to it," she said. Although the truth was, she wasn't sure if she believed it herself. "Come on. Let's get to work."

Ekemma stood on the banks of the Amazon with Pilar, Justin and the animal expert, Eduardo Munoz, waiting for a boat laden with fruit to arrive. Eduardo was young and spoke little English, but thanks to Pilar, conversation came easy enough. Munoz had arrived not long after Justin returned from Bogota, laden with equipment ready to catch a bat. He had a series of loose nets in different sizes, and an even more sophisticated piece of equipment referred to as a harp trap. It was made up of a thin metal frame with fishing line running top to bottom like a harp, and a tumble bag attached to the bottom. He explained to Pilar that the idea was to place some fruit on one side of the trap to entice the bat in, the bat would fly into the fishing wire and tumble down into the bag. Which sounded great in theory. Now they just needed to find the bat and set the trap. If all else failed, they would try to hit the bat with a tranquilizer gun and manually net it with the loose nets. Either way, now it was a waiting game.

"Catching bats, eh?" Justin said, searching the skies. "Never thought I'd find myself doing this. Wait," he said, looking at Ekemma and Pilar, "does this mean we can call ourselves vampire hunters now?"

Pilar raised her hand to his face and pushed him away. Justin laughed and Ekemma shook her head.

"I think we'd need to be chasing vampire bats to be called that," Pilar said. "We're chasing a fruit bat."

"But if that was a bite mark I saw on Sebastian's body, then it's not a fruit bat we're after," Justin said.

"Perhaps," Ekemma said, "but Sebastian could've been picking fruit when he was bitten by the bat in self-defense. Or he may have eaten some free fruit from that seller. I showed him a photo of Sebastian and the man said he'd seen him around but couldn't remember whether he'd ever given him free nibbled fruit before." She shrugged. "So until we have proof, it's a process of elimination. If we get a sample from this bat and it proves not to be our origin, then at least we have ruled out one line of investigation."

Justin nodded. "Alright. So as soon as we see one of these suckers, we pounce on it, then knock it out with the tranquilizer and take the blood sample. Piece of cake, right?"

Ekemma looked at him. "Let's hope."

Pilar pointed toward a boat on approach. "Is that fruit?"

Ekemma scanned the boat and nodded. "Yes."

Justin folded his arms. "Now we just need a bat."

"We don't want just any bat," Ekemma said. "We want the type that carries the Constant Strain."

"How many different types of bat were there in the Amazon again?" Pilar asked. "Nine hundred and fifty?"

"Yes," Ekemma said, "but the type of bat that came here yesterday is the one Aiko needs to study. If it knows it can get fruit from here, it will be back."

Pilar nodded. "Let's hope."

Hours passed and there was no sign of any bats. They'd paid for the fruit-seller's entire load and asked that he leave it in the boat, uncovered, on the banks of the river. He had agreed, and they all waited and waited, but nothing came for it.

"Maybe it's a timing issue?" Justin eventually said. "It was late afternoon, almost dusk when you saw the bat yesterday, right? Maybe that's when we stand the best chance of seeing it again."

"He's got a point," Pilar said to Ekemma.

Ekemma looked at the boat laden with fruit, then to the skies and the rainforest in the distance, then nodded. "OK," she said. "Let's leave Eduardo here on watch, while we go back to the hospital. We'll return in a few hours."

They nodded, then Pilar moved off to speak with Eduardo.

Bodhi and Helen, after breakfast, had now set up their sanitized hut to become a donation center of sorts. Before too long they'd had a line of people at their door and commenced the donations.

One by one the villagers entered, took a chair, held out their arm and gave a bag of their immune rich blood. Most of the villagers were stoic in their offering, but one or two seemed nervous or even terrified of the bigger needle required to take the blood and needed gentle coaxing, though it was difficult given the language barrier. Bodhi couldn't exactly crack jokes or say calming things, because they didn't understand a word he said. One young man even fainted, passing out cold, and Bodhi and Helen found themselves kneeling over him and bringing him back to consciousness, while many of the others laughed.

They handed over each blood bag to one of the armed

gunmen, who turned and took it away to wherever their cold box was being kept. Bodhi saw Helen eyeing them carefully. She didn't appear entirely comfortable with them taking the blood away. Bodhi wondered briefly whether these men would hold the blood for ransom or sell it to the highest bidder. Would El Patron believe that he owned this blood because he owned the village? He dismissed the thought as unworthy. He didn't know these people. He had to hope that El Patron would do the right thing.

When Bodhi finished his current patient, he stood to stretch his back out.

"I need a bathroom break," he said to Helen, peeling off his gloves and placing them in their biohazard waste container. "And some fresh air."

"No problem," she nodded.

Bodhi removed his mask and stepped outside the hut, pausing to stretch again and inhale the oxygen rich Amazonian air. It was nice to take in the green surrounds as a break from the wooden hut and bags of blood.

In the clearing in front of the hut, some of the older children were playing soccer. He watched them for a moment, smiling again at their prowess, but a hard stare from one of the guards soon moved him along. He turned and headed for the trees beside the hut.

He found a spot to urinate and stood there, looking up at the trees, searching for any bats and listening to the wall of sounds emanating from the dense scrub before him. Something fluttered in the corner of his vision, and he turned to see an enormous butterfly come to land on the trunk of a tree. It was almost the size of his hand, its wings a deep blue color, tipped black and marked with white dots. He watched, amazed by how beautiful it was.

It made him think of the countless birds flying over Parque Santander in Leticia, and the pink dolphins he glimpsed swimming in the Amazon. He thought of Helen's advice back on the boat, how he should enjoy the moments of beauty and wonder. And despite the pandemic that was spreading across the continent, despite the armed men around him, Bodhi understood in that moment what Helen meant, about soaking up the good to balance out the bad. He stared at the butterfly and smiled at the realization.

He zipped up and began the walk back to the hut, pulling a sanitizer tube from his pocket and cleaning his hands. As he tucked the tube back in his pocket, something bounced off his head. He heard the children laughing and saw the soccer ball rolling away on the ground near him. He looked back at the children, then smiled and nodded. They were enjoying taunting him, but he was glad that they at least weren't pretending to shoot him with toy guns this time. He decided to take it and play along.

"You got me," he said, holding out his hands. He walked over to where the ball landed and picked it up.

The children called for it. He raised it to throw it back, then decided against it. He put the ball back down on the ground, then kicked it to them. The children laughed and chased after it. One caught it with his feet, then maneuvered the ball along and passed it back to him. Bodhi lifted his leg, stopping it with his thigh, then used his feet to kick it back to the children. They swooped on the ball, kicking it between each other as Bodhi began to head back toward the hut. Soon enough though, one of the boys kicked it back toward him with pace. Unprepared, Bodhi reached out at the last second and tried to stop it with his hand, but it went right past him, much to the jeers of the children. He smiled at them, accepting that he would continue to be the butt of their jokes.

"Si, si," he smiled, then turned and jogged after the ball.

He was impressed with the boy's kick, as the ball had traveled a way off the beaten path and into the trees behind another hut. He waded in after it – the forest floor shrubs were waist high, sometimes shoulder high, and the dirt beneath his feet was sodden mud, pocked with the occasional puddle. He spotted the ball by the dented shrubs and moved to pick it up. As he did, voices ahead in the near distance caught his attention. He looked up, past the other hut, to a clearing, and paused at what he saw.

A long rectangular hut stood with open sides. Many of the villagers were inside, working away in surgical masks. He saw various tables laid out, saw some of the villagers working with tubs of leaves, and some with mounds of a sludgy paste. He saw drums here and there, and many watchmen, with their automatic weapons, standing around casually.

Bodhi's heart skipped a beat as he realized what he was seeing.

This was the drug lab.

He quickly looked away knowing that he had to get out of there before someone saw him.

But he was too slow.

Angry shouts exploded in Spanish, and all eyes turned toward him.

Bodhi's heart thundered against his ribcage and he held his

hands up asking for calm and pointing toward the soccer ball. Of course, nestled in the shrubs, they couldn't see it.

"I-I just came for the ball! That's all! I'm sorry. I'm sorry!"

But panic shot through him as some of the men raced toward him, weapons raised. Bodhi backed up quickly out of the shrubs, returning to the path, fighting the urge to run, terrified of being shot on the spot. Soon enough three of the armed men surrounded him, shouting in Spanish, pushing and shoving him and aiming their weapons in his face.

"I didn't know, I swear!" Bodhi pleaded, darting his eyes around at each of them. "I just came for the ball."

One of the men swung a mean punch that landed with a crack on the side of his face. The force sent Bodhi flying to the ground. He hit the mud, seeing stars. He tried to get to his feet, as the men kept yelling, then one landed a boot into his side.

Bodhi groaned, winded, as pain shot through his gut and he tried to crawl away. Someone grabbed his hair, yanking his head up, then they threw an arm around his neck and pulled him to his feet. Another blow and he tasted blood, feeling his mouth swell instantly. More blows caught him in the stomach and side, as more people seemed to be gathering. Shouts came from all around. Somehow through the din he caught the lighter tone of Helen's voice. Through the crowd around him he saw glimpses of her running toward them, and further on, the children standing there staring at him, open-mouthed.

One of the guards at their hut ran after Helen, grabbing her and pulling her back.

"Please!" Bodhi said as best he could with the arm around

his neck squeezing the air from him. "Please! It was an accident!"

A short command cut through the clamor and the punches stopped. The scarred lieutenant strode easily through the mob, a dark look upon his face. Despite the arm around his neck and the depleting oxygen in his lungs, Bodhi held his hands up in surrender.

"What is this?" the lieutenant said plainly.

"Ball," Bodhi managed. "Just… getting the ball." He motioned back to where the ball lay hidden in the shrubs.

The men around him started shouting accusations in Spanish. The lieutenant kept his cool gaze on Bodhi. One of the children, who had dared approach the group, started shouting in his higher-pitched voice. The men paused to regard him as he jabbered on. The boy turned and jogged to the shrubs, collected the ball, then kicked it back to the other children who immediately continued their game.

The lieutenant looked at the ball, then returned his full attention to Bodhi. "What did you see?"

"Nothing," Bodhi said. "I swear."

The men around him started to protest again, until the lieutenant silenced them with one small flick of his hand. He stepped closer, then leaned right up into Bodhi's face.

"No," he said. "You saw everything."

"Please," Bodhi begged, as the arm around his neck pulled tighter still. "I don't care…" his mangled voice croaked. "It was an accident… I swear."

"Bodhi!" Helen yelled, still struggling against her guard. "Let him go!"

The lieutenant looked back at her for two moments, then

muttered something in Spanish. Suddenly Bodhi was being dragged in a headlock over to her.

He squeezed his eyes closed, grasping on the man who dragged him, terrified he was being led to his death. Sweat flooded every pore of his body, his heart was ready to smash through his chest, and he gasped for air like he was drowning.

"Please…" he begged, tears wetting his eyes. "It was an accident… I just wanted the ball…"

Helen watched as Bodhi was thrown to the ground in front of her, then she was swiftly pushed down beside him. Panic shot through her. She didn't know what had happened. She'd just heard the yelling and stepped outside the hut to see Bodhi on the ground being kicked and beaten. Without a thought for her own safety she'd run to help him but had been stopped by the hut's guards.

She panted with exertion, eyes wide with the horror of the situation. One moment everything had been fine. They had discovered the villagers' rare natural immunity and had been taking the supplies they needed, and now this. She and Bodhi were on their knees in the mud, pleading for their lives.

The men were yelling and pressing the nozzles of their weapons against Bodhi's head. He was breathing heavily, his eyes on the ground, clearly terrified but trying to remain calm. The side of his face was swelling, his mouth was stained with blood, and he held his side, wincing. He squeezed his eyes closed and Helen wondered whether he was praying or whether it was just in pain.

"Please!" Helen said, holding her hands out to the guards. "Please, no!"

The guards turned their guns on her, right in her face, and she felt her stomach fall to the ground.

Bodhi looked up at them. "No! No, please, this was my fault! Leave her alone!"

One of the guards behind Bodhi stomped on his back. He groaned and fell forward. Helen threw herself atop him and wrapped her arms around him. "Stop! Stop it!"

Bodhi looked at Helen, sweat pouring down his face, mingling with the blood. "I'm sorry," he panted. "It was an accident."

"I know, I know," she reassured him. She knew whatever had happened had to be a misunderstanding. She knew Bodhi wouldn't have intentionally caused trouble.

A guard stepped forward, pushed Helen aside and dragged Bodhi up. The scarred lieutenant fixed him with an un-readable stare.

"I was just… getting the ball…" Bodhi panted anxiously, still wincing with pain. "That's all. That's all. I p-promise."

"It's just a misunderstanding," Helen said, trying to keep her voice calm, heart racing, palms sweating as she darted her eyes between the two. "We're very sorry if we've upset you… If it's OK with you, we'll just go back to the blood donations."

The lieutenant glanced at her, then unsheathed a knife from his belt. He held it up in front of her face, then moved to Bodhi and pressed it against his neck.

"I knew we should never have trusted you," he said. "American spy. You working for the DEA?"

"No!" Bodhi closed his eyes briefly, then opened them again. "I'm just an epidemiologist. A scientist. I swear to you."

The lieutenant scowled, then leaned back, sheathing his knife.

Bodhi panted. "I was just after the soccer b–"

The scarred man slapped Bodhi so hard his face snapped sideways. Helen gasped in shock, reeling back, as the man hit him again, and once more, this time with his fists. Bodhi gasped and cowered, trying to raise his arms over his head. The sound made Helen's stomach curdle and she tried to intervene but an arm around her pulled her back once more, and the cold touch of metal to the side of her head stopped her efforts.

"STOP!" she yelled, tears pricking her eyes. "PLEASE STOP!"

The lieutenant stepped back, not even out of breath. He gestured to the guard holding Bodhi, who released him and he fell to the ground. The scarred man straightened his shirt, then turned to Helen.

"Get back to work," he said shortly, then strode off.

Bodhi was lying curled over in a ball, hands over his head. He looked up, checking it was safe, then lowered his arms and pressed his forehead into the dirt as he caught his breath. Helen moved to him and helped him to sit up. His nose was bleeding, one side of his face swelling, but he was otherwise OK. Most of the blows he had taken were to his body. He looked back at Helen, panting with shock, with relief, with terror, with agony.

"I'm sorry–" he panted, his voice sounding thick and nasal.

"It's OK," she cut him off, grabbing his shoulders and pulling him into a hug. "It's OK. It's going to be OK." She eyed the guards around them carefully. "We're going to be OK."

The guards pulled them apart and to their feet, pushing them back toward their hut. Bodhi moved with pain, holding his abdomen carefully. Helen ushered him inside the hut first, then immediately moved for her med kit. Both of them stood there shaking and catching their breath, as she fumbled with an antiseptic wipe and dabbed at his facial wounds.

"It's OK. I'm fine," he said, taking the wipe off her. Helen didn't believe he was, but she had to respect his request for space.

She nodded, then took a moment to catch her breath and steady her heart before saying firmly, "Let's just finish taking this blood, so we can leave. Alright?"

He nodded, then gingerly moved to his workstation, cleaned his hands, then snapped on a fresh mask and pair of gloves, although it took him several tries to get them on his sweating, shaking hands. She placed a bottle of water down on his table, then gently squeezed his shoulder in comfort and support, before going back to her desk to finish what they'd started.

Bodhi's face was throbbing and his head and side ached, but he focused his efforts, working as quickly and as efficiently as he could. Every time his mind wandered off, thinking about what might happen to them now, he used his throbbing wounds to bring him back to the present. They couldn't leave until they finished, so he had to finish the job. The thoughts kept barging back in, though. Wondering if he'd screwed them both. Wondering if they would kill them now. Would he die here in the jungle, his body left to be picked over by the insects? Would he just be another picture flashed briefly on a news station, about a foreign health worker gone missing? He pictured his parents, their hearts breaking at the news. He pictured himself being the reason for this pandemic raging across the globe and wiping millions of lives away. All for chasing a stupid soccer ball.

"Bodhi?" Helen said gently, watching him from where she sat, prepping another patient for a donation. "Keep going."

He nodded and continued. Whenever he finished with a patient, Helen stepped over and took the bag blood from him, giving it to the guards, doing whatever she could to keep him away from them. He didn't like the situation, but he didn't argue either. He would do whatever it took to ensure there was no further trouble and they both made it home in one piece. After all, it wasn't just their lives at stake, it was countless others. He had to hope they would stop with his beating, that the beating was punishment enough and they would let them go.

When he finished his last patient, he looked to Helen.

"Shall I start packing up?" he asked her. She nodded, taking the last bag and handing it to the guards. She returned to her patient, finished with him, then she began to sterilize and pack away her gear. They worked in silence and the tension hung thickly in the air like a dense mist, the fear very present. Both their minds were clearly absorbed, wondering what would happen now.

When everything was sanitized carefully and neatly tucked away in their two backpacks, Helen turned to the guards on the door again.

"Lieutenant?" she asked them. "We're ready to leave."

One of the guards walked away, while the other watched them carefully, weapon deliberately on display.

The two of them stood there calmly, hands by their sides waiting. Bodhi was sweating, and when he looked at Helen he saw a sheen of sweat across her brow, too, that he knew was not from the humidity. They were in a potentially very dangerous mess. He looked down at the bloodstains that had splattered across his white shirt, saw the matching stains on Helen's shirt from when she'd hugged him.

He heard the lieutenant's voice in the distance, and fear shot down Bodhi's spine. The guard on the door motioned them outside. Helen looked apprehensively at Bodhi, then they both grabbed their backpacks and personal bags and did as ordered. Helen exited first, standing in such a way as though to shield him.

"We're finished here," Helen told the lieutenant firmly but calmly. "We just need our cold box with the blood, and then we can be on our way." She gave him an awkward smile, attempting friendship. "Leave you in peace."

He stared at her for a moment, before clicking a phone off his belt and making a call. Bodhi heard him say the word "Patron" and knew who the person on the other end of the line was. Bodhi's heart kicked up a notch. He tried to swallow but his throat was dry. He looked up into the sky above the clearing, suddenly wishing he was a bird that could fly away from this. Then he looked at the trees that surrounded him. Would the thick rainforest become a prison they could never escape from?

All the while the lieutenant spoke, he stared at Bodhi with murderous eyes. He heard the word "football" and knew they were discussing the incident and what to do about it. Bodhi dropped his eyes to the ground, but then decided against it, raising them again to meet the lieutenant's and hold his stare. Bodhi did his best to look apologetic, but not cowardly, to stand by his convictions, to prove that he was only after the ball and nothing more. He would not let this man see guilt or fault upon his face. It was an accident and he was not a threat to them.

There appeared to be a disagreement between the lieutenant and Patron, but the former soon gave in to his boss's commands.

He ended the call and placed his hands on his hips, glaring at Bodhi again.

"Get in the van," he said, then walked off.

Helen stepped forward. "We need the cold bo–"

"GET IN THE VAN!" he yelled, pointing toward it. His voice was so loud and fierce that both Bodhi and Helen flinched in fright.

Bodhi grabbed Helen's arm and began walking toward the black van. Two guards opened the back and they climbed aboard. Bodhi winced in pain, holding his side and wondering if any internal damage had been done. They placed their backpacks and bags down and took a seat either side against the walls, facing each other.

"We need that blood, or this has all been for nothing," Helen whispered, fear in her eyes.

Bodhi managed to swallow. "Why would they keep it?"

Helen shrugged. "To sell it? To barter with it?"

Bodhi exhaled and tilted his head back to rest on the wall. "If I had just walked straight back to the hut. If I hadn't played soccer with those kids."

"It was an accident, Bodhi."

He lifted his head off the wall. "An accident that could get us both killed."

"No one's blaming you. They let us come here," she said, her mind turning over seeking reason. "They wanted us to help their people."

"That was before I saw their lab, before I had proof of what they're doing here."

They heard footsteps and looked at the open doors. Two men appeared carrying the cold box.

"Oh, thank you!" Helen breathed, moving to help them. Bodhi did, too, but one of the men raised his gun in his face. Bodhi held his hands up and they both sat back, as the cold box was placed down. The men stepped away and the lieutenant appeared at the doors, staring at them coldly.

"Thank you, honestly," Bodhi said to the man. "I promise you we're not a threat. I can't tell anyone about anything because I don't know where we are."

The lieutenant said nothing, just gave them both that deadly glare of his, before he stepped back and the doors closed on them.

"Shit," Bodhi breathed. "I don't know if his silence is a good thing or a bad thing."

"They're letting us go," Helen said, her eyes on the doors. "It's OK, they're letting us go."

"Are they?" he asked, his elevated heartbeat only making the throbbing in his face worse.

The vehicle started, startling them both.

"We've got the blood and we're going home," Helen said. She reached out and clasped his knee. He was sure it was in reassurance, but he felt hope there, too, that what she said was true. "We're going to help save lives, Bodhi. You did good."

"Maybe tell me that once we get back to the team, huh?" Until he set foot on French soil again, he couldn't let himself believe it.

She gave a sad smile, then the two sat there in silence, rocking to the motion of the vehicle as they left the village behind.

CHAPTER TWENTY-ONE

Ekemma smiled upon seeing a bat finally come to land in the boat and begin nibbling at the fruit on offer. It was just past seven in the evening, and though they were exhausted from helping at the hospital, this made it worth the wait.

"Bingo!" Justin whispered, his eyes bright with excitement. He looked over at Eduardo and Pilar, wearing thick gloves as they each took a side of one of the loose nets. "Ready?"

Pilar translated and she and Eduardo began to sneak slowly up on the culprit, while Justin and Ekemma moved toward it from the other side with a net of their own.

A few meters out from the boat, Pilar and the animal handler paused and readied to pounce. They waited a few moments until the bat had turned its back, face deep in fruit flesh, then they lunged forward.

Sensing their movement, the bat took flight.

"Go!" Justin yelled, and he and Ekemma threw their net at the creature. They missed.

"Ahora!" Pilar yelled, and she and Eduardo released their net. They missed, too. "Dammit!"

The animal handler was fast, however, and he raised his tranquilizer pistol, taking aim. He fired a dart. It just missed. He fired a second time, his aim following the flapping bat in a smooth motion. This time the dart hit its mark.

They watched as the bat took the hit and flew on for a few wing strokes more, before it suddenly slowed, and its wings lost tautness. Then, suddenly it veered downward toward the water.

"It's going to drown!" Pilar yelled and she and Eduardo raced toward it, splashing into the water. Still airborne, the bat tried to flap its dopey wings to keep itself aloft but it eventually came down to the water with a splash.

Ekemma's chest tightened as she watched, but relief came when she saw the animal trying to flap its wings and keep itself afloat on the surface. Pilar plowed through the water, arriving at the animal quickly and scooping it up in her gloved hands. The animal tried to struggle, but the tranquilizer had taken effect, numbing its fight. She raised the animal out of the water above her head like a trophy.

Justin clapped in applause, "Nice save!" and Ekemma smiled.

Pilar grinned back, then turned and swam back to the shore, holding the bat above the water line.

"Sergeant Pilar Garcia, Vampire Hunter!" Justin announced in a booming voice. Ekemma laughed.

Pilar reached the bank with a sly smile on her face and handed the animal to Eduardo who nodded graciously with a look of amusement on his face. He moved away with the animal to dry it off, as Pilar squeezed the water from her clothes and looked at her GHA team members.

"Let's get this blood sample, shall we?"

Aiko sat with Lou by her side, staring into the comms screen with bated breath.

"You have good news for us, right?" Lou asked.

Ekemma nodded. "We have processed a sample into the sequencer. It should be uploaded into the GHA software now."

"Good," Aiko said, tapping away at her console. "Has it matched the Constant Strain?"

"No," Justin said, holding up his laptop screen, showing the DNA comparison between the virus and sample taken from the bat. "But it has matched something else on file."

Aiko scanned the screen with alertness, but when she saw the results, her shoulders slumped a little. "It's matched the virus found on the fruit from yesterday. It's not our strain, but there is a chance that it may be a relative or the original virus prior to undergoing several mutations. Either way, we need to study it more closely. We might still be able to use this to try and figure out the Constant Strain. You need to get that live blood sample to me as soon as possible. Right now, it's the only option we have."

Ekemma nodded. "What are our chances of getting a courier at this hour, Lou?"

"No." Aiko shook her head. "This sample is too important to leave with a courier. It's the closest live animal sample we have to the Constant Strain. One of you will need to personally control the chain of custody and bring it to me."

Ekemma looked at Justin and Pilar, then turned back to the screen.

"I'll do it," Ekemma said. "There's no more value I can provide to the hospitals now the WHO volunteers have arrived. And there is little I can do to help Helen and Bodhi, but these two may be needed here, so they should stay. I'll go. I'll take it."

Justin and Pilar nodded in silent agreement.

"Let me check what Gabe's contingency plan has for you," Lou said, tapping away at her keyboard and studying the screens before her. "Alright, if you hurry, I can get you on the last flight out of Tabatinga, Brazil. Just cross over the open border, get your stamp and by the time you arrive at the airport, your tickets will be waiting."

"Will do," Ekemma said.

"Aiko," Justin said. "Did anything come of the samples from Sebastian Dias?"

"I've been undertaking further study with my lab techs here and across the GHA network, and as I suspected, it has been confirmed that three viruses were present in his system. A strain of human-avian virus, a strain of bat virus, and the Constant Strain. I believe the Constant Strain is the result of gene swapping and mutation between the other two."

"So, he already had a human flu," Justin said, "then somehow got the bat flu, they met up in his cells, mutated, and the new virus is what's spreading like wildfire."

"Yes," she said, nodding. "The chances of this interaction happening, of a host having two viruses at the same time and creating a third, was not something that could be predicted. But this is why the virus has swept through everyone so fast and we were not prepared for it. And theoretically we have two virus mysteries to now solve: firstly, how the original bat virus infected Sebastian, and secondly, the new virus that is now spreading across the globe."

"Still, that's great news, right?" Pilar said. "If we know how this all started."

"Yes and no." Aiko hesitated. "Although the test results from Bogota have confirmed the boy was indeed bitten by a bat, we have not yet confirmed that this was how he caught the virus. We still need to rule out whether he ingested tainted fruit or whether the bite was what kick-started the infection. We also need to try to recreate the virus in live cells in order to study it and find a way to block transmission. Ideally, live cells will quicken this process for us. That's why I need that bat blood and the swabs you've taken. It may not be our culprit, but it's the closest thing we have so far and it may still provide us with useful information."

"Understood," Ekemma said. "I'll start packing."

"We'll escort you there," Pilar said.

Bodhi stood among the trees in the darkness, the insects of the Amazon performing a symphony of sounds around him, though he didn't find it relaxing. They'd been driving for hours and were having a toilet break. It was good to stretch his legs, though his body ached from his earlier beating. He'd raided some painkillers from their med kits, but he could do with a really long hot shower, or an ice pack or two. Through the darkness he could see the bloodstains on his white shirt. Earlier scenes flashed through his mind of the scarred lieutenant beating him. Fear still pooled in his stomach. He'd never been physically attacked before.

So far it appeared as though they were taking them back to Leticia, but he didn't want to get his hopes up. As far as he was concerned, they weren't safe until they were back with the team.

He zipped up his pants and turned to head back to the van but stopped abruptly when he saw one of the guards aiming his weapon at him.

Bodhi's heart leapt into this throat.

This was it.

They were going to kill him. Right here in the forest where no one would ever find him.

"No!" he said, holding his hands out as though they would protect him from a volley of bullets. "No! Please!" He stepped backward as the guard yelled at him in angry Spanish and took aim. "No!"

He heard a fluttering noise behind him, felt something touch his head as the guard took aimed and fired.

Bodhi yelled in terror, curling his arms up over his head and dropping to his knees

The gunshot was loud and it sounded as though a thousand creatures within the dark jungle around them startled. Two sounds stood out above the rest, though. One was Helen yelling his name, the other was a screeching sound. Bodhi looked up, realized he hadn't been shot. He heard the fluttering sound again, along with the screeching and a soft thud as something hit the ground beside him. He turned around to see a bat, crawling wounded along the ground. It had been shot.

"Bodhi!" Helen came running toward him, along with her guard. "Bodhi?"

Bodhi stared at the guard in shock, feeling as though he was about to have a heart attack from the stress. The man hadn't been going to shoot him, he'd been aiming for the bat.

The bat screeched in pain again. One wing had been shattered by the bullet.

Helen reached him. "Are you alright? What the hell happened?"

"I-I don't know…"

"El vampiro," the guard said, moving toward them. "Bat." He pointed. "Vampiro."

"V-vampiro?" Bodhi said, just catching his breath again. "Vampire? Vampire bat?" he added, looking back at the creature.

Helen pointed to Bodhi's bloodstained shirt. "It must've smelled that."

He looked down at the blood, then back to the creature. "Shit. It was going to eat me?"

"Drink, blood," one of the guards explained, mimicking teeth and sucking upon his hand.

Helen's body paused and she flicked her face back to Bodhi's. "Sebastian Dias traveled along here. Probably stopped right here for a toilet break."

Bodhi stared back at her and nodded, a cold feeling washing over him, dousing the fear and turning it into excitement. "He must've been bitten."

The guard moved to the bat and raised his weapon to end it.

"NO!" Helen yelled, pushing the man's weapon down. Shouting ensued from the man and his colleagues moved over. "We need its blood!" Helen begged him. "We need its live blood!"

"I'll get the gloves!" Bodhi said, running back to the van. As he did, one of the other guards raised his weapon at Bodhi.

"No, please." He held his hands up, motioning to the van. "Gloves." He mimed pulling them onto his hands. "We just need gloves. For the bat. El vampiro. El vampiro!"

The guard lowered his weapon a little, face confused, but he followed and watched Bodhi carefully as he climbed into the van and began rummaging through one of their packs for a pair of thick gloves. He found them, placed them on and ran back, still wincing from his earlier injuries, to where the others stood around the wounded creature, which continued to screech in pain. Bodhi carefully moved in and caught the creature, cupping it in his gloved hands. It tried to struggle, claw and bite him, but Bodhi held his thick padded hands firm.

They moved back to the van, where Helen donned a pair of surgical gloves and prepped a syringe to collect a blood sample from the creature. They did so with relative ease, then Bodhi released the bat back onto the ground.

"It's going to die," Helen said, eyeing it. "It won't survive that wound. Put it out of its misery."

Bodhi nodded and motioned for the gunman to end it. The man did so without a second thought, and Bodhi shuddered.

More words were shouted in Spanish and Bodhi and Helen were being shoved into the van again and the doors closed.

"So what do we do now?" Bodhi asked, his sweat-stained, swollen face looking at the syringe of blood that Helen held.

She shrugged. "Well, I've never undertaken sequencing

from the back of a moving van before, but I guess there's a first time for everything."

Bodhi nodded, and as the van began to move along once more, he started pulling out the items she would need and set about establishing a field lab on wheels.

They both worked in a ball of patient concentration as the blood sample was prepared. When finally the battery-operated centrifuge had finished separating the serum from the blood, they set about prepping the sample in a pipette with the necessary reagent. Bodhi angled the laptop to maximize the light, as Helen carefully input the sample into the DNA sequencer with the pipette. She closed the lid of the device and double-checked the software had initiated.

She looked at Bodhi. "Now we wait."

Bodhi nodded and checked his watch. It read nine-thirty, but that didn't seem right. His mind turned over as his swollen and bruised face still gently throbbed. Then he paused, as a realization hit him.

"What's wrong?" Helen asked, studying his face.

"It's nine-thirty," he said. "We should've swapped vehicles by now."

Helen stared at him in the laptop light. "Maybe we're taking the van all the way in." She looked at the cold box. "Maybe it's just easier with this box full of blood?"

"They switched cars for a reason."

"Yes, in case someone followed us from Leticia. They won't be looking for this vehicle."

He stared back at her. "I don't like it. Something isn't right. I think we're taking a different route."

The worry began to set in again. Bodhi wasn't sure how

much more he could take. He was exhausted, his body ached, and he was still recovering from thinking he was going to die twice already today. Now this. Why were they taking a different route? Was it even a different route or were they taking them somewhere different altogether? Somewhere they would never be seen again.

"If we go missing there are going to be a lot of questions asked," Helen said, obviously reading the worry on his face. "They can't risk heat like that on El Patron."

Bodhi nodded, but his body felt tense. "I hope you're right."

"Come on," she said. "Help me clean and pack up this stuff."

Bodhi knew she was trying to distract his thoughts, but he nodded and they got to work.

Helen heard the alert and looked at the screen before her. The results had come back, much faster than they'd anticipated. Bodhi moved quickly and painfully to sit beside her and they both stared, stunned.

"Holy shit…" Bodhi breathed, staring at the DNA results on the screen. "This is it… This has to be it, right?" He looked at Helen in the laptop light.

She nodded, her mind turning over the information before her. "The bat carries a type A virus that matches seventy-two per cent to the Constant Strain. The unmatched characteristics from the Constant Strain might well be the avian flu characteristics that Aiko identified, and the likely mutations that took place for it to become our pandemic virus. But… yeah." She felt a sting of tears in her eyes. "I think this might be our source."

She looked at Bodhi, his swollen and bruised face

accentuated by the dim laptop light and the surrounding shadows. He nodded, his own eyes shining with exhausted emotion.

"We have the original source of the bat-borne virus and we have immune rich blood." He stared at Helen. "We can help stop it. We can help stop this."

Helen nodded back, unable to stop the tear that ran down her cheek. She laughed and wiped it away, and he laughed, too, pressing his own eyes to clear the moisture.

"We did it, we only bloody did it," Helen said, closing her eyes a moment. "Oh God, we just need Wi-Fi to contact Lyon and let them know."

She checked the time on the laptop screen. It was almost ten-thirty. Her face fell with concern.

"What is it?" Bodhi asked.

"We definitely should've switched cars by now," she said. "We're definitely on another route." She glanced around the van's cabin, then held still focusing on her senses. "On the way to the village there was an incline, so we should be on a decline now. We're not. We're on another incline."

Bodhi stared at her. "They're not taking us back to Leticia."

"Maybe they're dropping us off somewhere else. Somewhere we won't be expected. Somewhere eyes won't be on them. Maybe we'll need to find our own way back?"

Bodhi said nothing. She saw the doubt on his face.

"Wherever they leave us," she said, reassuring him and maybe herself, too, "Gabe and Max will get us out of there in no time. If I know Gabe, he'll have our exit route already planned out."

"We need to get back to the team," he said quietly. "They

need what we have. They won't stop this pandemic without it."

Helen nodded. "We'll get back to them," she said more firmly. "We'll get back to them."

Bodhi checked the time. Another hour had passed before the van finally came to a stop. They collectively held their breath as the men in the front of the vehicle began speaking to others in Spanish briefly, before the vehicle moved on. A short time later, the vehicle stopped again and the engine turned off. They heard the men exiting the vehicle and walking around to the rear of the van. The doors opened and two men they hadn't seen before climbed in with blindfolds and rope.

Bodhi and Helen exchanged a quick glance before their hands were pulled forward and bound. They didn't resist. They both knew to do so would be useless. Bodhi's throbbing, swollen face was a constant reminder of that. Not to mention the men's weapons.

Blindfolded, the men pulled them from the vehicle, then led them along a firm path underfoot. He heard more voices of greeting in Spanish, before Bodhi heard the words "Patron". He knew Helen heard it, too, because he heard her audibly inhale.

Bodhi stumbled as he was pulled awkwardly up some stairs, stubbing his toe. Suddenly he was inside an air-conditioned building. He smelled food cooking, heard a dog barking, and more voices in Spanish.

Bodhi followed obligingly to wherever they led him, eventually coming to a stop, where the backs of his legs were kicked and he dropped to his knees onto the hard-surfaced floor. He groaned slightly, his body bent over, his blindfolded face staring at the ground. He heard Helen beside him, also on her knees, breathing hard. He tried to remain calm, but it was hard not to think the worst. His whole body shook, his heart raced, his throat turned dry, thinking this was finally it. They were about to be killed, and they would die holding everything the world needed to fast-track the fight against the growing pandemic. Would El Patron ever share what they had with the world? He thought of his parents again, of the grief that would fill them.

He heard Helen breathing rapidly and felt devastated by the thought that her husband would lose his wife after having lost their daughter just the year before. All because Bodhi had seen their stupid lab.

"She didn't see anything," he blurted. "It was only me. She doesn't know what I saw. You can let her go."

"Bodhi! No!" she said.

"I'm not letting you get hurt for something I did."

"And what did you do, exactly?" a deep voice asked calmly from nearby.

Bodhi paused, then looked in the direction of the voice. He felt the hairs on his arms standing on end. He swallowed hard, though it was difficult with his dry throat.

"I-I was playing soccer with the children. *Football*… The ball got past me… I was retrieving it and–"

"And…?" the voice asked. "What did you see?"

Bodhi's mind turned over. What could he say that wouldn't get him killed on the spot?

"I asked you a question," the voice said, closer.

Bodhi stilled his heart, caught his breath. "Nothing," Bodhi said calmly. "I saw nothing but the beautiful rainforest."

The silence sat for what felt like an age.

"Good. Very good," the voice said.

There was another moment of silence before Bodhi was suddenly pulled to his feet and dragged along to another room down a corridor.

"Helen?" he called, panicked.

"I'm here," she said, sounding equally panicked but apparently following.

Again they were stopped and dropped to their knees, but this time their blindfolds were removed. They found themselves in a sitting room of sorts. The furniture was expensive, the place well decorated.

The muzzle of a weapon pressed against Bodhi's swollen cheek, causing a wave of pain to radiate out.

"Good evening," a man's voice said. They looked over their shoulder to see a well-dressed man enter the room. The voice was different from the one they'd just spoken to in the other room. This man moved to stand in front of them, clasping his hands before him and looking each of them over. His skin was light, his age old, his English refined.

"Where are we?" Helen asked.

"That is not important," the man said. "What is important is that you are required here for the time being."

"We have blood in that van," Helen said. "The container will only keep it cool so long. We need to get the supplies to the hospital in Leticia urgently."

"You will get the blood to Leticia only if you do as you're asked."

"What do you want us to do?" Helen asked.

The man stared at them a moment. Though he seemed calm and restrained on the outside, Bodhi had no doubt that if he worked for El Patron, he could turn any second. The man nodded to their guards and again they were pulled to their feet.

"We will untie you now," the man said, "but if your movements displease me, you will be shot. Understood?"

Bodhi and Helen nodded, both swallowing their fear. The man motioned again, and the guards cut their bindings. Bodhi and Helen automatically rubbed their wrists.

"Come," the aged man said. "First you must clean up. You smell terrible."

Helen and Bodhi followed the man down a corridor into a bathroom where soap and towels awaited. The man motioned to the basin and one by one they began to wash their hands and faces. As Helen dried her face, she saw Bodhi studying his swollen and bruised cheekbone and nose. It was the first time he'd seen his face and she saw the shock present in his eyes. They both looked away from the mirror, however, when a rotund guard wearing a surgical mask and gloves appeared at the doorway, carrying their backpacks of field equipment. He unzipped them and began pulling things out until he found what he was looking for.

The aged Englishman stepped forward again. "Come," he ordered them, holding out the surgical masks and disposable containment suits the guard had pulled from their backpacks. They took the masks, gloves and suits and put them on, throwing each other curious glances, then followed him down a corridor, while the rotund guard pursued with their backpacks.

The Englishman came to a door, knocked softly, pulled on a surgical mask and gloves, then opened it and disappeared inside.

"Come," he said again from inside the room.

Helen entered to see it was a young girl's bedroom. There were dolls and teddy bears on the dresser, and there in the bed before them was the girl, maybe nine years old. She lay there in a fevered state, her breath rasping, her lungs rattling. Helen glanced at Bodhi in surprise, before turning back to the girl. She stepped closer.

"She has the virus," Helen said, a statement rather than a question. The sound of the girl's ragged breathing squeezed something inside Helen's chest. Memories of her daughter came flooding back; of sickness, of pain, of dying.

The Englishman nodded. "You will give her a transfusion of the immune blood."

Helen looked at him in shock.

"She is O positive," he told them. "You will start immediately."

Helen looked back at the girl, who started coughing, wet and phlegmy, almost choking. They heard a bang and saw the cold box being placed down outside the room.

"You believe this immune rich blood can help, yes?" the Englishman said.

Helen looked back at him and nodded. "Y-yes."

"Then you will start immediately," he said again, more firmly.

Helen looked back to Bodhi. "G-get the supplies we need."

Bodhi nodded and moved to their backpacks and began to take out everything they needed. Helen watched as he pulled out an IV line, syringe, and antiseptic swabs. He cleaned each thoroughly, then handed the items to Helen, before he turned to the cold box and searched through to find the correct blood type. Most of the village had been O positive, a popular blood type in Colombia, so it didn't take long before he found what he was looking for and resealed the box.

Helen, holding the required items, moved to the child. Helen's body was shaking slightly. She felt weird, all light, like she was floating on air. She realized it must be shock. For days now she had been running on autopilot, getting the job done, but with everything that had happened in the past twenty-four hours, her resilience was starting to crack. Seeing the devastation of this pandemic, being surrounded by violent men with guns, witnessing Bodhi's beating, fearing for their lives, and now this. Helen was being asked to save this young girl's life. Tears pricked her eyes.

She placed the items down on the bed and studied the child, examining her. The girl was sweating, burning up. She thought of Angie again; laying there sweating, burning up.

The girl opened her eyes at Helen's touch. The whites of her eyes were bloodshot from coughing. The moment the girl's eyes fixed on Helen's, Helen felt her heart shatter into a thousand pieces. She pressed her lips together, fighting to contain the emotion.

"Hurry!" the Englishman said.

Helen looked to him. "She should be in a hospital."

"There's no time. You took blood from the villagers, so you can give it back to her. Move."

Helen turned back to the girl, struggling to breathe. Bodhi reached out and took the antiseptic swab from Helen and began wiping the girl's arm. Helen stared back at the girl, but she couldn't move. She was frozen, numb, like she'd forgotten everything she'd ever learned. She didn't know what was wrong with her.

Yes, she did.

She was utterly terrified that she couldn't save her. Just like she couldn't save Angie.

What if she couldn't save this girl? She couldn't watch her die.

And if she died, Bodhi and Helen would die, too.

"Helen?" Bodhi asked, eyeing her carefully over his surgical mask. Her eyes moved to his, but she couldn't answer. Bodhi eyed her with concern. He knew something was wrong. He glanced over to the Englishman, then reached out and took the syringe and the IV line from Helen's hands.

"I'll handle this," Bodhi said confidently to the Englishman.

Helen nodded at him numbly, vaguely, then slumped down in a chair placed beside the girl's bed.

While Bodhi took care of the transfusion, Helen stared at the girl. She reached out and took the child's hand in hers, as tears swelled in her eyes.

"She's El Patron's daughter, isn't she?"

The Englishman didn't answer.

The young girl coughed and spluttered again. Her lungs were close to drowning.

Helen felt her frozen exterior began to crack. This girl needed her.

More memories came flooding back and as though on

autopilot, Helen began to do everything she could to ease the girl's pain; patting her face with a cool cloth, plumping her pillows to elevate her lungs, all the while Bodhi checked on the bag and the IV line. And then they sat in silence, waiting for the bag to slowly empty into the little girl, carrying with it a passive immunity that would hopefully trigger her own immunity to fight back against the Constant Strain.

CHAPTER TWENTY-TWO

Aiko stood with Davidson, Lou and Gabriel who'd just come on shift at the comms desk, waiting for word from the hot spot team.

"We should've heard from them by now," Davidson said, the tension he felt clear across his face and shoulders. "Why haven't we heard from them?"

The doors behind them banged and they turned to see Ekemma enter. Aiko felt herself jump to life.

"The bat blood!" she said, moving toward her to collect their special delivery.

Lou moved to welcome Ekemma back with a hug.

"Has there been any word from Helen and Bodhi?" Ekemma asked.

Gabriel shook his head, the concern etched across his normally cheerful face. "No. They're overdue."

"It was going to take several hours to get there," Lou said. "We knew they had to stay overnight, and it's going to take several hours to come back."

"Exactly," Aiko said. "They should've been back hours ago." She felt the tension rising within her, as though her spine was a taut piece of wire that could snap at any moment. Ever since Bodhi and Helen had gone into that jungle, Aiko hadn't felt herself. She'd been edgy, she'd struggled to sleep, and for the life of her she couldn't stop thinking about Bodhi. She didn't like this feeling at all. She just wanted them to return so things could go back to normal.

"It's important we all stay calm," Lou said. "There could be any number of reasons for delays."

"They had rain in the jungle," Gabriel suggested. "It might've slowed them down, blocked roads."

"Or for all we know," Ekemma added, "they found a village of sick and dying people and they're busy trying to keep them alive."

"Like I said before, Helen has a lot of field experience," Lou said, "and Bodhi seemed very resourceful. We need to trust they're doing their jobs and they're staying safe."

"We have every contingency in place," Gabriel nodded. "No matter where they show up, we will get them out of there swiftly."

"I hope they have good news for us when they do," Aiko said. "The virus Ekemma has brought back is only a relative of the Constant Strain. It's something, it's data, but it's not what we really need."

"Check in with the team in Leticia," Davidson said to Lou. "See if they've heard anything."

"If they'd heard anything they would've told us," Lou said.

"I know," Davidson said, "but we have to do something. Just check in with them."

"What happens if they don't show?" Aiko asked him, her voice lacking its usual power.

Davidson stared at her. "If they don't show we elevate things." He exhaled heavily. "We don't want to elevate things."

Aiko watched as he turned and walked away. She stared after him, feeling a tightness in her chest as to what he meant by that, and what it could mean for Bodhi's and Helen's lives.

Bodhi placed the last of the contaminated items they'd used for the transfer into the double-bagged garbage bag and handed it to a gloved guard. The girl was resting now, and the Englishman was ushering them from the room.

"The... the cold box..." Helen began, shaking her head as though trying to clear the fog inside her mind.

"It will be refrozen overnight and the samples kept cool," the man said. "You will remain here until morning. If she needs another transfer, you will do it."

"We're expected back in Leticia," she said. "We're already late."

"You will return when we permit it."

"Sir, if we don't return," Bodhi said calmly, gently, "they may come looking for us. We need to let them know we're OK."

"In the morning," the man said firmly, then turned to the guards and spoke in Spanish.

Bodhi and Helen were taken by the arms and led back to the bathroom to remove their containment suits and sanitize, then to another room, a bedroom with two single beds, and placed inside. The door was closed behind them. They looked at each other, then collapsed down onto their respective beds, Bodhi somewhat gingerly, holding his side. With each passing hour the bruises sat more heavily upon his skin.

The silence sat for a moment before Bodhi broke it.

"The life of El Patron's daughter is in our hands," he said, staring up at the ceiling.

Helen nodded. "We can't let her die."

"No pressure then," he said dryly. "I can't believe we're staying the night at El Patron's house."

"At least we know why he decided to help us. It wasn't to save the people. It was to save his own daughter."

Bodhi looked at her. Helen smiled back sadly. "You did good in there. Thank you. I… I just froze up."

He gave her a brief, sympathetic smile. "My parents will be pleased I got to play doctor for once." Bodhi stared at her, not sure whether he should say what came next. "She reminded you of… of your daughter, didn't she?" he asked gently.

Helen's eyes shone from across the room. She nodded. "Angie was a little older, but yeah." She placed her hand over her chest. "It broke my heart…" she whispered.

"You did good, too," he told her. "The blood is one thing, but she needed someone to nurture her. I couldn't have given her what you could. She needed that just as much."

"I wonder where her mother is," Helen thought aloud, staring at the ceiling.

"Maybe she was being kept away, to keep her alive."

Helen nodded absently, then sighed. "Love is something else, you know. We can't control how deeply we feel it. That's why it hurts so much to lose someone."

Bodhi stared at her, his mind turning over the pain Helen

must've felt, wondering if he'd ever feel the love she described. As if on cue, Aiko appeared in his mind again. Memories of happier days, laying in each other's arms, tangled in the sheets, and laughing as they joked about marriage and kids.

"The team are going to be beside themselves," Helen said, breaking his thoughts.

Bodhi nodded. "Let's hope they don't do anything we may regret."

Aiko stood by Gabriel, as he connected their comms to Pilar's. Ekemma, Davidson and Max stood beside them. No one could sleep.

"Still nothing," Pilar said, her face showing deep concern on one of the screens.

"What do we do?" Justin asked, his face intense.

Max rubbed his jaw. "There was rain in the forest—"

"Not enough to shut the roads," Pilar said. "I'm sure of it."

"Are you still being watched?" Davidson leaned in.

They saw Justin move to the curtains and peer out.

"Yeah, they're still there," he said, shaking his bladed leg with nervous energy.

Davidson exhaled and looked down at the desk.

"I think we should wait a little longer," Ekemma said, firmly but calmly. "Let's give them one more day. Anything could've happened to slow them down."

"Yeah, Kem," Max said. "*Anything* could've happened! They might need us." He shook his head. "What the hell were we thinking, letting them go into the jungle with these criminals?"

"We were thinking of saving lives," Ekemma said. "And this was our only chance to try to rush a treatment before this pandemic takes over the world. I saw the latest statistics. They're reporting several cases in Dubai now. That's *seven* countries. It's hit the international flight system. There are over three hundred dead, many more critically ill. Within hours, I have no doubt they will start reporting cases here in Europe. This is it, Max."

"He's right," Justin said, "we shouldn't have let them go. Helen and Bodhi are missing and we still don't have the answers we need!" Justin shook his head as he began to pace.

"There has to be a reason," Pilar said, rubbing her forehead, the tiredness clearly smacking at her and Justin, too. Neither looked like they had slept. "They know Helen and Bodhi are part of an international organization," she said. "They also know I'm here and that I'm part of the US military. I don't think they would openly take them into the jungle and make them disappear. They would know there would be serious consequences to that."

"But we don't know who took them exactly, or where," Aiko said, feeling her throat swell with emotion.

"We know enough," Pilar said. "We know it was people connected to El Patron, and I'm sure if we check in with the DEA or the Colombian government, we'll get more information than that."

"But are they going to care about two people who are effectively aid workers?" Max asked.

"One is American," Ekemma shrugged, "and one is British. Perhaps if it were just little Nigerian me, they wouldn't care, but them two?"

"Kem…" Justin said gently as he stopped pacing and looked back into the camera.

"It's the truth," she said to him.

"Alright, people," Davidson said, checking his watch. "I've run out of time. I can't stall reporting into Greta Meier and she won't be able to stall reporting into the Assembly. This may not be our call to make anymore."

"You need to make it our call," Max said, stepping toward him. "These are *our* people. If they go in there guns a-blazing and anything happens..."

Davidson stared at Max, then turned to Gabriel. "Contact me as soon as they get in touch. I'll try and stall, but I can't promise anything." He looked back to Max. "You want to stop this escalating? Then come with me."

Aiko watched Davidson leave and Max reluctantly follow, then she looked back to the screen.

Pilar sighed. "I'll try talking to our motorcycle friends again. Be in touch soon."

The screen went black.

"I'll go over all our contingencies," Gabriel said, moving back to his desk.

Ekemma looked at Aiko. "Do you need a hand with the virus I brought back?"

Aiko shook her head. "No." She turned and began making her way back to her lab. Right now she wanted to be alone.

Bodhi awoke to find himself alone. Helen's bed was empty. He quickly sat up, wincing at his side, then rubbed his face, forgetting about his swollen cheek and wincing at that, too. He groaned, then stood gingerly. Everything felt worse today; his body was feeling yesterday's beating. Holding his tender side, he opened the bedroom door. The guard outside, startled, aimed his gun at Bodhi's face.

"Sorry. Sorry," Bodhi said, holding his hands up. "Helen? Where's Helen?"

The guard stared at him.

"Er," Bodhi racked his brain for his small Spanish vocabulary. "Er, mujer. Mujer? Woman?"

The guard eyed him, then motioned him forward with his weapon. Bodhi followed him and realized he was being led back to the girl's room. The door opened and Bodhi saw Helen, masked and gloved, sitting in her containment suit by the girl's bedside, holding her hand. She looked over at him and he saw her eyes smiling over the top of her surgical mask.

"She's improving," Helen said, looking back to the girl. "Her temperature has come down slightly." She looked back to Bodhi. "It's working."

Bodhi felt relief sweep over him and found himself leaning his shoulder against the doorframe, catching his breath.

"That's good," he said. "I'm glad." He wanted to enter the room but knew he couldn't without his protective clothing. "Have you been here all night?"

Helen nodded. "I couldn't sleep. I couldn't leave her."

Bodhi felt a pinch of guilt, but after several nights of not a lot of sleep, last night he'd pretty much fallen unconscious with exhaustion. He was glad for it, though, because his head felt a little clearer this morning, even if his body didn't.

"You should rest," he said. "I can take over the watch, if you like."

Helen looked back at him.

He shrugged. "Teamwork. I'll go get my suit."

Max swallowed as Greta Meier stared at him and Davidson.

"So, it's been roughly fifteen hours since you expected them back?"

"Yes," Davidson nodded.

"There was rain in the jungle," Max added quickly. "This may have caused a disturbance to the roads back."

Greta nodded, considering him.

"Maybe so, but we can't sit on this," she said. "I will speak with my Colombian colleague and their ambassador at once."

"Greta," Davidson said, holding up his hand. "Please proceed with caution. I'm sure you appreciate this is a delicate situation. Not just for our team, but for people across the globe. If we upset this… drug lord, who knows what he might do in retaliation."

"I understand this, Peter," she said. "Has it ever been my style to go in guns blazing?"

"No," Davison said, then smiled. "Not at first anyway."

"Exactly," she said. "I'll simply have a conversation with the ambassador about our scientists who are… running late." She shrugged. "We shall see where this leads."

Davidson nodded. "Yes, ma'am."

Greta nodded and the screen went blank.

Max looked at Davidson. "How much attention will the Colombian ambassador pay the World Health Assembly?"

Davidson shrugged. "Colombia are members of the World Health Assembly. With Greta involved, I think there's a good chance she'll get through to the ambassador, and hopefully the ambassador to the rest of the government."

"But what will that mean for Helen and Bodhi?"

Davidson shrugged again. "Let's hope members of the Colombian government have ways to talk to this El Patron."

Max exhaled heavily. "They have to show up. They have to."

"The question is," Davidson asked, "if they don't show up, what do we do about this pandemic?"

Max's mind turned over. "If this remote village has a rare immunity to this new virus, there might be others out there. We'll have to make a plea for volunteers to come forward and roll out testing across the region."

"That takes time and resources, Max, and we're short on both."

Max rubbed his tired face. "I don't know, Peter. Robert used to make these kinds of calls, not me."

"Well, he's not here anymore," Davidson said bitterly, and Max noted the scowl on his face.

"What happened to him?" he dared to ask.

Davidson looked at him but didn't answer. Instead he stood. "Go update the team."

Max stared at him a moment, then left the room, heading back down to the main floor. Tiredness smacked at him, but he couldn't sleep. Every muscle in his body felt tight. He was used to pressure in this job, but never before had he dealt with a situation like this. Trying to stop a pandemic was stressful enough, but having to deal with Helen and Bodhi missing, a powerful drug baron, and possible military interference, was something else.

He marched over to Lou's desk. "Get Pilar back on screen and join Aiko up, too, in the lab."

Lou nodded and quickly did as requested. As soon as Aiko and Pilar appeared, she turned to Max eager for his update, as Gabriel rolled his chair closer and other staff gathered around to hear the latest.

"Greta Meier, through the Assembly, is going to speak with the Colombian ambassador."

"What does this mean?" Aiko asked.

"It means it's being elevated," Max said.

"But what does that mean exactly?" Aiko asked again.

"It means our senior people are talking to senior Colombian people."

"Could this result in a military operation?" Pilar asked from her screen connection.

Max looked at her. "Right now they're just talking."

"Yeah, right. For now," Justin said, then turned and moved off camera. Pilar glanced after him.

"Let's hope for Helen and Bodhi's sake," Lou said, "that they talk some sense into these guys."

"Let's hope," Max said, before he turned and walked away.

Bodhi heard a knock at the door and saw Helen appear. He'd been with the girl for four hours, holding her hand, cooling her brow, regularly performing standard observations. The improvement was slow, but there was improvement. The immune rich blood was fighting off the virus and teaching her own immune system how to fight it.

"How's she doing?" Helen asked.

"Better. Her lungs sound like they're beginning to clear."

Helen smiled. "Good."

"You didn't sleep long?"

"No," she said. "Something was happening. The guards woke me up, motioned me to pack up."

"Yeah?" He straightened. "You think they're finally going to let us go?"

"Gather your things," the Englishman broke in, appearing beside Helen. "You will leave one more bag of O positive blood with me, then you will continue on your journey."

"You're letting us go?" Helen asked him.

He studied her. "It appears people are starting to ask questions about your return to Leticia. Questions we don't wish to receive. So leave the blood, pack your bags and head out to the van."

Bodhi and Helen exchanged a look of both surprise and confusion. Did they hear right? Were they finally able to leave? Was this really happening?

Apparently, it was.

Bodhi stood and made his way toward the door, not needing to be asked twice. He removed his mask, gloves and suit, threw them in the trash, carefully sanitized, then stepped out into the corridor where their backpacks waited. He lifted his, wincing as he did, before they were blindfolded once more and led back toward the van.

Once inside, the blindfolds were removed again and the cold box loaded inside. Bodhi moved to check both the villagers' blood and that of the bat was still inside. It was, and again he breathed with relief. He closed the lid to see a man standing there, startling him. The man wore a simple white shirt, expensive gold rings, and an expression that made Bodhi's spine turn to ice. The man didn't have to introduce himself. Bodhi knew this was El Patron.

Were they actually being allowed to leave? Or was now going to be their end?

"Thank you for saving my daughter," the man said plainly, as if gratitude was an uncommon emotion for him.

Bodhi, stunned, wasn't sure what to say. Helen spoke for the both of them.

"Thank you … for providing us access to your people. Their blood will save many more people, like it did your daughter."

The man nodded, looking calmly between them. "You have seen my village and you have seen my face."

Bodhi carefully sat back against the wall, swallowing hard and holding his breath.

"As I have seen your faces," El Patron continued. "Mr Bodhi Patel of Washington DC and Mrs Helen Taylor of London. I hope you will never forget my face, because I will never forget yours. Or where you live. Or where your families live."

The silence held as neither Bodhi nor Helen breathed.

"I-I have a terrible memory," Bodhi stuttered. "I assure you."

El Patron stared at him, letting the silence hang in the air before a small smile slid across his face and he spoke once more.

"Good."

They heard a sound in the distance then, and El Patron and his men suddenly looked into the air. Bodhi soon recognized the deep thrumming of a chopper flying overhead, though it seemed to echo.

"Vamos," El Patron said to his men, then turned and casually walked away. A powerful, terrifying presence.

Just as the men closed the van doors, Bodhi saw two helicopters approaching in the distance. Military choppers. He looked back at Helen, in the dim light coming from the driver's window.

"Are they for us?" Bodhi asked. "Or for the pandemic?"

Helen shook her head, eyes wide. "I don't know. I'm not sure I know anything anymore."

The van started up, then began to move, wheels turning over on the dirt road, leaving the home of El Patron.

Bodhi and Helen stared at each other, disbelief displayed on both their faces. They suddenly exhaled loudly in a mixture of surprise and relief. While Bodhi clutched at his chest, Helen bent forward, leaning over her knees. Their panting in sheer relief soon turned into laughter, though, and eventually even a few exhausted tears.

CHAPTER TWENTY-THREE

Aiko felt her chest sink as the Leticia team reported there was still no sign of Helen or Bodhi.

Davidson exhaled. "Words obviously didn't work. I'm told they've sent helicopters up to circle the rainforest, flexing muscles as a warning to El Patron."

"Do you really think he's going to care?" Max asked.

"Well, put it this way," Davidson said, "the Colombian government doesn't want external interference. If they don't apply pressure for El Patron to release them, our governments will send agents in who can find them. They won't want foreigners snooping around El Patron, it could start a war. They don't want a repeat of what happened when Pablo Escobar was running things down there."

"Shit is about to get intense," Pilar said, on screen.

"It already is," Justin said.

"Justin's right," Gabriel said. "You two should pull back to Tabatinga. Get out of Colombia."

"I think they should pull right back to home base to be frank," Max said.

"They can't leave them!" Ekemma said.

"They're not leaving them," Davidson said. "They're just getting out of the way while the professionals find them."

Justin moved toward the camera. "We're not leaving."

"We've already put two of our team at great risk, Justin," Max said. "We're not risking you any further. So pack your things, you're pulling out."

A knock sounded on the door to Pilar and Justin's motel room. They both tensed and Justin moved to answer it, while Pilar slid her hand into her pocket as though placing her hand on a weapon. Justin peered out the curtains.

"Holy shit!" he said, yanking the door open. Helen and Bodhi stood there, looking sweaty and disheveled. They both had blood on their shirts and Bodhi's face was swollen and bruised.

Pilar jumped up and moved to them as Justin ushered them into the room.

"Helen!" Max barked, leaning down on the table. "Where the hell have you been?!"

"Is that blood?" Lou asked suddenly.

"Relax, relax!" Helen said, holding up her hand, asking for calm. "It's a long story. But we're fine."

"What happened to your *face*?" Aiko blurted out.

Bodhi looked into the camera and shook his head. "Nothing. I'm fine."

"You nearly gave me a heart attack!" Max said, despite himself.

"Yeah," Helen said, "we had a few of those ourselves."

"What was the delay?" Ekemma asked. "Did everything go alright?"

Helen nodded and smiled, her eyes shining with tears. "They have immunity. We have thirty-seven bags of blood. Get the hospitals on standby, get a courier on standby. Get ready to start replicating those antibodies, Aiko. We've got people to save."

"Will do," she smiled, her chest lightening.

"And Aiko?" Helen said.

"Yeah?"

"We think we found the source, too."

Aiko's eyes popped with excitement. "You did?!"

Helen nodded. "We're pretty certain it's a vampire bat virus, that these villagers had the natural immunity to. It must've bitten Sebastian Dias and mutated with another Type A virus already in his system, and that's what Sebastian spread to the world."

"Tell me you have a blood sample from the suspect bat," Aiko asked urgently.

Helen nodded. "Yeah. We do. One tried to eat Bodhi."

"That was the delay?" Davidson asked, a puzzled expression on his relieved face.

Helen sighed. "No. El Patron, the guy who controls the whole area, his daughter was sick. She caught the virus, she was very sick indeed. He insisted we take a detour to give her some of the blood."

Max's jaw went rigid. "So his daughter survives while other kids out there die."

"Max..." Helen said. "She was just a kid. It's not her fault who her father is."

"He's a drug lord! He doesn't deserve anything."

"He enabled us to get all this blood. He's helping others, too."

"He's scum, Helen! You know how many kids he's killed with his poison?"

Helen's face softened. "Max ... This wasn't your kid."

Max looked a little stunned by her comment. "Yeah? Well, she wasn't your kid either."

Aiko saw Helen's face fall.

"No, she wasn't," Helen said, nodding, clearly too exhausted to argue. "I could actually save this one."

Helen stepped forward and flipped off the comms.

Aiko looked at Max, who lowered his head as regret flooded his face, then he turned and walked away.

"I'll update Greta," Davidson said, eyeing Max before jogging up the steps.

Ekemma squeezed Aiko's arm. "Let's get ready for their data upload."

Helen and Bodhi stood in the motel room, still not quite believing they were back and safe.

"Garcia," Justin said, "help me with their things." The two stepped outside to pay the tuk-tuk drivers and unload all their gear.

"I never thought I'd be so glad to see this place," Bodhi said, slumping down carefully on one of the beds.

"I can't wait to get back to Lyon," Helen said, then she paused as she thought of Ethan. "And even London."

Bodhi nodded. "I need a hot shower and a soft bed first, but yes, I can't wait to get back, too."

"To see Aiko?" Helen asked, studying him.

He looked up at her, surprised.

Helen smiled softly. "You weren't just friends with her, were you?"

Bodhi didn't answer.

"She was worried about your injuries," Helen said. "She cares about you."

An uncomfortable look crossed his face. "Nah." He shook his head, averting his eyes. "The only thing Aiko cares about is her career and what her parents think. And her parents don't like middle-class Anglo-Indian Americans."

His comments were brutal, but Helen believed they came from a place of hurt. She pursed her lips and shrugged. "People change."

"Yeah, they do," he conceded, "but not her." He glanced at Helen. "You don't have to worry about it, it was a long time ago."

Helen studied him. "I'm not worried. I just know what I saw, and for as long as I've known Aiko, she's never looked like that at anyone."

Bodhi's face flushed with surprise again, but before the conversation could continue, Justin and Pilar began dumping their gear inside the room.

Justin placed the cold box down and looked to them both. "Alright, injuries?" He moved swiftly to Bodhi.

"We're fine," Bodhi said, standing again, moving stiffly and holding his side.

Justin squeezed his shoulder and studied his face. "Let me look you over," he said. "You copped a bit of a beating, huh?"

"It's just bruising."

"Hey, I'm the medic, tough guy. Let me do my job," Justin said, taking his shoulders and moving him to sit back on the bed.

"Sorry to say, but we need to get this blood to the hospitals," Helen said.

Pilar nodded. "We'll take care of it. You rest." She looked to Justin, who nodded.

"No, I'll come, too," Helen said, turning to Bodhi. "You upload all the results to the software, then confirm Aiko has it so she can start working. Then you rest."

"Then you get a check-up, Bodhi," Justin said, pointing at him.

"Are you sure?" Bodhi asked Helen.

She nodded. "We've got it from here."

Helen felt a level of comfort when she entered the Leticia hospital and saw several WHO volunteers assisting the local staff. The waiting room was still crowded, but she could see the difference the extra pairs of hands were making to the local staff.

They found Doctor Ramirez and she watched in relief as several bags of blood were handed to him. He looked down at them, then back at Helen.

"Thank you," he said.

Helen smiled. "Thank *you* for getting us in there."

He nodded, then fell silent.

"I know it's not much, but that's all we can give you for now," Helen said, "but… you know where to find more."

"Yes. I do."

Justin, who was watching, stepped forward. "The WHO

support teams will continue to work with you, monitoring your quarantine zones and helping to care for your patients, until the threat recedes."

"They'll help with containment," Helen said, "and hopefully, with that blood to work from, along with the live viral samples we've collected, we'll have antivirals and a vaccine for you soon, too."

"Thank you."

"No, thank you, Doctor Ramirez. We couldn't have done this without you. Truly. You've helped saved many lives... including that of El Patron's daughter." Helen extended her gloved hand.

A smile of relief spread across his face as he nodded and he took her gloved hand in his.

"Good luck, Doctor Ramirez."

He shook her hand. "And you."

Bodhi felt the exhaustion rising up over him again, and as much as he didn't want to do this comms chat, he knew he had to. As soon as he confirmed that Lyon had the information, he could shower and he could rest.

He watched as his tablet screen connected with Aiko's. She appeared, her face showing signs of exhaustion, too, though her eyes were curious. Strands of her long dark hair had fallen from the normally perfect bun she tied it up in. It was interesting to see. He was so used to her being so perfect and in control, and for the first time she looked nothing but. She almost looked as though she'd spent the past few days in the field with them. Maybe she had, in spirit. Helen's words cycled around his mind.

"Hi," Aiko greeted him, her expression much warmer than last time they'd spoken alone.

"Hi," he said back. "Er, Helen wanted me to check you'd received all the results that I just uploaded."

She nodded, her eyes darting to another screen close by. "Yes, thirty-nine blood samples, stating blood type, all with presence of the bat-borne virus particles and antibodies. The bat-borne virus does appear to be the foundation of the Constant Strain virus." She looked back at him. "While we work on creating monoclonal antibodies from your samples, the WHO is going to see if we can obtain more blood and sample other people in that immediate region, too."

Bodhi nodded. "Good luck to them. Helen and the team are distributing what blood we can, and we'll get the rest to you as soon as possible. What we have won't spread far at all, but hopefully the WHO can procure more in time or we can reproduce it quickly enough to deliver to the hot spots."

"We should be able to turn around the antivirals fast once we get our hands on the immune rich blood."

Bodhi nodded and the silence sat, as she studied his face. He felt uncomfortable beneath her gaze.

"Your face looks bad," she said. "You should have Justin–"

"It's fine."

She stared at him.

"I was a med student, remember?" he said.

Aiko nodded. "Yes. I remember. But you should still get checked over."

They stared at each other.

"Well," Bodhi said. "I gotta go, so…"

"Right," she said gently.

"Right," he said, then moved to end the comms.

"I'm glad you're OK," she said suddenly. Her eyes were down on her console, but then she lifted them up again.

He stared at her a moment, then nodded. "Me, too."

Bodhi ended the comms. He sighed and laid back on the motel bed, staring up at the ceiling.

He closed his eyes, wishing for sleep; he was too tired to deal with thoughts of Aiko right now.

Strangely enough, he noticed how quiet it was, and found himself missing the sounds of the deep Amazonas.

Helen was glad when her feet touched the ground in Lyon. It had been thirty hours since they'd made it back to Leticia with the blood. That was as long as it had taken to sort out things in the Leticia hot spot, then catch several commercial flights back. It didn't bother Helen though. She'd used most of those hours on the plane to sleep. Not that it had been exactly restful. She'd never dreamed so many dreams; of the rainforest, of El Patron's fevered daughter, of the children playing football, of the automatic rifles, of Bodhi being beaten, of him handling the transfusion like a pro when she couldn't, and of course, she'd dreamed of Angie. Her daughter had been laying in a hospital bed, but she looked as she had before the cancer. She was happy and healthy, and she smiled and laughed at her mother. And when Helen had awoken from the dream, she'd had tears running down her face.

Upon landing they headed straight for home base, noting how cold it was compared to the South American humidity. They had to check all their gear in with Max and clear themselves back from the operation. When they arrived at the GHA facility, Lou was waiting for them with a selection of French patisseries and a huge smile.

"It's so good to see you," Lou said.

"It's good to see you," Helen smiled, turning around to see Max and Justin bumping elbows as Lou moved to Pilar. Helen noticed Aiko looking at Bodhi, who was still moving rather stiffly and holding his side. Helen saw the two exchange an awkward nod of hello. Max turned to Helen and placed his hands on his hips.

"Welcome back," he said genuinely.

Helen smiled and gave him a nod. "It's good to be back." Max had a fire to him, but Helen understood where it came from. He cared, a lot, and sometimes he just didn't know how to express it well. Sometimes he voiced the things no one else wanted to say, though, and that was a useful trait to have; his courage. He was also a man who had the courage to admit when he was wrong.

"You did good," he told her. "It was dangerous and damn stupid, but the outcome was very good."

She smiled and bumped his elbow. "Don't go changing, Max."

He discreetly beckoned Helen away from the others. She followed, curious, and he turned to face her, looking as though he was trying to find the right words to say.

"I'm sorry for what I said about your son," she jumped in first. "You have every right to hate El Patron and what his kind do."

"And I'm sorry for bringing up Angie like that," Max said. "Saving that little girl was the right thing to do."

Helen took a moment, looking down at her feet, swallowing

away the lump in her throat. She'd done so well keeping it together for so long, but now somehow there were cracks in her facade and the emotion was beginning to leak out. But the truth was, Max of all people was the one who would understand the most, what it might feel like to lose a child. She reached out and squeezed his arm, and he squeezed hers back.

"Now, I saw pastries," she said. "Don't keep me from them."

Max broke into a smile. "Never stand between a woman and food. That's what my ex-wife told me. I'll never learn."

Helen laughed and they moved back to the group, as Peter Davidson emerged from the boardroom. Standing on the upper tier, he leaned on the rail and stared down at them.

"Welcome back," he said, then looked to Helen. "Could you spare a moment?"

She stared at him. "Sure."

She excused herself and made her way up the stairs toward him. He ushered her through to the boardroom and closed the door.

"Take a seat," he said.

She did and stared back at him.

"Sorry, I know you just got back," he said, "but we need to report to Greta Meier."

Helen nodded and Davidson logged in to a video conference. The screen connected and Greta Meier appeared. She looked elegant and poised as usual. She smiled.

"Helen," she said warmly. "It's so good to see you. We were worried about you and your team for a while there."

"I won't lie, I was, too."

"I believe you have good news, though?"

"Yes, Director Meier," Helen said. "We believe we've the tools to slow this pandemic and will soon have the means to stop it altogether."

"Yes? It was spread from a bat bite?"

"Yes and no," Helen said thoughtfully. On the journey back, in between sleeping, she'd been catching up on all of Aiko's notes. "Our Patient Zero, Sebastian Dias, was indeed bitten by a bat and infected by an A type influenza virus, but we believe that he was also carrying another avian A type virus at the time. The two viruses mutated, swapping genes in a reassortment, which enabled this new virus to evolve, creating an antigenic shift, which started this new virus, that we're calling the Constant Strain, spiraling out of control. The boy spread it far and wide in his travels before he died. But we managed to get a blood sample from one of the original bat-borne virus hosts, a vampire bat, and between this sample and the samples collected from the boy and the sick, our team plus our extended network of scientists are working on a way to block transmission, using all this information. But we also managed to track down a small village of people who hold a rare natural immunity to the *original* bat-borne virus, and we have now sourced blood donations and are replicating the antibodies to roll out to the affected communities, which will help ease the burden in the short term while we work on vaccines. So we have the information at hand to tackle this pandemic from both sides and establish a set of protocols for future treatment and containment. I'm told the monoclonal antibodies will soon be pushed out to all the hot spots, which should see the death rates drop dramatically, and strong quarantine measures are being put into play across all connected nations. Of course we still need to investigate exactly how Sebastian became infected et cetera et cetera, but that will be in my full report."

"Very good," Greta said. "You've done very well. And I have to say, the attention you've brought to the GHA has been useful. I've been asked many questions about what we do from these countries. I think this will help us next time we find ourselves working there."

"I'm glad to hear it," Helen said.

"I know you must be exhausted, but as soon as you can, please issue me with your close-out report, so I may take this to the World Health Assembly."

"Yes, director," Helen said.

"Greta, please." She turned her eyes to Peter. "I will speak with you later, Peter."

"Of course," he said, and ended the comms.

Davidson sat back in his chair and exhaled loudly. He turned to study Helen.

"You look tired," she said kindly.

He nodded. "It's hard to sleep when your team is missing." He studied her. "What about you though? Are you OK?" he asked gently.

She nodded. "I'm just glad to be home."

"You consider Lyon home now?" he asked curiously.

She paused, her mind thinking over Ethan and London, and the guilt set in again.

"So," she said, changing the conversation. "Is this where you strip me of my Acting Director status?"

Davidson stared at her. "Why did you head out into the field? That's why we hired Bodhi Patel."

"Force of habit," she shrugged. "I wanted to give the new guy a handover and… I don't know. Maybe I'm a little protective of my team. I wanted to make sure he knew what he was doing."

Davidson studied her. "Well, that habit is going to have to change…"

She nodded, dropping her eyes to the table, wondering what disciplinary action he was going to take. She had, after all, put the team in a dangerous situation, despite the risk paying off.

"If you're going to stay in the role," he finished.

Helen looked up at him. "What? What does that mean?"

Davidson exhaled. "It means I'm going to recommend you for the job permanently."

"You are?"

He nodded and sat forward again. "Listen, it's not going to be easy. What Robert did–"

"What *did* he do?"

"You're going to have a lot of eyes on you," Davidson continued, ignoring her question. "There'll be auditors all over you, checking everything the team does. But right now, I think you're best placed to handle that, rather than bringing in someone new who doesn't get what we do here, who doesn't understand the people we have."

"Come on, Peter. It's driving me crazy. Tell me: what did Robert do?" Helen asked again. Davidson hesitated, but then relented.

"He stole from us," he said, sitting back again. "He stole funds from the GHA to pay off gambling debts."

Helen's face fell. "He bloody what?"

Davidson nodded and Helen felt her body begin to tighten with anger.

"That son of a... How much?"

"A significant amount."

Helen exhaled heavily, shaking her head in disgust. "Here we are begging and pleading for every penny, so we can save lives and he–"

"Yes. He did. And that's why there will be a lot of eyes on you, all of us, for a while. But I know you can handle it. If you can handle a drug lord and dangerous men with guns, you can handle this." He sat forward again. "And I know you're the right person for this job, because you *care*. You care about what the GHA is trying to do, and you care about the team," Davidson reiterated, then considered her for a moment. "But it will take sacrifices. If you're going to lead this team, you can't be disappearing into the wilderness again. You need to be here, overseeing everything. They can't be calling me to step in. Understood?"

Helen nodded, realizing how perilous her actions had been. If they had failed in their operation, the GHA could have been shut down entirely.

"So," Davidson said. "Is that a yes, you'll accept my nomination for GHA Director?"

Helen sat back in her chair, her mind ticking over. She felt a sense of ownership of the team, a need to guide and protect it; what they did, what they stood for. She thought of Robert again and anger flashed through her. He'd squandered their much-needed funds. No wonder things had been so tight. She couldn't let that happen again. Too many lives were at risk. But Davidson was right, if she was to lead the team in its entirety, she needed to have full oversight. She couldn't be incommunicado in a jungle somewhere. If she wanted to steer the team, it would take a sacrifice. She thought of Ethan, then. He may not be happy if she grew roots in Lyon, but at least she would be based permanently somewhere. Perhaps it was time she stopped running away and finally dealt with Angie's death and her crumbling marriage? Regardless of however it turned out.

"Yes," she said to Davidson. "Yes, damn it, yes."

"Yes?"

She nodded. "This team has a lot of potential to make a big difference, Peter. We've worked too hard to throw it away. Shutting us down would be a huge mistake."

"It would," Davidson nodded. "Now we just need to convince Greta Meier and the auditors of that."

"Leave it with me."

Davidson smiled. "So, what did you think of Mr Patel? Should we get him in here and see if he wants to join us permanently?"

Helen nodded and smiled. "Yes. Let's get him in here. And maybe those petit fours and a cup of tea?"

Davidson laughed.

Bodhi walked up the steps toward the boardroom, following Assistant Director General Davidson. His heart was thumping in his chest, wondering why he was being called into the meeting. Were they going to fire him for nearly getting Helen killed over the soccer incident?

Davidson ushered him through to where Helen waited,

incongruously sipping a cup of tea and dusting her fingers of sugar from a French pastry.

"Come in, Bodhi, have a seat," Helen motioned. Bodhi sat down in a chair between Davidson and Helen, wincing a little as he did.

"So, how're you doing?" Davidson asked, eyeing his purple-brown cheekbone.

"I'm good."

"You've had your injuries checked out?"

"Yeah, Justin checked me over back... back in the field. Nothing broken. It's just some bad bruising."

"I'm sorry you went through that," Davidson said. "What happened... that's not an ordinary mission."

Helen placed her cup of tea down, clearing her throat. "Well, actually..."

Bodhi and Davidson looked to her.

"Unfortunately, outbreaks can occur anywhere," she continued. "Politics, civil war, hurricanes, floods, man-eating animals, men with guns, *drug lords*. We never know what we're walking into. Every operation is dangerous because we're facing the worst serial killer of all. Viruses. If we're lucky, that's all we're dealing with. But often, all these other things can occur to make what we do that bit trickier, that bit more dangerous. It's hard, seeing the devastation some communities go through. But we can make a difference. No matter how small we may think it is, the impact can be huge. Not just for these communities, but for mankind in general. It's not an easy road, but as they say, no risk, no reward, right?" she finished with a smile.

"Spoken as though you were Director General Greta Meier herself," Davidson smiled.

Bodhi nodded and noticed both Davidson and Helen staring at him. He paused, wondering if he'd missed something.

"Oh, Peter – we forgot to actually ask him the question," Helen said to Davidson.

"What question?" Bodhi asked, looking between them.

"What do you say, Bodhi?" Davidson said. "Would you like to join the Lyon team on a permanent basis?"

Bodhi continued looking back and forth between them.

"But I thought–"

"I've been asked to step into the Team Director role permanently," Helen said. "Which means we have a vacancy for a lead epidemiologist."

"Oh. Right," Bodhi said, exhaling with relief and feeling his entire body unclench. "I thought I was about to be fired."

"Fired?" Helen asked. "You did great. You were fast on your feet, offered me great support. You helped save that little girl's life. I think that medical degree will come in handy in the field. Justin can't be everywhere at once."

"Right," Bodhi said, still catching his breath and waiting for the world to stop spinning so he could catch up.

"Of course, we'd understand if what happened out in Colombia has turned you off," Davidson said. "It's important that the team are comfortable in their roles and are able to, not just physically but *emotionally*, do their jobs."

"You're smart," Helen told him, "you're capable, intuitive, analytical, and you fit well with the team. You're a natural choice. What do you say?"

When Bodhi had left Atlanta he'd been seeking something more. He'd been wanting to see the world, and that South American operation had opened his eyes to so much. Not all of it good, but he'd helped the GHA team fast-track a treatment for this new pandemic that threatened the entire globe. He'd helped to make a difference. He felt as though he'd accomplished more on that one mission than he'd done in the years prior, working in Atlanta.

Bodhi glanced out the window to the team below. He saw Justin laughing and slapping Max on the shoulder, who broke into a grin. He moved his eyes to Ekemma who also broke into a pearly smile, as Pilar shook her head and folded her arms, suppressing her own smile. Lou tapped her teacup against Gabriel's in a cheers motion, while beside them Aiko gave a laugh. He'd forgotten what it looked like, what *she* looked like, when she was relaxed and happy.

She was beautiful.

As though sensing his eyes on her, Aiko looked up at the boardroom window. Their eyes locked and her smile faltered briefly, before it came back, strong, like the sun emerging from clouds. She raised her teacup in a "cheers" motion. He gave a small smile back, then turned to Davidson and Helen.

"Yeah," he said, nodding. "I'd love to join the team."

ACKNOWLEDGMENTS

My sincerest thanks to Marc, Lottie and the teams at Aconyte, Z-Man Games and Asmodee for inviting me into this world and allowing me to help develop it and its characters for these Pandemic novels. Matt Leacock has created such an awesome series of games and it's an honor to be able to write the first novel in this series. Not only has it been a wonderfully fun experience, but also very educational and challenging! I hope readers enjoy this first outing, getting to know the team, and that they come back for more to see what happens next – not only in the world of the viral outbreaks, but also in each of the characters' lives.

A special thank you to Melissa Jane Ferguson, scientist and SFF writer (go check out her novel, *The Shining Wall*), for checking over my science so that it made some sense whilst also leaning heavily on creative license.

A special thank you also to Emely Maas, for her Colombian and South American expertise.

As always, I'd also like to thank my family and friends for their support, patience and understanding of how busy I always am.

Last, but never least, thanks to my regular readers for following me from book to book, world to world, and to any new readers I have picked up with this novel. If you enjoyed the read, please do leave a rating or review online to support the Pandemic novel universe and its future endeavors.

Thank you!

ABOUT THE AUTHOR

AMANDA BRIDGEMAN is a Tin Duck Award winner, an Aurealis and a Ditmar Awards finalist. She is the author of eight volumes of the award-nominated Aurora series of near-future space thrillers, the SF police procedural *The Subjugate*, which is being developed for television by Anonymous Content and Aquarius Films, and a Stephen King-esque mystery *The Time of the Stripes*. She's also worked as a TV and film actress.

amandabridgeman.com.au
twitter.com/bridgeman_books

CAN YOU SAVE HUMANITY?

Deadly viruses are on the verge of outbreak, putting the whole world at risk. It is up to you to find the cure.

In this exciting **cooperative** board game, you must work with your team to discover a vaccine. Can you stop the disease from spreading and save the world **together**?

2-4 | 45-60 | 8+

Find more cool games at **ZManGames.com!**

®, TM and © 2021 Z-Man Games.

WORLD EXPANDING FICTION

Do you have them all?

ARKHAM HORROR
- ☐ *Wrath of N'kai* by Josh Reynolds
- ☐ *The Last Ritual* by S A Sidor
- ☐ *Mask of Silver* by Rosemary Jones
- ☐ *Litany of Dreams* by Ari Marmell
- ☐ *The Devourer Below* edited by
  Charlotte Llewelyn-Wells
- ☐ *Cult of the Spider Queen* by S A Sidor
  (*coming soon*)

DESCENT
- ☐ *The Doom of Fallowhearth* by Robbie
  MacNiven
- ☐ *The Shield of Daqan* by David Guymer
- ☐ *The Gates of Thelgrim* by Robbie MacNiven
  (*coming soon*)

KEYFORGE
- ☐ *Tales from the Crucible* edited by
  Charlotte Llewelyn-Wells
- ☐ *The Qubit Zirconium* by M Darusha Wehm

LEGEND OF THE FIVE RINGS
- ☐ *Curse of Honor* by David Annandale
- ☐ *Poison River* by Josh Reynolds
- ☐ *The Night Parade of 100 Demons*
  by Marie Brennan
- ☐ *Death's Kiss* by Josh Reynolds

PANDEMIC
- ☑ *Patient Zero* by Amanda Bridgeman

TWILIGHT IMPERIUM
- ☐ *The Fractured Void* by Tim Pratt
- ☐ *The Necropolis Empire* by Tim Pratt